# THE
# WIDOW
## AND THE
# KING

Also available by John Dickinson,
and published by David Fickling Books:

THE CUP OF THE WORLD

# THE
# WIDOW
## AND THE
# KING

## John Dickinson

David Fickling Books

OXFORD · NEW YORK

A DAVID FICKLING BOOK

Published by David Fickling Books
an imprint of Random House Children's Books
a division of Random House, Inc.
New York

Published simultaneously in Canada by Random House of Canada Limited, Toronto, and in
Great Britain by David Fickling Books, an imprint of Random House Children's Books

www.randomhouse.com/teens

Library of Congress Cataloging-in-Publication Data
Dickinson, John.
The widow and the king / by John Dickinson.— 1st American ed.
p.    cm.
SUMMARY: When the hooded prince of the evil "undercraft" is released from a magical prison,
young Ambrose, the last descendant of a great king, flees for his life, not knowing who his friends
or enemies are.
ISBN 0-385-75084-6 (trade) — ISBN 0-385-75085-4 (lib. bdg.)
[1. Fantasy.]  I. Title.
PZ7.D55845 Wi 2005
[Fic]—dc22
2004013373

Printed in the United States of America
June 2005
10 9 8 7 6 5 4 3 2 1
First American Edition

*For Peter*

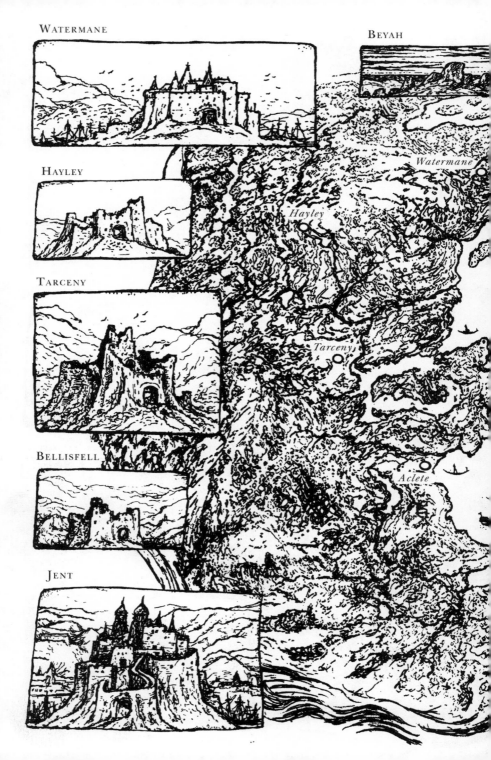

WATERMANE

BEYAH

Watermane

HAYLEY

Hayley

TARCENY

Tarceny

BELLISFELL

Aclete

JENT

VELIS

BAY

TRANT

TUSCOLO

DEVELIN

Velis

Pemini

Chatterfall

Bay

Baldwin

Tuscolo

Trant

Develin

Jent

# Contents

# PART I

## WASTELANDS

# I

## The Moonlit Throne

 man came among the mountains, hunting his son with a sword.

In the late afternoon he led his horse along one side of a great, empty valley. On his right hand the slope – all grey rock and patches of low thorns – rose steeply to a high crest. To his left it dropped eerily away, hundreds of feet to the valley bottom, where a stream ran with the opaque blues of glacier water. The path he followed was narrow, threading upwards along the hillside towards a distant ridgeline. A light wake of pebbles trickled down and away behind him, kicked from their places by the hooves of his horse or by his own armoured heels.

He was a short man, but strong. Within the iron frame of his helmet his face was deeply lined. His surplice was a faded blue and white. Under it, and through the long rents in it, peeped a coat of mail that was brown from weeks on the road. His back ran with the sweat of his climb.

Now and again he spoke to the horse that followed him.

3

'Hah-sa, Stefan.'

'Come Stefan, come.'

The horse was a great, grey animal, bred for carrying a knight across the plains of their home: not for these narrow places where nothing was level. It peered unhappily at the ground and picked its way with care, as it had done all day and for many days before this. On its back it bore the knight's high saddle, his bags and gear and weaponry. A spear clunked remorselessly in a long holster, flicking its tiny point of iron against the sky.

The sun was setting when they reached the ridgeline. Shadows welled in the valleys, and in the yellowing light of evening the hill-crests were like islands in a rising sea. Far ahead a high, round-shouldered peak rose to ice-fields that glowed in the last sun. A few carrion birds turned in the air, almost level with the man's eyes. Before him the ridge ran on, bare and rocky, dipping to a sudden end in—

– In a clump of tiled roofs and walls of dressed stone!

The walls were the same brown-grey colour as the rock on which they were built. That was why he had not seen it at once. That, and because it was the last thing he would ever have expected in this place. The path, running now along the very ridgeback, led down from his feet to a gate between two squat towers. There it ended.

A house – of all things, a fortified house! Here, after days of journey into the mountains?

The back of the knight's gauntlet scraped upon his metalled brow. Without thinking, he had put his hand up to rub his eyes. But this was not a dream. His feet were on stone ground. The evening air was chilly in his lungs.

There was no light showing in the building. There was

no smoke from any chimney, no movement or clink or call among its stones. The walls were old – even in this light, he could see that.

The very smallness of the towers seemed sinister.

A house – here?

The mountains were desolate places. Very few people came into them. In the days since entering them he had seen nobody; not even one of the poor, savage hill folk who lived here. Last night he had lain in an abandoned hill village. There had barely been enough room in those mean huts for him to stand upright.

The hillmen did not build places like this.

Nevertheless, it was a house. Men might be there now. And if men were there, they might know, or have seen, or be sheltering the one man he was looking for. Raymonde, his son, at last.

Yesterday he had found the remains of the horse. It had been dead perhaps a week, but still he had known it from his own stables. Raymonde had always been careless with animals.

Damn him!

A fugitive might travel far in a week, even on foot. But the dead horse had been the knight's first real finding in days. After searching and guessing for so long, a sign as firm as that one made him feel he must be close. There had only been one path from the deserted village that had looked as though it might go anywhere. It had brought him here. Now it wound down to the silent gate and stopped. There might be other paths, looping and curling out from the buildings across the hillsides, but none could go far. The ridge dropped steeply on three sides. There was no road off it that he could see but back the way he had come.

So, if Raymonde had followed this path at all, he might be here still. After all these weeks, he might be only a short walk away.

The knight drew a long breath. His throat was tight and his palms tingling.

Now?

But remember what he's done, he said to himself.

Remember, remember; all the sick, familiar litany that brought the rage trembling back into his limbs again.

Remember Varens, your child, his own brother – dead in your keep. Pale and dead and bloody; his eye dull and white fingers clutching at nothing!

Remember – Raymonde *did* that. Did it behind your back! The sneaking, snivelling, graceless, treacherous . . .

Remember Varens – laughing in the house, leading at the hunt, brave under punishment. Varens – *dead*.

Raymonde! You . . . Murder – theft – witchcraft! In *my* house!

*Did you think I would never come for you?*

Reaching up on tiptoe he drew his sword from where it hung by the saddle. It was a short weapon, but familiar to him, and the single oak leaf cut and painted on its pommel was the badge of a woman he had once loved. It settled into his palm and was ready there. He peered down through his armoured eye-holes at the gate that he had found.

Still nothing moved among the buildings. For a moment more he hesitated. But it was no use asking himself if he was ready.

6

*Remember!*

'Let's get it finished, then,' he said aloud.

He led the horse slowly forward. The clank and scrape of their movements sounded in the air. Anyone inside would hear him coming. There was no help for that – except the iron in his hand and the mail upon his body.

The gates were wood: rugged and old. One door was ajar. Sword in hand, point down, he stepped through.

No one lurked behind it. He jerked the other leaf open and grunted to his horse, which followed him big-shouldered into the gate-tunnel and out into the space beyond.

No one.

The knight stood in a small, paved courtyard scattered with dry goat-droppings. To his left the yard was bounded by a low wall, giving a clear view across the valley to the hills on the far side. On the other three sides were buildings with blank windows and doors shut fast. Between two of the buildings opposite was another arch, half-blocked by a goat-hurdle that had been pushed roughly to one side. He stole through.

Here was another court, surrounded on three sides by pillared walkways. And here again there was a low wall to the left, with a view of the darkening mountains across the valley. Shadows gathered in the colonnades. There were more doorways, but they were open. The rooms within were wells of darkness. There was a horrible stillness in this place.

Nothing for it . . .

He stole up to one of the doorways. If there was anyone within they would hear the scrape of his heels upon the stones.

7

Wait. Listen.

His heart was beating hard. Now, in seconds, surely . . .

'Let's get it finished,' he muttered again.

At once he moved, ducking through the opening with both hands on the hilt of his sword, and stepped immediately to his left to set his back against the wall. His thigh banged against something which rocked and gave. There was a huge clatter – things falling, things breaking in the darkness around him. He swore.

He crouched, with his heart still pounding, and groped. Nothing stirred. The room was empty. His fingers found the leg of the trestle table he had up-ended. In the doorway was a pottery bowl, broken. The remains of some liquid had spilled from it. He sniffed, and smelled the decay of food. No one had been eating *that* for days.

And Raymonde?

Carefully, deliberately, he checked the other rooms around the court. He found sleeping pallets, lamps, a child's writing slate, a crude cup-and-ball toy and the remains of a fire with ashes that were loose but cold. A small number of people had lived here – perhaps no more than two. They had lived not like the hill people, but in the manner of the Kingdom, down in the plains from which he had come. Then they had left.

Abandoned houses – or wrecked or burned or looted – were nothing new to the knight. There were so many now, in the fields of the Kingdom. But this house, and the hill village he had found across the valley, had been deserted only a few days ago. And a few days ago, Raymonde had been near this place.

Did that mean anything? There was no knowing. But if Raymonde had come here, he was gone again.

The knight cursed, wearily. He wrenched the great helmet from his head, and his pale, greying hair tumbled to his neck. He looked around him.

In the middle of the courtyard, facing away to the low wall and the mountains across the valley, was a throne. It stood on a platform of blocks. A flight of steps ran up to it from the far side. Faded carvings writhed upon its high back, obscure in the growing dusk. The thing was as large as the throne of the King in his city of Tuscolo, away in the heart of the Kingdom. But what king had ever sat here, high in the mountains, with not even a roof above his head?

The knight paced around it, half imagining that a man, maybe Raymonde himself, might even now be seated upon it, staring out at the peaks that were blackening with the night. But it was empty. There was space before it for a crowd to gather, to hear the words of their lord. Yet that, too, was empty, like all the house.

Darkness was gathering. The knight turned away. Now that he was sure the house was abandoned, the tension of his search was leaving him. After his surge of anger, the same heavy, empty weariness was stealing on him again, as it did time after time. He was exhausted, and lost. He had no idea where he would head tomorrow.

Near the throne was a fountain, with a wide bowl about waist height and a spout from which rose a thin stream of water. It must have been fed by some pipe from the higher ground much further along the ridge. He took his horse, patted it and led it to the fountain to drink. He removed its saddle, its harness and his gear. Then he took a lamp that he had found in one of the rooms and lit it with flint and tinder from his saddle bags.

In the silence he began to hum to himself. He was not a singing man, but noise was what he needed now.

In the outer courtyard he checked each of the store-rooms, finding a little grain, root vegetables, dried fish, dried meats, and firewood cut from the scrub of the hill-side. He went on to the gate, which he heaved shut and wedged with small stones. His breath came in gasps that echoed in the gate-tunnel.

When he had finished he raised his lantern and peered at the walls. Above the inner arch something was carved upon the keystone – a coiling serpent that snaked around and around a disc. The disc itself was blank, except for a break upon its left-hand side where a gash had been cut by some chisel.

The man grunted. He knew it.

'The Doubting Moon. Is that it, now?'

It was a sign to him, as sure as the dead horse had been.

'Tarceny!' he snarled.

It was the badge of an enemy ten years dead. And it meant witchcraft.

It meant the small, heavy book they had given him, with the moon upon the cover, the night the Count of Tarceny had died under the claws of his own demons.

*Take the book into the south,* the King had said. *Keep it in your home, and let none approach it without my permission.*

Poison of Tarceny! He could not read the thoughts his hell-beguiled enemy had written within it – nor would he have ever wanted to. He had locked it in a chest in a high chamber, and had locked the chamber door. He had spoken of it to no one but his own sons. And so down the years he had kept faith with his monstrous charge – until the day when he was abroad and Raymonde had come creeping along the corridors with the iron keys of chamber and chest in his hand . . .

Had taken the book and . . .

. . . cut – Varens – down . . .

. . . when the boy had stood in his way.

And the knight knew his honour was blasted. Men would damn him for what had happened in his house. And they would damn him again for what he must do to avenge it.

'Tarceny!' he cursed again, and felt his limbs ache with weariness.

And here was Tarceny's sign, cut into the gate of a house at the end of the world. That was not chance. Raymonde had been coming here. Something he had read in the book would have brought him. And what?

Again, there was no knowing.

Night had come. Around him the mountain-shapes rose like a huge, still sea. Treading in his bubble of light he made his way to where his horse stood. Company was company, even when it was four-footed and dumb. He found its nosebag and filled it with grain from the storehouse. Then he rooted in a sleeping room for more blankets, and lay down by the low wall with his head pillowed by his saddle and bags. He did not want to sleep indoors, here. If something came to the gate he had fastened, he wanted to hear it. If something disturbed his horse, he wanted to see. He was uneasy. It was better to be aware.

At last, with an effort of will, he blew out his light. He sniffed at the smell of the wick, and wondered how even such a thing as ordinary lamp-oil had found its way to this place.

Above him the stars stood clear in the mountain sky. Somewhere the real moon, nearing its full, must already be rising. An hour or so would see it lift above the ridges to cover the world in dark silver.

'Aun.' It was a voice of a woman, calling softly. 'Aun.'

With a long, breathless struggle, like rising through dark water, he woke. Fragments of a dream still flitted in his mind: Varens, living, laughing; the hall at home; the book safe in his hand. But he was no longer dreaming. He was awake, in the courtyard of a ruined house, almost a week's march beyond the nearest living hearth.

And he knew, with the empty jolt of his heart, that Varens was dead.

In his dreams, the knight thought, he might go home; but in the waking world, maybe never.

He cursed and struggled to a sitting position. The moon was up, paling the stars and pouring silver light over the courtyard. The air was chilly and his breath hung like a frosted cloud before him. It was almost never cold enough for that, down in the plains.

He was sick with half-sleep.

'Aun.'

It *was* a woman's voice, from somewhere close. He looked around. There was a figure, wrapped in a cloak, sitting on the lower steps of the throne. It took him a moment to realize that she had used his given name, as an old friend might. He had not heard it spoken for so long.

The moon was on her face. He knew her at once, but did not believe it.

'Am I still dreaming?'

She seemed to smile. 'No, you are awake.'

He had not seen her for ten years. It was hard to tell if she had aged at all, in this light. A very little, he thought.

'What are you . . . ?'

'Hush!' Her finger was on her lips. 'Come away,' she said, softly but urgently. 'Come away.'

Enemies? Close? As softly as his swimming head allowed, he rose and made his way to sit beside her on the throne-step.

'Speak low,' she said. 'And don't show yourself at the wall.'

'What is it?' he murmured.

'What you would call witchcraft.'

'Tarceny?' he asked sharply.

She put a finger to her lips. He held his breath to listen.

Silence.

Then a scraping noise from below the walls, like stone drawn across stone.

That wasn't a man down there, he thought. No man moved like that. It might have been a beast. But – he could not imagine what sort of beast it could be.

The noises faded into stillness.

'They are around the house,' the woman said. 'They know you are here.'

'Will they come in?'

She shook her head. 'Maybe not. I think their orders are to watch, only. But if they see us, it may madden them.'

He held his breath again, but now he could hear nothing.

Witchcraft. Raymonde had been coming here, with that book in his hands. What had he done?

And – and why was *she* here – she of all people, who had disappeared from the world ten years ago?

He bit his lip, and wondered if he was still dreaming.

No, it truly was her: Phaedra, the bride of Tarceny, after all this time. Her skin, which he remembered as olive-coloured, seemed very pale under the moon. Her long dark hair was hidden within a hood, but the arch of her brow was clear upon her face: clear, and soft as a cold kiss.

She was still listening – listening for something moving beyond the wall. No sounds came. At last she sat back with a slight sigh, and the cloud of her breath silvered in the moonlight.

'What are you doing here?' he asked. His voice was hoarse.

'I have been here since I left Tarceny,' she said.

Ten years – here? What kind of living could she have had here, scraping her keep from these rocky hillsides? After what she had done to bring down Tarceny, she could have been Queen. Or she could have been his own lady. And if she had chosen that, he would have pushed every damned obstacle out of the way to make it so. Instead she had come here.

Why *here*?

'Sometimes,' she continued, 'when the winters were

14

rough, we would go down to the plains. I still have good friends at Chatterfall, you may remember.'

Remember? Yes he did. But . . .

'We?'

'My son Ambrose and I,' she said. 'You knew I had a son, Aun.'

He had known, of course, but he had forgotten. Perhaps he had forgotten deliberately. That *she* should have had a son – the son of the Count of Tarceny!

His fingers had begun to fidget in his lap.

'And you, Aun. Is it well with you?'

What could he say?

'No.'

'You came here looking for someone,' she murmured.

He put his head in his hands and grunted, briefly.

'He has been here?' he asked.

'Yes.'

When? How long ago? Why didn't she say?

'He has read the book, Aun,' she said.

Such a gentle reproach, for what had happened in his house! But he had not yet spoken about Varens. He did not want to.

'Do you know what was in it?' she asked.

'You know I cannot read.'

'But he can.'

'I came – I came to stop him.'

He could not tell her what he was planning to do.

'It is too late, Aun.'

'Too late?'

'Listen.'

For a long moment they sat side by side. Then he heard

the noise again. Out on the hillside, below the low wall that bounded the courtyard, something was moving: something that slithered across the rocks. It was a heartless sound. It made him think of blind evil under the moon.

He half-rose to his feet, but her hand on his arm stopped him. When she spoke again, it was in a whisper.

'I had bound them, Aun. I came here and trapped them and their master near this place, after Tarceny died. I lived and raised my child here, so that I could be sure they could not escape. But your son read of them in the book. That is why he came . . .'

She hesitated. The knight looked sharply at her. For a moment he thought she must have begun to weep.

But no, she was not weeping. She was frowning; and concentrating, as though for some reason her words had begun to give her difficulty.

After a moment she said: 'Tarceny had written of them. That is why your son came . . .'

She was repeating herself. Did she think he hadn't heard?

He knew he was awake, now – fully awake; and she was there and solid beside him. She looked as clear and collected as ever he remembered her. And yet there was something very dream-like about this. She had begun to force her words, still in an undertone, but at the same time as if she feared he was not hearing her properly.

What was this?

'It was a week ago,' she was saying. 'Maybe it was more. I find it – hard to count time, now. He came up the path. He spoke well . . .' She seemed to smile, briefly. 'He would not say why he had come. But I was pleased to see him, because it is lonely here, and maybe because he reminded me of you. We gave him supper. He talked about the Kingdom, and the troubles that poor Septimus is having, holding onto the crown that you and I won for him . . .'

You and I, you and I, she was saying: those days of broken meanings, ten years ago, when she had vanished, and joy had vanished, and left him a sour, rewardless man who beat his own sons: a man to whom laughter and her voice returned only in his dreams.

But was he dreaming, or was she? The way she spoke made him feel as if *he* might be in *her* dream, a thing wavering on the very edge of her mind.

'But when I woke . . .' She was stammering now. 'When I woke he was gone. The door to my house was open. I remembered – that it was to you that the book had been given when Tarceny was killed. Then I followed him. I saw him on the skyline. I tried to stop him, but he struck me. He let them out, Aun. He let them out!'

'Who? What has he done?'

She gave a helpless gesture, as if this were something she had already explained, or had thought he understood. 'Them! Him!' she said, pointing to the low wall. Then she put her hand over her face.

'Ambrose fled,' she said. 'I had told him he should.'

An ugly, hollow feeling was growing inside him. What was it Raymonde had done here? Witchcraft, no doubt of it! Bad enough to drive a boy from his mother – and to empty the village across the valley too, maybe. He had been dreading what his son might do with that book in his hands. Now it had begun.

17

But what, exactly? What? *Them! Him!* What did that mean?

Hold fast. He must not be distracted, even by her. She had seen Raymonde.

'My son,' he said, keeping his voice gentle as though he was talking to someone who was sick. 'Can you tell me where he went?'

She stared at him. Her face was so close that, even in this light, he could see the veins in her eyes, the shadows beneath them and the little lines upon her skin that ten years ago had not been there.

'Can you tell me where he went?' he repeated.

'No, Aun!'

He felt the breath of her exclamation, warm upon his cheek.

'You must not look for your son,' she said. 'You must look for mine.'

What? No! He jerked his head away. At once she laid her hand on his arm.

'Aun! Ambrose is twelve years old – just twelve! They are hunting him . . .'

He did not need this! To turn aside; let the trail go cold; leave Raymonde's wrongs unanswered, when he was so close? To chase after a boy who might be anywhere? Hopeless.

'I cannot leave here, not yet,' she was saying. 'I – I am only beginning to learn how to move again. I cannot help him. You can. Aun, he needs . . . Aun, you *must* . . .'

Must? Why must he?

Why must this be put to him?

He would not look at her. He set his chin on his hand

and thought of Raymonde, while the woman he had once loved pleaded at his elbow.

'He is just twelve,' she repeated.'

'They are hunting him . . .

'I cannot leave!'

Again she was speaking as if in a fever or a dream, as if he were fading from her, and she was desperate to make him understand.

'No!' he said, and shook his head and shut his eyes. And again he said, 'No.'

Then he cursed and rose to his feet. He stood with his back to her, with his arms crossed in front of him and his shoulders hunched against whatever she might say next.

'Raymonde's been here,' he said. 'That's what matters.'

There was a long silence. He heard her let out her breath. In the quiet, his mind began to pick over what she had said, listening to her words for the first time. He turned.

'Did he hurt you?'

She shook her head. 'There is nothing else you can do for me.'

He looked at her; at her face in the moonlight. Her eyes were down. Dreaming or not, she had understood him well enough. He hated to see her so. With a sour feeling inside him he turned away from her again. After a moment he began to pace the courtyard. His mailed feet scraped loudly on the moonlit flagstones.

'I thought the Angels had sent you to me, Aun,' he heard her say. He did not answer.

The sky was clear. The moon was high overhead,

pouring its colourless light over the world. Around him the buildings were drenched in silver. The peaks watched him, their faces marbled in grey and white. His own shadow was black on the paving beside him, squat and armoured, clinging to him like grief.

He had left his living, his house and his manors, and maybe he would never return. One purpose alone remained to him. How could he give that up? How could he begin a goose-chase through the mountains while Raymonde, damned Raymonde, went free with his brother's blood on his hands and witchcraft that could bring the Kingdom down?

And – and what good, what possible *good* would it do? What good could a man like him do for any child? His name was evil and his fatherhood cursed. The boy would be better without a man whose sons became men like Raymonde. Better to let him go where he was going – to those friends at Chatterfall, as like as not. Surely they would do well enough for him there, if he could get to them.

And if he could not?

Well . . . all men suffered equally in the end.

It was Raymonde that mattered.

He had strayed to the low wall that bounded the court-yard. Without thinking, he looked over and down. Under the wall was a drop of twenty or thirty feet to a slope, strewn with great stones, that declined steeply away from him – far, far away into dimness at the bottom of the valley. The light of the moon silvered the rocks and low thorns with elusive depth, as though it struck through clear water. The mountainside was vast, and still.

*Don't show yourself at the wall.*

The enemy – witchcraft!

There, on the slope below him!

They were man-sized but not man-shaped. Or if they were men, they were bagged and cowled in such a way that they might have been any shape. They were watching him.

His blood was lurching. His hands gripped the stonework. Unthinking, his eye had begun to count them, as a man counts his enemies in the moments before the swords come out. Three, four . . . But *that* was not one of them. That was his own shadow – his head and shoulders rising above the shadow of the wall, which the moon had flung down among these creatures to look back up at him . . .

One of the figures moved. It raised an arm – perhaps it was an arm – towards him. In the uncertain light he thought that its fingers were longer and thinner that any man's. It seemed to be trying, hopelessly from down there, to reach him. A feeling of appalling grief – grief and horror – washed though him, as if the thing had drawn its fingers across his heart. He looked into its face and could not see the eyes beneath its hood.

His feet carried him away, stepping back from the wall. He tripped, but recovered. He was breathing hard. His hand went to the sword at his side, but it was not there. It lay beside his pillow, where his horse stood still in the moonlight. He was defenceless. He waited.

Nothing happened.

Nothing. They were watching, not attacking.

*I had bound them here, after Tarceny died.*

21

Fates, what things! What things – savage and lost and pitiful; *beckoning* to him!

In the moonlight he looked at his hands, as if they might lengthen before his eyes and twist themselves into the terrible shapes that he had seen clawing the air from below.

He was shaking.

They're down there, he told himself. I am not. I am still a man.

In his mind he saw the creature again, stretching its limb towards him. *Look*, it had seemed to say.

*Look. The man will let a son die. So that he may make his own son die.*

And his shadow had lain among them.

He drew a long breath, and sought to shake his mind of what it had seen.

Raymonde, he thought. But . . .

*Look. The man will let a son die.*

But . . .

But if Raymonde had found what he wanted here, then Raymonde would be returning to the Kingdom now.

So he must follow, anyway.

Whatever he did, he must retrace his steps through the mountains. And Chatterfall, he remembered, was a manor house at the northern end of the lake – a week's journey, perhaps, from where he stood; not more than a day's ride from Watermane and other gateways to the Kingdom. A child on foot, finding his way through the mountains, would go slowly. If he turned and made his way back now, he might yet catch the boy before he got to the lake. If not, it would not be very far aside to go to Chatterfall. A day or two out of his path – what difference would it make?

Cunning old mind, he thought again. You always are when you deceive yourself. What if you find the boy? If Chatterfall cannot keep him, what then?

What child deserves to be long in *your* care?

And yet – I am still a man.

And Angels! I am tired.

Slowly he made his way back to the foot of the throne where his bundles were lying.

'I think . . . Best you tell me about this enemy who is hunting your son,' he said.

There was no answer.

The throne-step was empty. She was gone – gone, and he had not seen her go. He looked around him.

'Phaedra,' he called softly, using her name for the first time. 'Phaedra.'

Nothing stirred among the shadows of the colonnade. No sound came from the dark doorways of that place.

'Phaedra – I will go.'

She was gone. And though he walked through the rooms and courtyards, calling softly, and sat up hour after hour by the moonlit throne, there was no answer but the emptiness of the mountains.

## II

### The Enemy

mbrose was still very small when his mother pointed out the carved moon to him, on the arch above the gate of their home. He was interested at once, because she said his father had put it there. He had never known his father.

So he would often look up at it, in the years when he spent so much time playing with his white pebbles in the outer courtyard. And later, when he was old enough to take the goats along the mountainside to the pasture or to go down to the stream and fish, he would pause beneath it for an instant before leaving the house. And sometimes he would go to it in idle moments, between chores or even during them.

The moon was a blank disc, chiselled in deep cuts on top of older, fainter carvings that he could barely see. It had a jagged mark on its left-hand side, and it lay within a coiled serpent that snaked around and around it. The serpent was Capuu, his mother said. Capuu was good, because he held the world together. Ambrose understood that the moon itself was not so good, even though his father had put it there. She hadn't told him why, but he thought maybe it was not good because of the mark on it. Or maybe it was like his family name, *Tarceny*, which was never used because she said people did not like it any more. But he didn't worry very much about that until some time after his tenth birthday.

Then a nightmare came to him without warning.

He dreamed he was a small child, awake in a dark room. Perhaps it was a room at Uncle Adam's house, far away at Chatterfall. There was a window, and the sky outside was paler than the darkness in the room. And something moved between him and the window. It was a shape, with a curved back or shoulder that could not have been a man's.

That was all he saw.

He woke in a rush, thrashing and crying. His heart hammered, and he stared around in the darkness, in case the thing he had seen was already standing beside his pallet.

The Thing! He could not remember what it had looked like. He thought . . . He did not know if this had been in the dream, but he thought that the curved shape had had long hairs on it, that stood up like bristles, and a neck that had slumped to a head that . . .

He hadn't seen the head.

But it had *been there*, in the room. It had been looking for a way past a line of his white pebbles; looking for a way to where he sat wide-eyed in the darkness.

'*Mother!*'

She rose, warm and sleepy, from where she lay on the other side of the room. And although he normally did not hug her very much, he curled up and clung to her like a little child. She murmured to him, and rocked him, and told him it had only been a dream. But she could not comfort him, because he knew it was more than that. Somewhere, long ago, he had seen the Thing before.

'You were safe, my darling,' she said after a while. 'They could not come at you.'

So he knew it was a memory. Something had really happened. Anything that had happened once might happen again. He clung to her tightly and could not speak. They both stayed awake until dawn.

'Very well,' she said at last, as if she had decided something.

With the light strengthening at the window she made him get up and dress. She led him out of the house before they had even had breakfast.

She led him along the path, down into the chilly mountain-shadow. Then they turned left and began a long scramble straight up towards the ridge that soared away above them.

They were climbing up towards the places where he was never, absolutely never, allowed to go.

She did not allow it, because it was dangerous. It was not the same sort of danger there was at the streamside, because once she had taken him down to look at the water in spate, and had made him promise to take care, she had let him roam there at will. And it wasn't the sort of danger there was from the occasional wolf or lynx that she pointed out to him on the hillside, either. She always seemed to have her eye on the ways over or round to that side of the ridge, and whenever she saw him on them, or looking at them, she would call him sharply away.

Now they were going there together. And it had something to do with his dream.

He did not want to meet his dream. Not even in daylight. Not even with his mother by his side.

His heart was beating hard with the climb, and his limbs felt hollow from effort without food. By the time they reached the top his whole body seemed to be trembling. He gathered breath, looking about him at the far mountain-scapes: ridges and silent peaks, veiled with wisps of cloud. Opposite him, the mountain Beyah rose high in the sunrise.

The ridge on which he stood was narrow. The ground was level for only a few paces. On the far edge was a tall white stone standing like a sentry among low thorn bushes. Beyond the sentry-stone the ground dropped again. He picked his way over to look down a slope he had never seen before. And he gasped.

Sunk into the hillside before him was a great, circular pool. It lay among steep, tumbled sides to which thorns and scrub clung in patches. At their lowest, opposite him, the cliffs were little more than the height of a man. But from the highest point, near where he stood, they fell some fifty feet to the bottom. And all around the cliff-tops stood a ring of tall, grey-white stones.

She put her hand on the nearest.

'Try it,' she said. 'Push.'

He put both hands on it. The surface was rough, and covered with old lines that must have been cut by men. He pushed. Nothing happened. He placed his feet carefully and pushed again, using his legs and all the column of his body. He might as well have been pushing at the mountain.

'It's not going to move,' he said.

27

'No, it isn't.'

Again Ambrose looked about him. Nothing seemed to have happened yet, but he was still nervous. The cold air made him shiver. At the same time he did not want her to know that he was afraid.

'I could get a lever,' he said stoutly. 'And I could dig away the ground.'

'You could. And in time you might move it. But I don't want you to. That stone is your safety, my darling. I've brought you up here to show it to you – and all its friends. Come, let's try the next.'

Her voice was calm. Puzzled, Ambrose followed her.

They picked their way down the rough, thorny slope to the next stone. This was balanced right on the very edge of the cliff. Surely, if he rocked it hard enough, it might go.

He tried. It would not budge.

'I am more anxious about this one than any of the others,' she said. 'But as you see, it is fast in its place.'

'What are they for?'

'They are a prison, my darling. And we are the jailers. Let us try the next.'

They went on down the slope. It was difficult going – it always was on the mountainside, unless there was a path. In the still air of the dawn their voices and the clatter of stones under their feet echoed flatly from the far cliff. Ambrose kept glancing into the pit. The surface of the pool was nearer now. He could see nothing in it but the reflection of the sky.

They tried stone after stone. Most were tall, like the first two. But others were lower, thin and flat like blade-bones, and two were simply boulders that crouched like beasts among the thorns. Ambrose was able to move one of the blade-bone ones just slightly – a hair's-breadth in the earth at its root. The rest might have grown straight from the mountainside.

They were approaching the lowest point in the cliff, opposite where they had started. A huge stone rose there, like the tooth of an enormous beast.

Pebbles rolled under Ambrose's feet. He swayed, and once more looked to his left into the pit.

*'There's someone there!'*

'Yes,' she said, and did not turn around.

There was someone there, standing among the low rubble that bordered the far edge of the pool: a thin figure, hooded in a grey robe, looking into the water.

There had been no one a moment before.

The figure was standing quite still. It made no sign as Ambrose stared at it.

'He likes the sunrise, even now,' his mother said. 'That's why he shows himself at this hour. If we had come at another time there would have been nothing for you to see.'

She was waiting by the next stone. He scrambled down to her and peered around it at the grey man on the far side of the pool.

He was still there, still looking into the water. Ambrose could see him quite clearly, across the fifty or sixty yards between them, standing motionless like one of the big heron-birds that waited bright-eyed by the stream for something to kill.

The rising sun was filling the bowl of cliffs with light. The pool held the reflection of the rocks, and of the grey figure, with barely a tremble on its surface.

29

'Who is he?' Ambrose whispered. His heart was still beating hard with the shock.

'Who is he, indeed? He is our chief prisoner. But that is only the end of his story, not the beginning.'

Her eyes were fixed on the man by the pool. Her jaw was set, as if she was looking at something foul or disgusting. Ambrose shivered.

'I was born to a high house, Amba. But to the man you see I am no more than a daughter of farmers – so he once said. What kind of man could he be, do you think?'

She drew breath, and spoke loudly so that her voice bounced among the cliffs.

'Ambrose, tell me the names of the first princes.'

She meant the seven sons of Wulfram the Seafarer, who had led the people over the sea three hundred years before, to conquer the land and live there. It was the very first story out of history, and he knew it quite well. But . . .

But the figure lifted its head and looked at him. Under the hood, its face was that of an old man with deep-sunk eyes. Ambrose could almost feel those eyes, resting like a weight upon him.

'Their names,' she repeated, standing strong at his side.

'Dieter, and Galen . . .' he began awkwardly.

'Louder.'

She wanted the man to hear what he said. Ambrose didn't. He could still feel the eyes that watched him. But he filled his lungs and spoke out as he had been told.

'Dieter and Galen. Marc . . .' He hesitated. Then he went on: 'Lomba. Hergest, Rolfe and Talifer.'

*Talifer*, echoed the cliff opposite. It was the name of

his own ancestor: the prince who had founded the house of Tarceny.

'Indeed.' She smiled, as if between them they had won a small victory. Still speaking clearly into the air, she began to walk down towards the big stone. 'You have told the names that men remember.'

'But . . .' Ambrose was still staring at the figure by the pool. Without thinking, he had begun to bite the knuckle of his thumb.

'But,' she said, 'there was one son who is not remembered. You are looking at Paigan, the living brother of all those first princes. And through all the years between then and now he has pursued his brothers and their descendants. He ruined them and brought them to evil in any way he could, until all the house of Dieter was destroyed, and so were the lines of Galen and Marc, Lomba and Rolfe and Hergest, and of the male line of Talifer only your father was left; and at last only you.

'And then we caught him – the hill folk and I.'

She gave a little laugh.

'Yes,' she said, calling across the pool. 'How was such a terrible prince caught by a daughter of farmers?'

*Farmers*, said the far rocks.

For a moment more the figure looked at them. Then it moved at last. It turned and walked with slow paces away along the apron of rock that fringed the pool. Over the still water Ambrose could hear the pebbles clatter lightly beneath the old man's feet. He watched, fascinated. Again he was reminded of the herons, and the jerky way they walked among the reeds and white snow-fisher flowers by the stream.

'He finds it galling, you see,' she said softly. 'For he

thought me no more than his tool. And now he is trapped. He cannot pass the stones.

'And pleasant company I wish him,' she called across the water, 'among those that are with him there.'

. . . *with him there*, said the far cliff.

The man paid her no attention. He paced on, alone by the water.

'Who else is there?' asked Ambrose urgently.

She looked at him.

'The things you remembered in your dream, my darling. Creatures he sent to kill you, when you were a child less than two years old.'

Ambrose stared around the enclosed pool. Nothing moved among the bright rocks. The surface of the water showed only the reflection of the cliffs and the grey figure standing beneath them. Ambrose swallowed.

The Thing! Here!

'You are right to be afraid, Amba,' she said. 'I brought you up here to tell you this.

'I know what you saw, because I have seen them, too. They are savage things, desperate and ill-formed. They come from deep within the pool. When they were free, they could appear anywhere in the land without warning.

'But also I have brought you here to show you that the ring of stones holds them in. They cannot escape unless the stones fall. Neither can he.'

This man, and his . . . Things. All his life they had been here, within a mile of the house! She had never told him there was anyone on the mountain but themselves.

'What does he eat?' Ambrose whispered.

'He does not need to eat.'

'Where does he sleep?'

'He does not sleep.'

The grey man paused on the far side of the pool. Once again he looked into the water.

'What's he doing?' Ambrose hissed.

'Waiting for you.'

Waiting for him.

Ambrose swallowed. Why him? It didn't seem right or fair. He had always done what he was supposed to. He watched the goats. He gathered firewood when they needed it, and even when they didn't. He prayed . . .

His mouth was open to protest when another thought came to him.

It came to him suddenly and clearly, like a whisper in his head. And it had nothing to do with anything that had been said before; and yet it seemed absolutely right and to the point. It was the thing to ask. It was the moment to ask it. So he did.

'What happened to my father?'

She frowned, sharply, at the figure across the pool.

After a moment she said: 'Come away.'

'But what happened . . . ?'

'I will tell you, my darling; but not at *his* bidding. Come away.'

She walked quickly away from the pool, down the hill-side below the tall stone. Ambrose followed a pace or two. Then he looked back.

The man by the pool had disappeared.

'Amba, come *on*,' she said.

He hurried after her. She led him swiftly downhill along a faint, narrow path that ran away towards the tip of the ridge where the house stood. In places it faded altogether beneath screes of grey pebbles. The footing was bad. But she did not slow her pace, and he slithered along behind her as best he could. He knew something had made her angry.

After a while walls appeared on the ridgeback above them. It was the house: their house. He had never seen it from this angle before.

Abruptly she stopped and seated herself on a boulder. She rested her chin on her hands, looking out and away to where the peak of Beyah was colouring with the morning sun. There was just enough room on the rock for him to squeeze onto it beside her. He wanted to be as close as he could, now that he knew what else lived on their hill.

'Let that be a lesson to both of us,' she said at last. 'Never taunt a man who is helpless: especially if he is not quite as helpless as he seems. I should not have done it. And I should have kept us well back from the ring. But I was angry for you, after what you remembered last night. And now he has paid me back through you.'

'I only asked . . .'

'He wanted you to ask, Ambrose. And you did. And it hurt me, for your sake and mine, just as he intended. No, don't worry. I will tell you. But first remember how easy it was for him to suggest it. Remember, too, that when you looked back you could no longer see him. He is often very hard to see. So now you understand why it is that you must *never* approach him. Above all you must never listen to him, or speak with him, no matter how important it seems that you should.'

'Yes,' he said.

'So,' she sighed. 'Your father.

'You know your father was Ulfin, Count of Tarceny. He was a fine man, handsome and masterful. He ruled a great march of land within the Kingdom . . .' Her hand waved away along the ridge. 'And he wanted to be King, because he saw much that was wrong with the Kingdom and believed that he could right it. To be King he needed power. He found this strange grey man, who now called himself the Prince Under the Sky, and who offered him power and claimed him as a son.

'What your father did not understand was that he was being tricked. The Prince had only hatred for him. He hated all his brothers and their descendants, because their settlements had succeeded where his had failed.

'Did you never wonder why there was a throne in the courtyard of our house? It was his. We live in what was once his stronghold. But it was not strong enough. His brothers abandoned him. He was overwhelmed here in the mountains by the very hillmen he had come to conquer. They flung him bleeding into the pool, meaning to make an end of him.

'Perhaps they thought he would be a sacrifice to appease their goddess. For the pool holds the Tears of Beyah, who in their legends is the mother of the world.'

Beyah was the mountain across the valley. But yes, she had told him that the hillmen thought her a goddess. Of course the hill-gods were stories, and you did not pray to them in the way she had taught him to pray to the Angels. But she had also said that they were something more than stories. So he frowned, and tried to grasp the story he was being told.

'But the Prince did not die. Instead the Tears gave him the power to live and work ruin. That was the power he offered to your father, long afterwards. The Prince offered it to him in a stone cup. I saw that cup. It was just a plain, rough-carved thing. But it held the Tears. And so, in a way, it held the whole world.

'Your father used it. He knew that using it was wrong, but he needed it, and he persuaded himself that he was just being clever. He knew other people would have called it witchcraft and evil, but he called it *under-craft*, which in his provinces is a word for cleverness. He wrote his thoughts on this in a book, which I do not have.

'Now this is the hard thing I have to tell you, Amba. In his war to become King, your father needed this "under-craft" very badly.

'So badly, that when the Prince told him that the price for it would be your life, he agreed.'

Opposite them the mountain of Beyah hunched against the sky. Fingers of light were creeping down its ridges like the runnels of tears; Ambrose remembered that very clearly afterwards, just as he remembered the tremble in his mother's voice when she said those words.

'He did not succeed. I had friends – Evalia and Adam diManey, who hid you at Chatterfall, and others whom you don't know. Your father was defeated by a man called Septimus, who was less masterly but more honourable. Septimus is King now.

'And in his last living moments your father turned on the Prince who had ruined him. And an angel spoke through him to our enemy. It said: *Paigan Wulframson, least of your father's sons. By the last of your father's sons shall you be*

36

*brought down.* Remember that, my darling, because as I have said you are the last of the son-to-son descendants of Wulfram. The Angel was speaking of you.

'You are the one who will bring that son of Wulfram down. He knows it. He tried to stop your father saying the words. And when he could not, he killed him.'

'You told me he was killed by his enemies!' he cried.

'He was, my darling. Now I have told you why. And now you see why I came here to catch this Prince, and why we live here, in the very house that he built for himself three hundred years ago. Because men have made themselves kings, one after another. Yet all the time he has been the hidden King, who moves men and kings like so many pieces on a chessboard. And he brings ruin on all of us. All the fields I grew up in are wastelands now, Amba. Wastelands. And the wars and troubles that wasted them had their seeds in what he has done.

'And if he were free, he would hunt you with every power he had, because you are the last of his father's sons.'

It was a lot to understand. She had told him before that he was descended from Wulfram, but she hadn't made it seem important and he hadn't realized that it was. He did not see how the mountain could have wept, or how the man by the pool could have lived for three hundred years, or could go on living where he was without sleep or food; waiting, and wanting to hunt him.

But what he thought about most of all, as he sat dumb and miserable on the hillside, was his father.

Ambrose had always wondered what his father had been like. He had often imagined meeting him, and finding ways to please him. Now he knew that his father had tried to kill him. He wondered what it was he could have done that had made his father want to do that.

She put her arm round his shoulders, and he let her.

Thinking didn't seem to make it any better. It just hulked at the back of his mind, like something horrible that he couldn't see but always knew was there. The things he wanted to ask would not form themselves. They stuck in his throat as if he might poison himself by saying them.

Other questions, less important, came more easily.

'So that man is my uncle?'

She frowned. 'Yes, in a way. He is your uncle across nine generations. But it is dangerous to think like that, Amba. I have told you how he carries his quarrel with Wulfram's descendants. You must not approach him.'

He was silent for a moment longer. Then he asked: 'Which angel was it?'

Now she laughed.

'My darling – what a question! The Angels move within us, fleetingly, and do not stay to introduce themselves. My friend Martin, who was a priest, called this one the voice of Umbriel, and that will do, I suppose . . .'

She often spoke to him about the Angels: Umbriel and Gabriel, Michael and Raphael; whom Heaven had sent to carry its light into the world. Seven-eyed Umbriel was his favourite, because at birth he had been given the Angel's name: Ambrose Umbriel. He had not known that she had actually met any of them. But it did not surprise him very much, because he knew she had lived in the lands of the Kingdom, and had met so many people there – kings and princes and knights and bishops. Why not angels, too?

Why not – after this?

And it didn't help anyway.

'I don't like it,' he said.

She sighed.

'I know, my darling. I took you up there so that you could learn what it was you were afraid of, and to help you be less afraid. And instead I've let him make me frighten you even more. And he's made us both miserable into the bargain. So it is, with him, even now. But there's nothing we can do but bear it, go on living, and maybe learn a little in spite of him. And that will be our revenge.'

Her arm tightened around his shoulders and gave him a little rock.

'We can begin now,' she said. 'With breakfast. Why don't we have a little of the honey today, to cheer us both up?'

'Yes please.'


Later, he went back to asking questions – many times, and often the same ones. She always answered, even when he did it just to distract her from being angry with him over something he had spoiled or something he hadn't done. She would finish scolding him, and then, after a few moments, she would say:

'Your father did not know you, my darling. At the time he had never set eyes upon you. And he did not really know the mind of the man he dealt with. Men can do very evil things to people they do not know, and when they listen to the words that that man speaks.'

'I'll get a bow and arrow,' Ambrose said once. 'I'll give the hillmen one of our goats for them. Then I'll go up and shoot him.'

She smiled.

'He would be gone before your arrow had flown half the distance. Don't you remember how he appeared and disappeared? There is a place he can go where no arrow can follow him.'

'Where?'

'Not far: into a dream of this world, I think. Anyway,' she added, frowning, 'the angel did not say "kill". I would gladly see him dead, but I do not know . . .'

'Then what am I to do?'

'I do not know.'

'Then how am *I* supposed to know?' he shouted at her.

'Mind your manners. I do not know *yet*. For the time being, we just go on living. That's all we need to do.'

He knew she had told him the name of the enemy; but he never had to use names much and he knew that his own was spoiled. So it did not seem fair that his enemy should have a name at all. He made no effort to remember it, and in his mind he called him 'The Heron Man', from the colour of his cloak and the way he had stood by the pool.

And he did as he was told, and stayed away from the ring of stones.


'Living' seemed to mean that his days should be filled with things she wanted him to do: fetching water from the big underground cistern; taking their half-dozen brown goats out to feed among the greener patches on the hillsides, and bringing them back up to the house again at the end of the day. Milking them, hand-feeding them, making sure they were penned into the outer yard. Cutting, carrying, and drying the goats' winter feed; cutting and carrying up firewood, carrying up and drying fish from the traps; and, of course, Taking Care. The older he grew, and the more he would do, the more she seemed to worry about him. She kept warning him not to fish when the river was high, for fear he might be swept away. She kept warning him away from the pot, for fear that he might burn himself. Of course he tried stirring it when she wasn't looking, and, as luck had it, he *did* burn himself. He didn't think that proved anything, but she did.

And when chores were done, there would be other things, before he could play or they could have supper. There was a slate on which she showed him how to write letters, and then words. He must write any word that she said, and form the letters correctly too, if he wanted to eat well that night. She had two small books of prayers to the Angels, and she made him read them until he knew them by heart. Even when they had finished with the slate, and he had begun to play with his cup-and-ball game while they waited for the pot, she never seemed to stop wanting him to learn things.

'You know, the hillmen say that the world is like a cup,' she said as she watched him one evening.

'That's because they live with mountains all round them,' said Ambrose, who could remember their last trip to the house of the people he called Uncle Adam and Aunt Evalia at Chatterfall, in the Kingdom where the great broad sky stretched in all directions.

'That's one reason. Now, the mariners of Velis say the world is like a ball.'

The ball bounced rebelliously out of the lips of the cup. Ambrose looked at her, crossly.

'Who's right, then?'

She smiled.

'Maybe they both are.'

'They can't both be right!'

'They can, because the world can be more than one thing. Perhaps the cup and the ball are each a dream of the other.'

'You're being silly,' he said.

'You're being slow. You should be able to catch much faster than that. Let me.'

She reached for the cup, and he let her have it. With quick movements she swung the ball into the cup *clip-clip-clip* three or four times, but then the ball bounced out, as it always did if it landed on the part that was a bit pointy. It tumbled free to the end of its twine.

Ambrose laughed. His mother sighed.

'I could have done it with my old one, in my father's house at Trant. I should have made this one better.'

'Why didn't you?'

'Amba!' she said reproachfully. 'Was I ever taught to carve wood? I did my best, and no one can do you better than that. If you don't like it, play with your stones.'

'Did you make those?'

'No. Someone else did that.'

'Maybe I will, then.'

'Mind your manners, Amba, or there'll be no supper.'

He knew he would not give up the cup-and-ball, because at least the cup-and-ball *did* something, while the pebbles just sat there, or got lost by themselves when he wasn't looking. But he wanted to let her think he was thinking of it. So he picked some up from the windowsill where he kept them, and turned them over in his hands.

42

'Why do the stones keep him in?' he asked. 'Why can't he walk between them?'

She took a pebble from his palm and held it up before his eyes. It was one of the more knobbly ones, with the same faint lines and traces on it that they all had.

'It's stone, isn't it?' she said.

'Yes.'

'It is, and it isn't. The hillmen say they are teeth from the mouth of the world-dragon, Capuu. Capuu is very strong. They cannot come past him – so long as the ring is left to stand.'

She watched him turning it in his fingers.

'You have got them all still, haven't you?'

'I think so.'

'That's not good enough, Amba, and you know it. Find them and count them out for me, please.'

He sighed, and she looked up sharply. But there was no point complaining. She had always fussed about keeping the pebbles together – even more than she fussed about keeping him away from the pot. He gathered them in fistfuls and counted them out on the table for her.

'Thirty,' she said, nodding. 'And mine makes thirty-one. Just as there are thirty-one stones by the pool. Each of these was cut from one of those stones. They have the same virtue.

'That was how we caught him, you see. I knew that he dwelt at the pool, because it was the source of his power. And I had found out what the stones do. So I came into the mountains with gifts for the hill village on the other side of the valley. They fear him, but they also hate him. One morning I approached the pool, with forty hillmen and their beasts. The ring was broken then, because one stone – the big one – had fallen and was out of its place. But I laid your pebbles across the gap before the enemy was aware of us. And so he and his powers were caught within the ring. Then we raised that big stone, inch by inch. It took us almost four days. Some of the hillwomen came and played with you and made you grass-dolls while a few yards away the rest of us were sweating and pulling on the levers and ropes that shut him in. And when it was done you and I went down to live in the enemy's house, and the hill folk went singing back to their village. And the enemy could do nothing.'

The hill people knew about living, Ambrose thought. They also knew how to play while they did it. Their village was perched on the opposite slope, some way along the valley. It was the only place within a day's walk where other people lived. Sometimes she took him there when she wanted things like baskets and clothes and tools, which the hill folk made much better than she could. On those days they had to leave at dawn, carrying items from the little store of trading goods that she had brought up from their visits to the Kingdom. They would walk and walk down their side of the valley to cross the stream at the bottom, and then climb up and up, following the path that wound backwards and forwards, and it was always more bends than he remembered before the little stone-built huts came into view.

Ambrose liked the village because going there was an adventure; and because of the little, bird-like hill folk too. They smiled (with very few teeth) and played music on their pipes for him, and sometimes gave him titbits of a kind that his mother did not make. They called him *hala-li*, which she said meant 'little king'. He supposed it was because they knew he lived in the house with the throne. He wondered if they also knew that he sometimes sat in that throne pretending to be a king addressing armies that would go out and conquer all the mountains for him.

In the summer after he was twelve, she began to let him go to make her trades on his own. He liked that, too. Bargaining was fun, using hand signs and face expressions and the very few words he knew of the language of the hills. And it meant that he could spend a whole day away from the narrow crib of his home and out in the beginning of the rest of the world. And when he was in the village he could look at the path that ran on away from it, along the hillside, up and down for days until it came at last to the Kingdom and the great lake, and to places like Chatterfall, which was the only other house he knew.

But he could never stay for long. He would have to start back in the very hottest part of the day if he was to be home before darkness. And he would walk and walk back the way he had come, until at last he would be climbing up the final stretch of path in the summer dusk. His feet and legs would be aching, and so would his shoulder if he was carrying anything heavy. The air would be cool and the mountain-colours fading.

And he would look up at the hillside above him, where the jagged ridgeline hid the pool and the stones around it.

And he would think: *He's still waiting.*

# III

## The Man Who Shaved

he had asked him to spell 'justice' on his slate and he hadn't formed the letters well.

'It isn't any use anyway!' he yelled at her. 'The letters don't *do* anything.'

'That's enough! I'll dress you in goatskin if I must, but letters are a thing I *can* give you and I will *not* leave the job half-done!'

'But there's only the prayers to read, and I know them already!'

'Amba, that's enough!'

They glared at each other for a moment. He was nearly as tall as she was now. But he still couldn't meet her eye when she was angry. He sat down, fuming, and looked at his slate again. He knew quite well what strokes she expected to see, but his fingers didn't want to do them. Neither did he.

'I'm never going to use them though, am I?' he grumbled.

'*Ambrose!*'

Now she was angrier than ever.

'You have *so* many things to learn still! One of them

46

is that if you do something you should always do it properly. So you can write it out now, or start again tomorrow on an empty stomach. It's up to you!'

He mumbled and hung his head. But the moment her back was turned he stalked out of the room and banged the door behind him. He hurried across the throne-court to the archway. Here his way was blocked by the hurdles that kept the goats from straying inwards during the night. He dragged them aside, passed through and replaced them firmly, as if he could wall his mother in with them. Then he strode, furious, into the outer yard.

Running out on her was happening quite often now. She kept saying that he was twelve and should be able to do more, and he kept thinking that he wasn't going to put up with it. And yes, it usually cost him his supper, but at this time of year he could wander the hillside while the light lasted and find berries to fill himself up a little. The trouble was that it never got him out of doing what he didn't want to do. Later that day, or maybe the next, he would have to get down to it – or miss another supper. So she always won.

She wasn't going to this time, if he could help it. This time he was going to do something – something so bad she'd think twice before ordering him around again.

The goats, which he had brought in from the hillside an hour before, were gathered in a small flock against the low wall. They lifted their heads and looked at him with their misshapen eyes.

He thought of opening the outer gate and driving them all out onto the hillside again.

But that would be stupid. Either he'd have to go and

get them all back later or, if he didn't, they might both starve that winter. No use.

He wanted to break something – a door, maybe. Or perhaps start a fire.

Start a fire? The tinder was back with her in the kitchen. He wasn't going back there.

No use, again.

He thought of going to the Heron Man.

He could do it. She would be furious, but he could do it any time he liked.

He thought about it again. The Heron Man, and his Things. He never saw them. But sometimes he thought he could feel that they were up there. They were up there all the time, day and night, like a cloud hanging beyond the ridge.

*Never approach him, never speak with him.*

Ambrose shuddered.

No use again, he thought.

But why not? The Heron Man couldn't get out. It ought to be safe. Ambrose could go up there whenever he wanted – whenever she upset him. He could talk to him as much as he wanted, from behind the ring of stones. And it was a man up there – a man like Uncle Adam, away at Chatterfall. Not someone like Mother. Maybe he was someone Ambrose could really talk to.

What was it like, to be as old as all the stories – three hundred years or more?

*Never speak with him.*

No father! Nothing! It just wasn't fair!

'It's only *you* that says he's evil!' he said aloud.

She was not there to hear him, so he could say it. He

48

might say other things, too. It was only *she* who had said that his father was wicked! It was only *she* who had said that his father had wanted to kill him! Why *didn't* she want him to talk to the man by the pool? *What* was it she was afraid he would say?

It wouldn't matter, so long as he stayed back from the stones. Nothing could reach him from inside the ring. He could talk, or taunt if he wanted to. She had done, the last time. Why couldn't he?

And if the Things appeared he'd just – just throw stones at them!

At once he turned and walked briskly towards the outer gate.

The goats crowded in under the archway after him, as they did whenever he took them to pasture. The gate-tunnel echoed with the sounds of their hooves, magnified to a great cavalcade. He pulled one leaf of the door inwards, meaning to step through and shut it quickly behind him. Then he stopped. The goats stopped, too.

There was a man on the path outside.

He was a complete stranger, who had stopped dead in the act of reaching for the door.

He wasn't a hillman. He was taller than they were – about as tall as Mother. He had long brown hair, a brown and stained cloak, and heavy, dusty leather boots. And his cheeks and chin were concealed in a thick mat of brown beard, which looked very strange to Ambrose. None of the hillmen had hair on their face like that, nor, so far as he could remember, did Uncle Adam.

And his eyebrows slanted darkly, even when they were lifted in surprise.

49

'Ho! Someone does live here after all,' said the man. His accent was strange. Where had he come from?

His clothes were good – much better than the goat-wool tunics or rough mantles Ambrose was used to – yet they were stained and needed mending. He carried a pack over one shoulder. His staff was freshly cut. Ambrose knew there was no tree in this valley the man could have got it from. He must have walked a long way. Altogether he had a wild, mysterious air. Ambrose was impressed.

'. . . I live here,' he said, recovering. 'So does my mother.'

'Your mother? Anyone else?'

'No.'

'Anyone come here – in the last month, say?'

'No one ever comes. Not for as long as I can remember,' Ambrose said.

The man dropped his pack heavily to the ground and looked at him sideways. Ambrose gaped back. Behind him, in the gate-tunnel, the crowd of goats waited.

'And how long is that?' asked the man.

Ambrose could not answer.

'How old are you then?' said the man.

'I'll be thirteen this winter. Um. Do you – do you want some water?'

'Thirteen?' The man raised his brows again. 'Good. Well, you're tall for your age, anyway. But then I was born to a line of runts. And, yes thank you – it's been a thirsty climb.'

Ambrose remembered that all the bowls and pails would be in the kitchen, and that Mother would be in the kitchen, too. He didn't want to have to go in to her again.

But the man reached into his pack and drew out a leather bottle, which he held out to Ambrose. Ambrose took it. It was empty.

'Wait here,' he said, and ducked hastily back inside the doorway. The goats were still there, looking at him expectantly. He tried to pull the door shut behind him, to block them from going out, but it stuck on the stones as it always did. He was about to try again when he realized that the stranger would probably think it rude to have the door slammed in his face. Maybe he thought Ambrose had been rude already. But there was no time to think about that. The man wanted water.

He scattered the goats back into the yard, slipped past the inner goat-barrier and walked softly over to the fountain. The door to the kitchen was open, but Mother did not call from within. He did not call either. Nothing like this sudden arrival had ever happened before. He wanted to keep it to himself for as long as he could. He waited anxiously while the thin stream of water filled the bottle, and then hurried back to the gate, thrilled by the chance of being able to talk to the man again. *You're tall for your age.* True, Mother sometimes said the same. But it had never sounded so rich with praise before.

The door was still ajar. He could see the light cracking from top to bottom of the outer arch. A couple of goats were back at the tunnel, looking interestedly at the opening. If he had left it another few moments they would already have made their way outside. He slipped past them and squeezed noiselessly through the gap.

The man had sat down with his back to the arch, intent on something in his hands. For a moment he did

51

not seem to realize Ambrose had returned. Then he looked up.

The thing in his hands was a book. The man closed it with a snap.

A book!

'Can I see that?' said Ambrose, eager for anything new.

'It's mine,' said the man, thrusting it back into his sack. As it disappeared Ambrose glimpsed a shape upon its cover: a blank disc with a mark upon the left-hand side.

'Is that a moon on it?' he said. 'My father's sign?'

'What? Your father?' The man looked hard at him. Slowly, his hands drew the cords on his pack closed and knotted them firmly. 'Who is your father then?'

'He died when I was a baby.'

The man's mouth drew into a wry grin.

'Lucky, aren't you? Wish mine had. Is that my water? Thanks.' He took the bottle, and drank.

Ambrose waited, puzzled but pleased at the same time. He wasn't sure why the man had put away the book, or what he had meant about fathers. But the man was glad to get the water, and didn't seem to mind that Ambrose had inadvertently half-shut the door on him.

The brown face of a goat peered through the doorway. Ambrose shooed it back inside. In a moment he would invite the man in anyway.

'Thanks,' said the man again. He seemed to have drunk the bottle dry. But he was in no hurry to get up. 'So . . . you've lived here all your life, have you? Seems to me I've been travelling for half of mine. Tell me now. Is there anywhere around here I might bathe?'

Ambrose thought. 'I could draw a pail . . .'

'All over, I meant,' the man said.

Ambrose stared at him. The man grinned again.

'I'm just a *bit* dusty, you see,' he said.

'There's the stream back down at the bottom of the valley,' Ambrose said. 'You must have crossed it. On your way here . . .'

He hesitated. He could tell from the man's look that that was not what was wanted. 'Or . . .'

'Or?'

Ambrose hesitated again. You *couldn't* go up to the pool. Not to bathe, surely. That would be . . .

On the other hand, he had been about to go there himself, hadn't he?

Why shouldn't they go – the two of them? It would be a real adventure.

But that would mean going *inside* the ring . . .

'Or?' said the man again.

'I think . . .' said Ambrose.

'Aun!' cried Mother. 'Is it really you?'

They both started at the sound of her voice. The man scrambled to his feet. She was standing in the gateway. For a moment she was smiling with delight. Then, as the man stood, her smile faded. She frowned.

'Your pardon, sir. I mistook you for an old friend.'

'I . . . grieve to disappoint you, madam. I am not he.'

The man finished with a movement that bent his body at the waist. Ambrose knew what it was, because she had taught him how to do it himself. It was a bow. It had always seemed silly to have to practise it when there was no one to bow to. This was the first proper bow he had ever seen anyone do.

'You must come in, sir,' she said. 'Ambrose, the goats . . .'

'I was keeping an eye on them,' said Ambrose, surly because he was being rebuked in front of the stranger.

They entered the gate-tunnel together, and Ambrose closed the gate firmly behind him. She led them across the outer yard to the second arch and unfastened the goat-barrier there. Again Ambrose fastened it behind them.

In the inner yard the stranger stared curiously around him – at the throne, the buildings, the fountain. Mother looked at him closely.

'Do you know the house of the Baron Lackmere, sir?' she asked. 'Your face recalls him to me.'

The man hesitated. Then he said, 'Your eyes do not deceive you, madam. My name is Raymonde diLackmere.' He bowed once more. Ambrose bowed, too.

She smiled again, broadly. 'Then sir, you are most welcome, for your father's sake and your own. And I give thanks to Michael, that he has guarded you on your journey, and to Raphael, for you are safe come.'

'Thank them indeed,' said the man. 'If I may know . . . ?'

'Your father knew me first as Phaedra, daughter of the Warden of Trant, and later as the Countess of Tarceny.'

'O-oh,' said the man slowly, as if he had suddenly understood something. He bowed again. Ambrose bowed again, too, and wondered when either of them would notice. At the moment they seemed to have eyes only for each other. Now the man was looking at her narrowly. Maybe he was trying to decide what sort of woman she was – what she knew, why she was here. And she was smiling again, smiling broadly, as if she had just been given a wonderful and unexpected present.

'Is your father well?' she asked. 'Has he sent you to me?'

'He is in good health,' the man said. 'And no, I am here by chance. My horse died and I was lost. I followed a path, not knowing where it would lead.'

'A strange chance! What brought you to the mountains at all, sir?'

'A whim, my lady, I assure you. If my father knows of this place, he has not told me.'

He was asking a question, Ambrose realized. *Did* his father know of this place? He had said he wished his father had died. Ambrose wondered what kind of father it was that the man had.

'To my knowledge he does not,' she said. 'We have not heard from one another in ten years. It was only the chance of your coming that let me think he might have had news of me. But now you are come, and welcome. Rest with us, and eat with us. Ambrose shall wait upon us both. It will be good practice for him.'

Ambrose bowed again.

'Is his water ready yet? she asked, coming into the kitchen where Ambrose was setting the table. She tested the small pot on the hearth with her finger. 'It should be warmer than this. A little longer, maybe,' she said.

'What does he want it for?'

Splashing sounds were already coming from the courtyard where the man, stripped to the waist, was washing himself from a pail that Ambrose had carried to him from the rain cistern.

55

'He wants to shave. Now, Amba. You've not seen a man shave before, have you? So you can help him. You'll need to get him some of the fat, and a sharpening stone, and as soon as the water is ready you can take them all out to him. I'll finish in here . . .'

She was happy, excited. She seemed to have forgotten their quarrel in her pleasure at the man's arrival. She went on talking while he rummaged for the sharpening stone.

'. . . Also, we'll need to make a bed for him by the hearth. So you'll have to move our pallets into the next room . . .'

'What has he got to do with my father?' Ambrose asked.

She looked surprised.

'Nothing that I know of, although his father had. Why do you ask?'

'No reason.'

He still resented the way she had taken all the stranger's attention from the moment she had appeared. He was willing to bet she would do the same over supper, too.

'So what did his father have to do with mine, then?' he asked a moment later.

'His father is Aun, Baron of Lackmere, and he was one of your father's enemies. But he was also a great friend to me. Without him, and without people like Adam and Evalia, neither you nor I would be alive today. The King owes him much, too. After your father died, the King sent him to take charge . . .'

She stopped.

A frown crossed her face, as though some smell had drifted into the room, and she could not tell what it was.

Her hand had stopped, too. She had been in the act of laying a knife on the table. The short, metal thing hung in her fingers, a few inches above the boards.

Slowly, she set it in its place.

'What is it?' Ambrose asked.

'Nothing,' she said. 'I remembered something, that's all.'

She looked at the table, as if she had forgotten what she was doing.

'Why,' she said aloud. 'Why does a man come riding a week into the mountains by himself? What sort of a whim is that?'

'Maybe he's bored at home.' Ambrose nearly added, *Like me*; but he managed to stop himself. She would know he was thinking it anyway – if she was paying attention.

'Riding his horse until it drops? I'd like to know . . .' She cleared her throat. 'What did he say to you when he first arrived?'

'Not much. He wanted water.'

'Water?' she said sharply.

Ambrose nodded out to the courtyard. 'To drink, and then wash in.'

'Oh, I see. Yes, of course he would. All the same . . .'

She was still thinking; staring at the table and thinking. Her mood had changed. She was looking the way she sometimes did when she was worrying about stores and whether there would be enough to get them both through the winter.

'Amba?'

'Yes?'

'You say nothing to him of the pool, please. This

57

young wolf has a right to our hospitality, but not to our secrets . . .'

Wolf? Why did she call him a wolf?

'And you must be careful what you do say. The less the better. Talk about shaving if you like. Let me do the rest, until we know more.'

'What do you think he'll do?' he asked.

'He'll have supper with us and go to bed and go on his way when he's rested.'

'But . . .'

'Never you mind what else he *might* do,' she said sharply. 'I don't doubt he is honourable enough . . .

'He'll tell us when he's ready, I expect,' she added.

Ambrose clamped his mouth shut. It was exactly as he had thought. She was going to enjoy the man's company, but he wasn't allowed to. It was *Take Care* again: don't go near the stream when it's high; don't burn yourself at the pot; don't talk to the only man ever to have come to the house.

She was bending over the pot in which the water was warming.

'That will do,' she said. 'It mustn't be too hot. You can take this out to him now. And help me put the broth back on the hearth. And when you've done out there you can come back with your bowl. I don't forget bad manners, Amba; but just for tonight I think you had better have a full belly despite them. And . . . yes, after you've done those other things, I want you to make sure you have all your white pebbles.'

Ambrose sighed inwardly. Those wretched pebbles again!

'They're all there,' he said.

'Don't argue, Amba. I want you to make sure. Now take this and hurry. I think he's waiting for you.'

Released at last, Ambrose took the water and carried it out, eager at least to see the mystery of a man shaving away his beard.

She had told him about great houses, where the boys of knights and nobles waited on their elders at table. She had played games with him, pretending to be a strict and stern lord, and making him carry her cup and bowl to her with his back stiff and his head high. So that evening he did as he had been shown, carrying the water, the dried fish and the weak root-broth in turn, first to her, and then to the guest. He stepped slowly and kept his face solemn, lingering each time to make sure the man had what he wanted, and to steal another close look at him.

He was still fascinated by the way the man's face had slowly changed as his beard had come away under the knife. It had become leaner and more pointed. The cheeks were hollow, and now they glowed an angry red. They must be sore, he thought. But the man had never complained. He had talked all the while in an easy, friendly way, asking questions about Ambrose and his mother, and the mountains, all of which Ambrose had thought harmless enough. And he had explained about shaving, and how to make knives sharp enough to do it. It had taken a long while, and yet it had all been over too quickly for Ambrose. He wanted the man to talk to him again. He wanted the man to look up from the table and speak to him now. She couldn't stop him answering if that happened.

The man was hungry. He took a large cut of the precious cheese that Ambrose brought to him. He took most of the dried fruits from the bowl that was to serve the three of them. He did not look up. Instead all his attention was on her, as he talked about happenings in the Kingdom. Most of hers was on him, except now and again when she gave Ambrose a sign to bring something to the table.

A nod of her head sent Ambrose scurrying for more dried fruits. As he ducked out into the courtyard with the bowl in his hands he heard her laughing lightly at something the man had told her.

Did she trust him now? Or was she just pretending? Ambrose had never known her pretend at anything. He didn't know whether she was any good at it. But she always seemed to know when Ambrose was pretending, so maybe she was very good at it indeed.

In the storeroom he took a moment to steal some of the dried fruit and stuff it into his mouth. He might as well reward himself for doing this chore. And if they weren't even going to look at him, they wouldn't see how his cheeks were bulging. Then he filled the bowl and hurried back.

'There is war coming in the Kingdom,' the man was saying as Ambrose came back into the room. 'It is the same thing again: the house of Baldwin rising against Septimus. This time it is the Lord of Velis who makes the challenge.'

'As though there had not already been enough,' she sighed. 'It was Baldwin's misfortune that the best of them were slain ten years ago.'

The man did not agree. 'Velis may yet prove a match for Septimus. A stronger king may be a good thing indeed.'

'At each rising men say the same, and the land suffers for it. I had believed your house was loyal to Septimus?'

The man looked at her, lazily across the table. Suddenly Ambrose thought he understood why she had called him a 'young wolf'. Ambrose had seen a wolf not long before, while guarding his goats at pasture. It had been standing still in the cover of some thorns, with a careless slope to its head and shoulders as though it were not thinking of doing anything; and piercing eyes that gave out the lie.

You always had to watch for the wolf.

'Sometimes, sometimes not,' the man said. 'Everyone makes their choice, don't they?'

'And they are judged for it.'

'Judged?'

'By men while we live, and after by the Angels,' she said.

'Hmm.'

The talk had stopped for a moment. There was something else here that the two of them did not agree on. Ambrose wasn't sure whether it was about kings or angels or both.

She looked up at him.

'Ambrose, you may go to bed.'

He bowed, saying nothing in case she realized that his mouth had fruit in it.

'Goodnight,' called the man over his shoulder.

In the musty-smelly chamber that he had made into a temporary bedroom for himself and his mother, Ambrose unrolled his blanket and lay down. He could hear their voices, muffled by the wall. He wanted to hear if they were still talking about kings and rebellions and exciting things like that, but he could no longer pick out the words. So he sulked, and his fingers played with the small pile of white pebbles he had made by his pallet, and he wondered why she had felt they might be needed all of a sudden.

Then, because he was tired, he slept. He did not hear his mother bid their guest a good night and come to lie down in the room beside him.

He did not hear the man rise and leave the house stealthily just before dawn. He knew nothing until his mother's hand was shaking him, urgently, frantically, in the grey of the morning that saw the end of his world.

'You must not follow me, Amba,' she said, in the last few moments by the hearth while she waited for ink to dry on a piece of paper before her.

Ambrose was still struggling to dress. He understood, with a sense of loss and bewilderment, that their guest was gone. He had no idea where or why.

She seemed to know.

'You must go across to the village and wait for me,' she said, as she knotted the paper into a little roll with twine. 'If I do not come today, you must go to Chatterfall and give this to them there. Here is coin for a boat at the lake . . .'

To Chatterfall? By himself?

'Quickly, now. Tie the purse to your belt. And you must take the pebbles.'

His fingers fumbled with the string. By the time he had tied the knot, she had already left the room.

The pebbles. He scooped them up from the windowsill,

piling them in his hands because he had no other way to carry them.

She was outside under the archway, pulling aside the goat-hurdle. He followed her. Because he was clutching the pebbles against his chest he could not pull it shut behind him.

'Quickly, Ambrose,' she called from the darkness of the gateway opposite.

He hurried after her. She had the gate open. The path along the ridgeback was a pale thread, leading away in the darkness of dawn.

She looked at him.

'Untuck your shirt and carry them in the fold in front of you. Try not to lose them. And whenever you are still, place them around you. Now, Amba,' she said, embracing him. 'I love you. Go quickly. Do not come back to follow me.'

So of course he followed her. Once he had gone a little way down the hillside and was out of sight, he doubled back. He saw her hurrying away along the faint path that ran below the house. He tracked her, moving swiftly, around the end of the ridge and uphill on the far side. She never looked behind her. He saw that she was heading for the pool. So he guessed that the man must have gone to the pool before them.

And still he did not understand.

So he was there to see her, scrambling uphill around the pool, calling to the man who was standing at the cliff-top; to the man who levered and strained with his staff against a sentry-stone.

From the cover of a patch of thorns Ambrose stared up in disbelief. Didn't the man know what he was doing? Didn't he realize how dangerous it was, even to be there?

The poolside was empty. The Heron Man was nowhere to be seen. Maybe he was hiding somewhere – in that dream that she had spoken of. Maybe their visitor did not know about the Heron Man. They had to get up to the man and warn him – make him stop before it was too late! They should have warned him the night before, only she had thought the pool and everything must be kept secret.

He was felling the stones!

How could he be doing this?

He heard the man shout something, angrily. The point of the staff had broken under the stone. The man drew it out and looked at it. He paid no attention to Mother, who came running and calling along the clifftop towards him. Ambrose saw her reach him, and clutch at his wrists. He heard her shouting at the man, begging him to stop. He saw the man wrestle one-armed with her, and push her away.

Then the man's other hand came up, swinging the broken staff into the side of her head with sickening force.

She fell.

Unbelieving, Ambrose saw her tumbling in the air. Her body bounced once among the rocks, outwards, like any pebble that tumbled down a hillside. Then she hit the water in a white splash, and disappeared.

Slowly the surface of the pool stilled. She did not reappear. On the skyline the man had bent to his work again, prodding and levering with the longer piece of his staff, as if nothing had happened.

And from his hiding place in the thorns Ambrose stared and stared at the pool, waiting for her to rise and struggle to the shore. But she did not.

Only when the first stone tumbled in a roar of rocks to the cliff-foot did he start, gather himself and run – run as though all the Things in the pit were already after him.

His feet carried him, slipping and skidding, back around the end of the ridge, under the walls of the house that had been his home. The goats were already out, spreading down and along the hillside from the open gate. They scattered before him, and bleated at him as he passed. He ignored them. White pebbles jumped from the fold in his shirt as he stumbled, and rolled away down the hillside. He ignored them, too, and ran on.

## IV

### The Fight at the Falls

hen Ambrose came down a looping track through pinewoods a fortnight later, he had just eight white pebbles in his hands.

He was tired, hungry and exhausted.

He could hear a waterfall, somewhere to his left among the trees. He remembered that from before, just as he remembered clearly this thick smell of pine trees in the sun. He was somewhere close to Uncle Adam's house now. He really was.

He hadn't remembered how far it would be from the jetty where he had said goodbye to the man with the boat. The road had gone on and on by the lakeshore, between reed-beds and high hills. He had begun to wonder if he was going to find the house before nightfall. But there was still an hour or so of daylight left, and now he was close. Now he knew he would get there before darkness came.

His feet hurt. They seemed to be hurting worse than they had before his long rest in the boat. Starting on them again had been agony. He hadn't bothered to put his shoes back on. They were no more than scraps of goatskin now, held together in places by twine. They flapped as he

66

walked and were no help at all. Still, he was moving as quickly as he could, shuffle-shuffle down the path, because he knew that the journey was nearly over.

Further down the slope voices began to mingle with the sounds of falling water. People were calling to each other, unworried, unhurried in the easy afternoon. He could see the sunlight through the bare trunks ahead of him. He could smell woodsmoke. The track was levelling. He hobbled on. He was approaching a clearing.

He stopped in the shadow of the last tree.

Was this the place?

He was looking across a sunny, grassy space decked with fruit trees. On the far side was the roof of a long, wooden house, rising above a cluster of sheds and a stockade. There were people in the clearing, moving slowly with baskets. Chickens clucked and wandered among the closely-nibbled tussocks, unafraid.

Was it? Surely it was. He wanted it so badly to be Chatterfall. And the sights prodded and ordered his memory until it agreed with what he saw. It had been like this the last time. After days of travelling through the mountains, down the river and across the lake, they had emerged suddenly from the pines into a clearing with fruit trees, and beyond them had been the house: Chatterfall – warmth and comfort and safety, waiting at the end of everything.

Only she wasn't with him, this time.

There were two women picking fruit in the clearing. The nearest was tall, dressed in working clothes, and her brown, grey-streaked hair was tied roughly back from her face. She was talking idly over her shoulder to the woman at the next tree. Ambrose watched her hands move among the low branches – twist and pick, twist and pick, placing the fruits carefully in her basket. He saw her stand on tiptoe to reach a high fruit. It was very ripe, and fell almost as her fingers closed on it. She lost it, and it dropped on the ground. It would be bruised now, and would spoil, Ambrose thought. Better eat it at once. He could almost taste the fruit from where he stood – warm, juicy and sweet with sun.

The woman seemed to think so, too. She said something, laughed, and then stooped to pick the fallen fruit from the tussocks. She put it to her mouth.

Then she saw him.

Ambrose stepped, hesitantly, into the light, and began to make his way towards her. He was trying to decide if this was Aunt Evalia. She wasn't quite as he remembered from his last visit, years before. He didn't think her hair had had grey in it then. Her long nose looked pinched.

She watched him as he hobbled towards her. She still had the fruit in her hand. She was frowning.

'What do you want?' she asked.

She did not know who he was. For a moment he wondered if he had come to the right place after all.

'Is – is this Chatterfall?'

They were looking at him warily, as if he might have some disease.

'What is it you want?' the woman repeated. 'If it's a meal, you can ask at the house and say I sent you . . .'

It was her.

'You're my Aunt Evalia,' he said.

She was not really his aunt. But there had been a time when she had told him he could call her that.

'What? Who *are* you, boy?' Her eye fell on his hands. 'What have you got there?'

She came closer, and he opened his grip to show her the white stones. She picked one out, and turned it in her long fingers as though she could not believe what she was seeing.

'Angels!' she exclaimed softly, staring at him. 'Is it – *Ambrose?*'

'Yes,' he said.

'But – what's happened to you? You're a skeleton! Have you been ill? Where's your mother?'

He juggled the stones into the crook of an arm, so that he could reach one shaking hand inside his shirt. He drew out the little roll of paper that she had given him in the last moments of leaving. Aunt Evalia broke the twine around it and read it. There were only two lines of writing. Ambrose saw her lips form an exclamation.

'Is she coming after you?' she asked.

'No,' he said.

He looked at the ground before his feet, and waited to be asked how he knew. He sensed her eyes on him, her mouth parting to press him further. He felt so weak that he thought questions would crumple him up altogether.

Perhaps she saw that.

'We must get you up to the house,' she said. 'When did you last eat?'

'This morning,' said Ambrose.

That was true. The old man in the fishing hut had given him a drink of water and a half-loaf of bread before they got into the boat together. And there had been fruit and another loaf at the same hut the night before. There had also been cheese, but his stomach had been weak after days of eating only berries, and he had felt sick at the smell of it.

'Look at his feet, mam,' said the other woman. 'He can't walk on those!'

Aunt Evalia looked down, and frowned. 'No. We must lift him. Help me, Vinney . . .'

'I'm all right,' he said, as they lifted him in arms that seemed so very strong.

'Mercy of Angels,' said the other woman. 'You don't weigh a feather!'

'Adam!' called Aunt Evalia. '*Adam!*'

They carried him between them through the gate in the stockade. The little yard beyond it was all earthy, just as Ambrose remembered it, with straw spilling out of the low byres and scattering in wisps across the ground. The place reeked of animals that were not goats. An elderly man whom Ambrose did not know was brushing down a horse by the door of the main house. He looked up, astonished.

'Where is Master Adam?' Aunt Evalia called to him.

'Gone down to the Creek Acre, my lady . . .'

'Please find him and ask him to come to the house as quickly as he can. You may take the horse. Thank you.'

They carried him into the dimness of the long room of the house. Ambrose remembered the odours at once: the rushes that lay all over the floor; the hearth, which did not smell like the hearth at home because here they burned big logs cut from wood that did not grow in the mountains; and the hairy-wet reek of Raven, Uncle Adam's huge, black fighting hound, who lay in front of the hearth watching them with yellow eyes.

Ambrose had always been afraid of Raven, because

he was so big, and because he growled. He was growling now, a low, frightening sound, as the women carried Ambrose up to him. But Aunt Evalia spoke to him sharply, and the other woman poked at him with her foot, and Raven heaved himself shaggily from the hearth and stalked out of the room, as if he was not going to stay with any strangers that he wasn't allowed to bite.

They put Ambrose down in one of the two big chairs by the hearth. The woman Vinney went off to find bread and water. Aunt Evalia knelt to peer at his feet.

'You came the whole way on your own?' she asked.

'Yes,' he said.

After a moment he added: 'I did get lost once. There was a bit I didn't remember.'

There had been so many places he hadn't remembered. The mountain paths had risen to ridge after ridge, beyond which would lie bare, empty valleys, without any tree or crag that he could recognize from the time before. And beyond each valley there would be another ridge, which he might or might not reach before night came. And then there would be another night.

'I didn't like the nights so much,' he said.

'My dear . . . you're here, and that is what matters. But you were lucky it was not winter.' Her long, clean fingers probed at his scabbed and filthy soles, and at the swollen tendon in his heel.

'Ow!' he said, and jerked his foot away. He couldn't help it. It hurt.

'How long is it since the pains started?'

Ambrose shrugged. 'I don't know. After the first day, I think.'

71

He had not known, when he had set out, what would happen to his shoes, and then to the feet within them; just as he had not realized how hungry he was going to become, or how hard it was going to be to sleep in the cold nights, on rocky ground with no blanket but the unmeasurable darkness full of sounds.

Aunt Evalia murmured to herself, and nodded. He could not remember her ever being angry or surprised before, but she seemed surprised now. Maybe she would be angry as well. Mother might have been angry, especially about the damage to his shoes. But he did not see what else he could have done. There had not been a donkey to ride this time. And he had had to keep going. He had kept going because he had known that he must find his way to Chatterfall.

And he had known that he *would* find his way, because it was the only place there was to go to.

'Vinney!' Aunt Evalia called. 'We will need more water, and bandages. And – yes,' she said to Ambrose, as she rose to her feet. 'I am afraid these must have salt. And salt!' she called again.

Vinney came back, bringing bread and fruit and water, and promised him broth when the pot should be ready. They washed his feet, and it smarted. Then Vinney took a palmful of salt from a small sack and Aunt Evalia put her hands around his ankles.

'This will hurt,' Aunt Evalia said. 'But you must bear it.'

It hurt more than anything Ambrose had ever known. He howled and tried to jerk his feet free. White stones fell from his lap and scattered over the floor as he reached down to snatch at her wrists, but she held him and spoke to him while Vinney rubbed the stuff mercilessly into his ragged soles. By the time they finished he was sobbing. Aunt Evalia lifted a bowl of dark liquid to his lips. It smelled strong, and sour.

'What is it?' he said, still wincing.

'Wine. It will help the pain. Drink it.'

He did not like the taste. And when he had finished his feet seemed to be stinging as badly as ever. But he could look around him at Uncle Adam's long hall, while Vinney began to load the pot with vegetables and herbs and – yes – bits of meat, to make his mouth water.

'It will be a while before it's ready,' Evalia said to him. 'But there's bread and fruit on the tray.'

'Thank you,' he said.

'We need Adam,' said Aunt Evalia. 'Where is he?'

The bread and fruit were at Ambrose's elbow. But he did not reach for them straight away. He remembered that he was no longer moving, and what Mother had told him to do whenever he stopped to rest. He leaned forward, and began to place the white stones, which had scattered on the rushy floor, one after another in a circle around his chair.

When he had finished, he looked up.

Aunt Evalia was watching him. There was a new expression on her face, as if she had suddenly been told very bad news. He wondered if she knew what the stones were, and what it was they kept away. Then he remembered that it had been Aunt Evalia and Uncle Adam who had helped to hide him from his father, and that the room where the monster had appeared in his dream had been at Chatterfall.

73

'What have you seen, Ambrose?' she asked.

He shook his head. 'I haven't seen anything.'

He hadn't seen anything. But he had heard things, on his journey out of the mountains: things that blundered in the nights around where he lay. He had listened with his limbs locked and his heart hammering, staring at the darkness for the shape that had moved in his nightmare; but nothing had come close enough for him to see. And nothing had stopped him getting to Chatterfall. So perhaps it had only been wild beasts after all.

Anyway, he was here now.

Aunt Evalia looked over her shoulder. The room behind her was empty. Vinney had gone out into the yard. She crouched down beside Ambrose and lowered her voice.

'Ambrose, where is the Prince Under the Sky?'

He looked away.

'Ambrose,' she said again. 'I can see you are tired, and upset. You can tell me your story when you are ready. But I need to know this now. Where is he?'

'I don't know,' he mumbled. 'He'll be out, but I don't know where.'

When she said nothing, he added: 'They can't get me. The stones keep them away.'

She looked at the white stones he had laid around him. A frown gathered on her face.

'There used to be more than this,' she said gently.

'I lost some,' he said.

He had spilled them several times, especially on that first day when he had had so many to carry, and had run and run without daring to stop and search for any he

74

dropped. And then later he had been so tired, and hungry. It had been hard to count them all, and know how many he had.

'It doesn't matter,' he added again. 'They keep him away.'

He was trying to sound brave. He wanted to reassure her, and himself, that it would all be all right. He had been horribly afraid, but now he had got here. So it would be all right.

He knew, of course, that eight stones were not very many at all – not enough to protect Aunt Evalia, or Uncle Adam, or Vinney, or anyone else but him if the Things came. But he didn't know what the answer to that was. He was exhausted, hurt, and hungry. It was difficult to think.

All at once Aunt Evalia knelt and put her face within inches of his own. Her hands were on his shoulders.

'Ambrose,' she said.

Her voice was level. But her fingers gripped him tightly.

'These pebbles may help. They can keep his creatures away. We must pray that they will. But remember that he is very subtle. Murder is the least of what he does. If he is your enemy – and he is – then there are many ways he can attack you. And whatever else diverts him, he will not forget about you. You must not forget, either. You must watch for him, all the time. And remember that he is often very hard to see. Do you understand?'

'Yes.'

'Watch all the time, Ambrose. It's important.'

'Yes – I know – yes.' He didn't want to think about it. He had watched, or tried to watch, all the long journey.

He thought he had barely slept. Now he was here. He wanted to rest, and eat, and rest. And she wasn't letting him. He covered his face with his hands.

Aunt Evalia put her arms around him and gave him a squeeze.

'Maybe we should not say any more until you're stronger,' she said. 'You're here, and we can help you. Remember that. And we'll be having supper soon. See if you can sleep a little now.'

He drew a long, shaky breath, and nodded. Then he bent down in his chair and began to rearrange the stones around him. He moved one a few inches to the left, adjusted another, looked at them, and put the first one back almost where it had been. So he went on around the ring. When he got back to the first one he started again. This time he did not finish. He shifted in the big wooden chair and pillowed his head on his arm. It was all so much more warm and comfortable than the rocks on which he had lain for a fortnight. The wine was stealing on his brain, and he was feeling sleepy.

He slept all that night, and most of the next day, lying huddled among his stones on a makeshift pallet by the fire. They roused him to eat, and murmured to him, and he fed and lay down again without ever having woken properly. Someone came and bandaged his feet, which brought back the pain. He protested sleepily, and people murmured to him again. When they had finished they went away. The fire was warm, and his pillow soft, and he lay for hours, feeling as weak as a sack of bones, and did not stir.

Once, when he lifted his head from his pillow, he saw

Aunt Evalia standing on the far side of the room, before the wooden chest that the house used as an altar. On the wall above the chest was a hanging cloth, with four great faces embroidered in it, like people, but with flaming hair, halos and staring eyes that pierced into the room to see everything that happened in the house. They were the Angels: Michael the Warrior, Raphael and Gabriel, and Umbriel with the book in which all things were written. Aunt Evalia's hands were open as she stood before them. She seemed to be praying. Watching her reminded him of his mother, and the way she had prayed at home.

They had not asked what had happened to Mother, yet. When he got up, he supposed they would. He hoped they would not ask too many questions about it.

He dozed again, and again people came and spoke beside him. This time they were not speaking to him, but to each other. It was Aunt Evalia and a man, sitting together by the fire. They spoke in low tones, as if they did not want too many people to hear. The man had a soft, wheezy voice that Ambrose remembered. He sounded gloomy. Aunt Evalia sounded worried.

'There's other news,' the man said. 'Velis and his rebels are at the gates of Watermane.'

'Will they come this way?' asked Aunt Evalia.

'Maybe, maybe not,' said the man. 'Watermane is strongly held. But certainly it is too close for comfort.'

'This will be his doing, I suppose.'

'His?'

'The Prince Under the Sky.'

'It's too soon, surely,' the man protested. 'The rising started weeks ago!'

Ambrose realized that the man must be Uncle Adam. He wanted to lift his head and look, but for the moment it was too heavy.

'One way or another he will have a hand in it now,' said Aunt Evalia. 'I know him. Chaos is what he loves. He will bring grief all across the Kingdom – the worst that he can, because the Angels have told him his time is short.'

Neither of them said anything for a while. Ambrose thought that he should get up, because Uncle Adam was there. Uncle Adam had always been important to him. There was something very fine about the fat, balding man, Ambrose thought. He still remembered and treasured the few words that had passed between them on his last visit. But his head and limbs and shoulders all felt very tired, so instead he shifted on the pallet and let his body rest again.

'He's waking up,' he heard Aunt Evalia say.

'Will that – Prince – know he's here? He'd have come by now if he did, wouldn't he?'

'The stones may be hiding Ambrose from him. But the Prince knows our house. He may come here anyway. Or send – others.'

'Hmm,' said Uncle Adam, sounding gloomier than ever.

'I had thought we would repair the riverbank tomorrow,' he said after a moment.

'No one must go out of call of the house.'

'Hmm.'

'There is still fruit to pick in the clearing, if you wish to be busy.'

'Me? Pick fruit? What will the men say?'

'I am behind with my tasks, because of Ambrose and

other things. I have thrown myself on your mercy. As ever, you have gallantly accepted and will come to my aid.'

'We will have to tell them soon.'

'I know. But I have not yet thought what to say. If any of our people take fright and run off we shall be worse placed than ever.'

They were silent again. Someone else had entered the room and come up to the fireplace. Ambrose heard a stirring stick moving in a pot, so probably it was Vinney, who had come in to check on the supper. Perhaps that was why Uncle Adam and Aunt Evalia had stopped speaking.

There was a cry from outside.

'See what that is, would you, Vinney?' said Aunt Evalia.

Vinney mumbled something. Her footsteps receded across the floor. After a moment Aunt Evalia spoke again. Her voice was barely more than a whisper.

'Adam. If the Prince has been loosed, it will be because the one who loosed him felled or moved at least one of the stones around his pool.'

'And so?' said Adam.

'So if the stones can be raised, his powers may be trapped again.'

'You mean us? Go into the mountains? All that way?'

All that way, thought Ambrose.

'Phaedra did,' Aunt Evalia said.

'Hmm. We'd need horses, chains, pulleys – what's the ground like?'

'I don't know.'

I do, thought Ambrose.

'A week's journey? Ten days? Winter comes early in the mountains. Do you know the way?'

'Ambrose does. But he needs to get stronger.'

'Will the Prince allow it? Or whoever released him?'

'Someone must do it, Adam.'

She's right, thought Ambrose. That was what they had to do. And together they could go back and shut the Heron Man away again. And then they could be safe. He would get up and tell them she was right, in a moment.

The cry came again, closer this time. It sounded as though someone was running. And now Vinney was calling inward from the doorway. Aunt Evalia and Uncle Adam got quickly to their feet. Someone else had joined Vinney in the doorway – the runner, Ambrose thought. A boy's voice was calling 'Maister! Maister!'

And then everyone seemed to be talking at once.

Ambrose opened his eyes. He looked up at the rafters and battens and straw of the roof of Chatterfall. From the dimness he guessed that it was evening again. Rushes had been lit around the room, casting their dull yellow glow on patches of wall and on a trestle table that had been set for supper. He must have slept the whole day away.

After a moment he managed to lever himself to a sitting position and look about him. He looked first for Uncle Adam.

Uncle Adam was at the doorway. He was fatter and more bald than Ambrose remembered, but still the same. At that moment he was talking to a boy of about Ambrose's age, who was dressed in a woollen jerkin and carrying a herding crook in his hand. The boy was telling him about something he had seen in the woods. The boy's voice kept rising, and Uncle Adam kept shushing him and making him talk more quietly. The boy was pointing out

80

of the door at the woods beyond the manor yard. His arm made a circling motion, as if he meant that whatever it was he had seen was moving around the house.

Ambrose watched Uncle Adam nodding and at the same time calming the boy at the door. He longed for Uncle Adam to come and talk to him instead. He had a story to tell, too. He wanted to tell it to Uncle Adam, and to see him nod like that and maybe grunt with surprise as he spoke of his journey out of the mountains, and the way that they could go back to shut the Heron Man in. He waited for Uncle Adam to look towards him.

Aunt Evalia passed, talking urgently with Vinney. 'A cloak for Ambrose . . .' she was saying. 'And – will we have any shoes that would fit him? No matter. He could not walk anyway. He must ride with me.'

Ambrose looked round. Ride? Tonight?

'Quiet!' Uncle Adam said. 'Quiet, all!'

Something had changed, Ambrose realized. Everyone seemed to be hurrying about, talking in undertones, getting things ready. Whatever attention they were giving him seemed to be about getting him ready, too. He did not know what he was supposed to be ready for. Maybe it had something to do with what the shepherd boy had seen.

Across the room the old groom came to help Uncle Adam put on a thick coat of padded leather that dropped to his knees. It strapped together at the back and bulged in rings around his body, making him look like a big, squat caterpillar standing on end. Adam was grumbling under his breath. Aunt Evalia passed Ambrose again, and gave him a quick smile.

'It will be all right,' she whispered.

They're worried about something, he thought. What is it?

Why wasn't anyone talking to him?

With a long clinking of metal Uncle Adam struggled into another garment. This seemed to be a shirt of bright links, which fitted over his leather coat. It had a hood of the same metal weave that he drew up around his head. Then he stooped for something that stood propped against the door-frame. Ambrose knew what it was. A sword.

'Vinney, Ambrose will need a pouch for the stones,' said Aunt Evalia. 'Please bring me the large drawstring purse. Quickly. And my cloak . . .'

The serving woman muttered and began to pull things out of a chest. Aunt Evalia went over and spoke in whispers with her husband. Ambrose saw her lay her hand suddenly on his arm. It ended with them both looking silently out of the window at the coming night. When Vinney scurried back across the hall with things in her arms, they shushed her and went on listening.

What were they trying to hear, beyond the endless sound of the falls?

Vinney scuttled over to him and laid a pale canvas pouch on his knees.

'What's happening?' he hissed to her.

She looked hard at him, as though whatever it was must be his fault. Then she was away, hurrying after something else she had been told to get. He watched her go, and saw that she was frightened. That frightened him, too. He gulped, and remembered that he was supposed to gather up the stones from around him. One, two, three, four, five, six, seven, eight. The big purse held them easily. It had a long drawstring that he could pull tight, knot, and then loop over his head and shoulder. He found that his hands were shaking.

'Ambrose!'

Aunt Evalia, now wearing a thick, brown cloak over her dress, was beckoning him to where she stood with Uncle Adam at the door.

His feet were still bare, apart from their bandages. He picked himself up and hobbled over to Aunt Evalia. She gave him a quick squeeze of the arm.

'Ambrose,' she whispered again. 'We must leave the house, and you must come with us. Be brave and do as we say. It will be all right.'

Ambrose looked to Uncle Adam, standing in full mail and holding his sword at the scabbard, and waited for him to say something. But Uncle Adam did not speak. His eyes stared unseeing at some point on the rush-strewn floor, as if he were trying to solve a puzzle that was too clever for him.

'Can I have the letter back?' Ambrose asked suddenly.

He could see it where it lay, among other papers on a little writing table against the wall. Now, if he was going to have to leave again, he wanted to take it with him.

Her eyes followed his, and saw it. 'Why . . . ?'

'She wrote it.'

'Oh.' Aunt Evalia looked at him, with a little frown. He could see that she had been wanting to ask what had happened, but there had been so many other things to worry about that she hadn't. He stood there thinking: *Not now. I don't want them to ask about her now.* But perhaps she guessed something, for she said: 'Of course, of course,' and went over to bring it to him. Then she put her arms round his shoulders and gave him a hug. He had not asked for that.

The letter was a narrow strip of paper. On the inside was the short message that she had written, in that hurried dawn when they had woken to find that the 'young wolf' from the Kingdom had slipped away and gone up the hillside.

*To My Dear Beloved Friend Evalia diManey. One has come to loose Him. I beg you take care of my son Ambrose. Your friend Phaedra, of Trant and Tarceny.*

It was her writing. He had left so many things behind. He did not want to leave this, too. He put it carefully into the drawstring purse.

With a finger on her lips Aunt Evalia led him out of the door. It was night outside. The moon had not yet risen. He could barely see across the yard to the stockade, the outbuildings, and the wooden fence-gate through which they had staggered together just the day before. A big shape loomed out of the night beside him. It blew heavily. It was a horse.

Arms caught him and swung him upwards.

'Up you go, sir,' whispered the old groom in his ear.

The horse snorted and sidled away from him. There was a stirrup, and he managed to get his foot into it. His raw soles screamed at once, but as soon as his knee took his weight he was flung upwards like a sack, and was able to struggle into some sort of perch in front of the saddle.

Someone was climbing smoothly up behind him. That was Aunt Evalia. The groom moved to the horse's head. Ambrose clutched at the animal's mane and perched there, swaying. He was sitting on a rolled blanket that must have been put there for him. Behind, he felt Aunt Evalia settling herself into her seat. Her arms reached past him in the darkness and found the reins.

'Quiet now, my dear,' she whispered.

He thought her voice had a tremble in it.

Suddenly the horse began to move under them. The groom was leading it over to stand in the shadow of the stable by the gate. There they waited.

At the door of the house a torch flared in the hand of a servant whom he had not seen before. The light showed him Uncle Adam, sitting on a great horse like a statue, in his metal shirt and helmet with a long lance in his hand. He was watching the gate. At the feet of his horse another shape moved – low, black and hairy. Ambrose realized that it must be Raven, and he shivered. He hoped the servant with the torch was holding Raven's leash, but it was too dark to see.

Once, he had asked Mother why Uncle Adam kept a dog like Raven. He was so much larger than the dogs that guarded the hill people in their village across the valley from home.

*'To help him fight if need be, my darling. He has no one else who can.'*

He twisted in his perch, trying to look back at Aunt Evalia.

'Are you going to fight for me?' he whispered.

'Yes, my dear. Be quiet, now. You must be quiet.'

She would not let him talk. That made it worse. Ambrose was frightened, and he wanted to talk. He wanted to ask what the boy had seen, and whether it had been the Heron Man or some of his Things. And he had begun to worry whether he should get off the horse again and put the stones out around him. But he could tell Aunt Evalia didn't want him to do that just now. Why not?

How did she know what they were doing was the right thing?

This waiting was horrible. It was as bad as any of the nights he had spent alone in the mountains. It was worse, because it was happening at Chatterfall, where he should have been safe. He thought he could hear sounds beyond the stockade around the house – branches stirring and clicking in the wind, or scrapes and noises that were not made by the wood, and yet were being made all the same. But it was hard to pick out anything against the endless roaring of the falls.

We're going to ride out, he thought. Uncle Adam, and Aunt Evalia and me; because the Heron Man is coming. That's what the shepherd boy was telling them. He had seen the enemy coming.

Why don't we go *now*?

But they did not. Perhaps they thought the enemy was already outside. They stayed still, waiting.

After what seemed a very long time, a new noise began – a low, shaking, growl quite unlike the falling of the waters.

It was Raven.

Ambrose tensed, and felt Aunt Evalia's arms around him tense, too.

A whistle sounded from somewhere in the wood. At once Raven launched into a volley of barks, flinging himself against the end of the chain-leash held by the man with the torch. Ambrose clenched his teeth against the sound, and waited for it to stop. But it went on and on. He wondered if the Heron Man would be frightened away by Raven alone.

From beyond the gate came a voice.

'DiManey! DiManey!'

Ambrose had not expected his enemy to speak. And the voice did not sound frightened.

'DiManey!' It was a big, roaring voice. Ambrose could not imagine the Heron Man shouting like that.

'Who's there?' bellowed Uncle Adam suddenly, from his saddle. At the sound of his voice Raven's barking fell to a low growl.

'Open your gate, diManey, if you want to keep your roof whole!'

'What do you want? And who are you?'

'You've one with you who is not yours. I want him, and everything he carries.'

He knows I'm here, thought Ambrose desperately.

When Uncle Adam did not answer, the voice called again.

'Open the gate! Open it, or we'll burn the house. We'll kill you. And your wife, your servants, your pigs, and everything you've got to the last chicken!'

Behind Ambrose, Aunt Evalia leaned in her saddle and whispered to the groom who held their horse's head. He dropped his hold on the bridle and felt his way towards the gate in the darkness.

Ambrose felt Aunt Evalia's grip around him tighten. Her arm was trembling. The horse beneath him shifted.

With a loud grunting of timbers the gate opened, swinging backwards and inwards until it struck against the wall of the stable. Shapes were moving on the road outside, drifting lightly in through the gateway. Steel clinked. Feet scraped on dry earth a few yards from where Ambrose sat precariously in his saddle. Faint moonlight showed him a row of man-sized figures, entering the yard cautiously. There were three or four of them. The nearest was barely ten feet from where he and Aunt Evalia sat on their horse in the shadow of the stable. If it was dressed at all it wore a dark cloak or armour from head to toe. Ambrose could make out no details, except for a single pale spot near the figure's shoulder that might have been a badge or cloak-buckle.

Aunt Evalia's breath was coming lightly, shallowly in his ear. Her grip on him was so fierce that his upper arm was numb.

'*Hah, Raven!*' cried Uncle Adam.

The big hound leaped forward at the invaders, baying to shake the woods. With another cry Uncle Adam kicked his great horse forward to follow, lumbering at them across the short space of the courtyard with his sword in hand. A volley of shouts answered him – men's voices bellowing in anger and alarm. The figure nearest Ambrose lifted an arm or weapon as great Raven leaped at it, rearing almost to the height of its head.

Now the horse beneath Ambrose started forward, heading for the gateway. He could feel Aunt Evalia urging it on, shouldering past the fight, trying to follow Uncle

Adam's great charger as it broke through to the gate. Cries of rage and hate exploded around him. There were other figures – man-like, horse-like – crowding the night in the roadway. There was a horse in front of him, and a man-shape, caught with one foot in a stirrup. The horse beneath him took him so close that he could have kicked the other animal with his left toe. Blows rang and beasts turned in the night. Somewhere, someone fell. For a moment Ambrose saw a horse, riderless, heading away into the night before him. He thought it might have been Uncle Adam's. But they were through their attackers. The road between the trees showed like a pale stream ahead of them. Still the horse carried them forward, picking up speed. Ambrose swayed with the beat of its hooves. He had never ridden on anything so big before. He crouched low, trying to cling to the horse's neck as Aunt Evalia clung to him. He was afraid of the fight at the gate, but most of all he feared falling at height and at speed in this darkness. Now the shouts behind were fading and the sound of the hooves rose beneath him. And above both he heard a sudden, long hiss that broke off with a snap. Aunt Evalia cried out. He felt her lurch forward, shoving him up towards the horse's neck. He had a moment to wonder why she was riding so badly. Then they were both falling.

He was flying through the air in darkness.

Bush-branches crashed around him. He yelled in pain and terror. Then his body struck something big, and hard, and he had no voice to cry with.

He rolled in the thicket. His head hummed with pain – he must have hit it on the ground, but he could not remember that. His arms were sore. His legs . . . He could crawl. Trembling, he clambered to his hands and knees.

Feet were running heavily towards him on the road. Two or three of the attackers were coming, jingling with metal as they approached. The horse had vanished into the distance. Aunt Evalia could only be yards away, but he could not see her. He did not know if she was hurt, or how badly. He could not hear Raven, or Uncle Adam.

The enemy! The enemy!

He crouched for a moment where he was, thinking that they might miss him. Then his nerve broke and he blundered away from the road through the thickets.

He was sure they were close after him. He thought they were crashing through the dark wood behind him. But he couldn't look, and he could barely hear against the noise of the falls. He scrambled uphill, to left and right, feeling ahead of him for the tree trunks that loomed suddenly at him out of the darkness from the distance of less than a yard. Again and again he tripped or ran into some obstacle – hard, bruising wood or tearing branches. His bandaged feet limped and stung as he forced them to carry him. His way was upwards, steeply upwards, and he was heavy on the slope and could not make himself go faster. Well before he felt it safe to stop, his legs gave up, and he leaned against a trunk on the edge of a small clearing, sobbing for breath.

As his lungs calmed, he could listen. Beyond the long pouring of the falls and the wind in the trees he could hear faint cries lower down the woods. If there were words in them, he was too far uphill to understand them, but they did not sound as if there was fighting. Calls were being answered by other calls. The words might have been *Look over there* and *He must have gone that way.*

The clouds moved in the sky, and the moonlight grew. He glanced around, fearfully. What he had thought was a clearing was in fact the road again. It had bent back to meet him above the point where he had left it. He could see the pale blur of its surface running among the darkness beneath the trees, curling uphill (perhaps) to his right, as it snaked on up the slope.

He did not know what to do. Run on along the road? Or hide in the woods, putting his stones around him as the only defence he had left? He was being hunted. There were shapes and shadows among the trees. Any of them might hold a watcher. Any of the shadows might be an old man, standing only a few yards from him, in a long robe and hood; watching him with eyes in deep darkness.

Nearby, something heavy moved. His eye caught a curved shadow, shifting against a background of trees to his right. His mind leaped at once to his nightmare, and he just managed to stop himself shrieking aloud. He started to move again, sliding as quietly as he could away from it among the trees, knowing that he was making too much noise and that he would be heard – if it had ears to hear with.

Suddenly, a shape erupted from the bushes by the roadside ahead of him, plunging downhill to cut off his escape. He yelped, springing away from it, and collided with a tree trunk in the dark. As he staggered the thing leaped at him and flung him to the ground. Something heavy and soft was feeling at his face. It found his mouth and pressed against it.

'Quiet!' grunted a voice.

Ambrose struggled and kicked. But the weight of the thing bore down on him and he could not free himself. Metal clinked. The thing was wearing a mail shirt, like Uncle Adam's.

'*Quiet*, damn you!'

Ambrose lay still, telling himself that he was only gathering his strength for another try. The grip on him eased a little.

'What's happened down there?'

It was a man's voice. Not a nightmare, but a man. Ambrose twisted to look up at the shape of his captor's head.

'Come on,' hissed the man. 'What's happened down at the house?'

'We – we've been attacked.'

'By whom? How many?'

'I don't know. Uncle Adam is fighting . . .'

'Who? Your uncle?'

'He's not really my uncle. But he needs help!'

'Up.'

He pulled Ambrose to his feet, and brought him out onto the road, turning him so that he faced along it to where the three-quarter moon was beginning to rise over the tree-tops along the slope. The man, who was no taller than Ambrose, peered at his face. He was wearing an iron helmet and a pale surplice over his mail. He was a knight, like Uncle Adam.

Behind him, under the trees, the big shadow moved

again. It was lighter than the darkness around it. There was a heavy, snorting noise.

'Sss, sss, Stefan,' said the knight, softly over his shoulder.

It was a horse – the biggest horse Ambrose had ever seen.

'What's your name?' said the knight.

Ambrose did not answer.

The knight shook him. 'What's . . . ? No, all right then. But what's the matter with your feet?'

Ambrose looked down at his bandages, pale in the moonlight.

'I walked from the mountains,' he said.

'That'll do. You're who I've come for. Let's go.'

Go?

'What about the house? They need help!'

The knight looked downhill. There was a cry from below, too far off to make out any words. A smell of smoke was gathering among the trees.

'That's not a fight,' said the knight. 'That's sack. They've fired it. I saw that as I came down the road – even before I heard you. Up, now.'

Without letting go of Ambrose for a moment, he had steered him to the side of the great horse. It towered over the boy in the darkness, far taller than the animal he had ridden with Aunt Evalia. (Aunt Evalia! Where was she? What did *that's sack* mean?) The horse breathed heavily, and shifted like a mountainside that was about to fall.

'Up.'

Once again he was being lifted up the side of a huge animal. He snatched at the pommel of the saddle and hung where he was until the knight caught his foot with one hand (*Ow!*) and heaved him on upwards.

'Sit up,' the knight said. 'Hold on to the saddle.'

Ambrose levered himself into some sort of a position. The saddle had a high back, as well as the pommel that he was gripping with both hands. It felt as though he had climbed into a living tree.

'Steady, Stefan.'

The knight took the reins and stood at the horse's head. For a moment he stood and did nothing. Perhaps he was listening, trying to hear through the trees and the noise of the water for other sounds in the night.

'Come, Stefan, come!' hissed the knight at the horse. The great beast moved forward, stepping at first and then breaking into a heavy trot. The man was running at the beast's head, grunting and jingling as he went. Ambrose clutched desperately at the saddle. He did not know who this man was. He did not know where they were going. Most of all, he was afraid of another fall.

A bend in the path followed. They were making their way on up the slope beside the falls. Down to his right he could see flickers of firelight, showing through the trees where he knew the house should be. They moved backwards as the road curved and climbed on. After a little he could glimpse the fire again, to his left now, as the road wound back across the slope. It was further away, harder to see through the thickets of trees. He wondered what had happened to Aunt Evalia, and to Uncle Adam, and Raven, and whether any of them would be able to look for him in the morning.

And what would happen to him if they could not?

'Walk, Stefan,' grunted the man. They slowed. The knight was breathing heavily. The road had got steeper. Maybe he meant to run again when they got to the top. He was looking over his shoulder again. Ambrose looked around, too. He could no longer see the fire. All sounds were lost in the roaring of the falls. But he could still smell the smoke that stole among the trees.

Perhaps it was the smoke that was making his eyes blur like this.

The road curved again, and levelled. The woods opened. To his left, below the three-quarter moon, rose the flat lack shape of a high hill. To his right was what seemed to be a great sleeve of lake, running away between steep slopes. This was the way he had come yesterday, in the sunlight, hearing the falls ahead of him and thinking that at last his journey was nearly over. Now the moon rose above the darkness of Chatterfall, and the voice of the waters would never cease from weeping.

## V

### The Knight of the Wastelands

t was weeping from the sky that woke him: rain falling in a light pitter-patter. He had been aware of it for some time before his mind rose from sleep. His body ached and his head swam. He was very hungry.

He lifted his head. It was light. He was lying in a small space, open to the sky and bounded by walls of tumbled, blackened stone. Lank weeds rose from the ground about him. Stones and the ends of charred timbers peeped sullenly from among them.

Slowly his mind made sense of what he was seeing. He was inside the remains of a house. There were gaps in the wall that might once have been windows and a door. But the roof was gone, and so it wasn't a house any more. Whatever had covered its floor had gone, too. There had been fire. It must have been a big one, to scorch the stones like that. Now only the lower walls were left, providing a little shelter from the weather.

What was he doing here?

He remembered that there had been a knight in the woods above Chatterfall. He had put Ambrose on a big

96

horse and led him for what seemed like hours. Then they had all stopped, and the knight had told him to lie down and get some sleep.

The horse was nowhere to be seen. But the knight was a few yards away, crouching by what must have been a hearth at the foot of a ruined chimney. He had a pot on it and was beginning to feed a fire with twigs.

Food? Ambrose rose on one elbow.

The knight looked across at Ambrose. He stopped what he was doing.

Ambrose sat up with a jerk. It was *him*!

It was the man who had struck Mother on the cliff-top! The one she had called a wolf!

Or was it?

Surely this knight was much older than that man had been. His hair was lighter – partly because there was grey in it. There were lines around his eyes and cheek muscles.

Yet it was the same face – the face on the man called Raymonde, who had come up the path to the house a fort-night ago: the same look, the same slanting brows.

Except that it had smiled then. It had smiled widely, and the eyes had been eager, and the mouth had been full of talk and of confidences. This knight was not smiling, and he was not speaking. He was frowning. He did not seem to like Ambrose's face any more than Ambrose liked his.

Ambrose looked at the knight and kept very still.

At last the knight cleared his throat.

'Eat first, hey?' he said. 'There are old strip-fields around this place. Things growing – grain, roots; maybe olives and fruit. See if you can find us anything.'

He still did not smile, although Ambrose could tell that he was trying to sound cheerful. For the moment, Ambrose thought it best to do as he was told. So he rose stiffly, and hobbled towards what must once have been a door out of the wrecked building.

'Keep your eyes open,' the man said. 'If anyone approaches, come quickly and do not call out.'

Among the things piled by the knight's saddlebag was a small, triangular shield of wood. On it was painted the head of a wolf. There was also a hand holding a bar or staff across its face, but it was clearly a wolf.

Ambrose limped out into the grey world.

The ruined house lay in low, rolling countryside, covered with scrub and a few trees. There were indeed strip-fields around it, and orchards, all overgrown. There were no berry-bushes of the kind that had fed Ambrose for most of his journey through the hills. Twenty yards away the great, grey horse was pegged on a long rope among yellow tussocks. It lifted its head and looked at him mournfully, as if to say that he would find nothing in that direction.

He thought of walking away across the brown land: of just walking and walking, as he had done for the last fortnight, and not coming back to the face by the fire behind him. But he had nowhere to go now. His feet hurt and he was weak. The knight had talked about food.

The smell of onions led him to a small kitchen garden, where he also found a few root vegetables that he did not recognize. They had gone to seed, of course, but Ambrose thought they could still be eaten. He pulled them from the earth and wandered into the orchard. There were some fruits hanging from the trees, but most were beyond his reach. He looked among the grasses for windfalls that might be fresh, and found a few. He also found the remains of a goat, still tethered to a trunk. It was dry and flattened among the long grasses. The eyes were long gone, and the teeth showed from the ragged lips and skin. Someone had cut its neck nearly in two, and then had left it there. He did not touch it.

He brought his findings to the knight, who scowled and poked among them. The man seemed to think that Ambrose could have done much better if only he had tried, but he made no move to go and look himself. He took the onions, tore the outer leaves off them, and dropped the remains into the mix of meal and water in his pan.

Ambrose gathered the eight white stones from the ground where he had been sleeping and put them into his pouch. He wondered what he was doing here, in a wrecked house in a flat brown land where nothing useful grew. Home was gone, and Chatterfall was gone, and for the moment there was nothing but the light rain on his shoulders, and the rising hiss from the pot.

The rain poured on, ceaselessly. He huddled into the slight shelter of the wall, as close as he could get to the flames without being in the man's reach. The broth, at least, was beginning to smell good. There had been so little to eat since leaving home.

At last the knight removed the pan from the fire.

'Well enough,' he said.

Ambrose reached out at once, hunger rising in him like a beast. The knight struck his hand away.

'Let it cool, you idiot,' he said. 'Did your mother teach you nothing?'

How could he talk about Mother?

The knight waited for an answer, then shrugged when he did not get one. After a bit he took a knife and cut up some of the windfalls Ambrose had found, throwing away the bad pieces. They ate them in silence. Then the knight picked up the pan and began to spoon the mess in it to his own lips. Ambrose watched mouthful after mouthful disappear into that sour, stubbly face. He couldn't help thinking that Mother had always served him first – unless he was being punished.

At last the man passed the pan over to him. He took the spoon, and gulped at it. It was just a porridge, flavoured with the onions, but at that moment it tasted very, very good. Ambrose felt it moving down inside him, warming him. He had not realized how cold he had become. So he ate every drop that he could spoon up, and then without being told took the pan to an old trough to wash it. He limped back to the knight, who offered him water to drink.

The rain was easing, down to a few spits from the sky.

'What happened here?' said Ambrose, suddenly. Food had made him bolder.

The knight looked around as though seeing the house for the first time. He pulled a face.

'Raided,' he said. 'It is common enough. All this land was fought over in Tarceny's rising, ten years ago, and Baldwin's rising after that. A house like this – it is built for defence, but if you have enough force and a bit of time you can always take it.'

Ambrose thought of the fire flickering through the

100

trees at Chatterfall. He remembered Uncle Adam, at the door to his house; Aunt Evalia, lurching in the saddle behind him; and his mother's voice, speaking beside the pool. *All the fields are wastelands, Amba.*

'So,' said the knight. 'Let's see what you're carrying there.' He held out his hand for the pouch of stones. 'Give it,' he said, frowning again.

Ambrose thought of refusing. But the knight snapped his fingers impatiently and held out his hand again. Reluctantly, Ambrose passed the bag over.

'They're mine,' he said. 'I need them.'

The knight peered into the pouch. He did not seem interested in the stones, but after a moment he drew out the strip of paper with Mother's writing on it. He frowned at the writing.

'That's her name, isn't it?' He held the paper at arm's length to Ambrose, jabbing his finger at the end of the line of writing. 'That's your mother's name.'

'Yes,' said Ambrose, warily.

The knight grunted, and handed the pouch to Ambrose. Ambrose was so relieved to get the stones back that for a moment he forgot about the letter. When he looked up the knight was stuffing it into his own pouch.

'That's mine!' said Ambrose.

'It says who you are. I'll take care of it. Now, boy,' he said, once again in that voice that tried to sound friendly when never a smile crossed his face. 'I met your mother in the mountains a week ago. I'm here because she asked me to come to Chatterfall to find you. Now we know Chatterfall's gone, we need to go somewhere else. That will mean riding south . . .'

'That's a *lie*!' yelled Ambrose.

The knight stopped, staring at him.

'She's dead!' he shouted. 'They're all dead! You're a liar!'

'That she is not! I saw her, a week ago. She said . . .'

'Liar!' Ambrose screamed. 'And it's *your fault*!'

The knight looked like the man who had hit her. He was so like, he *must* have had something to do with him. And he saw how the knight's face whitened – how he glared at the words. For a moment Ambrose knew that he was right. Then . . .

'I'll not be called a liar by you!' the knight shouted.

And angrily, deliberately, the knight leaned across and cuffed Ambrose hard around the ear. Ambrose's head sang. He put his hands to the side of his face. The knight's gauntlet smacked into Ambrose's other ear, and Ambrose reeled. Through his pain he heard the man say: 'I've not come days out of my way and business so *you* can call me names. You learn this lesson!'

Ambrose could not remember being struck before – not like this. Not at home, nor in diManey's kindly place by the waterfall. Both sides of his head throbbed, and he was fighting tears. His heart raged, helplessly, against the world and this evil man.

'Now get up,' the knight said. 'Someone attacked Chatterfall last night. Whoever it was will be out looking for you. We've made smoke here. We need to move. Get yourself together.'

'I'm still hungry,' Ambrose mumbled defiantly.

'If we see a whole roof today, we may get food. Otherwise there will be nothing until nightfall. Don't put your hopes up.'

The man had already turned away, and was stamping out the fire.

He had said it now. *She's dead.* He hadn't wanted to.

Saying it was like making it happen again: (her body turning in the air, bouncing outwards from the rocks with a noise like a wet sack dropping). Saying it made it real. Now the emptiness of the world was in him, as well as outside.

Oh, there were people like Aunt Evalia and Uncle Adam, who would embrace him and feed him in an afternoon, and be gone themselves before dawn. There were ill-faced knights who stole her last writing and beat him around the head. There were even berry-bushes, and as he was now learning, old strip-fields, that might provide a mouthful now and again. But they were part of the emptiness.

And all the fields were wastelands now.

The rain had lifted. The sky remained a thick, mottled grey that dulled the heart. They set off together on the horse along a path through the thorn-hills. It ran up slopes, over ridges, along valleys. Before crossing each skyline the knight checked the horse and looked back, but nothing moved behind them. Ambrose, perched once more upon a rolled blanket before the saddle, found his seat growing more and more uncomfortable. He hated the feel of the knight's arms around him. When at last the man spoke to him, he barely heard.

The man repeated himself. 'Have you not ridden before?'

He was trying to be friendly again. But Ambrose did not want to talk to the knight. It was his fault, too.

The man grabbed his collar and jerked him backwards.

'What's the matter with you?' he said roughly. 'Lost your tongue?'

Because of the way they sat, he could not force Ambrose to look at him. And Ambrose stared away across the brown heath, clamping his jaw shut. He felt the knight's anger rising, suddenly and violently, just as it had done over breakfast. He barely cared.

Nothing happened. After a moment the knight cursed him, set him straight in the saddle again, and kicked the horse onwards.

It was a long day, across that rolling, brown land. Now and again they dismounted at streams, standing in tight-lipped silence while the horse drank. And now and again they passed buildings: small groups of huts or a stockaded farm. Ambrose's eyes lingered on them as they approached, and his stomach thought of bread, and hot soup and maybe fruit – until he saw that the fields were overgrown and the roof beams blackened against the sky.

The knight steered his beast past each silent, empty doorway, and said nothing. He seemed to be a creature of the wasteland himself.

Late that afternoon they came to the top of a steep slope that fell through stands of trees. Below them was a great expanse of water, pale grey in this light. Ambrose could just see low shapes on the far side which might have been clouds, or might have been hills on a distant shore. To left and right the water ran on endlessly until it melded with the dull horizon.

It was the big lake again. Ambrose had crossed it only two days before, huddling in the bottom of the fisherman's boat on the last stage of his journey to Chatterfall. He was surprised to find that they had come back to it. He had thought they were moving away from the places where he had been. Perhaps it was a very big lake indeed. There was so much about the world he did not know.

On a low hill by the shore stood a great house. It had broad towers with banners that strayed in the wind. Its walls were a dull grey-brown, not very different from the dullness of the earth on which it stood. There might have been people moving down there, but Ambrose could not be sure.

'Bay,' the man muttered behind him. He kept the horse going downhill, away from the treacherous skyline.

Ambrose stared at the castle. So that was where they were going, he thought. It looked a huge place. Many people must live there. He had never been anywhere like this before. But the more people there were, the safer it might be. He could see that. He looked at the high walls, and could imagine that there might be food and warmth and safety within them. And now he could see an end to the journey, he longed for them to get there; because it would mean this day would be over and he might be able to rest and eat and sleep for however long he needed. For ever, maybe.

The wasteland-knight was following a path that descended from the ridge in a line parallel to the lakeshore. The horse plodded slowly onwards. Each time it came to a fork in the track, or to a stretch of open ground on their right, Ambrose thought the knight must be about to turn its head towards the house by the shore. It did not happen. He clenched his teeth, but would not ask his captor what he was doing.

On they went. The knight did not turn the horse. Ambrose watched helplessly as the castle fell back on their right hand.

The daylight dimmed. The path ran on into the evening. When they reached a low knoll Ambrose looked back and saw that lights were now beginning to burn on the distant towers.

Back there, guarded and defended, was light and warmth and food. And maybe there were people who smiled and hugged one another. Those walls still kept out the world, like an island of light in a dark sea. And the knight was taking him away from it. He had never tried to reach it. They were riding on, on into hunger and loss.

There was nothing that Ambrose could do. He could not steer the horse. He could not run on his lame feet towards the castle. He could not shout across that distance for rescue. He was nearly weeping as they crossed another ridge and left the lights hidden by the line of the hill. That was when he swore to himself that if the chance ever came to escape, he would seize it whatever it was.

Behind him the wasteland-knight moved them on to the south, and said nothing.

The chance came two days later.

There was another dreary dawn. Over breakfast the knight tried once again to be cheerful, and to get Ambrose to speak. When this failed, he suddenly lost his temper and cuffed Ambrose for 'dumb insolence'. After that there were long hours of riding, resting, and riding once more; all in silence. The lake appeared again, to their right. They followed the line of the shore, skirting woods of broad-leaved oaks and groves of olives. They passed ruined huts but saw no one, nor any animal, nor even a boat upon the water. There was nothing but the brown country, the horse's head, and the man whom Ambrose had branded 'Wastelands' in his mind.

Towards evening another castle appeared on a low rise above the shore. This was a mass of towers and pointed roofs, without the banners they had seen at Bay. Ambrose stared at it, from under the oak tree where the knight had checked the horse. He thought once more of food and warmth, shelter from the rain, and light when the evening grew dark around them. He thought of an end to loneliness.

This time the knight did not seem to be riding by.

'Trant,' said Wastelands, speaking for the first time in hours. 'Your mother grew up here.'

Mother had grown up here. Surely, surely, thought Ambrose, the journey was going to end now. And it was going to end among people who had known her, and therefore would be kind to him. He wondered what their faces would be like, what they would say when he told them who he was, and whether they would embrace him as she and Aunt Evalia had done. He thought he would not mind if they did.

They approached slowly. Ambrose watched the walls and the blank, unshuttered windows for signs of move-ment. But nothing in the castle answered his longing. No one called to them as they came on. There was no smoke or light as there had been at Bay.

A large black bird, perhaps a crow, flew heavily from a turret.

They crossed a low dyke and the remains of a stockade into an enclosure that ran down to the lakeshore. A bridge led over a ditch with a low film of water in it. Beyond it was an open gate like a tunnel between two massive towers. It was dark inside.

Wastelands dismounted and led the horse cautiously through the cavernous gatehouse into the courtyard beyond. The ground within was full of weeds and the smell of wet stone. There was no light or fire. Ambrose looked around the huge and gloomy buildings, and understood that the place was a shell.

Here was a house bigger and stronger than any he had known. He could not imagine how many people had lived in it – at least as many as in the whole of the hill village, and maybe more. And they had all known Mother, and maybe loved her. And yet it was empty: a dank ruin, just like the farms they had passed. All gone. All useless!

And Wastelands had known this! He had known there was no life here. That was why he had come to camp within its broken stones!

It was as the knight stood at the horse's head and looked about him that Ambrose saw the man's sword was still slung from the saddle. It was within easy reach. He could see it clearly, even down to the curious oak-leaf design that was cast upon its pommel. He stretched his hand for it. Wastelands still had not noticed. The sword came free, with a long, awkward scrape. Wastelands looked round.

Now!

Raging, gripping the hilt in both hands, Ambrose heaved and swung the thing over his head. It was heavy. He saw the knight look up into the coming blow, heard him shout, saw him step in, reaching up with a gauntleted hand to catch his wrist as the sword flailed over the armoured shoulder and thumped loosely into the mail on his back. Ambrose was already losing his balance, falling forwards. The man pulled, and he tumbled from the great height of the horse's back. The ground smashed the breath from him. He had lost the sword. For a moment he could not see. He put his hands to his head to guard against the attack that must be coming. Nothing happened.

'Get up,' said Wastelands's voice.

Ambrose rolled and looked around. The sword lay by him on the ground, unregarded. Wastelands had moved around to the other side of the horse and was fumbling with something. When he appeared again he was carrying the small triangular shield that had hung there. The face of the wolf grinned at Ambrose from behind the crudely-painted staff.

'Pick it up,' Wastelands said. 'Try harder, this time.'

Ambrose dragged himself to his feet.

'Pick it up,' said Wastelands.

The sword lay at Ambrose's feet. He picked it up. It was heavy. He had to put both hands on it. Wastelands waited for him, eyes angry, with the shield on his arm.

'You've a lot to learn,' Wastelands said. 'Time you had a lesson.'

The horse stood by, impassively.

Ambrose swung the sword. It was clumsy in his hands. Wastelands watched him. He did not flinch. He did not even move his feet or lift his shield. Ambrose realized he was well out of reach. He would have to get closer, on feet that were still sore. The knight could move that shield, too – far faster than Ambrose could lift the sword. And then what?

Ambrose's arms were weak, and the sword wavered in his grip. He knew he wasn't going to be able to hurt Wastelands. Wastelands knew it, too. He just wanted Ambrose to make the attempt. He was angry, but not because Ambrose had tried to kill him. That was only an excuse. That just meant that he could hit Ambrose as hard as he liked.

Ambrose knew he could not fight. And if Wastelands wanted him to fight, then he was not going to try. Making Wastelands angry seemed to be the only thing he could do.

He dropped the sword again, turned away and sat down.

'If you were *my* son . . .' Wastelands began. But he stopped.

He's angry because I'm not talking to him, thought Ambrose. He pretends he doesn't care, but he does. He's been getting angrier all the time.

'Be *damned* to you!' said Wastelands behind him. The man was angrier than ever now.

He'll hit me, thought Ambrose. He'll hit me, but he'll get nothing for it.

Suddenly the knight was crouching in front of him. His face, red with fury, was a few inches from Ambrose's own.

'If you were a squire of mine,' he hissed, 'I'd have you birched until you couldn't stand for a trick like that!'

Ambrose blinked. A fleck of spit had hit him. He looked Wastelands in the eye, and waited for the blows to begin.

'Right,' said Wastelands. He swallowed, as though his anger was something he could gulp back down inside himself. 'Right. You remember this. When you use a sword you must be clever. Clever twice over if you're on horseback. You balance your weight against the blow. And you look for the gaps in a man's armour, or for a weak guard. But first and above all you *must* be strong. You *cannot* use iron without strength in the arm. Do *not* try until you've got it!'

His hand caught Ambrose by the shoulder and hauled him to his feet.

'Now be useful,' Wastelands said. 'Find firewood. The roof of the chapel is whole. It will be dry in there.'

He was not going to be hit, then. Ambrose did not feel grateful; but he did feel surprised, and so he obeyed.

The old chapel was a good place for fuel. They built the fire together on its sheltered stone floor and crouched beside it. Ambrose set his circle of stones around him. Wastelands watched him in silence. But later, when Ambrose was feeding some of the pieces he had found onto the flames, Wastelands stopped him.

'What's that?'

Ambrose looked at the wood in his hand. It was a bit of a broken old chair – part of a leg, he thought. Once he would have been struck by the beautiful smoothness of the wood-join. Now it was only a little warmth.

'I know who sat in that,' said Wastelands. 'And he'd

not thank me for burning it. Nor would *he*,' he added, jabbing a finger at the wood.

Ambrose looked at the leg again. It was carved in the shape of a man. At first he thought that the folds cut around the shoulders were meant to be a cloak. Then he saw that they must be wings. The figure held an open book. On the book were a number of tiny lumps. Turning it in the light of the flames, Ambrose realized that they must be eyes.

It was the Angel Umbriel.

'We'll not burn that,' said Wastelands. 'It could mean bad luck.'

Reluctantly, Ambrose put it aside. It had been one of the best pieces he had found. It seemed a waste not to burn it, even for the sake of an angel. Even for Umbriel.

The Angels did not seem to have much part in his days now. He realized that he had not offered one prayer or asked for one thing of them since he had seen his mother fall. It was as if they had gone with her. And perhaps they had.

After a moment he said: 'Whose chair was it?'

The words sounded strange in his throat.

'Hmm? You've found your tongue at last, have you?'

'You said you knew who sat in it.'

Wastelands looked at him, as though there had been a lot he had been planning to say as soon as Ambrose broke his silence. But all he said was: 'I'll show you.'

He took a long stick, which burned at one end, and walked a few paces away from the fire. Ambrose got to his feet, picking two white pebbles from the ring he had set around him. Holding one in each fist, he followed. The stick gave very little light. It was a bright spark in the darkness, showing a few feet of stone paving. Shadows moved in the ceiling as Wastelands stopped by the wall.

'Here.'

He held the stick close to the stonework. There were letters cut there. They said AMBROSE.

There were oak-leaves carved around it, and the words WATCH FOR WHO COMES.

There were more words beneath, but his eyes were stinging with the smoke and he could not read them.

'He was your grandfather.' Wastelands said. 'Your mother's father. He was a good man, but he lived to see this house fall to his enemies, and he was slain shortly after.'

'And they did this?'

'This?' said Wastelands, raising his torch and looking around him. 'No. The house lived on then. This was done later. After we had defeated your father, the King, Septimus, gave all your mother's lands to Tancrem of Baldwin, to hold in stewardship until she should be found. It was foolish, for Baldwin was not loyal, and he wanted to keep the lands for himself. So the seeds of Baldwin's rising were sown even as your father fell; and the land was at war again within three years, when there should have been peace. Now Baldwin's brother, the Lord of Velis, rises to claim the throne, and Septimus must fight yet again to keep his crown from falling. And already both sides of the lake are waste. There are no farms that will feed so much as a knight and his dog. This kind house is empty, and many another with it.'

Remember, Ambrose. The wars had their seeds in what *he* had done.

He peered at the wall, feeling with his fingers. There were other names cut there, in a long row.

'Who are these?'

The torch was almost out. A single tongue of weak flame licked around its end.

'They are your mother's mother, and your mother's sisters and brothers. She showed me these stones herself. They all died before I came.'

'What killed them?'

'Chance, each one.'

Ambrose glared at him, angry at the answer. Even names in stone deserved more than that!

The knight met his look.

'How should I know? Sickness, childbirth – there's no end to misfortune in this world. If you want to know, you can ask your mother when you next see her.'

Then the light went out.

# VI

## The Wolf and the Wall

 hand was over his mouth.

As he lurched from sleep Ambrose thought it must be his own, and that it had somehow lost all feeling. But his arms were by his sides. The hand was someone else.

He started where he lay. It was dark. The hand pressed down, stifling his grunt. Metal pricked beneath his chin.

'Ssshh.'

A man was kneeling by him, holding a hand over his mouth and something sharp against his neck. He could see the shape, hulking black above him.

'Quiet now,' the voice said softly. 'Keep still.'

The man had a knife against his neck. Ambrose lay with his heart pounding and looked straight up above him.

He was in the chapel in his mother's house at Trant, lying by the wall where he had rolled himself in his blanket after the fire had gone out. Moonlight shone through the long windows and lit great pale patches of stonework above him. The white pebbles were around him, Wastelands asleep by a side wall.

'Up now. Quietly.'

He knew the voice.

Maybe it was because of the knife below his chin, but he knew it. He had a sudden, insane memory of a man who had shaved, and who had told him how to keep knives sharp.

It was the man called Raymonde! The one who had hit Mother!

How had he got here?

'Up.'

The hand lifted from his mouth. The knife stayed exactly where it was.

'I can't,' gasped Ambrose.

'*Up*,' the voice hissed.

'I can't leave the stones!'

For a moment the man seemed to hesitate. Then the knife dug against the soft skin below his jaw.

'Don't worry about *them*,' the man whispered. 'Worry about *this*.'

Ambrose could not think. The touch of the knife seemed to think for him. Slowly his limbs gathered themselves. They got him to his hands and knees; then to his feet. The man rose with him, and stood behind him.

'Walk that way. Not a sound.'

The knife was gone from his neck. He did not know where it was, but it must be close. Perhaps the man was holding it at his back. He limped forward, slowly, up the side aisle of the chapel. He could think about nothing but the knife, and the shelter of the white stones receding behind him.

'Left.'

Ambrose turned, and approached the dark, empty altar.

'Kneel down.'

Ambrose knelt on the altar-step.

'That's it,' the man whispered. 'You can pray if you like.'

'What – what are you going to do?' Ambrose stammered.

'Keep your voice down. We're just going to talk, that's all.'

Wastelands must be lying asleep, only yards away. Ambrose could shout to wake him.

If he did that, the man would use the knife.

And if he didn't shout?

Ambrose wondered desperately what the blow of the man's knife would feel like.

And *how* had he got in here? Wastelands had shut the gate! He'd rigged a tripwire!

'Careful now,' the man said. 'Do anything wrong and you'll be dead in seconds.'

Ambrose could not answer.

'Or it could be slow. I could give you a cut in the belly. You could sit and look at it for hours, wondering how long it would take.'

He's trying to scare me, thought Ambrose. That's all. He wants to scare me so I'll do what he says.

'Quick or slow. Could be either. Remember that woman you rode through us with the other night? Dead before I'd even turned her over and found she was a woman. Pity, that. Just my bad luck that I was the one holding the crossbow at the time. I'm sorry it had to be me.

'Pretty shot, though,' he mused. 'In the dark, and moving away. Smack, into the heart. That's quick. I could do the same for you.'

117

'Are – are you going to?' said Ambrose.

'So tell me why I should,' said the voice beside him.

'I – I don't know.'

A soft, sharp breath that might have been a chuckle.

'Not a bad answer,' he said, in that smiling, confiding way that Ambrose remembered. 'I don't know either. But old man Paigan wants me to. He seems to think I should. Why's that, do you suppose?'

'Who?'

'Don't you know? He knows you. He'll do anything to get you, if he can. Come on, now. Why does he want you so much?'

He meant the Heron Man. Of course he did. Ambrose swallowed.

'An angel told him I'd defeat him,' he said.

For a moment the man said nothing. Ambrose guessed that he was surprised. Of course, it would be surprising, if you didn't already know. Ambrose felt himself tremble. Maybe the man would be angry now, and stab him for it.

'An *angel*? Is that it? Well now, we are favoured, aren't we? What did this angel say? And why you, of all people?'

Ambrose gulped. When Mother had explained it to him, in that bright morning by the pool, he had accepted it. She had always told the truth. But when he tried to put it into his own words they just seemed silly.

'So what was this angel like?' said the man. 'Fiery wings, seven eyes? Did you see it?'

'I – wasn't there.'

'Of course not. No one ever is. But you do believe in the Angels, don't you?'

'Yes.'

'Nice to see you were well brought up. I wasn't,' the man said. 'But go on anyway. What did it say to him exactly?'

The knife was back, tickling just below his ear. The touch of the point brought the words out of him.

'L-least of your father's sons . . .' he stammered.

'What's that?' the man hissed.

'That's what it said! "Paigan Wulframson. Least of your father's sons. By the last of your father's sons shall you be brought down."'

'Oh.' The man seemed to relax slightly. 'And what does that mean, do you think?'

'I – I don't know.'

That was true. He did not know any more.

'Well now,' said the man, sounding as if he was enjoying the riddle. 'If you believe in angels, then you should take it seriously. *He* does. Maybe he was well brought up, too. Ironic, isn't it? Considering what he's done since . . .

'Least of Wulfram's sons, eh? Not very polite. But accurate. We all remember his brothers – Dieter, Rolfe, Talifer and the rest of them who founded the Kingdom. But who remembers him? That bit's clear enough . . .

'But the *last* of his father's sons – why should that be you? No, don't tell me. Your father was descended from Talifer, and all the other male lines have died out. So they have. So that means the line's going to stop with you, does it?

'Maybe around now, before your mother's altar?'

Ambrose could say nothing. The moonlight gleamed on the steps a few feet from him. He could see the individual grains of dust gathered there.

119

'I don't know if I believe in angels,' the man breathed. 'But if I did I wouldn't always believe what they say. They might cheat. They might lie. They might not be able to make happen what they say will happen. How do we know you're the last son, if I don't kill you now?

'Or maybe it's your death that will bring him down. Thought of that?'

Ambrose did not answer.

The man chuckled again. Then to Ambrose's surprise, he sat down on the altar-step beside him, as easily as if the two of them were back sitting on the throne-steps at home, watching the mountains turn gold in the evening sun.

'Defeat him? Good luck. I don't know about angels, but *him* I have met. I reckon he'd give them a run for their money. Maybe he's chased them all off already. He's something, I tell you. That pool-water of his. I didn't believe half what I read about it in your father's book, but it's all true. I can go where I want, see what I want, as quick as that. I got past the old gate just now, past your tripwire – no problem. And even if you'd been watching for me you wouldn't have seen me till I was on you. I could be walking beside you, and you'd never spot me unless you knew how to look. I've drunk it three times now. And already I've taken a city with it. I've got the man who's going to be King grovelling with thanks for that. See?'

'It's not witchcraft,' he added, as though he thought Ambrose would say it was. 'Your father's quite clear about that in his book. It's under-craft. You need to know how to use it, that's all.'

'It's tears,' Ambrose said, because he wanted the man to be wrong.

120

The man shrugged.

'Does it matter? What matters is that what he's promised me isn't going to last for ever. Not if I want to keep doing things with it. And I need to. So guess what he wants before he gives me more?'

The Heron Man. He wanted Ambrose dead.

'I've told him I won't do it,' said the man. 'And he laughed at me. So I came to have a look at you. But no, I still won't. I've got a better idea, haven't I?'

His voice trailed invitingly. He wanted Ambrose to ask what his idea was. Ambrose stayed kneeling on the altar-step, just as if the knife had never left his neck. He had begun to pray. Please Umbriel, help me. Help me. Help me . . .

'I like you, you see. I liked you the moment I laid eyes on you, bobbing at your gate and reeking of billy-goat. Why should I have your blood on my head? I've done plenty for him anyway. *Eight* stones I knocked over for him. Damn, but they were heavy! I've never worked so hard. And he lets me drink just once for each stone. Three gone already. Five left. And I have to sip it from his hands each time. Ugh. Can't help my lips touching his fingers. I suppose he likes that because I have to bow my head to him.

'And he didn't tell me he couldn't get you himself. I didn't know about your pebbles until I saw them. They made you pretty hard to see. If I hadn't spotted old Stefan outside, and got curious, I might still be looking. That's not fair, is it? He should treat me better. So if he asks me again, I may just put my price up.'

Again Ambrose glanced sideways. The man had fallen silent. He was pulling at his chin with one hand, looking down the chapel to the shadows where Wastelands lay. Ambrose still could not see the knife.

Please, Umbriel, if you are there. Help me.

'Look at the old oaf,' the man grumbled. 'Sleeping like a pig until I've got iron within an inch of his ear. Does he *want* me to slit his throat? What's he doing here, anyway? I thought I'd left him chasing in circles after me in the mountains. Has he started to beat you yet?'

Ambrose hesitated, confused by the way the man's thoughts had slipped so quickly from the Heron Man to Wastelands.

'Sometimes,' he said.

The man grunted. It might have been another chuckle. 'He does it because he knows he's no good, you see. No good for me; no good for you either. So he goes into a rage and then it's whack, whack. And he gets drunk, too. Nice man. He could never take it that he had been packed off home like old baggage after your father's fall. And all the time he was sitting on a book that could have told him just where to go, and what to do, to get all the rewards he wanted. But he could never read three words in a row. So in the end I got it instead. That about sums him up for you. At least your father was Something. *He's* nothing.'

'My father was evil,' Ambrose said. 'He wanted to kill me.'

Anything to show him he was wrong – even this.

And *now* this grinning man should be sorry! He should be *sorry* for what he had done! *Killed* her! Let *him* out! Left Ambrose to struggle all the way to Uncle Adam and Aunt Evalia – and then killed them too!

The man pulled at his chin again. Perhaps he was

sorry – a very little bit. But all he said was: 'So that's something we have in common, isn't it?

'Your father wanted to kill you,' he went on. 'Mine . . .' He jerked his chin at the sleeping knight. 'Mine wants to kill me. We should stick together, you know.'

Ambrose stared away into the shadows that concealed Wastelands's sleeping form.

'Now *your* father,' said the man softly. 'He made himself King. Sons of kings can be kings themselves. Did you ever think about that?'

'No,' said Ambrose, confused.

'I have. I told you I'd been having ideas. People need kings, you see. The worse things get, the more they think they need one. And things are bad, believe me. As it happens, I'm making a new king right now. That's what I got the water for. And we've started well. No one thought we could take Watermane, but I did it. I did that for him. Winning unexpectedly like that – it'll bring a lot of people over to us.

'But this king – I can see he's going to be a handful. I could be his friend one day, and called a traitor the next. I might be looking for someone better, soon. And if you can show you're Wulfram's stock, that would swing some scales.'

Ambrose sat quite still, trying to understand what the man meant. Someone better? Someone from Wulfram's line – to be King?

'No,' he said at last.

'No?' The man smiled. 'You can do more than that, little Wulf,' he said easily. 'I'm being a friend to you. I could be your only way of staying alive.'

123

Ambrose clenched his jaw. He could hear the threat. But now he could think, too.

Wulf? Wolf yourself!

'I mean it,' said the man. 'You're being hunted, didn't you know? Those fellows who came down on Chatterfall the other night – they're still on your trail. They've been given good reasons for wanting to catch you. We stirred up a regular hornet's nest after you there. How do you think you're going to get away – two of you on one horse, and a big, white one at that, which will stand out a mile in any country?'

Ambrose met his eye. The only way the enemy would know about Stefan was if this man had told them.

He didn't want to kill Ambrose. He didn't want to slit Wastelands's throat. But he wouldn't mind if somebody else did it for him.

*Wolf yourself!*

The man must have seen what he was thinking. He scowled.

'Come on. You need me. I don't need you. And if I did, I could just take you.'

His knife was in his hand again. Ambrose drew breath.

'After what you've done?' he said deliberately.

'What's that supposed to mean?' said the man sharply.

'You killed my mother.'

The man was silent. Then he said: 'Don't be stupid . . .'

'You killed my mother,' Ambrose repeated. 'And Aunt Evalia.'

He knew the man had been sorry. So he knew his words would hurt. They were the only way of hurting that he had. And he didn't care about the knife any more.

'Damn it, I didn't mean that she should fall . . .'

'You *killed* her!'

The man swore. He seized Ambrose by the shoulder and dragged him to his feet. Ambrose clenched his teeth for the knife-blow. It did not come.

The man released him. They stood, inches apart, glaring at one another. At the far end of the chapel Wastelands was stirring, mumbling, 'What – what?' in his blankets.

If you say anything, Ambrose thought, I'll say it again. I'll shout it. I'll run after you screaming it in your ear. Call me a wolf? You're the Wolf! That's what you are!

'*Sorry*,' said the Wolf savagely, and turned away.

And he walked through the wall.

For a moment Ambrose thought that the light had grown. There was a sudden deadness to the air, as if it gave no echoes. Before him Ambrose glimpsed a landscape of brown rocks under dull light – some place completely different from the silver-and-dark aisles of the chapel around him. He saw the man beginning to pick his way through the rocks that could not be where they seemed to be. Then the chapel wall rose in front of him again, blank and patched with moonlight. The man was gone.

'What's all the noise?' growled Wastelands in a voice heavy with sleep.

Ambrose stood by the altar with his heart beating hard. He wondered how close the man – the *Wolf* – had come to stabbing him. For a moment Ambrose had almost wanted him to. But the Wolf had hated to be reminded of what he had done. And he had gone.

Gone? Where? Into a dream, Mother had once said.

He could do that because the Heron Man had given him water from the pool. That was how he had appeared so suddenly.

The Heron Man must be able to do that, too.

If the 'Wolf' could find Ambrose, so could the Heron Man.

As fast as he could Ambrose limped back down the aisle to huddle within the ring of pebbles. Some of them had been displaced. Angrily he jammed them back into their ring.

'What's the matter there?' Wastelands growled.

He had lifted his head and was looking at Ambrose. In the moon-shadows his head was a shape, and no more. It was the same shape as the Wolf's had been. It could almost have been the Wolf, lying there. Wastelands was like the Wolf, who was his own son. And he wanted to kill him.

Ambrose shrank into his blankets and said nothing.

'Go to sleep,' grunted the man, and settled again.

Ambrose was left in the darkness.


The moonbeams lanced through the high chapel windows and fell around him. He sat bolt upright in the ring of stones with his eyes wide.

Sleep? Ambrose thought he would never sleep again, if he could help it.

What if the Wolf changed his mind, and came back to stab him? What if the Heron Man came? What if Wastelands woke properly – what would he do? He wanted to kill his son, just like Ambrose's father. Only the Heron Man could have made him want that.

So the Heron Man had caught Wastelands, too.

The Heron Man was everywhere. He touched everybody. The pebbles kept him away, but what use was that when he could whisper to a man and send him stealing out of a dream to put a knife at Ambrose's neck?

He was like a huge shadow, looking down into the world, standing still, still, until it struck. And where it struck, lives wriggled and went out like fish in a heron's beak. One after another, they went out suddenly and without warning: Uncle Adam; Aunt Evalia; Mother. So suddenly. So meaninglessly.

Ambrose sat sleepless, and thought about his mother. She had known everything, it seemed. She had comforted him. She had given him everything that he had had: everything he had eaten; everything he had learned; everything he had played with.

*'I could have done it with my old one, in my father's house at Trant. I should have made this one better.'*

*'Why didn't you?'*

In her father's house at Trant. And here he was, in the ruin of her father's house. He wished that he hadn't spoken to her like that.

The moonbeams inched imperceptibly across the stones of the chapel. Where the light fell on the wall beside him there was a word all on its own. *Ina.* Ambrose thought it was a girl's name. He had no idea how long she had lived, or what kind of person she had been. He knew nothing about these people, or this place which must once have been his mother's home. She would have done. Now it was a shell: all dead, all gone like her.

*Ina,* said the silent stone in the moonlight.

At last he picked up one of his own white pebbles and drew it across the stonework. It left a faint white line. Then he began.

Scratch. Scratch. Scratch. The sound of the stone scraping was loud in that quiet place. Stroke by stroke, forming the letters as she had taught him, he carved her name on the wall beside that of her dead sister.

*Phaedra.*

## VII

### Crossing

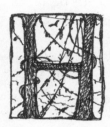is fears followed him the next day, and
grew as the hours passed. His eyes
searched the flat, treeless land as they
rode on under the grey sky. The wind
blew at them, tugging at the knight's
coat and throwing fine dust against
Ambrose's cheek. His vision blurred with it, and still he
stared and craned around him. He felt that he should
be seeing something that was not there to be seen.

He could picture it quite clearly in his mind's eye: the
figure of a man in a grey robe – not at a poolside now,
but as seen across the level grasslands with its cloak flap-
ping like a scarecrow on a winter's afternoon. Maybe it
was moving towards him. Maybe it was still. But it should
be there; and it wasn't.

Not seeing it was worst of all.

Around noon the skies began to clear. The track led
them past a living farm, and across a broad valley they
could see first a hamlet and then a manor house, all with
their roofs whole. In the mid-afternoon they came upon
a large village, crouching within its stockade in the valley
bottom. At its gates crowds of people were moving around

a collection of animal pens. Carts and awnings were set about, with men and women selling things from them. Wastelands left Ambrose to hold Stefan and went into the fair looking for horse-meal and food for themselves.

Ambrose watched the people buying food from the woman at the nearest cart. At another time he would have been curious. He had used coins only once, when he had thrust the whole of his mother's purse at the old man who lived by the lake, and had asked to be taken across the water. Here, he saw that each coin had a value, and that people counted them out carefully – so much for a plucked hen, and so much for a rabbit – and argued over what each purchase was worth. He even thought he saw the woman bite the coins she had been offered.

But he did not want to go close enough to be sure. He kept looking about him, watching the people as they passed; and especially those who wore hoods, or whose faces he could not see.

The wind blew up the valley, silvering the grasses. Ambrose stood with Stefan, big and reassuring beside him, and waited for Wastelands to return. He did not trust Wastelands – that angry, half-evil man – and after what the Wolf had said Ambrose felt more wary of him still. And yet he disliked Wastelands less than he disliked being alone. As time went on and Wastelands did not appear, he became nervous.

His hand stole to the pouch at his belt. Through the cloth he felt the stones within it. *Click*, they went. It was a reassuring sound. He did it again. *Click*.

Feet sounded, running through the crowd. It was

Wastelands, hurrying up to him with his mail clinking as he came.

'Mount up, quickly!'

He was empty-handed and breathing hard. Something had alarmed him. He lifted Ambrose, who swarmed gratefully into his perch. The knight heaved himself up behind him. People had turned to stare at them.

'Let's move!'

Wastelands urged the horse into a trot, looking back as he rode.

'What's the matter?' asked Ambrose.

'We've been seen. At least, I was.'

'Who?'

'No friend of mine – or yours, for that matter.'

There was a long, steady rise in the track. Wastelands checked his mount beneath the ridge, looking behind him again. Ambrose could see the road running back along the valley to the village and the cluster of dots that was the fair. It seemed to him that some of the dots had spilled down the road towards them. They were moving. They might have been men riding. At that distance, Ambrose could not tell how many they were.

'They will see us for sure as we cross the ridge,' said Wastelands. 'And we are two, on one tired horse. It only wants some of them to be well mounted. But there's nothing for it.'

They surged forward over the skyline. The noise of Stefan's hooves, harness and clinking iron battered at Ambrose's ears, and he heard nothing of the distant pursuit.

A furlong after crossing the ridge Wastelands turned off the road. The thorns and scrub were low, and gave

131

little cover for a moving horse, but he found a coombe of dead ground, and they threaded their way along it, emerging cautiously and then cantering across open land to find more cover. They saw no one. They followed the low ground among pathless rises, almost doubling back on the line of their journey, because that was where the cover took them. An hour later they crossed another ridge, and Wastelands seemed to relax in the saddle. Still he rode as they had done that first day after leaving Chatterfall, staying off paths and watching the land for enemies. Ambrose watched, too, for a cluster of black dots on the move, but above all for a lonely figure in grey who might walk at his very elbow without being seen.

Unless he knew how to look, the Wolf had said. He was not sure that he did know.

The afternoon wore away. The enemy did not reappear. On a hilltop in the shelter of a stand of trees Wastelands abruptly stopped the horse.

'Better rest him while we can,' he said. 'We may need everything he has before long.' They dismounted, drank water, ate their last dried fruit and unrolled their blankets, but Wastelands did not start a fire and did not take the saddle off Stefan's back.

Ambrose crouched in his ring of pebbles. There was no wind, and no sound at all but Stefan grazing what he could from the heathy ground. Wastelands sat wrapped in his blanket with his back to a tree and closed his eyes. Ambrose looked at him: this man who must be in part the enemy's man, and yet was the only help to be had. He thought it strange that someone like that could be tired.

'What did you see?' asked Ambrose suddenly.

132

'A man called Caw,' said Wastelands. 'One of a band of outlaws. They were knights and fighters for your father: consorts of his witchcraft, and they still wear the Doubting Moon badge. They'll be the ones who attacked Chatterfall. That was three, four nights ago. So someone's made them want you badly, for them to have kept to our trail so from their own country. Good tracking. Ve-ery good tracking,' he added, as if he thought there might be some more sinister explanation.

'Are they men?' Ambrose said.

'Yes – what did you think they were?' said Wastelands sharply. But at the same time his eyes searched Ambrose's face as if he thought Ambrose might indeed know more than he did.

Ambrose had not known if they were men or worse. The memory of his old nightmare was as real to him as the shapes he had seen in the gateway at Chatterfall. But he knew the Wolf had found him, using what he had called 'under-craft' and Wastelands now said was witchcraft after all. The Wolf must have told these hunters where to look for them. Ambrose wondered if he should tell Wastelands about the Wolf.

'I think they're getting help,' he said tentatively.

'Ugh,' said Wastelands. His brows slanted sharply. His eyes, Ambrose saw, had fallen on the white pebbles. Perhaps he was already guessing about witchcraft. His face was hard, and ugly.

Ambrose's courage deserted him. Speaking to Wastelands of his son might only bring the Heron Man closer. He said nothing.

'Let us say they know we are going to Develin,' said

Wastelands at last. 'They'll have reached the bridge by now, and they'll know they're ahead of us. If I were them . . .'

Ambrose watched his face as he explored the paths before him. He did not seem to like what he found there.

'They'll know we've left the road, and are between it and the river. They can watch the bridge, the road, and the bend where the river reaches the road. And they can sweep the banks. If there are still fifteen of them, they can do all that. They may have allies, too . . .'

At least one, Ambrose thought. Your son, the Wolf.

'We cannot go to ground. We have not the provisions. We *must* reach Develin. We *must* cross the river.'

'Can't you fight them?' Ambrose asked.

'We don't fight. We run.'

Crop, crop, crop, went Stefan on the hill grasses. Clouds had hidden the low sun. All the land was dimming. Somewhere just beyond the reach of eyes and ears men were hunting them with drawn swords. Somewhere, very close maybe, the Heron Man paced in the evening. And Wastelands said nothing.

And now Ambrose wished, glumly, that they had not passed so much time in silence together; although he did not know what he could have said to earn himself any friendship from this man. Maybe someone else could have done. The shepherd boy who had spoken with Uncle Adam had known how to make men listen to him. Maybe it was only Ambrose that men like this despised.

He wondered what it would have been like if it had been his own father there, resting his back against the tree; and whether his father would have helped him or handed him over to the Heron Man. And he wondered, too, what Wastelands would do now.

Still he wished that the man would speak with him.

After a while he asked: 'What is Devling?'

'Who?'

'Dev . . . The place you said.' It had been the first time Wastelands had said where they were going.

'Develin.' The knight rose and pointed into the evening. 'Look where the river runs – you can see a stretch of it down below. Where it bends – there. They have lit the lights.'

In the distance Ambrose could see a thin pale ribbon that must have been the river. On the far side of it was a shape that bulked like a small hill, with a star upon its crest.

'It is a great house. Larger than Bay or Trant, although not so old. There are few left in the Kingdom that can match it for wealth, and none that match it for learning – if you share your mother's taste for books.'

It was a castle – the third he had seen since leaving Chatterfall. And this one had lights, and life within it.

'I have been thinking to ask them if they would take you as a page. They would be well able to teach what you need to know – and to bat away any raiders that come. They've no love for your name, mind you. But I have no friends in places like Bay or Velis or Tuscolo. Whereas I did once make common cause with the Widow Develin. I think she will remember. *If* we can get there . . .'

Ambrose waited for him to say more, but he seemed to be thinking again.

The darkness was growing. Ambrose moved the little white stones outwards to give himself room to lie down.

One, two three, and so on up to eight. Eight stones. And the Wolf had felled eight stones by the pool. Suppose he could go to the pool now, and put one pebble where each of the stones had been – would that keep the Heron Man in? Ambrose could not imagine it. They would have to be very far apart. And how could he get there anyway? It was going to be hard enough to get to the castle across the river. The pool was a world away.

He huddled within the ring, his head on a fold of his blanket.

Still the knight was silent. Perhaps he was no longer thinking, but watching. Perhaps, with the enemy as close as this, he was going to watch all night.

Hours later, Ambrose was woken by a hand on his arm.

'Up,' said Wastelands. 'It is time to go.'

Ambrose thought he must be dreaming, because Wastelands's head had changed shape. Then he realized that the knight was wearing his helmet. He shook himself, heavy with sleep. It was still dark. The old moon had risen – little more than a fingernail.

'Dawn's not far away. If we go now, we'll reach the river under cover of darkness. Then we shall see.'

Ambrose fumbled for his stones and his blanket. It seemed to take an age to bring them together. The horse was anxious. The knight tightened its girth and replaced its bit in the darkness. Then he strapped on Ambrose's roll and they climbed once more into their places. Ambrose was still struggling with sleep as they rode off into the night.

They moved slowly, in a dream-like journey downhill. Ambrose swayed and nodded in the saddle, lurching in the fringes of a doze. He wondered when they would be able to lie down again. Stefan picked his way, following no path that he could see. The shape of the horse's head, the points of its ears, showed against the sombre land. Was it getting lighter? He thought perhaps it was. The air seemed very damp. The moon had disappeared, veiled by some cloud. The ground had levelled, and still he could see almost nothing at all. His world was sounds: the constant squeak and jingle of harness and arms; the plod-plod of the horse's feet, softening as the hooves bit into wet ground. There was water-noise; and now, and for some time, there had been the voices of birds: large water-fowl, quacking and hooting in the coming dawn. He could not remember when they had begun.

The river was there, away to their right. Wastelands was following the line of it, steering his horse as close as he could to the bank and then edging away again when they stumbled into boggy ground. Something flew *splatter-splatter-splatter* away across the surface of the water, quite close. The sky was much paler, and yet the air was still thick and impenetrable. He could see the head of the horse clearly, his own feet, and a few yards of ground. And then the world was a dull grey wall of river mist. All around them birds clamoured in the unseen dawn.

On they went. He could not see the water; he could not even make out the near bank, although he could hear reeds rustling close by. He wondered what they were looking for, and when things would change. Nothing did. His neck and limbs ached with weariness, and yet he was no longer sleepy.

Sounds had a strange quality in this mist. A large water-bird exploded from under Stefan's feet in a shudder of

137

brown feathers and vanished into the mist, trailed by honking cries. A moment afterwards, as Wastelands brought the startled horse back under control, they heard the same noise again. It seemed to come from fifty yards behind them. The soft plod, plod of hooves, the squeak of harness and the clink of mail surrounded Ambrose as the horse picked its way along the riverbank. He wondered if the mist was so thick in places that sounds bounced off it, as they might do from a wall of rock in the mountains. Now Wastelands was checking their mount. It stilled, waiting.

The sounds of horse-noises continued. Behind them, to their left.

A voice called, and Ambrose's heart bolted.

There was a rider, at least one, in the mist some twenty yards away. The same horse-noise, the same squeak, the same clink of mail. The rider called again, a question. Ambrose could not catch the words. They were muffled by helmet or hood, and muffled again by the fog. The voice was unhurried, bored, even. Behind him, Wastelands grunted loudly in answer, and stirred his horse to move slowly forwards. His arm was a bar of iron across Ambrose's chest. He leaned forward and whispered.

'Pick your feet up. Get beneath the cloak.'

Ambrose's eyes were straining at the mist. He thought he could just – maybe – make out the shadow of a rider over there. His heart was hammering.

Pick your feet up. In this mist, a horse and rider would be a shape and no more. The hunters had not yet realized that their prey was among them. But if they saw a second pair of legs, a second head, they would know at once. Stealthily Ambrose tried to draw up his feet and sit

138

cross-legged in his perch. His seat was precarious. He swayed, and almost fell. Wastelands clutched him, cursing under his breath. Ambrose swallowed, and tried again. He eased his left leg over the horse's neck and onto its other shoulder, so that he sat sideways with both feet towards the river. He bowed his head into the knight's armoured chest, and felt the big cloak draw around him. Propped like that, with his back to the loitering enemy, he could see only from the corner of his eye, to the head of the horse and the whiteness beyond it. His ears told him that there were two riders close, one now drawing ahead of them, another coming level. There were others beyond – how many? *We do not fight. We run.* They were not running. They were moving in company with their enemies, who could loom out of the mist and discover them in the time it took to draw a breath. Ambrose wanted Wastelands to urge the horse into a gallop – to carry them fleeing like a wildfowl along the riverbank, aimlessly, with the cries of the men in pursuit behind him. Wastelands did not. He was watching, letting the enemy draw slowly ahead. He must be hoping that they would not guess that he had been among them. Then, maybe, they could turn Stefan and slip back the way they had come.

How long? How long must they walk like this?

A voice called from ahead. Ambrose clenched his teeth and hunched his shoulders, but all that happened was that somewhere in the mist a horse picked up pace and rambled forward at a heavy trot. Voices came to him, conferring. They were coming nearer. Wastelands was idling his horse up towards his enemies. There were close, close. Could he see them? The lightest pull on the reins, and Stefan stilled. Another horse lumbered past – very close, this one.

139

Clutched under the cloak Ambrose could only see the mist over the water, and a single, thin black line curving away into it – a rope, suspended from two points somewhere out of sight, sagging under its own weight. A rope across the river.

Up ahead, somebody was dismounting. There was a slow paddling of hooves as other riders moved on into the mist. Metal rasped in a scabbard. That was Wastelands drawing his sword. What was happening?

After a moment Wastelands slid down from the saddle. Ambrose felt himself swaying as the man nudged the horse forward. Plod, plod. There was someone else moving in the mist. There was a tall structure of beams, from which the rope Ambrose had seen swept lazily off across the river. Down there, where the water must be, there was a darker shape, low and wide. A raft, or jetty.

A ferry!

At the foot of the beams, the shape of a man was stooping, sawing at something with a knife. Ambrose could hear the gasp of his breath. The other riders had left him to cut the ropes, and had gone on. As they came up the man straightened and looked up at Ambrose on the horse.

'Heavy stuff,' the figure said. 'You got an axe?'

Wastelands struck. Something whisked through the air and crashed loudly into metal. The man-shape disappeared. Ambrose swayed, lost his balance, and found it better to jump than fall. He hit the ground with both feet and stumbled.

'Quickly,' hissed Wastelands. 'Take his head.'

He meant Stefan. The horse backed as Ambrose reached for its bridle, but Ambrose caught it and tugged.

From the bankside the knight was grunting at the big animal. It came. Its hooves thumped loudly on the jetty of wooden boards. Slipping and scrambling, Ambrose lugged it on until the boards moved on water beneath his feet, and he realized they must be on a raft. The knight was cutting a mooring.

'Hold him!' the knight said.

Ambrose gripped the bridle with both hands and faced the horse, who shifted nervously, and then stilled when it realized the raft was tilting with its weight.

'Hold, Stefan,' said the knight to the horse.

The water noise increased. The river was all round them.

From the bank there came a cry – a wordless sound, full of pain and warning. The rope-cutter had dragged himself to a kneeling position, with his hands on his jaw and the side of his head. He cried again. In the mist ahead there were answering shouts. The raft was no more than a low platform of wood with a knee-high rail. There was a frame of poles at either end, each with a great eye through which the rope ran. The rope made a roaring sound as Wastelands began to pull the raft along it, out onto the water.

'Easy, Stefan,' the knight grunted over his shoulder.

There were horses, moving at a canter on the bank behind them. Wastelands heaved at the rope. They were already many yards out into the stream. Behind them, on the bank, the shapes of horsemen loomed – one, two, three. They were looking towards the raft, pointing. One seemed to set his horse at the river, but it baulked. There was a clickity-winding sound, carrying clearly across the water.

'Get round,' said Wastelands. 'Get round to his head.'
Ambrose had no idea what he meant.

'Get round to Stefan's head. Put him between you and the bank. Quickly!'

The horse shuffled uneasily, and the platform swayed as its weight shifted. Something hissed at him out of the air, and there was a dull, ringing thud from the bank that must have preceded it.

'Drop us in the water and you'll never find us!' shouted Wastelands at the bank.

'Do I care?' came the answer. 'Come back and we'll not shoot again!'

It was the voice – the big, roaring voice from the woods of Chatterfall.

But with each pull the shapes of the horsemen were fading into the mists behind them. The rope began to pulse with a dull, throbbing sound.

'They're cutting it,' gasped Wastelands. 'Hold Stefan.' He heaved and pulled. For a while nothing changed. Both banks were lost in the mist. It was impossible to tell how far they had to go.

Then the barge seemed to be swinging in the thick, brown current that swirled past them. Behind them, the rope trailed loosely in the water. The horse shifted unhappily.

'Saved me a job,' said Wastelands, panting. 'Now they can't follow us.' He had stopped pulling, and was trying to loop the unwieldy rope around one of the poles of the raft. 'What we need is just a bit of luck.' He stood, staring into the mist. They waited. Ambrose had the impression that the raft was travelling downstream, but also across the current. The rope ahead was taut. Loosed behind them, the current and the rope between them should bring them to the far bank at a point below the ferry. If only the ground was firm, and the bank could be scaled, they would escape.

'They've helped us, then,' he said. He had not thought that the enemy made that sort of mistake.

'A little. We could have been spilled in the water. They didn't think . . .' He tried to rub his face with his glove, but his helmet was in the way. 'They must have known we were close. They were sweeping the bank to remove any means of getting across. But they weren't expecting to find us. When we gave them the slip they were angry and didn't think. Nor did I. I should have stopped to knife that fellow, and we could have got away with all the time we needed.'

'I thought you had killed him.'

'I tried to. He had a chinguard. All the same, I did not expect him to get up again like that. I should have cut his throat. I was in a hurry, too.' He finished with a grunt that might have been a laugh. It was the only sound of good humour that Ambrose had heard from him in all their days of travelling.

He had not been afraid, Ambrose thought. He had walked among his enemies. He had kept going in the mist. Purpose like that could be a weapon against the Heron Man. As the raft drifted slowly in among the reeds on the far side of the river, Ambrose felt, grudgingly, that it was almost something to admire him for.

# VIII

## The Widow

hey emerged from the gatehouse into the outer ward of Develin. A high, musical trumpet sounded from the towers above them, and was answered almost at once by another trumpet, blowing from the gate on the far side of the great enclosure. A soldier in a clean, red-and-white-checked surplice hurried on before them, taking news of their arrival to the inner castle. Two more, carrying long pole-arms, walked at Stefan's head.

Ambrose looked around. On either side the white walls of Develin circled about him, closing their great embrace at the gatehouse behind his back. They blocked out all view of the world beyond. Along the foot of each wall ran a village of huts and sheds, with people – many people – busy outside them. There were animals and children running. Men looked up from mending a cart-wheel, watched Stefan pass, and went back to work. They were not afraid. Within these walls they had no need to be.

The inner gatehouse was massive, tall and bright with whitewash. There were many people about it – more

144

red-and-white-checked guards, more children, women arguing as they led out laden donkeys. And again there was music. Just within the gate a small band of men were playing stringed and wind instruments together in a light, jolly tune. They must have been practising, because the man who was their leader suddenly stopped them and spoke to them. Some of the children were watching. When the players started again they began a play-dance, linking arms and skipping in time together.

The inner courtyard towered with buildings. The cobbled spaces between them were alive with movement. People climbed steps that swept up to great doors. Faces peered down from long windows. Serious-looking men in dark green took Stefan and led him towards a trough. Ambrose stood close to Wastelands's side and felt very small. He had never seen so many people before.

Guards at one of the doors were gesturing to them, beckoning them to come up. Ambrose followed Wastelands up the steps. The soldiers spoke to Wastelands. Two of them led the way in. They passed down high-ceilinged corridors that were lit with rushes, even though it was bright day outside. Ambrose hurried along after the others, climbing stairs and squeezing his way past all sorts of people, richly and strangely dressed, who turned to look at him as he went by.

And now there was yet more music, swelling suddenly down the passages. It was a group of men, somewhere close, chanting the same words over and over on a single note. Their voices were as light and sweet as honey. Ambrose gathered his breath with the others outside a big, iron-studded door, and listened to the song as it rose from a nearby stairwell. The music was utterly strange to him: strange and beautiful and terrifying. He wanted it to stop. And yet he felt that if it did stop, he would yearn for it to go on.

The door opened. Ambrose followed Wastelands into a small, crowded chamber, full of faces and bright cloth. His eyes were caught at once by a broad-faced, broad-shouldered woman, seated in the middle of the room.

She wore black from head to toe. Her skin was pale and slightly blotched. Her dark hair was flecked with grey. Her face was round, and did not smile. He knew at once who she was, although he had never seen her before. She was the Widow of Develin.

About her stood a half-dozen men. One was a monk, who was almost bald, in a plain brown robe with a cord knotted around his waist. The others wore rich gowns, furs or doublets, and two were in mail. The chamber was hung with red tapestries; silver candle-sticks stood upon the joined-wood dressers. Here too the lamps were lit, although it was barely noon. The air was thick with a sweet smell, which must have come from the men's clothes or from some oil they had washed in. The sounds of singing still filtered in from beyond the closed door.

Standing before these people Ambrose felt ragged and filthy. Wastelands looked like a brigand, with his mail stained from the weather, his hair lank and the thin coat of whiskers that drooped from his mouth and chin. His voice sounded harsh as he addressed the room, speaking in strange, formal words about their journey.

'You have proof of the boy's line, at least?' said the Widow dryly, after Wastelands had fallen silent.

146

'I find it in the boy's look, which for me recalls both his mother and his father,' said Wastelands. 'Sir Martin, whom I see standing beside you, served in their house once. He will say if it is not so. Also, I found the boy at a house of his mother's friends at Chatterfall, which Sir Martin may know, too.'

The bald priest nodded. His eyes were bright as a bird's and never left the knight's face. He had the most prominent Adam's apple that Ambrose had ever seen.

'And he carried this.' The knight drew from his chest a crumpled piece of paper and offered it to the Widow. 'I do not read. I do not know what it says. But I know his mother's hand and I know the name of Tarceny.'

The Widow looked at the paper in the knight's hand, impassively. She did not reach to take it, but nodded to the priest at her side to accept it for her. Ambrose wondered why she might treat the knight so distantly, when he had claimed to be her friend.

The priest looked at the paper.

'Well?' said the Widow.

'My lady,' he said. 'It is her hand, as I remember it. But more than that, what is written here seems to address a matter that concerned her deeply, and me too when I served at Tarceny. I doubt not that this came from her – or that the boy is who Lord Lackmere says he is.'

The Widow shifted in her chair.

'So, Lord Lackmere – let us suppose that you have indeed brought me the son of the man who killed my man twelve years ago. You ask me for shelter for him, and a place at my hearth. Why should I do this?'

'Because you can,' said Wastelands. 'Because I ask it,

who was once your friend against your enemy. Because this boy's mother would ask it, who did more than anyone to bring your enemy down.'

'You talk to me of friends and enemies, sir,' said the Widow. 'Yet you have been both to me, and now I think are neither. My strength and charity are not endless. Let me ask another thing. News came to me yesterday that the city of Watermane has fallen to the soldiers of Velis. Did you know that?'

'No.'

Ambrose could tell that the knight was puzzled by the question.

'It was unlooked-for. Watermane is not a place to be knocked over with rush and a few soldiers. Yet I hear that armed men appeared suddenly within the walls and opened the gates to Velis before the garrison was aware. What do you think of that?'

The knight shrugged.

'Treachery. Or . . .'

'Or?'

'Or maybe witchcraft.'

The Widow leaned forward. The faces of the men around her were a wall against the man who stood before them.

'The last I heard of such a thing was in Tarceny's rising,' said the Widow, coldly. She glanced at Ambrose as she spoke, and he realized that she was talking of his father. 'Then there was a time when it seemed no strong place could hold against him. His soldiers appeared in Trant, and in Tuscolo, and in Pemini, one after another, and they fell. I never heard that the cause was treachery.'

Ambrose looked at his feet. He felt more uncomfortable than ever.

'I am told that your son Raymonde came to Velis before Watermane fell, and gave him counsel. I did not know that Lackmere was famous for its wise words. Are you not proud, Baron?'

The knight's face had hardened. Beneath the straggling moss of his beard, the lines around his mouth might have been cut in stone.

'I did not know that he went with Velis. I thank you for telling me.'

'I would be surprised at that, but these are surprising times. I recall that when Tarceny fell, certain things were given to certain – trusted – lords for them to guard and see that they never came to light. I remember it was said that by these things or through these things it was possible to work witchcraft. I know that one was a cup. But I heard, too, that one was a book. Lord Lackmere, I ask myself very much where that book is now.'

'And if I said to you that things given to my charge by the King are of concern to myself and the King, and no one else?'

'Not even to the unfortunate people of Watermane?'

There was a long silence in the room. Ambrose could hear the *whuff, whuff* of the oil burning low in the lamps. Wastelands and the Widow glared at one another. The counsellors stood around their lady. Their faces were fixed on Wastelands.

This is a crime, their eyes said. And it is your fault. Your fault.

Ambrose wondered if they thought it was his fault, too.

It was the Widow who spoke first.

'And at this time, sir, you come to me with the brat of Tarceny, as though he were a pawn that might be made – something else. With your enemies hard on your heels, and you ask me for shelter. Well sir, in the past you did draw sword when I had need of it. For that I have listened to you. This is what I say.' She leaned forward in her heavy, carved chair.

'I shall have space for one of you – one – in my house, as long as you will it. The other shall leave my gates before night falls, and go where they may, for I will not help them. It is for you to choose who will stay and who will go.'

Ambrose thought, gloomily, that he should not have been surprised. The Widow was his father's enemy. Everyone had hated his father. He wondered why Wastelands had brought him here at all. And he wondered, too, whether Wastelands would now stay here and let him be sent away. Ambrose had little reason to like the knight, and yet in the last few days he and his horse had become all the world he knew.

'A fair bargain,' said Wastelands slowly. 'For myself, I would trouble you no longer than my horse will feed. Take the boy and raise him as a page, until such time comes as he may serve you in another fashion. Or you and I may meet again to decide what is to be done.'

'If this is your word, then his way will be for me to choose and no one else,' said the Widow.

After a moment, the knight nodded.

When the Widow spoke again, her voice was less harsh than it had been.

'I am content. Sir, you may go.'

'Does my lady not even ask what I will do? I will tell you. First, to Lackmere. Thence, as swiftly and with such force as I may, to Septimus.'

'A curious choice, sir. I do not remember that you were so quick to take arms for him in Baldwin's rising.'

'He had been unjust to me after Tarceny's fall. He favoured Baldwin over-much, and reaped what he sowed. That was not my quarrel. This is. And it surprises me, my lady, that you do not see it as yours.'

Now the Widow was angry.

'Do not presume with me, sir! My house and my people are mine to dispose of. We do not look for wealth or power here, more than we have, but for lasting things that you would not understand. Ride with Septimus, Velis, or stay at home – I care not. But this I lay on you, since you remain to trade words after I have dismissed you.

'Sir, your house is not in order. The blood of one son has been shed. The doings of the other are not to be spoken of, and yet may bring us all grief. This lies at *your* door, sir, and it is for *you* to put it right!'

Once more the two locked eyes across the room.

'I shall do – what is necessary.'

'With wisdom, sir. With wisdom. Act without it and worse may yet fall.'

Wastelands was about to answer when the monk broke in.

'My lady, if I may, and before the baron departs, I have a question for him.'

'Ask it, Martin,' said the Widow.

'What of the boy's mother?'

Wastelands drew breath. Ambrose could see that he

151

was angry – more angry than he had ever known him, because of what the Widow had said about his son.

'He speaks not of her, save to say that she is dead,' he said slowly. 'Yet I myself met with her after he had left her, in a place in the mountains. I did not see her come. I did not see her go. But I saw her breath frosting on the air, and she spoke with me. This was no ghost. I will swear it on the Flame of Heaven!'

He bowed and left the room. His mailed heels clattered spitefully in the corridor outside. At a nod from the Widow, a guard followed him. Ambrose stood on his own, among all those strange people. His legs were trembling. He felt weak. He felt ill.

The Widow was still looking at the door through which Wastelands had disappeared. Suddenly, she chuckled. The men around her stirred, and some of them smiled.

'In truth,' said the Widow. 'We must bite a coin to know whether it is good or not. What shall we say of this penny that has turned up again?'

'That he was indeed bitten, my lady, and felt so when he left your presence.'

'But the taste in my mouth, Hervan. Is it good or not, do you think?'

The counsellor, a dapper man in a red doublet and gold chain, pulled a face.

'Any man who arrives suddenly with a pretender to two great houses, and possibly the throne, deserves suspicion. I would have laid money that he wished to enlist us in some plot, or at least to ransom or use the boy for some end of his. Your offer of haven for one tested him, as no doubt you intended . . .'

'Flatter me not, man, but I did.'

'Yet he asked nothing for himself, and so, for my judgement, did he prove his purpose honest. From what he said of the boy's mother, I judge that he very much desires that she should yet be alive, whatever the truth may be. Perhaps it is some feeling for her that has led him to act as he has done.

'More, he said that he would now ride to aid Septimus against the rising of Velis. If he is honest in this as well, we may judge that a plot for the crown was never part of his thinking.'

'Padry?' said the Widow.

'I would say so,' said a fat man in a green gown, whose round face bore a fringe of clipped beard. 'Though I would also say that his resolve to join with Septimus came upon him when he learned that his son followed Velis, and not before.'

'Indeed,' said the Widow. 'How far is the Kingdom fallen, that for the son to take one side is cause for the father to take the other!'

'Yet I thought also that he meant to test *you*, my lady,' said the counsellor in red. 'With his talk of riding to Septimus.'

There was a subtle change in the stance of the men, as though this was something they knew the Widow did not want to discuss.

'Did he, or do you?' said the Widow, eyeing him sourly.

The red counsellor bowed. Ambrose wondered if the man was about to get into trouble.

'Septimus will send for your help, my lady. He has lost much. You will have to make some sort of answer.'

'Have I not enough weary business that I must make war as well?' cried the Widow. 'War, yet again? Will it never end?'

The men were silent, waiting for her.

'Septimus is poorly placed now,' she said at length. 'What Lackmere can throw into the scales will not save him. We all know that. Even what we here could do might not be enough, and yet would cost us everything for a king who has never paid heed to his support in the Kingdom. No, I will not stir for Septimus.'

There was a slight murmur among the men. Ambrose had only half-understood what they were saying, but he could tell that not all of the counsellors were happy with that answer. The Widow must have felt it, too, but she was ignoring it. She was looking at him.

'It is a bad time to be a pretender without friends.'

Answer fairly, Mother had always told him. Tell the truth, fairly, and least harm will come – although that had mostly been about when she caught him stealing honey from the store.

'I don't pretend to anything,' he said, and his voice was hoarse.

'Call me "My Lady" or "Your Grace" when you speak with me. Do you pretend to be hungry, boy?'

His mouth was open to answer at once, when a thought came to him.

It came to him suddenly and clearly, like a whisper in his head.

*It is a trick*, it said.

It was a trick.

He swallowed, and looked into the eyes of the Widow.

'I'm not pretending about that, my lady,' he said.

Someone grunted. Surprise? Laughter? He did not know this place.

The Widow leaned back in her chair. 'So. We will have food brought up to you.' She looked at the man in the green gown. He nodded and, still smiling, made his way out of the room.

'Can you read?' she asked.

'Yes – my lady.'

'Read this.'

In her hand – it seemed to have come from nowhere – was a small book. She held it out to him with her finger marking a page. He had to take three steps towards her before he could focus on the tiny, beautiful writing.

'There is no treasure but Truth,' he began slowly. 'There is no Truth but Wisdom. There is no Wisdom, but from Learning, and Learning is won by the devotion of hours, years, days and nights to the works of Nature and the Treasures of Truth that others have gathered.' The page ended there. He looked up at her, wondering if this was another trick. But it seemed not.

'Good. Someone has made you not altogether worthless. Do you know it?'

'No – my lady. Is it a prayer?'

'Of a sort, yet it is addressed to no angel. Nevertheless I see that you read fairly; and that, hungry or not, you can think as well.' She jerked her chin to the low stool by the fire in the room. He made his way over and sat in the warmth, conscious of his damp and ragged clothes, and the aching famine inside him.

They were still watching him. He shifted on the

stool, but there was nowhere else he could go.

'Your cut-throat friend would have me make you a page,' the Widow said at length. 'To learn gentle manners and how to empty a man's skull of his brains with a sword. I will do better for you. In my house I keep places for forty-nine scholars. Their family is no matter to me. The poorer the better, so long as they have the wit to study with my wise men, and carry out into the world what they have learned. You will join them. And for your safety, and my peace, I think we shall not speak to any of your line. You are an orphan, found by a traveller, and brought to my charity. That is a story common enough in this cold time. We shall choose a new name for you . . .' She paused, and looked around at the men.

'His mother's father was of Trant. Trant's badge was the oak-leaf, if I remember. Shall we call him Acorn? Wisgrave, what do you think? Acorn?'

'Is it not a little obvious, my lady? Better a name with no reference to his family, no meaning at all.'

'All names have a meaning in my house, sir. Hervan – what is your thought?'

'That it might be both more true and more safe to make a name of the signs of both houses, the Moon and the Oak. So I say *Monak*, which will mean little to those who do not understand.'

'Except that you all but call him *Monarch*, and I would have no whisper of that.'

'Perhaps *Monk*, then . . .'

It was a game, Ambrose thought. The moon was for his father and the oak-leaf for his mother. The men were tossing them and his name between them, and the winner would be the one who could make his name disappear. His name was almost the last thing he had.

'Since you have called the Monk, we should let our Monk speak. Martin, help us . . .'

The bald monk smiled.

'Let us use my friend Hervan's idea, my lady, and yet change it just a little. If we mix the words for Oak and Moon in the old speech, we reach the name *Luquercunas*, which . . .'

'Which stretches the mouth too far . . .'

'Which, as I was about to say, my lady, we may shorten swiftly to *Luke*.'

'A point to you, sir,' said the Widow. 'I think you have it.'

'Luke,' said the red counsellor eagerly, 'recalls a heathen god of the sun, as I think my friend Martin will allow. The sun stands for royalty, and therefore . . .' He let the end of his sentence dangle in the air.

The Widow smiled wryly. 'In truth,' she said, 'the boy's calling shines through all effort to obscure it. No, sirs, "Luke" is plain, and yet speaks to those of us who have understanding. Enough. But I want no talk that the son of Tarceny is in my house – not even to those close friends and counsellors of ours who chance not to be here this morning – or men will say that I am plotting to put him on the throne. Hervan, you will instruct the guard who left with Baron Lackmere in this as soon as we are finished. And you, boy. Understand that it is a risk for me and all my house that you are here. It pleases me to take this risk, and to forgive you the wrong your house has done me, because I hold you innocent. But from now on your name is Luke, and you do not know your father. Be faithful to me in this, and study well, and I shall consider myself repaid.'

Ambrose nodded, supposing that he could not disagree.

'Here is food for you, then.'

The man Padry had been standing at the door for the past few minutes, with a small tray in his hand. He placed it on the ground in front of Ambrose's stool – nervously, as if Ambrose were a stray dog that might bite. Ambrose looked at the tray, and his mouth tickled at once with juices. There was a loaf, and legs of cold, small meat of a kind he had never seen before. He gave up trying to follow the talk, and wolfed at the food. There was wine, too, of a rich pungency that swam in his head as he drank his way cautiously toward the bottom of the bowl.

He understood that the Widow had tested him, swiftly and ruthlessly – not only with the reading, but also in the question: *Do you pretend to be hungry?* It had indeed been a trick. If he had just said 'yes' or even 'no' – which, under her stern look, he might have done – he would have got nothing. But somehow his brain had picked it up. It almost made him shiver to think how close he had been to going wrong. But he had got it right. He could be pleased about that. And now he was being fed.

And with food moving into his belly he could look at the world differently. He could see, through a square window behind the Widow's chair, the brown lines of hills that he had travelled to come here. Out there were the comfortless places where barns stood ruined and fields all run to seed. That was where he had seen his mother fall, crumpling under the blow at the clifftop. That was where Wastelands was going, where enemies still roamed with steel in their hands. The walls between there and here were deep, hard stone. He could measure the casement of the window with his eye. The depth of it was longer than his arm's reach – maybe twice as long. And now these people had taken his name, and put it beyond the walls with all the rest. They had made him into someone else. He could still feel his sadness, but it had moved a little further from him. Here inside there was fire and food. He was beginning to feel warm, and braver about being left on his own.

And he was beginning for the first time to feel sorry for Wastelands. He wished, now, that they had liked one another better. He felt that they should have done. Perhaps it had been his fault that they had failed.

The bald monk had passed Mother's letter to the Widow.

'She writes *He is loose*,' he was saying. 'I think I can guess who she meant by *He*. Pity that she has told us so little.'

The Widow looked at the writing. 'So what has she told us, Martin?'

'Enough to support our fears about the fall of Watermane. Velis, or one close to him, may be following the same road that Tarceny did ten years ago.'

'Then Velis is in great peril.'

The monk seemed surprised.

'Indeed, my lady. Although I own that I thought more of Septimus, who for all his faults is a man of honour and must contend against this thing.'

The Widow sighed. 'Septimus is finished. I can do nothing for him. I say that to you now, sir. If I must fight the ghost of Tarceny, then fight I will. But I will do it in my own way – in wisdom, not war.'

They were standing around her, waiting for her.

'Martin, I would that you go to Velis.'

'I? And say what?'

'Not as an ambassador, but as a counsellor. I shall write a letter for you to carry. You are my gift to him. I release you from my service, that you may serve him as you have served me. Watch for witchcraft, for untruth, for wanton cruelty. When you see them, speak against them. Velis is a pup, suckled on war. If he achieves the throne, he will need your help to bring peace.'

'As – as I am commanded, my lady.'

'Good, then. It remains therefore that we prepare our answer for Septimus when he should send . . . What is it, Martin?'

'My lady – if I am to accept this charge, I beg leave to withdraw.'

'What, to put your head in a bucket, sir? In faith, but I thought you stronger of stomach!'

Ambrose saw that the Widow wanted the monk to laugh with her, and also that the monk was not in a mood for laughing. He smiled, tightly.

'I would speak again with the Baron Lackmere before he departs. He may tell me more of his son's doings than could confirm our guesses. Also I would speak with him of the mother of – of our Luke here. She was friend to me, too.'

'That one? You have strange friends, sir, but I love you for it. And yes, you may withdraw. You will find that scoundrel in the kitchens, I guess. Yet come you back here straight. Now I must lose your counsel, I feel that I want it sorely.'

The monk turned to go and found his way blocked. A man stood in the doorway wearing the red and white chequers of the Widow's house over his mail. He bowed.

'What is it?' said the Widow.

'A party of armed horsemen, my lady. They have come across the bridge and are approaching along the gate road.'

'Armed horsemen? Who?'

'We see no banners, my lady. But the watch has counted fifteen or sixteen horses.'

'My lady,' said one of the others in the room. 'I guess that these may be Lackmere's pursuers.'

'So. Is Lackmere aware?'

'He is gone, my lady,' said the newcomer. 'This past half-hour. He mounted and rode as soon as he left you.'

'Gone? Did he not even stay for meat?'

The Widow rose and peered through the window as if expecting to see through its narrow scope the figure of a horseman fleeing across the hills. Her fingers still held the letter, but she had forgotten it.

'I did not mean that he should part without even a drink from my wells,' she said.

'Yet if these are indeed his pursuers, my lady, and they serve someone of rank, then it is better that he is not found within our walls.'

The Widow glared at the counsellor who had spoken. 'Well,' she said. 'If they wish to parley, then I will speak with them. Maybe I will win that old rascal another half-hour yet.'

Her eye fell on the man in the door. Ambrose saw at once that there was something more he would say, and did not know how to.

'The Lady Sophia, my lady . . .'

'At her lessons, at this hour, I hope.'

'She . . . we think she may have gone out beyond the walls . . .'

There was a moment's silence. The men around the Widow had stiffened like deer that scent a wolf. Ambrose trembled.

'*So!*' barked the Widow. 'You are telling me that my feather-brained daughter has played truant again and gone frolicking among the daisies, is that it?'

'My lady . . .'

'At the very moment when a troop of armed men, who may well be brigands, have chosen to ride up to my gate as bold as you please, sir?

'And that you have allowed her to pass, although you knew that I would not let it?

'*And* I guess, that this is not the first time?'

The man could do nothing but bow.

'Angel's knees, sir! Do I have walls for no purpose? Gates, guards, all useless?'

'I have ordered a sortie, my lady. Thirty armed men on horse . . .'

'I doubt it will come to that. But when this is past, I do not think the Lady Sophia should remember this day with pleasure. Nor should the guards who let her out, knowing she should be at lessons. And you and I, sir, will speak of this again this evening. Now, show me these brigands who think to crack their lances on my gate-bells!'

She stood among them: a short, round woman in black among those tall and colourful men. They bowed to her as she passed, her black shawl lifting slightly in the air of the room. The armoured men and the red counsellor followed her through into the passage way. Calls sounded in the corridor. Somewhere, someone began to run. The noises receded.

Three men remained in the room with Ambrose, muttering among themselves.

'It would be easier if we knew who they were,' said a greybeard in a blue gown.

'She will not take sides,' said the bald priest, Martin. 'She has made that plain. So she will be careful. For all that, I guess that these people – from Velis, or someone else – will receive little help from her.'

'And Lady Sophia?'

'Will find it easier to sleep on her front tonight, I suppose.'

They laughed, in spite of the tension in their voices.

'You think she is not in danger, then?'

'Oh, I fear she may be. But I tell myself that it is not for her that they came. Nor do I think that they will prove to be just brigands.'

'So you know who these men are?'

'Fifteen riders? I might make a guess.'

There was a pause. Ambrose looked up. He thought that a moment before they all had been looking at him. The man Padry cleared his throat.

'I think it falls to me to show the boy his place in the house. Ha, er – *Luke*, if you are ready?'

'Fifty scholars now, and only ten masters,' said the

163

other man. 'And more councils in a week than we used to see in a month. We shall have our hands full. But I would rather be here with five hundred young ingrates than follow you to Velis, Martin. That's a thankless task she has given you.'

'She has spoken of it before, although I had half-hoped she had forgotten. It was not a surprise. Yet I am sorry that I shall not have the pleasure of instructing our fiftieth scholar.'

Ambrose, who had been picking himself up to follow the man Padry, stopped. The monk was watching him. This was the one who had known Mother. There was something like sympathy in his eyes.

'Come, boy, come,' said Padry from the door.

The monk nodded in dismissal. Ambrose left. Padry was waiting in the corridor, tapping his foot.

'Come on, boy!'

Outside the Widow's chamber the sound of singing swelled again. It floated up the stair and seemed to flood the corridor. Maybe all these stone passages were always filled with music, just as they were always lit with lamps. But there were other sounds, too. From somewhere below came the sound of men hurrying in mail. Horses were snorting and turning in the courtyard. Through narrow windows Ambrose glimpsed red and white pennons dipping on the ends of lances. Somebody called an order, and another voice cursed him and yelled at him to keep his voice down. Ambrose scampered after Padry, infected by urgency as the sortie armed in the courtyard.

They came to a landing with stairs running up and down, and a door that opened on the far side into what seemed to be a long corridor with wooden walls. Padry listened. His mind was plainly on the fighters, and the threat to the house. But the sounds from outside were less now. Probably the Widow's fighters had all moved down to the outer gate. Perhaps the parley was already beginning. Padry turned back to Ambrose and smiled, absently. Then he looked away over the boy's shoulder and began to speak.

'This is the School Stair,' he said. 'Through this door is my lady's library, which with great generosity she has placed at the disposal of her scholars. Remember that each book is worth the harvest of several farms. Therefore you may come here only in the hours between Nones and Vespers, and no flame is permitted here at any time. You may take down and handle any work from the presses at will, so long as they bear directly on your studies, but you must make no attempt to unfasten them. Certain quires and bound volumes of exceptional value are kept in locked chests. These you may only examine at the direction of a master. This is the rule for all scholars. If you break any part of it, we will thrash you in due measure. We will thrash you also if you do not study. Above is a dormitory where you will sleep, and where we masters have our rooms. My lady has gone to much expense to see that the dormitory is divided into cells, one for each scholar. Remember that we will thrash you if you are outside your cell after curfew, and double if you are found in the cell of another scholar. Also, since the partitions are only of wood, we will thrash you if you snore . . .'

He must have said these words many times to students before this. Ambrose supposed that they would have known

165

what words like *Nones* and *Presses* and *Quires* meant. He did not; nor was he sure whether the threat of a beating if he snored was a joke. He did not laugh.

'So much for food for the mind,' said Padry, beginning to descend the stairs. 'Food for the belly you will have too. I will show you the refectory, which is also the scholars' hall . . .'

Ambrose ducked through the low doorway on the landing and peered down what he had thought was a long passage, with many other passages opening off it. Now he saw that the walls of the passage were not walls but the ends of great open cupboards, with benches between them. The cupboards had shelves, festooned with light chains, and in the shelves were books, folded papers, scrolls, more papers – so many things. A crowd of young men were gathered at the nearest bench, with a scroll open on a broad shelf that was part of the cupboard. One of them was reading aloud. The others craned over his shoulder. Further down the room other groups were doing the same thing. The buzz of low voices filled the air.

The nearest boys had noticed Ambrose. Their eyes had turned to him all together, like a many-headed beast. The voice of their reader stopped. Ambrose recoiled onto the landing.

'. . . We take our meal after Vespers, which at this time of year is at sundown,' Padry was saying as he diminished down the stair.

More sounds came flooding up from below – knives on blocks, and voices arguing. There was steam, and wood-smoke, in the air. The corridors still hummed with the distant song.

So many rooms, so many people! In a place like this it was possible for men to be singing, and for crowds of boys to be reading in the school, while in the outer court-yard thirty armed horsemen sat tense, waiting for an order to charge. And somewhere down at the foot of the stair there were yet more people who fed them all.

Ambrose hurried after the man Padry, feeling his courage deserting him again. Wastelands was gone. Stefan was gone. He had never been among so many people, and he knew none of them. There had been one man who had known Mother – the monk in the brown robe – and he too was now being sent away.

Brown robe, or grey robe?

No – it had been brown robe, surely, tied at the waist with a rope.

Yet – yet had there not also been a *grey* robe, there, among the men in the council chamber?

*It is a trick!*

Ambrose stopped, gripping the stair-rope. Suddenly his heart was going very hard.

That thought – when the Widow had been testing him – where had it come from? Like a whisper in his head that he had heard before?

There had been a half-dozen of them: Padry, the bald monk, and the man with the faded blue tunic, all of whom must have been masters at the school. And the red coun-sellor, and two men in mail . . . There had only been one monk, because earlier the Widow had talked of '*the* monk', and had turned to Martin . . .

It was too late to go back and make sure.

He forced his legs to carry him on down the stair. But

as he hurried after Padry through the uproar of Develin's kitchens, his mind's eye showed him more and more clearly the memory of another figure by the Widow's chair, silent, in a grey robe and hood. And watching.

And none of them had seen it. And it had spoken to Ambrose, whispering in his head about the Widow's test.

He had passed because of the Heron Man.

The white stones clacked at his hip as he walked. He put his hand on them. He thought he was about to be sick.

The Heron Man! How could he be *here*?

# PART II

## WISDOM

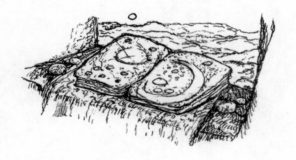

## IX

### The Company of the Moon

he Lady Sophia Cataline diCoursi
Develin was not frolicking among
daisies. She was holding up her skirts
and trying to creep forward among
bushes and tall weeds to a hiding place
from which she could see the riverbank.

She was not feather-brained either. There were several
reasons for what she was doing. One of them was that she
was sure the Widow would have a fit if she knew what her
sixteen-year-old daughter was up to.

Like everybody else at Develin, Sophia thought of her
mother as 'The Widow'. It was right for her. It made Sophia
think of a great, black spider sitting over everything and
covering them all with her webs. And it was a sort of revenge
for her own name – Sophia, for Wisdom – which her mother
had chosen for her at birth. She hated it. When her mother
was finally dead she would have herself called . . . well, *something* different. She would have liked to be Cataline, but her
governess had once told her that that had been the Widow's
choice, too. She did not feel that any name her mother had
chosen for her could truly be hers. There were days when
she did not feel 'Sophia' at all.

She knew well enough that she was outside the walls without escort (which was forbidden). She knew that outside the walls horrible things could happen, without warning, even on her mother's lands. Outlaws, vagabonds, raiding parties – they all came from time to time, although they almost never approached the castle. Her tutors had warned her that the children of rich houses might be taken for ransom. They had not told her that less fortunate people might be killed outright, for little reason. Nor had they told her that a child of any standing might be raped. She had worked these things out for herself, from the clues that filtered daily into the walled enclosures of the last great house in the south of the Kingdom.

But it was a bright day, after the heavy mists of the morning. The wind was stirring the reeds and trees, and harrying the white clouds south and eastwards off the land. Her heart had been bursting to get out from the close pen of the castle walls, if possible without the snooping eyes of someone who had been told off from other duties, with much dithering and consultation, to watch her.

Then a group of the scholars had gone out to fish, laughing with their rods over their shoulders and whooping in the gate-tunnel. That had been enough.

Sophia did not think much of the Widow's scholars. This was partly because they were her mother's. Their presence in the house, and that of the solemn-faced masters under whom she must study, were just another expression of that great oppressive Will that was Always Right and yet understood nothing. But also, she did not like them. They hung around the courtyards in groups between and after their studies. The older boys picked on the younger ones when they thought no one was looking. And they talked coarsely when Sophia passed, and meant her to hear what they said. She had fought against being taught as they were taught, and, when she had lost that battle, she had fought to have her lessons in private rather than in their company. So it was galling to her to see a group of them free to enjoy themselves when she had appointments with Father Grismonde for instruction in Dogma, and then with Master Denke for Rhetoric and Law. It was simply not fair that poor scholar-boys could go freely where she might not. She would not accept it. She had waited a few minutes and then, with a wink to the gate-sergeant, who was a friend, had followed.

It was time for some fun, and a little revenge.

The scholars went fishing when they could, for sport and food. Sophia disliked fish, which rarely appeared at the high table. But she had found that when they were fishing some of the scholars would wade right out into the river. They would take off their shoes and hose, leaving their legs naked to their loin-cloth; then they would gather up the tails of their shirts in the crook of one arm to keep them dry, take their rod in the other, and splash out into the waters, bellowing to one another about the chill. Then, if she found somewhere to hide, she could watch the parade of bare buttocks moving a few inches above the river's surface, almost as white as the clouds that drifted over the land.

It was a thrill to see them without being seen; and a double thrill to imagine what her mother would say if she knew.

Her father might have laughed, she thought. Perhaps

he still laughed, if he was watching her from where he rested under the Angels' wings. But the Widow would scream and froth. (And then, perhaps, she would get a nosebleed. Hah!)

This time Sophia was going to get closer than ever before.

The trouble with not wanting to be seen or heard was that movement was much more difficult. Her heavy skirts caught on briars. It was hard to keep her balance. She could hear the voices of the scholars, a stone's throw away on the bank. They would be fumbling with their hooks and bait. She took a long step forward, felt her skirt catch on something (again!) and swayed. The wind gusted among the bushes, and under cover of its noise she wrenched angrily to free herself. She felt the threads pull, and knew she would have to make up some story about a nail or splinter around the castle to account for the damage. Why did things *never* work the way they were supposed to?

She could glimpse a few yards of bank now, between the bushes. A man's foot and lower leg (still fully clothed) stood in thin mud. She crouched, and found she could slip forward for a better view.

This was it. This was secret. From outside they would only see the bush. No one would know what was on the inside.

Once, very long ago, Sophia had sat upon her father's knee at the writing desk that now stood in her mother's antechamber. She could not have been more than four years old, because her father had died before her fifth birthday. She remembered him laughing as she had pulled at his beard, and then he had stolen her ribbon because without meaning to she had begun to hurt him.

'Look,' he had said, and had opened a drawer of the desk.

He had put the ribbon in the desk and closed the drawer. She had cried out that she wanted her ribbon, and had pulled the drawer open. The ribbon had not been there, and Father had laughed again.

Then he had taken her fingers and showed her how the secret drawer worked. Press the catch, pull the drawer, and out came the secret drawer with the ribbon in it. Push the drawer back and open it again without pressing the catch – out came the ordinary drawer, with nothing in it. The secret drawer remained deep in the desk, and no one knew it was there.

That drawer and that memory were important to Sophia. They were things that she knew her father had given her. They told her – and *he* told her, as he watched her from among the Angels – that she could keep secret inside herself. Her mother, and her mother's people, could call and pull at her as much as they liked. Out would come only the ordinary Sophia. She alone knew her Self, as it was hidden within.

She was close, very close. She could hear the voices of the scholars, the squelch of their feet as they moved on the muddy bank – even the ring of a dangling hook as it struck upon some buckle or stone. But through the low branches she could only see the one man, crouching now as he busied himself over his rod. The others were screened from her by the leaves of the bush. Maybe some of them would wade out into the stretch of river that she could see.

She recognized the man in front of her, because he was older than most of the others. He had been at the

175

castle for years (lapping at the Widow's charity) but had never spoken with her. She did not know his name. He had a lean face, lightly bearded. His hair, which was a tired blond colour, was long and gathered into a pigtail at his neck as if he were a tinker. His clothes were a faded green, but his belt was of good leather and there was a pouch at his hip which must hold his bait. Either he or the breeze had wound his line several times around his rod. He was now unwinding it, carefully because of the bright hook on the end. Somewhere close, someone cursed as they tried the same thing, but the man said nothing. Sophia lay full length under the bushes and willed him to take his trousers off.

Round, round, round. Now the hook dangled freely in the wind, and there was more line yet up the rod. It would have a long reach. Sophia thought, with disappointment, that maybe the man would not be wading into the water at all, but would fish from some spot on the bank. Any moment now he would turn and be gone, and she would have to struggle on to another hiding place for a more rewarding view.

But he did not turn. His hands had stopped what they were doing. He was looking towards her bush. He seemed to be looking right into her eyes where she lay. Her heart bounced.

If I don't move he can't see me. He can't possibly see me.

She saw him frown, and rise to his feet. He was coming her way.

She backed quickly among the undergrowth, snagging on branches, scrambling. She heard the man's voice calling, curious but not unfriendly. For the moment she was screened by the bushes. But he'd come round them and then see who it was that had been spying on them.

She didn't care if they told the Widow. She would be beaten for it, but it would be almost worth it (she thought) for the horrors her mother would suffer at her behaviour.

But she did care about the scholars. It was suddenly obvious to Sophia what they would think if they saw her. She could imagine how they might treat her, or talk about her, or invent bawdy stories of her to tell to one another. And if the scholars knew it would be all around the castle by nightfall. That would change the way people thought about her for ever. So much for being secret! She wasn't going to get caught if she could help it.

That was why she took to her heels and ran towards the road.

When she had been small, she had run everywhere. She remembered nursemaids who had called her 'little hare' and pretended to be big hounds chasing her with deep yelps around the chairs in the hall. But she had not run for years – barely since she had become a woman. And her skirts were wet and heavy and her breath came in gasps. Behind her, she heard the man call again. He was not running yet. She pushed through the last bushes, leaped a ditch and emerged onto the road.

There was no cover here, and nowhere for her to hide. If she had been thinking at all, it was that she might walk briskly back towards the castle, with her head high, pretending that anything that had happened at the bank was nothing to do with her. As long as she could get far enough away by the time her pursuer appeared, he might not be sure who she was or what she had been doing. It might not work, but she could not run all the way to the house and she did not have time to think of anything else.

Then she saw the horsemen.

They were approaching her at a walk from the direction of the castle. She could see at once that they were not of Develin. There was something unfamiliar about their armour and horses – ragged outlines that she did not know. The head of the leader was bare, his hair long and disordered. The hilt of a great two-handed sword danced over his left shoulder as he rode. She could see no banners.

These could not be outlaws, surely, jingling towards her in the afternoon sun? They were barely half a mile from the castle gate! Beyond them, the long, white line of the outer wall and the pile of buildings around the upper court were in plain view. Her home looked so close that she almost felt she could touch it.

Half a mile? She could not possibly reach the gate if they *were* brigands. They would be on her in moments. She had no idea what to do.

She stood there, watching them come.

Behind her, the bushes parted. There was a soft thump as the fishing scholar leaped the stream. He stood beside her. She heard him whisper something – maybe it was an oath. He had seen the horsemen, too.

Then his hand touched her shoulder.

'Kneel down,' he said urgently. 'Help me with my tackle.'

They crouched on the wet grass by the verge. He placed the rod between them. There was nothing wrong with it that she could see. She put her hand out to pull, uncertainly, at the line. He was untying the hook. They were two peasant people, busy with their fishing gear as they might be on any day of the season.

Her hair, her dress, her shoes if they saw them! There was no chance that she would be taken for a peasant woman. She could hear the horsemen coming. She could feel the weight of the horses as their hooves crunched wetly on the earth. They were close enough to speak to her. Why hadn't she run back into the trees?

'Don't look up,' muttered her companion.

She could not help it. She looked up as the first horseman came level. She waited for him to check his mount, draw his sword . . .

He did not. His horse plodded onward, slowly. She could see – she could almost touch – the dark, mud-matted coat of its legs as they stepped past. An armoured foot, a cruel spur, swung before her eyes. He was still riding forward. He was not looking down but ahead, intent on the road. He was an old man, armoured in black mail, with a great mane of white-grey hair and grey stubble. His big war-helm bumped at his saddle. He had passed them. Another was on them – dark leather and rusty mail, black cloak pinned with a white round badge at the shoulder. Sour eyes flicked down at her from under a fringe of white-grey hair. Then he was looking ahead again, and his horse had not broken from its stride.

One by one they passed, as Sophia and the scholar cowered by the roadside. Their armour was old and stained, but good; their horses a mix of strong beasts and common nags. Battle-axes and morning stars nestled among the pots and pans and bags hung at their saddles. These were not ordinary outlaws. Several of them seemed

179

to be knights of some sort. And each one wore the same white round badge, with a fleck of black upon it. The faces were gaunt, and so many of them seemed old. Hard eyes watched the road ahead of them. They would be terrible enemies, Sophia thought.

Now the last one was passing, a man much younger than the others. His head, too, was bare, and his coarse, brown hair blew around his face. He wore no badge. He looked down at her as he drew level. She met his eyes and knew that he saw through her pretence at once. She saw his hands jerk the reins. His horse checked, and sidled in the road towards her.

'Raymonde!' bellowed the voice of the leader from far ahead. He had not even looked around.

The horseman was still looking down at her. Then he winked. His hands shook his reins, and his body swayed as his mount surged on after the others.

She watched them go, dwindling along the roadway.

She found that she was already on her feet, and could not remember when she had stood up. Her companion rose beside her and let out a long breath.

'Thank the Angels!' he said, looking after the armoured company.

'Who were they?'

'I don't know. There was a house that had such a badge, but it was broken years ago. And this is far out of that country.' He thought. 'They came from the castle. They were not wearing their helms. They had business with the Widow, perhaps . . .'

His voice was slow, and had the faintest soft trace of the east-country in it.

'Even so,' he added, 'I've not felt my head so loose on my shoulders since I first met your mother.'

So he knew exactly who she was. Of course he did. And she saw from his look that he also knew she would get into trouble for being out on her own when such a troop passed by.

She looked at him mulishly, and he smiled.

She hadn't thought his face was handsome. She did not like beards (even beards that were little more than pale stubble about the face and chin). His eyes were grey and slightly sunk, and for a moment they were still wide with the danger that had just passed them. But they relaxed as he looked down at her, and a light came into them with his smile.

Something about the way he smiled stirred an old, friendly memory of her father before he had gone away.

'There's the postern door in the river-tower . . .' he said.

The postern led straight into the cellar corridor under the living quarters. Once it would have been guarded and used daily for unloading stores from barges that docked below the walls. But there was very little river-traffic now, and with this new uprising there might soon be none.

'It will be bolted.'

'I was saying, I could go in by the gate and unbolt it from the inside. If you waited a little, it would be open when you tried it. There's an old boat-shelter on the river-bank, which I use now and again. You could reach it and not be seen, perhaps?'

It would be difficult. No, it would impossible, with the garrison alert and alarmed as it would be. And the moment

181

anyone saw her they would tell the Widow, for the credit of it.

She saw him understand that, too.

'I've a cloak and hood on the bank you can wear,' he said. 'Nice and long and ragged. You'll look like a true fishwife. It's the best we can do.' He turned to go.

'Your pardon, sir . . .'

He looked back.

What was she thinking of? She didn't call scholars *sir*. She was talking to him as if he were a priest – or a knight. Perhaps that was because he carried himself like one.

'What is your name?' she asked.

'Chawlin.' He leaped the ditch without waiting, and disappeared into the bushes.

She followed him far enough to be concealed from the road, and waited.

She was scared, but unrepentant. Yes, she had nearly been caught, and caught by people far worse than her mother's cronies. It had been the worst possible chance that those horsemen had been on the road just then. But she had got away with it. And with a little good luck now, and the help of this scholar, she was going to get back inside the walls without anyone knowing she had been away.

The scholar had not asked what she had been doing by the bank. If he guessed, he did not seem to mind. And if he was doing so much to help her he might not even tell the others. He was taking a risk for her, indeed. If they were discovered he might well be punished. She wondered if he hated the Widow, and was doing this to spite her. But it did not sound like that. It was more as if he just knew what it must be to live as the Widow's daughter. She thought again of her father, chuckling among the Angels.

And he spoke well, she thought. His voice was soft and slow, and it was laced with words like *perhaps*, as if the thing he was most sure of was that nothing could be sure. To anyone who endured the implacable certainties of the Widow, that was refreshing.

She stood among the bushes, waiting for him to return.

Only a few minutes ago she had been creeping past this spot on the way to the bank, eager to spy on a row of half-naked boys. She had not seen the horsemen. She had not seen the scholar smile. It seemed to her that so much had happened in a short space of time. She wanted to think about it. And her reasons for coming here seemed rather childish now.

Perhaps she had not been fair about the scholars. They were not all louts and props to her mother's vanity. She felt now that she wouldn't mind the company of some of the older ones – the ones who were really men, like this man Chawlin, and not just boys grown big. Maybe they all talked together about what they had heard in the classes – and laughed gently at the foolishness of the masters. She was sorry that she hadn't had the chance to find out.

That was the Widow's fault, she thought. Everything became a weapon or a battleground around *her*. She spoiled a lot of things, when you looked at it.

Sophia looked up as the man came pushing back through a screen of bushes.

'What did you mean about when you met my mother?' she asked.

He hesitated. 'That's a long story, and there's no time

183

for it now. Another day would be better.' He held out a torn, brown cloak. 'Are you ready?'

'Yes.'

'When you reach the shelter, wait a quarter hour and then come up to the castle wall. Bring my rod with you. Make sure you are well in under the wall, out of sight of the keep-watch, before you approach the door. Once you are through the door, bolt it again and leave the rod and cloak in the old storeroom that's first down the passage. I'll come back for them later. You understand?'

'Yes.'

'Good luck, then.'

Her success was her downfall. In her elation at passing the door unseen, she thought she could escape punishment altogether. So when she was called to account for her disappearance and missed lessons, she claimed that she had been in the library, and had lost track of time there. But this story collapsed under the evidence of the rents in her dress (which, as Hestie, her governess, reminded her all red-faced, would now have to be mended, and who was to do *that*, pray the Angels?). So she confessed instead to an adventure in the castle attics. And for that she was beaten anyway, with extra for the first lie and several strokes over because the Widow, who had heard more than one story from the gate-guard, did not really believe her even then.

It was Hestie who gave her the beating, with her thin little cane of thornwood. Sophia could have forgiven her for that, because it was the Widow who had made her do it. But then Hestie saw fit to say that if Sophia could not learn her duty she would be no better than the Whore of Tarceny, who had fled a royal betrothal for lust, and caused all that war and misery and suffering and the death of Sophia's father to boot. And that was *not* fair, because she would never do anything like the Whore of Tarceny, and Hestie was as good as saying that she would murder her own father or at least did not care about his memory, and she *did*, more than any of them.

Next morning (still sore) she found that her private lessons had been taken away. Her mother had sent one of the masters on an embassy, she was told, and the rest were now unable to indulge her. Worse, Hestie was again saying that she must be escorted whenever she moved outside the living quarters, let alone the castle.

*And* when she came to take her place at the scholars' benches (arriving late, because neither Hestie nor she knew how the lectures were organized), she saw that she had been put with a group of younger students. She felt that she wouldn't have minded so much if it had been with people like the man Chawlin and his peers. But these boys were at the very beginning of the middle studies that her tutors always thought she neglected. Feeling that she was still being punished, she slid into the last place in the back row and sat beside a long, dark-haired boy who could be no more than twelve or thirteen. There she started to sulk.

The master was Padry, who until yesterday had attended her twice a week to tutor her in Astrology and Mathematics. He gave her no sign of recognition. Either he hadn't noticed her when she came in, or he was pointedly treating her like any other of the rabble of scholars in the class. He stumped around the room in his heavy green robe, expounding the System of Croscan in almost exactly the same words that he had used in her private lesson last month.

'Everything that is, springs from one source, which is the Godhead. It scatters into the world like shards of light broken by a glass.

'And like light, it reflects back to our eye that sense of the Godhead in what it has become – if we have the wit to see it.

'Therefore everything that is, has meaning.

'We are surrounded by meanings. Many things – perhaps most – may have more than one meaning, depending upon the time and situation in which we behold them. Thus it may be true that the flight of a swan may foretell the fate of a man. But which swan? Which man? And at what hour has the swan this meaning, and not another?

'So that we may find order, and a true path for our understanding, Croscan proposes a system of twenty-one signs. Taken together these signs describe our descent from Heaven and our return to it. Taken singly, each may be a gate to the myriad of Heaven-sent meanings that surround us. By Midwinter you will know all twenty-one signs and their meanings. After that we will begin to explore outwards from each sign into the world of signs that surrounds it.'

The first sign is Fire, thought Sophia. Already blood was beginning to bang around inside her skull.

'The first sign is Fire,' said Padry. He raised one arm ponderously, revealing the gaudy red and gold flame-pattern that curled up the inside of his gown. (Sophia,

186

who had seen him do this before, was unimpressed.)

'Fire is bright; and yet it is formless, ever-changing. It gives light, and light is truth. Therefore fire is a sign to us of Heaven, of the unknowable Godhead that lies beyond the world, and beyond the Angels that were sent into the world for our sake. For this reason a flame burns endlessly on every altar in the land.'

Oh, get on with it, thought Sophia. The second sign . . .

There was a soft clicking sound from the boy on her left.

'The second sign is the Sun. On the first arc of Croscan's path, the arc of Descent, the Sun stands for Kingship. Why? It is magnificent. It rules the day. But more than this, it is *of fire*, the heavenly sign. And just so is Kingship touched by Heaven, for it is the duty of a king to bring the truth of Heaven to his people, above all in the form of justice.

'Now consider the purpose of a sign. In these days the faithless cry that the Kingdom is fallen to a wretched state. The Learning Houses are wasted, and Kingship itself is threatened. All true. But look to the sun! What does the sun tell us? It shines still, above all the misery of the world. Heaven has not ordained that it should leave us. Why then should Kingship leave us? Let the sun be a sign to us that right Kingship is still possible, and may still bring the land justice, and with justice the peace that flows from it.'

Sophia gritted her teeth and set herself to suffer. The ill-smelling scholars on the bench in front of her were starting to shift and fidget. The morning stretched ahead of her like a corridor with no end.

187

Something clicked from the boy on her left again.

'Stop it,' she muttered. 'I'm starting a headache.'

'Sorry,' said the boy, as if he had barely heard.

She looked at him. This was someone she had not seen before.

He had a fine, pale face under the black curls of his hair. Yes, about twelve or thirteen, she thought. Many scholars his age would still be learning and re-learning their Grammar with Father Grismonde, but they must have thought that this one had come far enough to join the middle class. He was alert; yet he kept glancing around the room, frowning into corners as if he thought they should not be empty. The clicking came from a pouch in his lap, on which he kept one hand all the time. Maybe he had knuckle-bones in there, or stones.

Sophia nudged him.

'I said, stop it,' she hissed.

He stared at her, as though he had only just realized that she was there.

'I can't,' he whispered at last.

But he sidled a little further away from her along the bench, and next time made his noise more softly.

'. . . Whereas the sun does *not* change its form, the moon *does*. We are now well into the last quarter of this moon. It will rise tonight, and the next night, but ever later and thinner. In a few days it will not rise at all. The world is creeping to the dark of the moon, and the dreary influences that stir in its shadow. What does this sign tell us? On the arc of Descent, the moon's shifting light shows us Truth *as men perceive it* – fitfully, and sometimes not at all.'

The fourth sign, thought Sophia wearily.

'The fourth sign is Man . . .'

Ambrose lay in his narrow cell, at the end of his second day at Develin. The room was dark. He knew that beyond the thin boards of the partition by his ear lay another boy, and a pace beyond him another, and another, and so on all around him. And in other rooms of the castle, on and on, one after another: people, sighing and turning and sleeping. So many people! And almost all of them asleep.

Ambrose could not sleep.

He had placed the white stones around his pallet. He reached out and touched the nearest, to be sure it was still there.

He can't get me, he thought.

Someone was snoring. It was impossible to tell which bed the sound came from. He wondered if the masters patrolled down the dormitory, cane in hand, listening to the noises from each cell, so that they might burst in and thrash the offending scholar.

And in the morning everyone would rise, and get up and move about in these chains of rooms. So many people: voices, voices, and movement all around him, in a way he had never known before. And all the while he was trying to watch for someone he had barely seen, and listen for a voice that he could not hear.

Who had it been, passing under that archway? One of the masters? He did not know. What had the voice in the corridor been saying? He had not caught it.

Had there been someone behind him, when he had paused by the well?

For a moment he had been sure of it. For a moment. He reached to touch a stone again. They were still there.

His thoughts wheeled slowly, drifting with images from the day: a boy who had asked him where he had come from. Another boy, who had laughed at the way he spoke; the master called Padry in the class today, saying that things stood for other things; the girl who had glared at him when he had clicked the stones.

She had been different from the other students, not only because she was a girl but also because the cloth she wore had been very fine. Also she had been angry. She had reminded him of the lynxes that roamed the hill forests, scornful and sallow-eyed. A lynx. And it was he who had made her angry. He supposed that if he lived among as many people as this, he would not be able to help making some of them angry, whatever he did.

And the air in scholar's hall had been echoless, as if they had all been sitting in a wide landscape where nothing grew and there was never any wind. He remembered that feeling from before, when the Wolf had disappeared from the chapel at Trant. And somewhere just beyond his hearing he had thought there was a voice, speaking into ears that were not his. He had not heard what it said. And he had looked and looked for the Heron Man. And he had seen nothing.

He reached out and touched the stone again. It was pale in the darkness, like the moon. The moon had been put there by his father. But it meant something else now – something about truth. There had been no sign for a father among the things Padry had listed. That was a piece that was missing.

At last he slipped into a dream.

He dreamed that he heard someone weeping, far in the distance. And as he listened the sound grew, and changed, and became the hooves of horsemen, riding towards him on a wasteland road. He sat, waiting for them on his scholar's bench, knee-deep in long grasses at the road side.

The horsemen passed. Their faces were pale and bright-eyed, and they looked steadily before them as they rode by. Beside him on the bench a lynx turned to look at him, wild with sallow eyes.

The moon will rise tonight, the lynx said.

In a few days it will not rise at all.

# X

## The House of Wisdom

nder the high roof of the chapel of Develin Sophia lit a taper for her father. She placed it in the stand before the great banner of Michael, which hung from the full height of the wall to the chapel floor. Above her the Angel stood armoured in the fabric, sword high, summoning all the qualities of courage and war. Ranged around the altar were the banners of the other angels, each with a stand of tapers before them. Under Raphael there was a blaze of lights, set there by those who sought the Compassion of Heaven. There were also many before Umbriel, because in this place men were always wanting Truth. Before Gabriel too there were a few. But under Michael, at this moment, there was only hers.

People did not value warriors in this house, Sophia thought. Even though Father had been one. But she at least would remember him.

The chapel around her was dark and almost empty. She bowed her head.

She had very little to remember. The ribbon, the drawer, and the last time she had seen him – cased in

192

metal, from head to foot, like a statue of polished iron. She had still been very small, and she had only glimpsed his eyes and cheekbones, through his open visor. Yet she had known him at once, and known that he was smiling at her.

They told her later that he had died in battle against the men of Tarceny. He had been thrown from his horse in the rout of his followers and crushed in the press. She had dreamed and dreamed that it was not true, and that he would return at last to wear the flower-garlands she made for him. He had never come.

Sophia remembered these things. Then she counted to twenty, because even though she couldn't remember any more she felt she should keep standing there for him. Then she lifted her head.

Her maid Dapea was waiting a few paces behind her. There was no one else in the long chapel. The hour for supper was approaching. One by one the scholars and the castle folk would be leaving their chores and duties, deciding that it was not worth starting something new in the time that remained. They would be beginning to gather in the courtyards, where they would loiter idly, gaming or gossiping, until the hall-bell rang.

So the library should be nearly empty, too. And she was already dressed and braided for the evening, so she had time to spare. This was the moment she had been waiting for.

'Follow me, Dapea,' she said, and led the way back down the aisle.

Outside, at the top of the chapel steps, she paused. As she had expected, there were a number of people in the upper court, sitting or drifting around. A large group of scholars was already playing at knuckle-bones near the great hall. She smiled sourly and began to pick her way down and across to the school.

The school was a plain, rectangular building that jutted into the court from one end of the living quarters. It had been a barracks once, but after her father's death, when the Widow had found the world empty, she had installed the school there: to seek, as she said, some path away from the folly of men.

There it stood, that sulky, square block. And everybody – all her mother's people – cried what a great work it was! Within its walls thrived Alchemy, Arithmetic, Astrology, Dogma, Geography, Grammar, History, Law, Medicine, Philosophy and whatever else the Widow thought was a right path of enquiry. The library was as large as any in Jent or Tuscolo. Eleven masters and forty-nine scholars lived here, and lived for learning alone. Where else in the land was there the like?

Sixty mouths to feed, thought Sophia. Mouths to bodies that would never grow food, carry burdens or bear arms. And tonight, all the scholars would crowd into the great hall with the rest of the household – counsellors, clerks, craftsmen, guards and stable hands – and everyone would cram together at the trestle tables and sit, longing for their meat, while two of the Masters took turns to stand up and dispute formally with each other about Kingship or the Law or whatever had excited them most in the last few weeks. And barely anyone would listen. And no one might eat until they had finished. And in a month's time it would happen again; and the same the month after. For the Widow held that the school was a light both to her house and to the Kingdom, and must burn as brightly as she could bring it to.

Oh yes, thought Sophia. And that is why they sit here talking about Kingship while the Kingdom tears itself to pieces, is it?

The hypocrites!

When she's dead, I'll sweep them all away.

'Here comes lady high-and-mighty,' said one of the boys sitting on the step of the scholar's hall.

A few yards from them, Ambrose looked up. The girl whom he thought of as 'the Lynx' was crossing the court-yard towards the school. She was followed by another girl, who was clearly her servant. The Lynx stalked past him without looking down. Her companion, a dark-haired girl, smiled at Ambrose as she followed. He was surprised, and forgot to smile back.

Their footsteps diminished up the library stairs.

'Do you think she'll take her meals with us now, as well as her lessons?' asked the second boy, a shock-headed fellow of about fifteen.

'What? Stale bread and rotten vegetables?'

'And the nice rat-meat in the sausages.'

Ambrose knew both the boys by sight. That was why he had sat near them. He wasn't sure if he actually wanted them to notice him. He did not know what he would say if they spoke to him. (He himself saw nothing wrong with the food that they ate here.) But their presence was a comfort. So too were the three white stones he had placed around him – one behind him and one on either side.

The Lynx was gone. Other figures crossed before the school in ones and twos. More people were coming into the courtyard to join those waiting for the supper. Ambrose's eyes flicked warily around, hovering on doorways and patches of shadow. A burst of harsh laughter broke from among the scholars playing knuckle-bones. A man emerged from a doorway carrying a long pipe. He was one of the older scholars: a tall, blond man with his hair tied back into a pigtail. Ambrose had seen him before, standing by himself in a circle of scholars, telling a story while the crowd hung on his words. Now he was on his own. He sat cross-legged by himself and began to play. Ambrose listened.

There was so much music in Develin: chants and dance-tunes and musicians practising their instruments for some performance before the Widow. Ambrose liked some of it, and some of it he could not begin to understand. It took him a moment to realize that this tune was different.

It was different because he knew it.

The man was playing a melody of the hillmen: a lament with long, slow notes like someone stepping downwards on a stair in the sky. It was strange to hear it among these stone courts and windows, all alive with people. It told him once again how far he was from home. For some moments the air of the courtyard ached with memories of the mountains, bitter and sweet all at once. Ambrose felt a lump in his throat, and swallowed against it. He wondered how the player could have learned the tune.

And then it stopped. A group of three men, walking by, had paused to speak with the man. He was answering them. At the other end of the step the shock-headed boy

196

was whispering to his friend, and pointing at the white pebble beside Ambrose. Ambrose could not hear what he was saying. The second seemed to be laughing at something. Ambrose did not like that.

'No!' said a deep voice behind them.

Ambrose jumped.

'Truth and untruth?' muttered the voice. 'No, do not tell me that.'

Someone was approaching from the darkness of the scholars' hall. Ambrose could hear a heavy, sandalled tread upon the rush-covered floor.

He heard it through a gathering deadness in the air – a dull, echoless quality as if the walls of Develin were about to part like curtains and show him a land of nightmare.

He froze.

'As well say,' continued the voice, 'that because the light draws a shadow, we must put out the light.'

A figure appeared in the doorway. It was not the Heron Man.

It was a master whom Ambrose had not seen before: a tall man with a great, hatchet head and a face that sagged in thick circles one below another from his eye-pits. He wore a heavy red gown, and glowered down at Ambrose as if deep in his thoughts. There was a slight flurry as the other two boys stopped sniggering and looked attentive.

'Who were you talking to?' said Ambrose urgently.

The door behind the man stood open. The sun struck through the broad arch and lit a few square feet of the long room where the scholars ate and took their lessons. Beyond that, the shadows were empty.

'I may address myself, if there is no other worthy,' the

man said. He frowned. Perhaps he was surprised that Ambrose had spoken.

'I have not seen you before, boy. Are you a new scholar?'

'Yes – I came three days ago.'

'Three days ago, *Master Denke.*'

'. . . Master Denker,' repeated Ambrose, unsure if he had heard the name right.

'And you will stand when you speak with a master or an officer of the house.'

Ambrose got to his feet, risking another glance at the doorway as he did so. Surely there had been someone else?

Through the echoless air he heard the man speak again.

'Since you are here and idle – and impudent of mood – let me see what you know. What organ is king of the body?'

It was a question. He must answer.

'I – I don't know,' he stammered, '. . . master.'

The man towered over Ambrose. He seemed to be waiting for Ambrose to try again. Ambrose did not know what to do.

'You put your left foot forward,' said the master. 'And touch your heart to show that you tell the truth.'

Ambrose's limbs did as they were told.

'Now breathe, to strengthen the voice.'

Ambrose breathed.

'Now tell me that it is the heart that is king of the body.'

'The heart is king of the body, master.'

The man was right, he thought. His voice *was* stronger.

He tried another glance at the doorway, from the corner of his eye. There was still no one there.

'And why is the heart the king of the body?'

There was no one there. But a thought came to him, as clearly as if a voice had spoken over the man's shoulder.

*You cannot answer.*

The eyes of the master, ringed with sagging flesh, poured their gaze over him. There was a large wart on the right side of the man's nose. Ambrose's jaw was limp. He could make no sound.

'Why is the heart the king of the body?' the master repeated. But his gaze had swung upon the other boys. The scholars scrambled to their feet and placed their hands on their hearts as Ambrose had done. The master stopped in front of the shock-headed scholar and lifted an eyebrow.

'The heart is king of the body, master, because it is the seat of truth,' said the boy, roundly and clearly, as if he were speaking to a gathering of twenty men. 'Truth among men is law, and the King is the Fount of the Law, who gives justice to his subjects.'

'Indeed, Justice is Truth. How is it exercised?' The master's eyes were upon the other scholar.

'Through Punishment and Pardon, master,' the scholar said.

'Very good. And which is the greater?'

It was Ambrose's turn again. There was a moment's silence.

The other boys were looking at him. Ambrose saw the muscles on their faces tighten with alarm. Something bad would happen if Ambrose could not answer.

199

*It will be a beating*, said the whisper in his head. *Your first.*

The Heron Man!

'Which, of Punishment and Pardon, is the greater?' repeated the master, as if he thought Ambrose had not heard him.

Pardon, thought Ambrose. It must be Pardon. He remembered his mother saying something . . .

*Did she? Did you ever listen to her?*

The voice in his head teased and confused him, like a bystander jeering as he stood under the eyes of the master.

*You never listened. And then you left her.*

Go away! Ambrose's mind screamed at it.

'Come now,' said the master sharply.

*You did not listen. And then you left her. Now you cannot answer, and now you will be beaten. They will lay a thornstick across your back and peel your skin. Your flesh will swell, black and aching with pus.*

Go away!

*You deserve it because you left her.*

Ambrose struggled to shut the voice out of his head. The master's face loomed over him. The muscles around the big eyes were hardening with impatience. Ambrose's skin tingled as if it could already feel the cane swishing through the air.

*If you want to answer, ask me. I am all you have now.*

He opened his mouth again. The little corner of the courtyard was still and grey.

*I helped you to answer the Widow. I would do it again – if you asked.*

No!

200

*Ask me.*

*Ask me. You must.*

Seconds passed. His mind was blank. He could not think. And he would not. If he thought he would see her turning in the air. If he thought he would feel the thorn-stick on his back. The unseen eyes were on him, waiting for him to save himself. And he would not.

*Is* that *your answer?*

The air thickened with contempt. But he would not think any more.

At last the master sighed. He began to pace, with a slow, rolling step, before the boys.

'Pardon and Punishment each have their place,' he said.

'Men may pardon if they choose, and punish where they have the right, as a master punishes a bad pupil.

'Yet men also punish without thought and without law, for wrongs that may be real or imagined. Such punishment is itself a wrong to the one who is punished.

'And what man will pardon one who has wronged him, so long as his enemy is living? For first he is angry, and when he wearies of anger he fears that he would be seen as weak, and preyed upon. This we know as feud.' He stopped in front of the first scholar. 'Is it not true?'

'Yes, master,' said the scholar dutifully.

'And yet,' Denke went on. 'If one who has the right – let us say the King – interposes in a feud between two men, and holds the wrong against himself, and yet pardons it – the feud must end, must it not?

'That first pardon – the forgiveness when men are wearied of their quarrel, when all face ruin and yet none

201

have the will to forgive – *that* is the seed of peace. With peace there may be law, and with law, justice; with justice, pardon and punishment as they are deserved.

'Therefore Pardon is the greater.' Now he stood in front of Ambrose. 'Do you agree?'

The big, steady voice had cleared the mists in Ambrose's mind like wind. Pardon was the greater. He had known it.

'Yes, master.'

Once more the flesh-ringed eyes looked down on him. 'What is your name?'

He almost said 'Ambrose'. But that name had been taken from him. He hung his head and said nothing.

'Three days?' said the master, with the lift of an eyebrow. 'In another three days, if I question you, see that you show me you have understood. This is what we teach here.

'But for this reason, this time, I give pardon for your lack of wit. Do not forget again.'

With a grunt, the master strode off across the courtyard. As he left it seemed to Ambrose that the air lightened, as if something oppressive had passed on with him.

'That,' said one of the boys softly, 'was nearly the stick for you.'

'Lucky it was him,' the other murmured. 'He can scare the juices out of you, but he doesn't flog half as much as some.'

'And he's got something on his mind this morning, hasn't he?' said the first.

Twenty paces away Denke was again speaking as he went, as if someone walked beside him whom the boys could not see.

Ambrose realized that he was cold. He was clutching himself as if some gust from the mountains had blown over him, heavy with ancient tears. And he knew that he had known the answer the master wanted, and could have given it – if he could have forced his way past the dry, scornful voice in his head, which had been so quick, so right; and so familiar.

'Your name's Luke, isn't it?' said the shock-haired boy.

'Yes,' Ambrose mumbled.

'I'm Rufin. This is Cullen. Look – it can be hard starting in this place. We know that. We've all done it. You stay close to us. If you get stuck again, we'll try to give you a hint.'

'Thanks,' Ambrose said.

He knew the boys wanted to be kind. Maybe they would be able to help if someone asked him questions again. But they could not help him where it mattered.

He stooped for his stones. They were still there. His fingers trembled as he touched them. They could stop the Heron Man from reaching him. But the Heron Man had not tried to reach him. All he had done was to speak to him. And at the sound of his voice Ambrose had felt helpless – helpless like a bird under the eyes of a snake. The only thing he could have done would have been to beg his enemy for aid. And now the Heron Man despised him. There had been no mistaking that. Maybe he had always despised him. Ambrose wondered what he would do next.

He wanted to get away.

'Suppose the King is the source of forgiveness,' said Cullen, still watching the master. 'Then who forgives the King?'

'We all can,' said Rufin. 'When he's dead.'

They did not seem to be paying Ambrose any more attention. After a little Ambrose left, slipping into the shadow of the School Stair. He did not know where he was going. He did not really care.

What mattered was getting away from the courtyard.

At length, on a shelf of the third press in the library, Sophia found what she was looking for. Like the other books and quires it was chained for safety to the iron bar that ran beneath its shelf, so she had to spread it out on the reading shelf immediately below the place where she had found it, some way from the dimming light of the window. Dapea settled patiently on the bench on the far side of the library aisle. No doubt she thought that Sophia had become especially dutiful after her last beating, to be reading at this hour.

Well, let her. The quire had nothing to do with Sophia's legitimate studies. She had been thinking about it for most of the day. Now she had time, an empty library, and for escort a maid who could not read. She composed herself.

And then someone else came slipping along the bench to sit beside her.

Maddening! This was exactly what she had wanted to avoid, and why she had waited until now to come up here. Scholars were always clumping together over the same book, especially when anything up to a dozen of them might have been instructed by their master to consult a single work. Indeed, the fastest way of finding what you wanted in the library when it was busy was not to look along the shelves but to go and snoop at what your class-mates were reading, because the chances were that they had found it before you.

And here they were – well, one of them, anyway. It was the clicking boy, peering around her arm at the quire before her. Without thinking, she drew her hand across the page to hide the words on it.

'What are you looking at?' he asked.

('Nothing' would be a stupid answer. It would also be stupid to try to hide what she was reading. He would have to be told enough to make him lose interest.)

'It's just a set of heraldic records,' she said, and lifted her arm for him to see. 'In order of precedence, and listing the badge of each house.'

'Let me see.'

She made room for him, keeping her impatience locked in the secret places inside her mind. He looked down the long list of entries. At length he put his finger beside one. She glanced at it, and the word *Moon* leaped from the page at her.

He had found it – almost at once. He had found what she had been looking for.

She peered at the entry, spelling out the words in her mind.

*Tarceny. Sable, a Full Moon Argent defaced, commonly named the Doubting Moon. Motto, The Under-Craft Prevaileth.*

Hairs prickled on the back of her neck. She had half-guessed that this would be the answer. Chawlin had looked at those pale badges that the horsemen had worn, and had said they came from a distant house that had been broken. What house could that be? The scroll told her that it was Tarceny.

Those men had been Father's killers. They had passed by her so close she could have touched them.

'Why are you looking at this?' said the boy.

The Widow had spoken with them from the walls. She hadn't charged them, routed them, hanged them. She had *spoken* with Father's *killers*!

She cleared her throat. 'I'm under private tuition,' she managed to say. Her voice sounded weak in her ears.

'That's not true. Not any more.'

She gripped the edge of the desk and willed herself not to shout at him. She knew that an argument in the library would do her no good. Everyone in the house knew she was still in disgrace, and being treated like any other scholar. Scholars were expected to share texts. She would only draw people's attention to the piece she had been looking at. In any case, it wasn't really the boy's fault if he knew no better than to speak to her like an equal.

'A group of riders appeared at the gate a week ago,' she said carefully. (Truth, she found, was often the best way of keeping the whole truth secret.) 'They wore that badge. I wanted to know who they were, that was all. What is your name?'

He took a moment to answer. Then he said: 'I'm called Luke.'

'Are you here for a book? Can I help you find it?'

'I want to look at this with you.'

She frowned, puzzled. Her mouth was open to frame

a question when another movement in the room caught her eye. Padry, the Master of Astrology, and also the scholars' Master of House, was peering round the corner of the press at their backs, like an old dog with nothing to do.

Sophia's heart sank. Now *he* would want to come over and see what they were looking at, and then he would want to talk about it, and maybe even ask questions. And she had already told this boy about the company of horsemen, so the boy would think it strange if she gave different answers to Padry. But the last thing she wanted was to remind the Widow's masters that she had been missing at the time those men had appeared at the gate.

Sure enough, here he came, sidling his bulk along between the bench and the press behind them in his idle curiosity. And she could not brush the quire aside or even shift it to show a less incriminating passage, because this idiot boy was leaning his elbows on it, caught in something he was reading. His finger had moved down to the last lines on that page. Padry stopped just behind him. She could only hope that the master did not see the entry about Tarceny, which lay open to the eye before them.

Padry peered over their shoulders. She saw him begin to read. She saw his face change. Her heart sank again.

Suddenly his hand gripped the boy by the shoulder.

'Who set you to this? Who?'

To that moment Luke could not have been aware that Padry was in the room. He jerked, and turned pale. Something like a shriek escaped from him.

'Who said you were to study this?' said Padry again, shaking him by the shoulder.

Luke seemed to stop struggling when he realized who it was that had seized on him. But his breath was coming in gasps.

'N-no one, master.'

'No one indeed! Come with me. You will be taught to attend to your *studies*.' Ignoring Sophia, he marched the boy out of the room, still gripping him by the elbow. Sophia watched them go, with her mouth open and her heart thankful that Padry had pounced so swiftly upon the wrong offender. The sounds faded down the stairway. Dapea, her maid, was sitting bolt upright on her bench, looking dumbfounded.

'Angels!' she said. 'Is he going to beat the poor boy? And what for?'

He almost certainly would, thought Sophia. For some reason he had looked as though he had caught Luke tearing up a page to make paper. She wondered if Padry was actually going to start punishing the boy immediately, outside the school hall. But a door slammed, and all sounds were cut off. The silence swelled in behind it, troubled only by the sounds and calls of the household gathering in the courtyard.

Poor boy, yes.

'That's my fault,' she said grimly. 'Although I don't know why it mattered.'

There was nothing she could do. She returned to the table where the quire lay with its long list of badges and names of infamy.

Tarceny. *The Under-Craft Prevaileth*. (What was under-craft?) *Sable, a Full Moon Argent defaced*.

The Doubting Moon!

The Widow had spoken with them – spoken with them and let them go. Did she not even care about Father any more? She wore black every day, summer and winter; she spoke his name and cited his memory over and over. But she didn't care enough to *do* anything for him.

Sophia did not know. When it came to the Widow, she could not trust even her own feelings. That was something else the Widow had done to her.

Who could she trust? She wanted to talk to someone. But if she told anyone that she had seen these riders pass, she would risk another beating.

The scholar Chawlin. He knew, of course.

Well, why not? She had been looking forward to seeing him again. Here was a reason to seek him out. He would be at the Dispute tonight, with everyone else. She might catch his eye then. It would be very soon now. In fact she should be on her way already.

She reached to gather up the incriminating quire, and paused once more. Her eye skipped down the page. It surprised her how many families must have been destroyed since the scroll was written. She found the Leaves of Bay – they were strong, still. She found the Eagle of Baldwin, which must now survive only on the shield of Velis. At the bottom of the page she came to the entry that Luke had been reading.

*Trant. Vert, an Oak Tree Vert upon a Sun Royal Or. Motto, Watch For Who Comes.*

Green and gold. Another vanished family, with its arms preserved on this scroll long after they had lost their

209

meaning. She had heard the name before, but could not remember where. Luke would have done well to take the motto's advice. He had neither seen Padry nor heard him approach.

She could have warned him, she thought. She should have realized that Padry's appearance might mean trouble for him as well as for her. But she hadn't been thinking about him at all.

She rolled the quire up briskly, as if the noise it made could drown the little worm of guilt inside her. There was nothing she could do.

# XI

## Cellar and Stair

he great hall of Develin was in uproar. The tables hammered with knife-butts, bowls, dishes and the fists of feasters. The high-timbered roof was filled with wispy smoke. Cressets burned all down both sides of the hall, set between the great red-and-white banners that dropped to the floor. Music flowed from the small minstrels' gallery, barely heard in the noise of supper.

Padry was in his place at the high table, some way to Sophia's right. But scan the lower tables as she might, she could see no sign of the boy Luke. So they almost certainly had beaten him, and had left him lying in agony on his pallet. She pursed her lips.

Chawlin did not seem to be among the scholars either. Now why not? No one at the school could miss the Dispute supper without the very best of reasons. Nearly everyone else seemed to be there. Why wasn't he? She had been hoping for a chance to signal to him – a lift of an eye, the quick gesture of a hand – that she wanted to talk. And he was not there.

She was surprised how disappointed she felt.

'Now say, Master Wisgrave,' called the chamberlain Hervan on her right. 'Why is a man of wit the better of a man of word?'

On Sophia's left, the Widow turned to listen. Sophia kept her eyes on her food.

'I suppose that the man of wit—' began Wisgrave.

'Knows better than to answer!' cried someone, to laughter.

'And yet *this* man of wit takes not his own counsel!'

Every evening the counsellors paraded their cleverness before the Widow. Hervan and the other officers loved to show they were the equal of the masters, and the masters loved to show they were not. And the Widow would best all of them – partly, Sophia thought, because she was the Widow, and they had to let her. For sure, no other woman would be allowed to – or would want to. Sophia just endured it. Hestie, a plain knights' lady, hated it. She had begged and pleaded and grovelled to the Widow to be released, because she could not bear sitting tongue-tied while everyone around her took turns to show how clever they were. So she too was absent tonight, eating alone in her chamber, as she did whenever she could.

And because of that, Sophia knew, she would be without an escort after the supper broke up. In theory she was to follow the Widow and her counsellors as they went from the hall to the living quarters. But no one at high table would make it their business to see that she did. There would be a chance, then, to go where she wished and do as she wished – even to go running after a lone scholar in some dark corner of the house if she chose. It was, of course, exactly the sort of thing that Hestie was trying to prevent. So it would serve her right (and the Widow as well) if that was exactly what Sophia did.

She would too – if only she could work out where he was. And she could. He must be on cellar guard.

There had been a bungled attempt to break into the cellar and steal wine from the butts. The culprits, a group of scullions, were now completing their third day with their ankles fast in the castle's stocks, but still the repair of the cellar lock had not found its way to the top of the blacksmith's pile of jobs to be done. And as long as the men-at-arms kept breaking buckles and riding their horses until the shoes dropped off, there was no saying when the repair could be made. So a cellar guard had been set up – a pool of reliable men to take turns watching over the barrels until the door could be made fast again. Scholars were not usually given castle duties (especially not ones that tempted the throat); but Chawlin had been in the house a long time, and must be known and liked beyond the school. He was just the sort of man who would be called on to take his turn. He might well be there now.

And if he was, he would be on his own.

The corridors would be dark. She might even have to feel her way in places. And of course it would be forbidden. It would mean another beating, if she was caught.

And she was still going to do it. She really was.

At last the high table rose. All the masters and officers gathered to attend their mistress on their way to the council chamber. Sophia dropped quietly to the back of the group and stepped away into a side corridor. It would be a while at least before anyone shifted themselves to find her.

The sounds and lights faded behind her. With a hollow

tingling in her chest she passed as quickly and quietly as she could along an empty passage. If anyone had asked her, she would have said she was going to the chapel. But ten yards short of the chapel door she came to the cellar stair. No one was around. She slipped like a cat into the shelter of its darkness.

At the foot of the stair was another passage, barely lit. At the far end the cellar door blocked her way, big-timbered and strengthened with iron. It had a forbidding look. But the lock was broken. That was the point. From under the door filtered the light of a lamp. The man she was looking for might be in there.

Now, Sophia.

The door swung under her hand, and he was.

He was alone, sitting in the quiet with a lamp and food by him. He must have finished eating a few moments before. His eyes were wide.

'It's only me,' she said.

She had made him jump. That wasn't surprising. Sophia didn't like it when things came suddenly out of the dark either.

His hand was holding a long pipe. He had been in the act of lifting it to his mouth to play.

'Don't stop,' she said. 'I'll listen.'

After a moment he shook his head.

'What can I do for you?' he said.

She walked down the short flight of steps and sat on the last one, as though it were the most natural thing in the world that she should have sought him out at this hour.

'Those men we saw. They were from Tarceny,' she said.

'Larceny. She saw the impact of the word on his face. He sighed.

'I did think so.'

'My mother should have had them killed,' she said, putting her chin in her hands.

She was watching him intently, trying to read what he thought of her sudden arrival. For a moment she thought he was going to send her away. But he said nothing, and did nothing except go on frowning. His face looked drawn. He was looking at a patch of the floor by her ankle. He must be thinking about something. Or . . .

'Are you unwell?' she asked.

He shook his head again. 'The name's a bad memory, that's all. And I've not slept so well since seeing those fellows on the road. It'll pass, I think.'

'They were evil, those people.'

Now he smiled tightly to himself, as if thinking, *Poor child, what could she possibly know?* And still he did not answer. Still he was looking away, as if he wished the darkness were not so close. She could see he did not want to talk about this.

'Tell me a story then,' she said.

Once more she had surprised him. And it was her turn to smile, now.

'I've been finding out about you, you see,' she said.

'Well – yes, I do tell stories, if people want to listen. Is that what you came for?'

'Tell me about meeting my mother.'

'So. But that's not one of my usual ones.'

'You can tell it to me.'

He looked at her again. He would be guessing at the

215

impulses that had brought her down her at this hour. To hear stories? Unlikely. Disobedience, for sure. And what else?

'You said you would,' she insisted.

Well he had, hadn't he? *Another time*, he had said – back there by the road after the men from Tarceny had passed. Let him think what he liked. His tale would tell her more about him in any event. That was what she wanted.

At last he smiled again, more broadly this time, and his head shook slightly as if he could see no harm in it.

'Well,' he said. 'You've brought me the gift of your company, and I'm glad. Guard duty is lonely duty. Yes, I'll tell you, if you like. It was in Baldwin's rising – five, six years ago. You'd be too young to remember why it started, I guess . . .'

'Tell me.'

'Well.' He drew breath.

'Now Baldwin was a proud man, and headstrong, and his family had suffered in Tarceny's rising. The King had given him wardenship of the whole of Tarceny's lands west of the lake, but it was not enough. For what the King gives in wardenship, the King may take away if he pleases . . .'

Sophia listened. There was a funny, fluttery, bouncy feeling inside her as she watched him. She saw how his head turned, following his thoughts, with his hair and little bristles glowing in the lamplight like the lining of a cloud that hid the sun. She hadn't been sure if he was handsome, but now she was. Yes, definitely. The light and memory played on his face, and his eyes looked steadily into the shadows of the cellar.

216

And she had succeeded. She was with him on her own, with time – a little time – to stay.

As for *Poor child* and *You'd be too young* – she'd show him soon enough. She was not too young to know what she was doing, anyway.

'. . . War is a habit for the great houses – one they find hard to forget. And so Baldwin came to blows with his king.

'I was one of Baldwin's squires – warden of a small keep in the very north of the March of Tarceny, under the mountains. When the rising began I sent Baldwin soldiers, but otherwise I was not troubled until the King Septimus and his allies – including your mother – drove Baldwin across the lake and besieged him in Tarceny. Then he sent me his treasure to safeguard, and a few other squires whom he thought would keep watch over me and it until he escaped to join us.

'Of course, he did not escape.

'Soon we received summons from the King to surrender, and to hand over Baldwin's gold. We sent back defiance, because at that time we did not know which way the fight would go, and we knew that no one could come after us in strength until it was settled. We waited to hear whether the King or Baldwin would prevail.

'So the next message we received came from neither of them, but from your mother.'

He shook his head, ruefully, like some chess player remembering defeat at the hands of a master.

'She offered gold if we would surrender. The messenger had it with him. That did not matter. If we had wanted it we could simply have taken it. But your mother knows what moves men. She also offered land.

'She offered a manor, for each of us, in Develin and around. The gold only served to show that the promise of land was real. It was our first year's harvest, her message said.

'Now you must remember this: it is land, and only land, that makes a knight. Horse and armour can get you a knight's honour. Wealth can get you a knight's horse and armour. But it is land, year upon year, that gets you wealth. The morning her message came there were nine squires with me. A week later we were five, with not a blow struck. A week after that I was alone, and most of the treasure already gone with my fellows.

'She was as good as her word to them. A half-dozen still live in comfort on the lands of Develin or her allies. I, too, might have turned coat, perhaps. But . . .'

He hesitated. Some thought or memory had put him off his stride.

'You were loyal,' Sophia said.

He pulled a face. 'Baldwin and I did not love each other. But we were together in the taking of Tarceny. More, I was one of the few who saw how Tarceny died. I saw what killed him—'

'What?'

'I'm not talking about that,' he said.

After a moment he lowered his voice, and went on.

'So. Among the treasure Baldwin sent was something of Tarceny's. As I say, Baldwin and I never loved one another. But he knew what I knew. He sent it to me.

'He sent it to me,' he repeated, almost to himself.

The silence lengthened. The story seemed to have lost itself in the darkness of the cellar.

'Has she told you about it?' he asked suddenly.

'About what?'

'No, then. Wise of her, I suppose.' For a moment he sounded disappointed.

'So,' he continued. 'Tarceny's. And I knew Baldwin despised me. And yet he had sent it to me because he thought only I could be trusted with it. That mattered – more than land or gold. I fled with it.

'And your mother caught me.

'She caught me in the broken country between the north of the March and the Seabord. By then, Baldwin was dead and Tarceny a smoking ruin. She and some others were on a mission to make peace for the King with Baldwin's brother, in Velis.' He smiled, grimly. 'Septimus,' he added, 'is ever trusting where he should not, and forgiving where he should not. It will be the death of him. It takes more than a good man to make a good king.

'I had been on the run for ten days when her horsemen appeared on the track behind me. I was sore, cold, hungry – I was not thinking well. I just kept walking, and they rode up on me, much as that crew of Tarceny did to us the other day. I remember your mother passing me in her litter. "Look up," she said to me.' He made a noise, somewhere between a grunt and a chuckle. '"*Look up.*" I felt my neck about to leave my shoulders. That is what I expected for failing to surrender when I had the chance. A jerk of her head, and it would have happened. Instead she spoke to me . . .'

'Something about filling your mind, and maybe your belly as well?'

'Very like that. Of course she took . . . Ah no, it was

as well. I did not trust myself by the end, but I trusted her. At all events, she has been pleased to suffer me here since then. So I have buried myself in books and classes, and people may say what they like of me. Another man might have taken to the church. But knowledge is rarer, I think.'

He looked up, and she saw that the story was finished.

'Thank you for telling me,' she said.

'Thank you for coming,' he said gravely. 'And for listening, too. Talk is better than music, in the dark. Though as I say, it's not a story I tell, and I'd ask you not to repeat it to anyone. Your mother—' He broke off.

There were footsteps, coming down the stair at the far end of the corridor outside the broken door.

'That may be my relief.' he said. 'Now, you don't want to be found here. Go down that aisle into the shadows, and I'll take him on a quick tour of the cellar. As soon as we are off at the back you should get up the stairs. Be careful!'

He might be in trouble too! He would be in far worse trouble than she. Hestie would not forgive a scholar who was caught alone with the Widow's daughter in a dark place – however innocent they both might be.

He must have known that. Yet he had let her stay, and talked, and hatched this plan in his mind as they talked. She had not seen any of *that* on his face. And . . .

The footsteps were coming closer. She fled.

Ambrose lay in pain. His back ached and throbbed. He could barely feel the pallet beneath his cheek. His eyes were open, but in the dimness of his cell he could see little. He had lain like this for hours. It was getting worse, not better.

He was half-naked. His fingers could not have put his

220

shirt back on, even if his skin could have borne it. He had been clutching it when they had thrust him into his cell, but it was gone somewhere now. He must have dropped it on the floor when he had collapsed onto his pallet.

He had dropped his stones somewhere, too.

He could not move. He could not think – in his pain, and the darkness.

It was late. But Sophia waited nonetheless. She hung in the lee of the Wool Tower, listening to the sounds of the house preparing for the night. Somewhere around the living quarters Dapea and Hestie were almost certainly searching for her, candles in hand. So long as she was only a little while longer they might keep it to themselves, for her sake and theirs. But if they did not find her they would have to confess to the Widow that she had run out of their control again, and that would mean trouble for everybody.

Still she waited, intent on wringing a few more moments from the evening.

He was handsome. He was brave and experienced. He had been in the desperate battles on the edge of the Kingdom, not for greed but for loyalty and truth. He had rank, and grace. He was as clever as any of the preening, attention-seeking officers with whom the Widow surrounded herself. And yet he was so different from them! He was humble, even. Why did he endure living among the moth-eaten masters and the sons of merchants? None of *them* would have had the wit or the will to keep her out of trouble – twice now.

He had liked it that she had come, hadn't he? And now that she had left him, she wanted to see him again at once.

221

And if she waited, she would.

The bouncy, fluttery feeling inside her was stronger than ever now, as though she was unusually happy and yet had no idea why. It was because she was doing something that was forbidden, and knew that she would get away with it, if only she kept her head. But it was more than that. It was like the secret glow she used to get from her favourite daydreams, of finding her father wounded and forgotten in some cave, where she would nurse him back to health.

Like that. And it was because of him.

She was beginning to wonder if she might start a private – a *very* private – little fantasy about him. Why not? Life would be so much richer if . . .

Where was he?

He appeared at last, swinging the lantern thoughtfully as he crossed the upper courtyard towards the school building. She saw him start and look hard at her when she stepped from the shadows to join him, but he said nothing. Perhaps she had given herself away by waiting for him. She did not care.

'There's something else I wanted to ask you,' she said.

There weren't nearly enough things to ask him, or to talk to him about, and keep him talking while she stayed with him. But she had managed to think of one – one at least that might show him she was more than the child he had taken her for. And it would help her feel less guilty, too.

'Yes?'

'There's a new scholar, called Luke,' she said. 'Do you know him?'

'I think so. Dark hair, about thirteen years old. Arrived a few days ago?'

222

'Yes.'

'What of him?'

They talked in low tones, for other people were moving in the courtyard in the deepening evening. A flare of light marked the brazier at the inner gate. Somewhere on the towers above their heads there would be others, warming the armed watchmen as they began the long pace that would carry them on into the night.

'I don't think he's finding it easy here. I wondered if you could help him.'

'Shouldn't you talk to Padry about that?'

'He's suspicious of the masters. You can tell. He gets nervous if they come too close. And Padry was severe with him today, in the library. I think he may have been beaten.'

'Beaten? I see. What's his family?'

'None that I know of.'

'An orphan, perhaps. Well, since you ask, I will see what can be done.'

He ducked through the side door of the school. The passage within was dark. She knew he expected her to leave him. But she followed him, because she could.

And now he had agreed to watch Luke, and she had made another reason for meeting and talking with him in a day or two's time. *Since you ask*, he had said. And he wouldn't have suggested she talk to Padry if he had thought she was just a child. Nor would he have listened when she told him that Padry would be no good. She hugged these thoughts to herself as they climbed the stairs towards the landing and the door back into the living quarters, where they would part for the night.

\* \* \*

Something moved in Ambrose's cell. A hand gripped his shoulder. He gasped with the pain of it.

'Come on,' hissed a voice. 'Where are they? Quickly!'

The hand was shaking him – shaking him hard. His shoulder yelped. Maybe he cried out.

'Wake up, damn you. Wake up – it's coming!'

He rolled on his pallet. The man was crouching beside him.

'Up! Quick!'

And then there was something else.

Rising, lurching at the foot of his bed! It was big – bigger than a goat, at least. A head like a man's, moaning from an open mouth! An arm like a spider's, horribly long, flicked towards him. His blanket jerked, caught by a sharp claw. Ambrose pulled at it, screaming. He looked into the eyes of the Thing.

The man shouted and threw something. The cell was filled with pebbles that crashed against the wall and rattled upon the floor.

'Did you hear that?'

Chawlin stopped on the stair and raised his lantern.

There had been a cry – two cries – from the floor above them, and the sound of something hitting wood with force.

Drunks? thought Sophia. But the school should be virtually empty. Most of the scholars would still be in the great hall, with any wine they had managed to save from the meal. The masters would be at council with the Widow, most likely debating the evening's Dispute all over again.

They listened. The building was quiet once more. Cautiously they made their way up to the landing.

Something gleamed for a moment at the top of the next flight of stairs, and disappeared.

'What was that?'

'A cat?' she suggested.

She had seen the eyes of cats glow like that in the light of a lamp, like bright coins or marbles floating in the air, because their bodies did not show up in the darkness.

'A cat? Maybe . . .' He raised his lamp again, and began to climb the next stair, slowly. Once more she followed, realizing that if it had been a cat it must have been further up the stair than she had thought. And if it had been that high, then the eye should have been smaller than it had seemed. And it should have been white, or green. Not *red*.

Chawlin had reached the top of the stair with his light. He was looking around him. She could see from the way he stood that there was nothing up there.

'It was somewhere here,' he said. 'I thought it slipped back up the corridor when we appeared, but . . .' He sniffed. 'Do you smell anything?'

Was he asking her to smell anything out of place in a house of unwashed scholars? She took a long breath through her nose. But – perhaps – there was a scent on the air that she had not been expecting.

'Yes, I think . . .'

Chawlin sniffed again, and began to look around him – at the walls, the floor, even the ceiling. Sophia stood a few steps down, still searching for the smell. She thought it reminded her of stone – wet stone, like at the edge of a pool.

'Damn!' whispered Chawlin suddenly. 'Damn!'

The lantern swung in his hand and its light danced on the blank walls.

'Well,' he said, sharply. 'If there was anything, it's not here now.' He seemed to think for a moment. 'You should be in your chambers.'

'I'm going . . .'

'I will see you to the living quarters.'

He was coming down the steps, motioning to her to move, as though she would need an escort down the single flight of stairs and the passage to the living-quarter door. All at once he did not want her to be there. He did not want to be there himself. She turned, surprised, and preceded him down the stair towards the landing. She thought he looked behind him more than once as they descended.

'Damn!' said the Wolf in the darkness of Ambrose's cell.

His voice shook. He was staring at the blank wooden partition where, a few moments before, the monster had reared out of the shadow. From his pallet Ambrose stared at the wall, too, waiting for it to reappear.

All around the cell his white stones lay scattered. The Wolf must have scooped up the pouch and hurled them at it as it seized upon Ambrose's blanket. Ambrose felt his heart beating with a sick, heavy pulse. His back had begun to smart again, too. He must have jerked around suddenly as the Thing came. Now he was paying for it.

'Filthy beast of a . . .' muttered the Wolf. 'Are there more like that?'

'I – didn't see it,' Ambrose said. But he had.

He had seen it. He could still see it, pulling at him; with eyes larger than a man's and yet horribly human. And the long leg – or arm – and the drooling mouth. And the eyes. The eyes!

'It's out in the corridor, I think,' said the Wolf, tightly.

Ambrose held his breath. He knew the Wolf was afraid.

They listened.

Sounds carried dimly through the partition and the dormitory door. A murmur of voices. Feet on the stair, descending, fading.

Silence.

There had been people out there. Surely they would have cried out if they had seen it?

After a little the Wolf said: 'Maybe it's gone then.' He drew a long breath. 'Ugh. Lucky for you I came.'

Ambrose turned and lay with his face on his bolster again. His back was throbbing heavily, each mark beginning to pound its slow rhythm on his skin. His breath was shaking. He knew the man was right. If he had not been so sick and stunned from his beating he would have been more aware. But suffering as he was, he had almost felt that it did not matter whether the monster got to him or not. And it nearly had.

The room reeked with a smell like old water.

'You've got to take more care,' said the Wolf. 'You'd just dropped the pouch on the floor here when you lay down. Any time you're like that he can get you if he wants. And you can't tell what he's going to do. I thought he was going to play with you for a bit. But maybe you've annoyed him somehow. Or he's bored with you. You can't tell, see?'

227

'He's here, isn't he?' said Ambrose.

The Wolf did not answer for a moment. Then he grinned, and stroked his lip with a thumb. 'Maybe – sometimes.'

'What's he doing?'

'I only said *maybe*. And you've managed so far, haven't you? Up to today, anyway. What did they beat you for, as a matter of interest?'

Ambrose tried a different position on the pallet.

'I was reading something about my family,' he said, wincing. 'The Widow doesn't want people to know that I've got any.'

'I guess they thought you were giving yourself away,' the man said. 'So really they were trying to help you. It's ironic of course. He knows exactly who you are, and where to find you. So do I. And if I wanted you I could have you. Do you know I had Develin's own daughter sitting right under my hooves at the roadside, the day you came here? The Widow would have swapped you for her quickly enough, I guess. But those old fools from Tarceny weren't interested. I didn't like them anyway. They'd stopped being useful. They thought they ran me, when I should have been running them. So I've given them the slip. There's no sense in spending months chasing round the south while my King forgets about me. They were so sure you'd gone with my ape of a father. I hope they get him in the end, but I don't think they will. He'll be off to Septimus now . . .' He paused, following some line of thought. 'It doesn't matter. Septimus will have to fight, soon. Then we'll see.'

'Why did you help me?' croaked Ambrose.

'I'm sorry for you. And I said we should stick together. I don't forget that.'

*You killed my mother.*

Ambrose knew he should say it. He knew the Wolf was waiting to see if he did.

'Some of the things he makes me do – I don't like them,' said the Wolf.

'If you're going to live, you've got to make the best of things,' said the Wolf. Then, carefully, he said: 'I've never been a mother myself. But I don't mind. You need some-one to look after you.'

Ambrose felt his mouth move, but no sound came.

'Maybe a brother would be better,' said the Wolf. 'I had a brother, but I lost him. Brothers should look out for one another.'

Ambrose could not say yes; he dared not say no. Saying anything at all would hurt, more than ever.

'Anyway, you need to keep me on your side. That's your best bet. Then I won't give you to him. If we stick together, we can make him treat with us properly.'

'. . . What do you want?' said Ambrose at last.

'Oh – there's something you could do.'

Of course there was something. The Wolf had not come just to save him. He had some other reason for work-ing the Heron Man's magic to be here. He was waiting for Ambrose to ask what it was.

But even talking hurt so much now.

'It's one of your father's things,' the Wolf said at length. 'You've got your pebbles. They don't interest me. I've got his book. But there's another thing. Are you listening?'

'Yes,' gasped Ambrose.

'He's shown it to me. I know it's in a big castle, where people still live. It's locked away in a chest in a high room, not guarded. I've searched Velis. It's not there. That leaves just Tuscolo, Bay and here. All those houses had a part in Baldwin's fall. I was passing, so I came to have a look. I might have got it, too, if I hadn't stopped to help you. Now I've used my water for this time and I've got to go on. So you owe it to me, really. If it's here, you can find it for me.'

The man drew closer, speaking in a murmur.

'It's a stone cup. Find it for me, and I can help you. Understand?'

'Yes.'

'You'll tell me if you see it?'

'Yes.'

'That's a pact, then,' said the Wolf. He sounded relieved. 'Let's make it work. Now lie still and let me put these pebbles out for you. No good letting that thing come straight back the moment I've gone. How many should there be? I've got eight. So, one at the feet, right. Three up each side . . .'

Go away, thought Ambrose, as the Wolf groped and grovelled in the darkness of the cell. Please go away.

'You'll have to roll over, so I can get them on your other side,' the Wolf said. 'How far apart can they be?'

'I – don't know.'

He shrank from the touch of the Wolf's hand. The man was kneeling over him, smelling of sour leather, trying to jam the pebbles in between the pallet and the wall.

'There. That's the best we can do. Now you get better, and look hard around this place when you can. I'll be back when I'm able. In the meantime, look after yourself. Don't think of wandering off. Winter's coming. If you leave the castle, chances are you'll starve. Don't go talking to those idiot masters either. Or anyone. They'll think you're mad, or possessed, or maybe up to witchcraft. The one thing they won't do is believe you. Stay here. Stay quiet. Keep out of his way. Hear me?

'And take care of those stones,' he added. 'Or he'll pick your pocket before you know it.'

I should have said no, Ambrose thought, when the darkness had swallowed the Wolf.

I should have said no, and I didn't.

## XII

**Loss**

ebbles?' said the tall scholar. He peered disgustedly into the pouch. 'Is that all?'

'Give them back!' yelled Ambrose.

He tried to reach the pouch, but other hands were holding him. The little sunlit courtyard was full of grinning faces.

'Pebbles!' said the leader. 'Baby's toys! Who said it was going to be money?'

He looked around him at his fellows. No one answered him.

'Well it was one of you,' the leader said.

Ambrose jerked in the grip of the boys who had grabbed him, and almost broke free. But another hand caught him by the collar, and he swayed helplessly.

'These your toys, baby?' said the leader, dangling the pouch by the long drawstring. He was a lanky fellow, with a long jaw and curly brown hair. Ambrose had seen him and his friends hanging about the courtyards and the halls many times. He had never dreamed that they would pounce on him like this.

'Give them *back*!' said Ambrose.

'Baby wants his toys back,' said the leader, swinging

the pouch. 'All right then. Here you are.'

Ambrose felt the hands release him. He stood awkwardly. The tall boy held the pouch out to him in his palm. Sullenly, Ambrose stepped up to take it.

As he put his hand out the boy tossed the pouch neatly over his head. Behind him, someone caught it. Ambrose whirled. The gang spread out around him.

'Here, baby.'

'Give them back!'

Ambrose charged at the boy who held the pouch. It flew to his right. He lunged for it, but too late. Another scholar had caught it, laughing.

'Here, Boley!'

'To me! To me!'

'Give it *back*!' screamed Ambrose. He charged again. The pouch whirled high over his head. He spun. A boy was standing there, with the pouch in his hand. A boy he knew.

'Cullen – give it. Please!' he cried.

But Cullen flung it, laughing.

'Whoa!' cried someone, as the pouch thumped into his hands. Pebbles went flying from its open mouth and landed in the dust.

Ambrose screamed and lunged again. Again the pouch disappeared before he reached it. But he carried on his charge and collided with the thrower, wanting to smash him into the earth. The boy staggered with the impact.

'Hey!'

Thick arms wrapped around Ambrose. His head was buried in the boy's chest. His fingers flailed and found the boy's belt. His knuckles banged against the hilt of a knife that was stuck there. He was being forced to his knees. Raging, he felt for the knife again. His fingers closed on it. It came free. At once the shouts around him changed.

'Look out!'

'Grab him! Grab him!'

For an instant there was space around Ambrose. He brandished the knife, and charged the tall leader. A foot tripped him and he went sprawling. Someone landed heavily on his back. He flailed with the knife, but his arm was pinned.

'Get it! Get it!'

Fingers were prising at his grip. He could not hold the knife. It was gone.

'Off there!' said another voice. 'Boley, off!'

'He tried to stick Lex!'

'Off there! You want to land in the stocks? Get up!'

'He had a knife, Chawlin. He was knifing Lex!'

'*Up*, damn you.'

Slowly the weight on Ambrose's back lifted. He got to his knees and looked up into a group of faces. Some of the oldest scholars had appeared in the middle of the crowd. One of them, a man with a pale, stubbly beard and his hair tied back, was weighing the knife in his hand.

'They're mine!' Ambrose said fiercely. 'They stole them. He *made* them steal them.'

'We'll come to that in a minute,' said the man. 'Whose is this?'

The boy Ambrose had wrestled with held up his hand. The man handed the knife to him.

'Put it away,' he said curtly. 'What was stolen?'

234

'Nothing was stolen, Chawlin. He just went crazy!'

'So what was stolen, you?'

Ambrose realized that the man was talking to him.

'They took my stones. *He* told them to take my stones.'

'Angel's knees, Chawlin! It was just a game with some pebbles. He went crazy.'

'Pebbles?' The man looked around him dubiously. One of the white stones lay in the dust of the courtyard at his feet.

'All right,' he sighed. 'Give him his stones back, whoever has them.'

Wordlessly, they piled stones into Ambrose's open hands. One, two. Three. Four, five. The pouch was added on top. It was empty.

'Now you all find something useful to do. Or I'll have something found for you. If there's more of this, you will be in the stocks for brawling . . .'

'They've still got some!' said Ambrose, trying not to weep. 'There's three missing!'

'Oh, Angels! Would any of you be hiding more of those stones? No? So off with you.'

The group drifted away. One or two of them shot glances at Ambrose as they went. There was a burst of laughter at something one of them said. Then they were gone through the low archway.

'See they don't hang about, will you?' said the man to his fellows. They nodded, and followed. Ambrose and the man were alone in the small courtyard.

'So what is your name?'

'I'm called Luke,' said Ambrose.

'I thought it would be,' said the man grimly. 'Well,

Luke, since we will both be late for afternoon study, we had better be out of sight.'

He jerked his chin over Ambrose's shoulder. Behind Ambrose, in the curtain wall, was a small turret with a door facing in to the courtyard. Ambrose felt the man's hand fall on his shoulder.

'Come on.'

The wall-tower housed a spiral stair that climbed up past arrow slits to the wall-walk, and on to an empty, roofed platform above it. The roof screened them from being overseen from the higher towers along the wall. The man lowered the trapdoor into place, cutting off the stair and the way to the courtyard below.

They stood facing one another on the turret platform. Some of the beams that supported the roof were low enough to make the man bend his head.

Ambrose recognized him. This was the one who told stories to the other scholars, and who had played the hill-tune in the courtyard. Now that he was close Ambrose saw that his face was pale and his eyes small. The man had slept badly last night – maybe for several nights. Ambrose knew about that. He had not been sleeping well either.

'So what was it about, Luke?' said the man quietly.

'They took my stones.'

'And you drew the knife, perhaps?'

'They weren't giving them back.'

'Angels! Are you an idiot? You'd have had them back in the end. Why was it worth a knife?'

'I didn't get them back. Not all of them.'

*Who said it was going to be money?*

'He told them to take them,' Ambrose said.

236

'Who?'

*The one thing they won't do is believe you.*

Ambrose shrugged. There were just too many people here to make sense.

'So you are an idiot. You go around clutching a set of pebbles as if they're precious, and of course someone wants a bit of fun with them. Is that worth a knifing? Do you know what the Widow's people will do to someone who uses a knife in this house? And what if someone else had drawn a knife? One of you could be dead now, and the other on their way to a hanging. As it is, Lex and his friends will tell the masters enough of this to bring you any trouble you want. But had you even *touched* one of them with it, your life would have changed for ever.'

Changed for ever?

Suddenly, Ambrose shrieked with laughter.

He couldn't stop laughing either. His lungs whooped and shuddered with it. He sensed the man's astonishment, and then his growing anger. But he couldn't explain.

Hands caught him roughly by the shoulders.

'Enough! You – Luke! Take a hold of yourself!'

He could not. He shook in the man's grip. His throat howled and his eyes misted. Part of his mind could hear himself, uttering cry after cry, jerking against the man who held him. He felt it beginning to hurt – his throat, his shoulders, his half-healed back. He could not stop. The man had shifted his hold. He was not trying to shake Ambrose any longer. He had one arm round Ambrose's shoulders and was bracing him against his own body, as if he were pinning a struggling goat while its coat was trimmed.

237

Ambrose sobbed and sobbed, for what seemed like a long time.

Gradually he became aware that they had both sat down. He had his face buried in the man's shoulder. He was still sobbing, but more easily, now, and with real tears instead of the fevered laughter and weeping with which he had begun. The grip on him had eased. The man was rocking him, awkwardly, as if he was embarrassed by what he had to do. He wasn't speaking. He had not tried to speak to Ambrose for some time.

At last Ambrose gulped. 'You're – you're the Piper, aren't you?'

'What do you say?'

Ambrose tried again.

'Is it you that plays the pipe?'

'Yes,' said the man. Perhaps he was a little surprised. 'I play a pipe. It is not the only thing I do. My *name* is Chawlin.'

It was another rebuke: a gentle one this time.

'I heard you in the courtyard, a week ago,' said Ambrose. He knuckled at his eyes, but his vision was still blurred. 'You played the Lament.'

'The Lament? The hill-song? You know it?'

'Can you – can you play it again?' He wanted the hills. He wanted home and the clouds massing on the peaks in the evening. He wanted her broth and to see her stirring it, and the way things had been before his life had changed for ever.

'My pipe is in my cell. But . . .' The man scratched his head. 'There is a story to it, about the gods of the hill people. I might tell it, perhaps.'

'Yes please.'

'It is a sad one.'

'I know.'

Ambrose knew the story. He knew it very well.

'So,' said Chawlin.


*Beyah was the Mother of all the World.*

*One day the sea-men came and killed her son. On that day she turned her back on the people of the world and mourned. Her grief was so great that no one dared approach her.*

*Only Capuu, the great dragon who lies round the rim of the world and binds it together, came to speak for her other children, and beg her not to forget them.*

*She would not answer him. But as her tears fell he caught one in his lips, and she was angry, and struck at him for that.*

*She hit him full on the mouth. And yet he did not lose the teardrop. He held it between his broken teeth. He flew with it back to the world. There he laid it before the people, and told them that it was all that Beyah had for her children now. It was all her grief and all her rage – the world as she saw it, through a curtain of tears.*

*And as he spoke, he spat from his mouth the teeth that Beyah had broken in his jaw. He spat them in a ring around the teardrop that he had laid before the people. And he said no more, but returned to the rim of the world, and drew his body around it, and held it together.*

*And the teardrop lay where he had left it, with his teeth around it in a ring. And the people turned from it, sorrowing, to live their lives within the embrace of Capuu.*

239

*Nor did any of them dare approach the tear where it lay.*

*For only the bone of Capuu can bear the grief of the world.*

'Thank you,' said Ambrose, hoarsely. Tears were still coming, but he wanted them to come. It was the same story that she had told him, so many times.

'It is a strange thing, the Lament,' said Chawlin, after a while. 'I have talked with the masters of it. We think it must be about the sorrow of the hillmen who were driven from the Kingdom when Wulfram came . . .'

Chawlin had said the murder had been done by the sea-men. Mother had said that it was done by giants, and had reminded him how much taller than the hillmen the people of the Kingdom were.

'. . . They had cities then; but the cities burned. They were driven from the rich lands. They died in thousands. The survivors fled to live in pockets in the mountains. They could not return. Maybe, in the story, the goddess would stand for their grief. The world had turned its back on its children. But they also talk of the dragon Capuu – a strength that lasts. He is like what the masters here call Faithfulness. For the most part, of course, the masters mean faithfulness to the Angels. But the hillmen do not know the Angels, and yet they too show faithfulness. So it is something near that, perhaps.'

*Capuu does not loose his hold for pain,* she had said. *Or all the world would die.*

'Did you live in the hills?' asked Chawlin.

Ambrose nodded, but said nothing. He did want to talk – about his mother, and maybe the father he hadn't

240

known, and all those things. But the Widow had forbidden it. And he did not think he could form the words without weeping again. And that would hurt.

'So,' said Chawlin, after a short wait. 'How did you come here?'

'I walked out of the mountains,' Ambrose said dully. 'Then a man found me. He brought me to the Widow. She tested me, and said that I could become a scholar.'

'What man was this?'

'The Widow knew him. They had been friends, but she did not talk to him as if he was still a friend. She called him – I can't remember what she called him.'

'A knight?'

'Yes. A baron, I think.'

'Ho. Would you remember his badge?'

'He had a blue-and-white shield, with a wolf and a staff painted on it.'

'Lackmere!' Chawlin was startled.

'Yes.'

Yes, that was what the Widow had called him. The name meant little to Ambrose. His strongest memory of him was of riding in the mist – the clink-clink of mail, the enemy close, the hands on the rein that would not change their course. That had been purpose, in a world where all purpose seemed lost. Maybe it had been faithfulness, too.

'Michael's Wings! And I fought under Lackmere once. And yes, so – so . . .' He pulled at his chin, thinking. 'So he was here, and I never knew. I wonder what he's doing now.'

'I think he is with Septimus.'

'Is he? So . . .'

241

Chawlin was looking at him, closely.

'So. Your name is Luke, is it?'

'I'm called Luke.'

Chawlin was still looking at him. Ambrose shook his head, trying to clear the reek of his memories. He remembered how Wastelands had made him stand in the moonlight when they had first met. Perhaps people could guess who he was just from his face. He must not let Chawlin guess. He kept his eyes on the floor. A cold tear edged down the line of his cheek and ran to the tip of his nose.

'Well, Luke. I think I have a few things to say to you. Will you listen?'

'Yes.'

'First is this. Not long ago someone spoke to me about you. As it happens they came when I was feeling grey and lonely, and even a bit scared – like you, perhaps. We talked, and that was good. There is a little of the Angels in everyone, I think. Sometimes you see it.

'But one of the things they said was that I might look out for you. So people care for you. I do too now. You hear me?'

'Yes.'

'Good. Second, Luke, is this. This is a good place. Food, warmth, people who care: if you've crossed the wilderness, you'll know how much that means. But more than that, this is a place where people are looking for hope. That's what the school is trying to do – find meanings, find ways to better the world. And it's true what they say. There's almost nowhere else left that's doing this. It's the last place in which you can really learn. That matters, too. It's a good place. It could be good for you.'

242

Ambrose nodded.

'And my third, Luke, is that you have learning to do. Do you understand me? You can do it here if you are willing. You must not fight the school. You must learn from it.'

'I know,' said Ambrose.

Food, warmth, people, hope. Yes.

But there was also the Heron Man.

'Can I learn to fight as well?'

Chawlin frowned. 'What do you mean? What kind of fighting?'

Ambrose shrugged. 'Any.'

Anything was better than sitting helpless inside the diminishing ring of stones. Only five now: too few, certainly, to wall the Heron Man back into his pool, supposing he could ever get there. Could five be enough to protect him, even? Perhaps they could, if he slept curled up. But that wasn't what he wanted. He wanted to hit back. Learning how would be a purpose of sorts.

Chawlin was still frowning.

'Well, first we must see you past this matter of the knife. If we can put that behind us . . . I could show you a little war-skill, perhaps. Not during lessons, or we'd both lose our places. And not in the house either. It would be better if we could meet down by the riverbank. There's a shelter there I use. The Widow may forbid it, if she hears of it. But she may not hear of it and she may not forbid it if she does. Have you used a sword before?'

'Once. It was too heavy.'

'Only once? When was that?'

He was trying to find out about Ambrose again. Ambrose just shrugged.

'It was on the way here.'

Chawlin was about to ask something else, but the sound of voices in the little courtyard interrupted him. He crossed to the inner parapet, peered down, and sighed.

'I thought so. They have come to look for you. And since they are here, we had better go down.'

He heaved the trapdoor open and led the way down the turret stair.

In the courtyard stood Father Grismonde, a stocky priest with a white beard whose normal duties were the teaching of Grammar and Dogma, and leading the Widow's house in prayer. There were two men-at-arms with him. Ambrose could tell by the stony way Father Grismonde looked at him that he had heard about the fight.

Chawlin's hand was on his shoulder.

'It'll be all right,' he murmured. 'At least, it should not be too bad. No one was hurt.'

Father Grismonde said nothing as they came up. One of the men-at-arms took Ambrose by the elbow and led him towards the arch out of the courtyard. The other walked at his side. Behind, Chawlin fell in step with the white-bearded priest, speaking softly. Ambrose could not hear what was said. Chawlin was not being rebuked for missing lessons, anyway. He was asking a question. Father Grismonde answered him shortly.

'Good luck, Luke.' said Chawlin. 'I'll come to see you at sundown, if they let me.'

Ambrose turned to reply. He meant to thank Chawlin for staying with him.

But beyond Chawlin, for a moment in a doorway, there was someone else.

244

Who was that? A man in a robe?

Someone else had been in the courtyard! Who?

The man-at-arms was moving him on. Chawlin had smiled and turned away. Father Grismonde was frowning.

Who had it been? Padry?

Padry was away from the castle. He knew that.

Denke, the Law-master? Or one of the masters that Ambrose did not yet know?

Of course not, he thought wearily. Of course not.

He had been there, all the time. And Ambrose hadn't seen him.

The archway threw its shadow around him. The short tunnel echoed with the scraping of the men's feet upon stone. Ambrose's hand stole to the pebbles in his pouch.

He had only five of them now.

Sophia sat at her mother's feet, in the council chamber of Develin. Her dress weighed on her. Her hair was pulled tightly into place and heavy with jewels. She had made Dapea take special care over it that morning. She thought that all the counsellors were eyeing her secretly, wondering why she was there.

Yes, why? Why am I doing this?

Her throat was tight with nerves.

The room was full. Most of the officers of the house were present. So were Father Grismonde, Pantethon the Master of Histories, and Denke the Master of Law. Only Sophia and the Widow were seated. The Widow's chair had no footstool, so they had dragged out the low wooden chest that normally rested against the wall to act as one. Sophia had tried the lid before she had sat down on it,

245

because she had been afraid of pinching herself. It was locked. It always was. She knew the key lay in the hidden drawer in her mother's writing desk. She felt awkward, to be sitting there in the middle of the room, perched upon the secrets of Develin.

Why was she doing this?

On most council days she found something else to occupy her, just in case the Widow thought it time that she learned more about the business of the house. But that morning she had gone to her mother and asked permission to attend, saying (with some truth) that she was interested in the winter progress around the manors, which she had heard was to be discussed today.

'Come and be welcome,' the Widow had said shortly. 'Speak if you have something to say. Otherwise listen, and learn what you can.'

Sophia listened, and learned little. There was an hour of gloomy talk about the war between King Septimus and Velis. Everyone thought the news was very bad. Looking around, she guessed that quite a number of the counsellors still wanted the Widow to take sides against Velis, but none of them dared say so. Others seemed to think it was already too late.

Then there was an interminable discussion about the progress: which of her manors the Widow and her followers would visit; the numbers of horses and guards that should come with them; and above all, which of the party would be able to sleep under a roof, and when – for no house in the Widow's lands but Develin itself could shelter all the cavalcade. The men talked round and round on very little things and never seemed to finish. Sophia wondered why her mother did not simply decide matters one way or the other, as she did at other times. But the Widow seemed listless today. She did not force herself upon the debate.

Then someone re-opened the question of who would be in the party. From there, they began to discuss the scholars. Then someone else mentioned Luke.

The direction of the talk changed at once, and the mood of the Council with it.

'My lady, I regret it, but he is not fit to be at the school.'

Sophia could feel her mouth going dry. They were coming to the moment.

'How is he not fit?' asked the Widow.

*She will not want to turn him out of the house, I think,* Chawlin had said. *She will look for a reason to keep him. If you can give her one, she may take it.*

'His attention is fitful,' sighed Pantethon. 'And it is plain that he likes not his masters . . .'

'So different from my other scholars,' the Widow murmured.

'But it is Father Grismonde whom you must hear on this, my lady. There is a matter . . .'

'Grismonde?'

'My lady,' said the white-bearded priest. 'I own to being disappointed. When I first saw the boy, I thought he had an air of the unearthly, and indeed I wondered if we might have the seeds of one who would in time talk with Angels . . .'

'Do you recruit still, sir? I thought our monasteries already over-full.'

247

'*However*, my lady, it is now plain that his uncommonness is a plain corruption of the mind, and that it brings dangers to those near him.'

'What! Then you should exorcize him, my friend.'

'My lady jests. I have seen too many cases of madness in men to suppose that they are all the work of ill spirits . . .'

Father Grismonde stood in the middle of the floor, with his white beard jutting and eye fixed on his mistress's eye. He knew that the Widow was trying to put him off. And plainly he was not going to let it happen . . . *Not the sharpest wit*, Chawlin had said. *But a stickler for what he thinks is the truth . . . I doubt he will let it drop.*

Sophia's heart sank. She would have to say something for Luke.

And what could she say?

She looked helplessly around the room. She saw Hervan the chamberlain. He was watching Grismonde closely, as though the old priest was going to say something dangerous without realizing it.

Hervan knew something about Luke that the others did not.

If Hervan knew it, so must the Widow. What was it?

'It is for Padry to approach me if he thinks a scholar has passed beyond remedy,' said the Widow. 'So far, I have heard nothing that might not be improved with a cane.'

'My lady will recall that she has sent Padry to Tuscolo in the hope of buying books before the war closes its gates. In the meantime, a serious matter has arisen, for which I have placed the boy in custody.'

'Very well,' said the Widow. 'What is it?'

'Some scholars took from him a pouch of pebbles, and threw it among them in sport. It should have been a harmless game, but he drew a knife . . .'

'His?'

'I do not know, my lady.'

'If it is, it should be taken from him,' said the Widow. 'Knives may trim pens, but I will not have a scholar carry one if he thinks to use it on a fellow. And certainly he should be beaten for this. Now . . .'

'Padry has already had him beaten, and he is no better,' grumbled Father Grismonde.

'My lady, if I may?' said Hervan, the chamberlain.

'Please, Hervan.'

'It is of course for the masters to advise on good order in the school,' said Hervan smoothly. 'However, if this matter had arisen among the household, I should have asked first if any had been injured, and whether there had been intent to cause injury.'

'By good fortune, there was no injury,' said Grismonde. 'As for intent . . .'

'Then,' said Hervan, overriding him, 'perhaps the matter is not as grave as it first appeared.'

'Indeed, Hervan,' said the Widow. 'Thank you.'

Sophia relaxed slightly on her makeshift stool. The masters were losing. With luck she would not have to speak in front of the Council after all. She was a little sorry, now, that she would not be able to boast to Chawlin about how clever she had been. But mostly what she felt was relief.

Father Grismonde was looking nonplussed.

'My lady, I do not know how—'

'Enough, Grismonde. You may beat the boy, but let it be.'

'And if the trouble stems from the pebbles the boy carries, the pebbles should be taken from him as well.'

Sophia looked up. Which counsellor had said that? She could not tell. But whoever it was had slipped their point in just as the matter was closing . . .

'So be it. But I will not have him turned off. Enough.'

And now it was closed. The Widow had not spoken so firmly all morning.

Sophia's voice almost died in her throat. But not quite. 'M-madam.'

She craned backwards to look into the Widow's frown. 'Yes?'

'May I speak on this?'

The Widow did not let people argue when she had made a decision. But this was the first time Sophia had ever raised her voice in Council.

The Widow sighed. 'Quickly then.'

Sophia paused. The thought of Chawlin's face, his feeling for this bewildered boy, surprised her with its strength.

'First, I beg that you do not take these stones from him, madam. I believe that they are all he has left from his family, for whom he is grieving.'

There was an intense silence. She could not see the faces of the counsellors; but there was an air in the room like – like ice. Fury, outrage, surprise: the Council – or someone at least – was staring at the back of her neck. (*Why this? Why you?* She could almost smell it.) The oil lamps hissed and spat thickly. She kept her eyes fixed on her mother.

250

The Widow shrugged.

'Very well. Aught else?'

'It is said – it is said he mislikes his masters,' said Sophia, astounded at herself. 'I think it may be because he has not been served justly.'

'How not?'

'He was beaten for studying something he had not been set to study. But Padry was mistaken. It was not Luke who was looking at the text, but I.'

There were murmurs around her. Strangely, the worst moment seemed to have passed.

'Padry is not here to answer you,' said the Widow. 'But I had not heard that studying more than one had been set to study was a crime in my house, so long as the texts are not sullied or torn by the careless. What work was this?'

'The lists of heraldry, madam.'

'And what did you learn?'

(Boldness, now, because if she lied they would know she was hiding something.)

'The name of the company of horsemen who came to your gate a month since.'

She saw her mother's face change. And Hervan's beside her.

The Widow, and Hervan. What did they know?

'They were from Tarceny,' Sophia said clearly. 'And, madam, I have a question that I wish to ask you.'

Was she truly going to do this here? In front of all the Council?

'Ask.'

'Why you did not have them slain, and so avenge my father?'

251

There was a moment of silence. Then the Widow sighed again. Perhaps she had been expecting – or fearing – something else. She looked to her counsellors.

'Grismonde, perhaps?' she said.

Father Grismonde cleared his throat. For a moment Sophia hoped that the priest would still be cross enough to snub his mistress.

'My lady, you know that in the school we allow three remedies for evil done. They are Faithfulness, Forgiveness, and Force . . .'

The Widow nodded. Sophia groaned inwardly. The two of them were going to pretend to be friends again. And it was she who had given them the chance!

'As with any remedy in medicine, each may apply in its own place,' said Father Grismonde. 'And each may be fatal if employed at the wrong time or in the wrong case. Among your masters there is dispute over which is greatest. Some will argue that it is Forgiveness, or Pardon, that should have primacy. I prefer the order in which I have given them . . .'

This isn't about *evil*, Sophia thought angrily. This is about Father!

'Yet there is no disagreement among us that Force is the least of the three,' rumbled the old priest. 'The most over-used, and the most like to add harm to harm. Each slaying leads to another slaying. If Man never forgave nor forgot, but pursued his enemies and the sons of his enemies and the servants of his enemies, the slaying would not cease until the last of us were slain. Every year, now, it seems to me that more die at the hands of men than are born from mothers' wombs.'

'Truth,' said the Widow. 'And still it continues. We have heard that Septimus fares at last to meet Velis, to what end we may all guess. And an innocent boy has been beaten in my house . . . Indeed,' she went on, with a weariness in her voice that Sophia would only remember long afterwards, 'I think sometimes that it were better we did nothing at all, for it seems no good comes of anything we do.

'Well, enough of this. At least I may make amends to the boy Luke. We have agreed that there should be scholars among us when we make our winter progress. Let him be in their number. He is young for it, but if he is grieving still, a change may help him, and also help him to learn more care for his fellows.'

'. . . And you were right,' whispered Sophia, when she met Chawlin afterwards in the darkness of the keep stair. 'You were right about everything! Even about him coming on the winter progress.'

'Ah. I thought your mother might want an excuse to keep an eye on him.'

'So who is he?'

'I don't know. I have a guess. But as long as it is no more than a guess, it is maybe better not to talk about it. Anyway, you seem to have done well. In fact, you did very well.'

That wasn't flattery. That was honest respect, and she loved him for it.

'Training,' she said, trying to sound dismissive.

'More than training. It's a hard thing to re-open a matter in a debate like that, even when you know they have ended in the wrong place. I don't think another beating would have done him anything but harm.'

'I even saved his pebbles for him,' she giggled.

'More to the point, you held your own in Council. Your mother will be pleased with you when she thinks of it.'

His praise, and the knowledge that they must part in an instant, lifted her. She stood on tiptoe on the step below his, and put her hands around the back of his neck.

'I had good help,' she said.

'You . . .'

'No, I'm going to.' And she reached up to kiss him. She felt the scratch of tiny stubble-hairs on her lips.

And he did not protest. He did not stammer or back away. She felt the sudden tension in him ease as she released him. He shook his head, unbelieving in the dimness of the stair.

'So where did *you* come from?' he asked, almost of himself.

Then there were feet on the stair below them. They parted abruptly, Sophia climbing, Chawlin going on down to meet, delay, and talk gaily with whoever it was that was coming up towards them.

Sophia crossed her arms as she climbed, holding her elbows where his hands had caught her for a moment. She could almost feel his fingers still, through the heavy cloth of her council-dress. Something had happened: something new, different, unexpected. It had happened to both of them. They couldn't pretend it hadn't.

And all the blood in her body seemed to be singing.

## XIII

## Winter Progress

nd the day you're married, mam,' Dapea chattered, as she folded another of Sophia's travelling gowns for the trunk, 'we'll be packing like this and we'll never come back!'

Sunlight filled Sophia's chamber, flooding in from the broad window. The pale walls and plain wood of the bed and wardrobe shone with it. The subtle golds and reds of her wall-hangings retreated in the uniform glow, as if they were embarrassed by the light.

The house was humming. From the courtyard below rose the sounds of people calling, organizing, ordering wagons and bundles for the long winter tour of the Widow's estates. And all through the rooms around them other people were packing too: shouting, quarrelling, excited at the long-expected change of routine.

'I shall not be married yet a while,' said Sophia cheerfully. 'Half the houses they might have matched me with have been broken. And half the rest are beyond forgiving.'

'The time will come, nonetheless.'

'I can wait,' said Sophia. She chose three combs for the trunk, but left her best behind, because the chances of losing or damaging it during six weeks of travelling around the Widow's manors were too high for comfort. 'Indeed,' she said with some malice (because she knew Dapea loved the thought of new places), 'you may be married yourself by then, and tied to a farm and a row of babies in Develin.'

'Oh, there's no one for me,' said Dapea, cheerfully. 'And I'd have none as would stoop so low as to want me.'

'No? Not with all these handsome officers and sergeants that we feed here? Or what about . . .' Sophia put her head on one side, pretending to think. 'What about these scholars – merchants' sons and the like coming to the school from all over the Kingdom? One of them might take you to a fine place.'

'Same answer again, mam. And they're too young.'

'Some are, some are not. Have you looked at the older men? There's that fellow Tadle, for one . . .'

'Oh no, mam! He's a drunk!'

'That's hardly fair. But if you don't like him there's . . .' Again she pretended to think. 'What's-his-name – the one you said told stories. Chawlin.'

She tossed his name into the room as lightly as she would toss a cloth into the trunk that Dapea was packing for her. But she thought that Dapea looked at her, and she glanced hurriedly away.

'Pleasant enough,' said Dapea. 'But he's never amounted to much, has he?'

'That's hardly fair, either,' said Sophia, cursing herself silently. 'Well, what about – what about Jehan the gate-sergeant? Is he manly enough for you?'

'Oh, mam – he's *ancient*! Spare me!'

'You're very cruel to them all, Dapea.'

Had she given herself away? Perhaps not, this time – but only by a hair's-breadth. If she mentioned his name again in Dapea's hearing, her maid would be instantly suspicious. And if she uttered it to anyone in a tone that was the slightest bit wrong, they would know. So Sophia clamped her jaw shut and kept Dapea furiously busy for the rest of the morning, to make sure that the girl did not have time to wonder.

It was one thing to have a secret fantasy about a man. It was quite another to find herself thinking more and more about him, and to spend hours wondering what he thought of her. For it did seem that she was seeing him more often – even if it was just that she was noticing him now when before she had not. She would turn round, and there he would be – in a passageway, or sitting with a group of other scholars, or helping in some household task. Perhaps he would avoid her glance, and she would pass on, fuming inwardly at the impossible gulf of custom and station between them. But sometimes he might look up, and their eyes would meet for an instant, across a courtyard or a crowded room; and she would be sure – sure – that he was pleased that she was there, and would have spoken to her if only they could have been alone. Then they would both turn away, as if other matters drove them.

And what was he? Why didn't people like Dapea see him as she did? Was she deluding herself about him? Surely not. But if he had the quality she saw, why would he be hiding it? Could he be a secret enemy? A spy?

Or what if . . . what if he was the kind of man who would catch the affections of the Widow's daughter deliberately, and then kidnap her for ransom or worse?

257

Oh, don't be silly, she said to herself. If he had wanted *that*, he would never have had a better chance than the day they met on the roadside. Yes, it was risky. But it was not that sort of risk. She could manage it. And after their rescue of the boy-scholar they shared something that no one else knew about. He had become a part of her secret self. Surely he must know that. Maybe knowing it would change him.

And so the thoughts went on, around and around in her head. And the less she could speak with him, the wilder they became.

Sometimes her feeling was so strong that she thought all the world would see it. And they must not. For Hestie and the Widow and all her counsellors would banish him at once if anyone guessed what she felt. No one, no one at all in the house, could be allowed to know. So she made rules with herself. She tried not to see him every day. If she managed somehow to pass close to him, she would let at least one day go by before setting out to see him again. And only once a week – well, maybe once every two or three days – would she look for a chance to talk with him alone.

Then she found that he would be among the scholars on the winter progress.

Her first instinct was to shout and turn cartwheels down the corridors. He'd be there – in the same party as she, for the length of six weeks. They could see each other every waking hour! She could find any number of chances to speak with him!

Her next thought was that the Widow would also be in the party, and even though Hestie would not be going, there would be plenty of officers and counsellors and other busybodies. How could Sophia pass six weeks under their noses without anyone suspecting?

What was he thinking of, putting himself forward like this?

At last she saw him in a corridor, managed to distract her escort with an errand, and caught up with him in time to ask. But all he did was laugh. He said (unconvincingly, she thought) that he had wanted to keep an eye on Luke, and also to see the manor of Ferroux, because it had once been one of the most ancient houses of the Kingdom.

'Now I'm going to have to sit through every manor court we hold on the tour,' Sophia complained, 'to show everyone that I'm being good.'

'You've no reason to behave any way other than you would,' he said solemnly. 'But all the manors will come to you one day; or to your husband. You will learn more in the courts than if you sit listening with us, perhaps.'

'Don't talk to me about husbands!'

He laughed again, and she was angry with him. Surely he knew she wanted him to talk about his feelings for her; and yet he had not.

Travel meant discomfort. Luxuries had to be left behind. Boots and clothes became caked with mud. Bodies ached after long days on the road. Nights were cold or crowded. Even the Widow's greater keeps and castles struggled to find space for a full third of the house of Develin when it came. Some places, like the keep at Gisbore, endured the caval-cade for a week; others, the small manors and the villages, for no more than a day or two. Sophia resented those little two-roomed houses, where the Widow would sleep in one and she in the other, with Dapea lying on the narrow floor, armed men pacing at her window, and everyone else scattered under village roofs or canvas within two stones' throw of where she lay. Then the darkness seemed close, and the snorts and snores of sleepers were loud, and she felt that she could not stir or even sigh in her bed, because the Widow would hear her from the next room, and guess what thoughts were passing through her daughter's head.

Still, Develin and its encircling walls could wait for her return. There were fresh sights for her eyes every day – hills, woods, villages, the people in and around them, the dogs that barked and frisked as the riders came in. She saw Chawlin, walking in the cavalcade, sitting with other scholars around some master or, in some out-of-the-way moment, showing the boy Luke how to use a quarterstaff. He was alive, and close, and she was alive, too. And each morning brought new things, and new sights to see.

In the mild air of a December afternoon she approached the circle of scholars where they sat in a meadow, under a broad tree. She was in a good mood because the manor-hearing had ended early, and she was not going to have to spend any more of her day in that packed, reeking barn while the Widow dealt with mill-rights and water-rights and harvest-dues, and all the people crowded around to see their lady and hear what she had to say.

She could see Chawlin, sitting cross-legged among the scholars with his back to her. Of course she could not do what she most wanted to do, which was to go and sit next to him. But with Dapea at her shoulder she picked her way around the circle until she could settle on a great root almost opposite, so that she could look across at him (and he at her, if he liked) as if it were the most natural thing in the world. There, with her back to the trunk, she faced out over the river-meadows and the low buildings of the manor at which they were staying as if she were a queen in a small court of her own.

Father Grismonde stood in the middle of the circle. He had broken off from something he was saying about the Angels while he waited for her to sit down. He seemed to think she had taken rather long about it.

'My lady honours us with her presence,' he grumbled. 'We were grieved to be without it this morning.'

'I was at the manor court, master,' she answered, remaining seated.

'Indeed. And it is of justice that we are speaking now.'

Father Grismonde, it seemed, was not in a good mood at all.

'And whom,' he asked, still grumbling, 'whom did the Widow's justice serve today?'

Sophia blinked. That was an improper question, surely – even when it came in debate, and from one of the Widow's masters.

'Why – those who received it, sir.'

'Did it? Did it indeed? Tell us then, of those who received it.'

Sophia frowned. The truth was that she had paid no more attention to the details of the hearings than she did to Father Grismonde's sermons. For most of the time she had been counting warts and missing teeth among the villagers.

'There were two families that won redress against the

manor mill for short shrift. Then there was a complaint among the villagers about who had the right to fish which part of the stream. And . . .' She hesitated, trying to remember. 'The rest were fines, mostly.'

'Of course. And who received them?'

'The manor lord, sir.' And the Widow would have a share. They would all know that.

'So – some small good done, and profits to the judges. And perhaps my lady can tell us of the case at Thale, two days since.'

Angels! Why this inquisition? They would all know about Thale, anyway. Unlike most cases, that one had been interesting.

'The manor of Thale is in dispute, master. The former lord's cousin claims it as inheritance-right. But a knight from Gisbore asserts that his father was wrongly dispossessed of it.'

'And the Widow's ruling?'

'That it is vacant, sir, and for her to dispose of at her pleasure.' It seemed perfectly fair to Sophia. The more vacant manors in Develin, the better. She was already keeping a list of them in her head. Land was what made a knight. She had begun to have ideas about who that knight might be.

The urge to look across to where Chawlin sat was very strong.

'So!' snapped the priest. 'Do we learn from this that neither claimant had a right to the manor?'

What under Heaven was biting him? Was he still smarting at her from the Council last month?

'So my mother has ruled, master.'

'And why should she have ruled thus?'

'In her wisdom, sir,' she said carefully.

You could think what you liked about the Widow's justice. (Sophia had seen the poor court-clerks knitting their brows and shaking their heads just slightly each time the Widow went against their advice). But no one, not even old Grismonde, would dare fault a judgement once it had been given, surely. It was time for him to shut up.

'Of course I do not mean that better earthly justice exists,' the priest muttered. 'I know no other lord that judges so fairly . . .'

Hypocrite, snarled Sophia in her mind.

'But indeed!' Grismonde went on, speaking now to the whole circle. 'If this justice we see is the best there is, then we may learn from it what justice itself truly is as men practise it!

'I asked – whom does this justice serve? To the judge go the fines. To the judge goes the manor – no doubt in time to be restored to whichever claimant promises most in arms or dues.

'More, to the judge go the eyes of all who are judged. We know that a lord who does *not* travel and give justice in his lands risks losing them – whether to his own tenants, to a powerful neighbour, or to a simple adventurer who arrives of a morning with a sword and a loud voice to make the landsmen listen.

'So justice serves the earthly lord more than any of the people who are judged.

'Look around at these barns and fields. What do we see? They are the Widow's, because she judges them. Is this the justice of the Angels?'

263

What's this? thought Sophia. He can't – he *can't* be preaching rebellion against the Widow! What is he doing?

Around her she felt the stillness of the other scholars. They were staring at Grismonde, fascinated by the sight of a master suddenly abandoning all discretion.

What was he going to say next? What was he going to do?

'Look!' said Grismonde.

He's provoking us, Sophia assured herself. He wants a debate. He wants someone to answer him. But it wasn't going to be her. She had said enough already. And besides . . .

*Besides, what if he was right?*

The thought slipped as easily into her mind as if a voice had spoken it in her ear.

What if he were right? And in a way, he *was* right. He was just saying the things they all knew without saying. And everyone talked so much about justice. And everyone talked so much about Kingship.

*And what if it was all lies?*

And so much of it was lies. Justice fed itself.

Grismonde's finger shook as he pointed towards the buildings like the wing of a soaring hawk. His face was red. His voice trembled.

'Look. What do you see?'

Around her scholars shifted. Some were staring at the barns. Some were hanging their heads. No one wanted to catch Grismonde's eye.

Link by link, the thoughts in her head supplied the words that Grismonde had not spoken.

If this is justice, then what is truth? What is Heaven?

What is the King? What can we hope for, if justice is a lie?

Link by link, like chains lifting a trapdoor down to a dark pit. If justice was a lie, thought Sophia, then the truth would destroy everything.

'Master . . .'

She looked up.

It was the scholar Luke, of all people. He was on his feet.

Grismonde had swung upon the boy, beard bristling. Sophia saw Luke swallow, and (as if by afterthought) touch his heart.

'Master – I see that the Widow's barns have roofs on them.'

Grismonde's face was like thunder.

'What?' he barked. 'If a barn has no roof then it is not a barn, surely?'

Luke wavered, but kept to his feet.

'Then . . . where there is no justice given, there are no barns?'

Images shot into Sophia's mind: of fields – these fields – blackened and destroyed by raiders. It had happened so many times: baron raiding baron – even village the next village. It had not happened here.

That was what Luke meant. It had not happened here; because here there was still the Widow to judge over them.

'Ho!' cried Chawlin suddenly, and clapped his hands in applause. So did someone else. Some of the scholars were grinning ruefully. It was simple, their faces said. It was really very simple, the moment you looked at it the right way.

'And – and where a lord pardons,' Luke went on, 'he's not taking anything, is he?'

Slowly, the anger faded from Grismonde's face.

'No indeed . . .' he said. 'No, he does not.' He drew his sleeve across his brow. 'No. Fair answers, boy, as far as they go. Good.'

He cleared his throat.

'And we have digressed. Let me return to the justice of the Angels.'

He drew breath, and fell back into the steady cant of a master who lectures a sleepy class.

'It is told that Umbriel keeps a great book, and his pen is witness to all we do. Suppose, now, that we could peer over the Angel's shoulder, and see his page before us. Every thought, everything seen and unseen that weighs on the least of our deeds. How should we read a book in which all things are written . . . ?'

Long after the ring had dispersed, Ambrose remained sitting beneath the tree. In the distance he could see people moving among the village buildings and by the big wooden lodge where the Widow was staying. But he would not go down to them. Not now.

He did not dare.

The sun was low and the colours were beginning to fade. Grey plumes of smoke drifted from the huts. A chill had crept into the air. Around him lay the leaves that winter had stripped from the branches. They were brown and dead; but their shapes recalled the memory of the oak they had been. Among them his ring of five white stones nestled like travellers that had found good camping for the night. And he was going to stay within it for as long as he could.

Still he could feel the forces that had beaten against him in the moment he had stood to speak. *Fool!* they had said, from every eye in the class. *What can you say? Why interfere? Sit down. You are nothing!*

His fingers were trembling.

I knew he was here, he thought. The Heron Man. And he was.

I didn't see him, but I heard him. Justice and lies – that's what he was saying to Grismonde. He was saying it to all of them.

And I stopped him.


'Is he right in his head, do you think?' Sophia asked.

She was sitting beside Chawlin in the shadow of one of the wagons, sheltered from view by the great wheel and by the coming obscurity of night. From the manor house behind them rose the clatter and smell of supper preparing for the Widow and her closest counsellors. Sophia knew that she would soon have to get ready to appear at table. She would have to start looking for Dapea, before Dapea came to find her.

Chawlin stirred. 'Luke? I don't know. Am I right in mine? Are any of us?'

'It was a serious question.'

'I know.' He rasped his finger across his stubbly chin. 'He's certainly less closed up than he was. Did you know it was his birthday while we were in Thale? Some of us went and begged honey cakes so we could have a celebration. At the end he stood up and thanked us like a gentle-born. So he is thirteen now – not far from being a man. And there's always been a lot to him that we don't see. He walked out of the mountains by himself, for one thing. I know that country. That would have tested anyone . . .'

'But is he?'

'As I said, I don't know. Either he does not want to speak or he has been told to keep his mouth shut. He's lost his family. Then something bad happened to him after he came out of the hills. If you get that far, and think you are safe, and then it goes wrong . . . Yes, it may have unhinged him. He has that way of looking at you as if there might be someone standing beside you. Ugh! I don't like that. But . . . well. You saw today. Of all of us, who was it that answered? And it was a good thing for Grismonde that he did.'

Sophia frowned. 'What was the old toad thinking of?' she complained. 'That was sedition – or very nearly! If I had gone to the Widow . . .'

'Please do not.'

Chawlin was looking at her earnestly. He seemed to think she meant it.

'He let his ideas run away with him,' he said. 'That was all. There are queer places in any head. And the more you think, the more queer they may be. Grismonde's been worried for some months now. But so have other masters and counsellors. He was ashamed of himself afterwards. I doubt he will trip himself up like that again.'

'Don't worry yourself. I'd never tell *her* anything.' She was cross that he even thought she might.

And he must have sensed her anger, because he fell silent. That depressed her more. She would much prefer to talk: either to convert him to her view, or be converted to his, it didn't matter. What mattered was that there shouldn't be this silence between them, in these very few moments when they could be together. It made her wonder again what kind of man he really was.

'What's the matter with them – the masters?' she asked.

Chawlin sighed. 'They're worried, as I said. There are some ugly thoughts running around. I've heard them ask – among themselves – why we believe the things we do. Like Grismonde today: why should we believe in justice? Most of all they ask: what's the point?'

'What's the point of what?'

Chawlin shrugged. 'What we are doing. The school, and if it does any good.'

'I've wanted to know that for a long time.'

Chawlin sighed again.

Sophia was impatient. Moments alone with him were so precious! She had come wanting to steal a kiss from him, as she had done last month on the stair after Council. She had wanted to laugh secretly with him at Grismonde and Luke, and maybe even hold him and feel the strength of his arm and chest. Yet here he was all sombre and grey, and talking only of depressing things. She couldn't kiss him when he was like this. It would be like kissing a tree stump.

She sat beside him, resenting the moments that passed so silently between them.

'I did not think to hear it in a class, like that,' Chawlin said. 'But maybe it was only a matter of time. And sooner or later it'll get said in front of the whole house. Then it'll be too late, whatever the Widow does. I think . . .'

He paused. Sophia glanced at him.

'I think we should have gone to help Septimus,' he said.

'It's too late to say that now, isn't it?'

'Now that it's too late we may see it and say it. I've never been able to find out who swayed the Widow against it. Someone must have done. And maybe it would have been a disaster, but maybe not. At least we would still all know why we do what we do. Now . . . well, there may be a bad time coming . . .'

Sophia had had enough.

'I must find Dapea,' she said.

'You're angry with me,' said Chawlin.

She stopped halfway to her feet. Because he was asking her not to leave.

For three heartbeats she looked at him. Then she sat down again, slowly.

'I want to know what you want,' she said.

'What I want?' he repeated.

She waited for him, tingling with the suddenness of the moment.

You know what I mean, she thought. Why are we together? What do you think will happen? What are you: spy, fortune-seeker or . . .

. . . Or lover?

So many words, and all impossible – for both of them!

'I could get you Thale,' she said slowly. 'Had you thought of that?'

He looked away, abruptly. 'No!' he grunted. 'And no, you couldn't, I think.'

'I could get you a manor. Maybe more than one.'

She was not sure what she was trying to do. Maybe she just wanted to pull him out of his torpor. Maybe she was trying to find out if he was a fortune-hunter.

Or maybe she meant it.

But if so, how could she persuade the Widow to honour it? Unless she meant he should wait until the day when the manors all finally came to her.

'I do not want it!'

'Then what *do* you want?' she hissed.

'What do I want?' he repeated. 'What do I want?'

He was staring in front of himself, unseeing.

'I want what I am most afraid of,' he said.

'Michael's Knees! What does that mean?'

He sighed.

'If I tell you, you must understand that I'm not asking for your help.'

If he told her, she thought, then yes, he did want her help – even if he did not want to want it.

'Tell me,' she said.

'I said I had seen what came to kill Tarceny. I did not say, I think, that I fought them. There were three of us there – myself, and Brother Martin who has now left us, and Tarceny's woman . . .'

'You met her? I had no idea!'

'She was there. And then they came for him – the monsters he himself had conjured. They were terrible. If I dream . . . Aagh – the *cockerel*!' He broke off, staring ahead of him.

It was a moment before he began again.

'I wonder if you can imagine what it was like, years later, when I was given Tarceny's cup. Every hour I

271

carried it, I thought of those things. I was very, very afraid.

'And yet all the while I knew there was something more within it – something very deep. Maybe it was deep enough to – to let me understand the whole world, so much that I would no longer be so afraid of what I'd seen. I don't know. I just don't know. Because I Never. Dared. Touch it.'

He sighed.

'When I met your mother I was almost glad to give it to her. Now – well, dreams do not go away. Or if they do, they come back worse than before. Things remind me. Those riders we saw – and other things. I wish now that I'd taken the chance when I had it, but I hadn't the nerve. And maybe I wish I could have left Develin after I'd given it up, but I hadn't the strength . . .

'I don't want manors, Sophia. Manors mean nothing. And peace and warmth and food mean very little now. I want to *know*.'

He broke off. Someone was coming. They both froze. A man, walking by, paused by the wagon tail. Craning from her place Sophia caught a glimpse of a gold-rimmed cloak and knew that it was Denke, the Law Master. She thought there was someone else with him, too.

Denke did not look their side of the wagon. He stood, head bowed and arms hugged round himself, as though he were listening or deep in thought. Sophia held her breath.

And in the long moments that followed, with her eyes on the corner of the master's cloak, she thought about what Chawlin had said to her.

It was as if he had lifted his shirt and shown her a great, shocking disease upon his skin. A stain of Tarceny – so close, on the man beside her! The man she . . .

He had used her name. Sophia. He hadn't done that before. It sounded so different when he said it.

Chawlin. Witchcraft. Tarceny. She needed to think.

Suddenly Denke groaned aloud – a hopeless, aching sound – and walked slowly on. Sophia watched him diminish in the sinking light. She saw, with some surprise, that he was alone after all.

Somewhere among the huts a voice was calling. It would be Dapea, out looking for her.

She had to think.

She looked at Chawlin, and saw that he had heard Dapea, too.

She cleared her throat. 'I've got to go. But . . . but I want to talk to you about this again. I promise I will.'

He nodded slowly and said nothing. She did not know if he believed her. She did not know if she believed herself either. She gathered her skirts and left.

In the dusk of the village buildings there was no sign of Dapea, who must have gone searching in another direction. Sophia slowed her pace, walking with her head high as if she had all the time she needed.

*I don't want manors, Sophia.*

All right, she thought crossly. He doesn't. And what does he want? Nightmares from Tarceny! *Aagh – the cockerel!* What did that mean? Behind the sureness and the smile there was another Chawlin – someone who huddled and quivered and jumped at shadows. No wonder he was drawn to the boy Luke. And twice now, when he had been

273

closest to the centre of his thoughts, he had talked about that thing, that cup from Tarceny. He must be fascinated by it. And frightened, too.

Chawlin. Did Tarceny taint *everything* it touched?

If he didn't want manors, then he didn't want her. Without land he could never be accepted as a suitor.

But he *did* want her. Or at least, he hadn't wanted her to leave. He talked to her about things he would never dare mention to anyone else. That mattered.

And, she thought (with her jaw set); and if he was afraid, was it not brave of him to want to confront his fear?

Or was he just wishing that he was brave enough?

She did not know. But she had promised she was going to hear him again. Yes, she had. So?

So she was going to. It was risky, but it always had been risky. She could manage it.

She could manage it, because he made her better than she was. She felt herself to be braver, cleverer, and more loving, just because of the moments he spent with her. She could never have turned the Council for the boy Luke if he had not encouraged her. She must remember that. And now that she had given her word she must be true to it, Tarceny or no Tarceny. It was the faithful thing to do.

It lightened her heart a little, to think that. And she wouldn't forget about the manors either. It was too good a plan to be wasted.

She paused in the shadow of a hut, and peered into the big yard before the Widow's lodge. From inside the lodge came the sounds and smells of supper preparing. The yard appeared to be deserted. Dapea was not there.

So much the better, thought Sophia. She could be standing by the door when her maid returned, and scold her for being tardy.

She stepped forward confidently. As she did so, a shadow moved in the yard. But it was only Denke, still pacing aimlessly about with his head bowed. She called a greeting, but he was lost in thought and did not look her way.

And he did seem to be alone.

# XIV

## The Light at Ferroux

he house of Ferroux was the oldest in all
the south. Rolfe, a son of Wulfram, had
raised his roof there in the conquests
hundreds of years before. Its name was
in a hundred songs.

Little remained of his building. The
manor that stood in its place was a small one – barely able
to support the Widow's company for two nights. There was
no township or settlement, no keep or even a lodge in that
place. Not a third of the Widow's following could camp
within the stockade. Yet it pleased the Widow and her
masters to pass Midwinter there.

At dusk trestle-tables were set in a horseshoe pattern in
the meadow outside the stockade. Braziers stood at inter-
vals behind the benches. They gave light and warmth, and
their fire marked the feast of Midwinter when, the story
went, Gabriel, Messenger of Heaven, had brought the
Flame to the wandering peoples in the lost times before ever
Wulfram and his sons took ship across the seas. Before the
high table the manor knight bowed and welcomed his lady
to that ancient house where, he said, the memory of the
King-fathers ran deep in the stone – even if the meat and

the wine were no better than their children could make.

'Both true,' said the Widow, not unkindly, and her people laughed.

Then the Widow raised her hand, and a tall candle was set in front of her. On it she cut, as she did every month in her home, three lines, one below the other near the tip. A lighted taper was brought, the candle lit, and a screen of thinnest horn placed about it to shield it from the breeze. The light shone dully through and played upon her face. Around her the Household of Develin settled to hear its ritual of Dispute.

Ambrose was late coming to the tables, because he had been practising in secret some strokes with a staff that Chawlin had shown him. He knew that arriving after the Dispute had begun might earn him a beating. But he felt that the Heron Man was very close now. He did not think that his unseen enemy would let him answer back again. Perhaps next time he would attack. Whatever he did, Ambrose wanted to be ready.

He slipped quietly up to the scholars' benches, clutching a white pebble in each fist. There seemed to be no space left for him. As he hesitated, the last scholar turned and saw him. It was Lex, the leader of the gang in the courtyard of Develin. He frowned. For a moment Ambrose thought he would call out and give him away. But to his surprise the scholar shifted inwards along the bench, leaving a space beside him.

'Come on,' he muttered. 'For once, this should be worth hearing.'

Ambrose crept in beside him. 'Why? What's happened?' he whispered.

Lex looked at him in astonishment. 'Where've you been? It's been all around the camp since sundown.'

'What?'

'Septimus. He fought Velis and was broken. His head's on a spike on Tuscolo's walls.'

Septimus. The King. The man who had defeated his father. So he too was dead.

It seemed to Ambrose that an unnatural stillness had fallen among the people. He felt the back of his neck creep, as if some cold throat had breathed upon it. A damp wind flustered the braziers. The night was cool and echoless.

The King was dead.

And what had happened to Wastelands?

'Master Denke,' called the Widow.

A little along the high table, the Master of Law rose to his feet. He wore his heavy red gown and a cap with a long peak. In the half-light he looked like a great, misshapen hawk. His voice was deep and powerful in the open air.

'You know, my lady, that Father Grismonde and I had already chosen that our dispute should once more address Kingship. With the news that has been brought to us this night, we think it doubly right to do. For in the past we have allowed ourselves to consider only single merits or strategies that may benefit a king, like single jewels upon a crown. Tonight it is the whole crown that I will speak of. I ask only that I may be heard to the end.

'Let me begin with a tale you all know, of the king of ancient times who sent to a wise man asking how he might keep his kingdom. And the wise man, without saying a word, turned away from the messenger and began to cut down all the tallest grass stems in the field around him. The messenger carried this sign back to the king, who took it to mean that if he would keep his kingdom he must slay and put down all the greatest men around him, for it was they who might threaten his rule.

'Now I have debated before with my colleagues the division of guilt between the wise man and the king for the crimes that then followed. Remember, each snick of a grass stem was taken as a sign that a family must perish, down to the youngest child and least of their servants. That is not our purpose tonight. But this fable carries in it a truth about Kingship that we all know in our hearts, and yet dare not speak . . .'

Because only a third of the full house was present, Ambrose and his fellows were closer to the high table than ever they were at Develin. Because the tables were set out in the open field, and not in the long hall of the Widow's castle, he had a clear view. He looked along the faces, to left and right of the Widow, and he knew every one of them – the Lynx, a counsellor, Denke, another counsellor, and Padry. On the left, Father Grismonde, Master Pantethon . . . The face he always looked for was not there.

The light and shadows wavered as the words rolled from Denke's mouth.

'There has never been a king who has not won, or held, or lost his crown without the use of iron to draw blood. There has never been a king who has not purchased the iron of his followers with land he has stolen from others. There has never been a king who has not called this theft justice. To do anything in his kingdom, a king must have power. To gain power, he must do evil.

'To keep power, he must do evil. And the evil that any king does to maintain power is greater than any good that power might do . . .'

Murmurs stole along the benches. Denke was indeed addressing the crown itself! Without Kingship there could be no hope. And yet there were heads on the high table that nodded as he spoke. The Widow looked inscrutable, and the shadows of the candle were stains upon her face. Had she known he would do this? Surely she would not have allowed it!

The candle reached the first mark; the Widow raised her hand. Denke finished and sat down. Father Grismonde rose to oppose him.

'It is a dismal vision that my friend Denke has drawn for us,' Father Grismonde began. 'Yet it is better that we should now confront such thoughts together than struggle with them each alone. And my friend has gone too far.'

Someone near Ambrose sighed, as if with relief.

'No, no. Such thoughts are lulling. They deceive. Think of the fable that Denke has told us. Think how much we assume from the image of the grasses. A grass stem causes harm to no one. It bears seed, even flowers perhaps, or has a graceful beauty as it waves in the wind. Had our wise man stood among a pack of wolves and slain or chained the fiercest among them, would we fault him for the message he sent? The wolf is savage. Man is savage. The wolf is treacherous. So is man. The wolf . . .'

'The Wolf,' murmured a voice in Ambrose's ear, 'is child of the Wasteland.'

Ambrose took a moment to understand. Then he gaped.

'What?'

It was Lex who had spoken. In the light of the braziers he was looking at Ambrose under low brows. Ambrose stared at him.

Silently Lex turned back to watch the high table.

'. . . and man is hungry,' Grismonde was saying. 'Who then shall chain the man that is wolf?'

Wolf? Wasteland? Why had Lex said that? How had he known?

What was happening?

The last paleness of evening was gone from the sky. The braziers ruled now, yellowing the tables and the heads of the people who sat at them. Before the Widow the candle flickered. Her face was close to it, watching it intently as it burned towards the second mark, when Father Grismonde would cease. Even in the flare of the braziers Ambrose could see the light that it cast upon her, and the darker pits that it threw beneath her chin, above her nose, and in her eyes: light and shadows together as the candle trembled.

'Look,' said the voice from Lex beside him. 'He is here. Look.'

It was not Lex's voice. It was no voice Ambrose knew. When it spoke, his head swam as if he had drunk wine. He could feel the seams of the world loosen. His mind caught glimpses of brown depths that lay behind them.

'Who are you?' he whispered.

'Light draws the shadow. Look!' said the voice that was not Lex.

281

'. . . and look!' cried Father Grismonde.

He was pointing to the manor buildings. 'Look! The roofs of Ferroux are whole! I myself have struggled with doubts, but the roofs are whole!'

He turned, still pointing, and blinked at his audience, as if they must see the tremendous force of his argument.

Men stared at him.

'The roofs are whole,' Grismonde repeated. 'There is rule here. So should there be in the Kingdom!'

Somewhere along the scholars' table, someone tittered. Grismonde looked around at the faces and seemed to realize that his listeners no longer understood him. He faltered.

'And – and if all this is held too weak to weigh the scales for Kingship,' he pleaded, 'then what is the alternative? What of Pardon? Denke himself,' he exclaimed, recovering his pace. 'Denke himself has taught us that there must be one to punish wrongs justly, and give pardon where it may be given. Without Kingship, who shall see our quarrels ended? Shall we look to each other? Yet who shall be the last to punish, who the first to forgive? Force would be first. Faithfulness would fail. Our blood would run and run. There must be one who *judges*.

'So I ask my friend Denke – if what he has said is true of Kingship, what then of Law? Of the very discipline he teaches? For how can Law be, without one who lays it down, one to judge among the strong men, and one to whom the weak may appeal against the strong?'

'Hah!' cried Padry at the end of the high table, and his palm banged upon the boards. But no one joined with him to celebrate Father Grismonde's point and his applause died lonely, like a candle in a night wind.

The Widow raised her hand. Father Grismonde sat. Denke rose for the short reply that the marks on the wax stem allowed him.

'To argue from thatch to Kingship is the thought of a simple mind. It is unworthy of my friend Grismonde.'

The tables stirred. Insults – however justified they might seem – were not permitted in Disputes. Denke lifted a finger, commanding silence.

'Where a king finds the roofs are whole, he may burn them and so do evil.

'Or he may leave them whole, and take wealth from under them, to give him the power to do his evil elsewhere.

'These are the only choices he has.

'What is the Pardon of such a king worth? In Develin we have told one another that men weary of their quarrels, and the word of a king may bring the peace. And we have lied.

'We have lied because we have said only what we imagine Should Be. We have shut our eyes to What Is.'

Utter stillness gripped the tables.

'And so to the Law, and the question he poses me.

'I must say that there may be Law, somewhere, among the Angels perhaps. There may be Law among some other people, who will one day come across the sea after all our bones are buried. For we were not the first in this land, and it is sure that we will not be the last.

'But among men as we are it is Law that bends before Power, and not the other way about. Such law is not Law but mist and memory. Our hopes were false, and we must now forget them. From our kings comes not pardon but punishment. It is a punishment that we have deserved.

'In our three hundred years, we have known no Law that has held, nor hope that has not failed.'

He sat down again. The listeners were still, appalled by what he had dared to say.

'Indeed,' said the Widow at last, 'I had not heard this before.'

Barely a breath was drawn around all the firelit meadow. The Widow lifted the hood from the candle and blew out the flame in front of her.

'I see that Denke has gained his argument,' she said. 'And I see that his words must cost him his place at my table.'

For a moment no one moved or spoke. Then Denke rose once more and bowed to the Widow. As he walked slowly away towards the darkness of the buildings his back was stooped and his head low, as if he were bowing still.

The Widow shrugged. Her face said she had ceased to care about anything. Her voice sounded old and tired.

'Let us eat now and console our bellies, since our minds cannot be at ease.'

A soft thicket of murmurs rose along the tables. One master had gibbered like an idiot. Another was dismissed in disgrace. All this in the House of Wisdom!

And Law had been denied by the Master of Law!

'Look,' whispered the voice in Ambrose's ear.

With the loss of the candle the Widow's face seemed shadowed. Her head bowed towards her plate, as if she found it very heavy.

And the man beside her!

No, that was Father Grismonde, of course, sitting crushed with his hands over his eyes.

But beside him?

Ambrose's eye flicked along the row of masters and counsellors. He saw them. He knew them. Yet, now – now it seemed that beside each one he looked at would be a pale, cowled old man, bald as a nut inside his hood, with eyes that did not fling back the light.

As if in a tunnel of days he saw them – in quiet rooms, in shadowed halls, on paths among dry fields, where each had met unseeing in their turn with the man in the grey robe. They had spoken with him in their minds and listened to the words from his mouth.

He was here. The light drew the shadow. The light was Develin. The shadow was the Heron Man. And the Heron Man had them. He had them all!

'Ambrose Ulfinson,' said the voice beside him.

Once again Ambrose jerked around to face Lex. No one knew his name here! No one anywhere knew his father's name!

The thing behind Lex's eyes was looking at him.

'The father of this house will wait in the garden. He will speak with you. Go and hear him.'

*Paigan Wulframson. By the last of your fathers' sons shall you be brought down.*

Ambrose gripped the board. Dimly, he heard the talk rise along the benches. Voices were calling for the meat and wine. Scullions carrying hampers were beginning to move down the tables, handing out bread. A cauldron of soup had appeared.

The face of Lex was still looking at Ambrose.

'*Go!*' said the Angel within it.

Ambrose fled.

\*　　\*　　\*

In the shadows beyond the firelight, in a garden of vegetables and herbs, were the remains of a cracked pavement. On it there stood an old fountain with a wide, dry bowl, very like one that Ambrose remembered in his mountain home. Here he came, stumbling among the rows of planted roots. He crouched with his back against the ancient pedestal and laid out his five stones around him.

Then he drew his knees up to his chin, and let his mind reel like a world in flight.

*Look!*

He had looked, and he had seen the Heron Man at the tables.

*Ambrose Ulfinson. The father of this house will wait in the garden . . .*

It had not been Lex's voice. It had not been the Heron Man's voice.

The Angels move within us, fleetingly, and do not stay. *He will speak with you.*

Ambrose swallowed. He did not know what to think.

The one thing he was sure of was that he had been sent here, by a voice that he could not disobey – a voice that had spoken names that had never passed out of his own head. *The Wolf is child of the Wasteland.*

It had sent him here to meet someone.

Who?

Ambrose looked around him. There were plants, and bushes, and shadows of bushes. Nothing else stirred. Behind him the firelight played and voices rose, arguing, as wine made its way along the tables. The old knight who held the manor was there, and could not leave while his guests ate. Could he be the father of the house? Ambrose

286

was not sure if he even had any children. And anyway, the manor wasn't his. It was the Widow's. It was part of Develin. And the lord of Develin was long dead.

Who then was the 'father of the house'?

The Heron Man was here, in the court of Develin. He had been here all along. He was speaking to all of them – the Widow, the masters, the counsellors. He had been doing it for weeks.

The Heron Man had spoken to everyone! He had them all!

Everyone except him.

The father of the house was going to speak to him, here in the garden.

Slowly, the awful thought seeped more and more strongly into Ambrose's mind. There was no one else it could be. It had to be the Heron Man. The Angel had sent him here, to meet his enemy face to face. The Heron Man was coming to him.

Keep out of his way, the Wolf had said.

You must never approach him, Mother had said. You must never listen to him, or speak with him, no matter how important it seems.

*He will speak with you. Go and hear him.*

'Why?' he cried plaintively.

Nothing answered him.

Why?

The light draws the shadow. Develin was the last light in the Kingdom. But the Heron Man had been among them all the time. Now the light was going out. Ambrose remembered the face of the Widow as she had puffed out the candle.

287

'Your house is not in order!' he said aloud.

They were the words she had spoken to Wastelands, even as the Heron Man stood beside her chair.

*He will speak with you. Go and hear him.*

He listened, and heard nothing but the voices at the tables. He looked, and saw only the herb-fronds glowing dully in the light of the fires.

He did not have his staff.

Time passed. Ambrose ordered his five stones again, setting them as far out around him as he dared, and waited. It was cold here, away from the brazier on the longest night of winter. The babble from the firelit meadow had reduced. The Widow must have retired. So must many of the house. The talking had gathered into clumps where those who had no early duty still clung to their bowls and places. And the firelight at his back flickered on the shrubs and bay-bushes, and showed him the shadows that lay among them.

At last he heard voices approaching, murmuring to each other: a man and a woman. Ambrose knew the man's voice. It was Chawlin.

'. . . seeing each other too often,' he was saying. 'It will do no good. We need to think what we are doing.'

'You're just depressed,' said the woman. 'Who wouldn't be, after hearing all that awful stuff at the tables? All the more reason to find company we like.'

Chawlin let out his breath, like a long sigh.

'You're so much younger than I am, remember. You're the future. You should not think to offer me . . .'

'What do you think I am offering you?'

Her voice was low, but pressing. Chawlin hesitated again.

'Sophia, look at my face. Look at it.'

'I like it,' the woman said firmly.

'No, listen! You don't know me! Can you imagine, talking to me as you are now, and seeing wounds, great red wounds, appear on my face?'

'What do you mean?'

'. . . and you know it's something in your mind, not real, because I am still talking to you and laughing with you and all the time you can see the flesh curling up from the rents, and the blood all down my skin?'

'Chawlin!'

'I've seen it. I've dreamed it, and thought it was a nightmare. There was a time when I saw it, waking, day after day, on friend after friend, and knew that I was mad. That thing from Tarceny I carried – just a plain stone thing. Until I gave it away, it was bringing all that back. And now I'm dreaming again . . .'

Something moved, to Ambrose's right, at the edge of his vision. It was not a man.

'I think you're being very brave,' said the woman.

Ambrose breathed in, slowly. There was a smell in the air, thick and characterless, like water at the edge of pools. He huddled backwards under the shelter of the old fountain. His heart was beginning to work, hard.

Fifteen feet from him, a shape stirred in the shadow of a bay tree.

Ambrose swallowed. Carefully, he looked away, watching from the corner of his eye.

It was smaller than a man – perhaps the size of a child all wrapped in a cloak. There was something bird-like about the way it had moved, and very light, as if it were made only of bone, or had no body at all. Within the shadow of its face or hood something – perhaps it was an eye – glinted red from the distant fires.

How long had it been there? It was watching him. It had seen that he had seen it. An arm – a limb like an arm – began to stretch out towards him.

'Sophia,' said Chawlin's voice. 'You must be more careful.'

'I'll do what I like . . .'

'Chawlin!' cried Ambrose.

There was a brief, stunned silence.

'Who's there?'

'Chawlin, help me!' Ambrose scrambled to his feet. He had to grip the fountain with one hand to prevent himself from overbalancing in his narrow ring of stones. With his other he reached out to them, begging for help.

'Luke!'

Chawlin was there, and with him was the Widow's daughter – the Lynx of Develin. They were standing very close to one another. They were holding hands. They must both have jumped when he called.

'Luke!' hissed the Lynx. 'Go away!'

'I can't!'

'What do you mean? You're not wanted here. Go away!'

'I can't,' Ambrose said again, trying to keep his voice low. 'Can't you see it?'

'What?'

They hadn't seen it. They hadn't smelled it.

'There!' he said, pointing at the shadow by the bay bush.

There was another beyond it, he now saw, to his left.

And he thought a third had been moving on his right, but it was gone for the moment. He did not know where.

'This is a bad relapse,' muttered Chawlin.

'For Umbriel's sake, Luke!' said the Lynx. 'It's just a cat. Please go away.'

Ambrose did not move.

'I'll have you whipped!' she said furiously. 'Go. Away. Leave us alone!'

'I can't!'

She must have been astonished, because she did not answer. Ambrose heard her draw breath. Then she exclaimed loudly and marched off into the darkness.

Chawlin hesitated. 'What is it, Luke? What are you seeing?' There was a note of unease in his voice.

'There! By the bay bush. You see it if you don't look at it. Can't you see?'

Chawlin stayed where he was.

'There – there's nothing there, Luke. It was a cat, that's all.'

'It's still there!'

'No! No, Luke. You just heard what I was saying and you frightened yourself.'

'Chawlin, help me!'

'Help yourself!' said Chawlin roughly. 'You've done enough damage already.'

He left, moving quickly with his arms swinging. He passed the bushes and boulders where the reeking, shadowy things crawled, and walked by them as if they were not there. He did not look back until he reached the edge of the garden. Then, when he was no more than a shadow among shadows, Ambrose saw him turn.

'We will have our bout by the woodstore tomorrow morning, Luke,' he called, in a different, more cheerful tone. 'Do not forget. And when we get back to Develin, I will see if I can get my hands on some real iron. You will like that, hey?'

He was gone.

They didn't listen, thought Ambrose, furious. They didn't see!

No one did. No one saw the Heron Man, moving among them. No one saw what he was doing in Develin.

'Cat?' muttered Ambrose savagely. 'What kind of *cat* are you?'

He picked a flaked of cracked paving stone from the ground beside him, and, looking away, flung it as hard as he could at the thing that crouched by the bay bush.

He was sure that he hit it, but there was no sound of a stone striking or falling. It was as if he had thrown the stone into a loose canvas sack.

It wasn't moving. It was watching him, like a big dog that expected something. They were all watching him.

They can't pass the white stones, he told himself.

He might try throwing one of the white stones. That would do something, he was sure. But he might never get it back, and then he would only have four.

*Andoh*, said the Thing before him from the darkness.

Ambrose jumped.

*Andoh.*

The word was followed by other sounds, deep and lipless. Ambrose felt the stone behind him tremble at the voice. He sat frozen as the Thing stole closer to the white stones. It groped at the edge of the ring. His toes and knees were drawn up as tight as he could to get away from it. And again it spoke, with a horrible, wheedling, pleading tone, as if it were saying, *Please, please, please . . .*

*Please, let us in,* he thought it was saying. *Please, let us reach you. Please, let us tear you so that the flesh curls up from the rents and the blood runs down your face.*

'Go away!' he yelled, despairing. Just as the Lynx had cried at him: 'Go. Away.'

Then he cursed it.

He could curse, now. Weeks in Develin had taught him the filthy, obscene words that the scholars flung at one another when they were angry. He used them all. He raged at it, the ugly, shapeless stupid thing that mouthed at him out of the darkness. He raised his voice and heard it crack with the effort. And he stopped, gasping for breath.

It could not pass the stones. It could not reach him. The Heron Man could not reach him. He could sit here all night if need be.

Away to his right, something like an insect the size of an ass heaved itself up among the scented leaves.

*Andoh,* it cooed.

Then it said a word that sounded like *Anson*; and other words, and *Anson* again.

The bushes parted and another came, lumbering out of blackness. A fourth (or was it a fifth?) flitted after it.

They were crouching in a ring around him, so close he could have reached over the stones to touch them. Huge eyes danced with the dying fires on the field. Their voices made him shrink. Long fingers, thick with hairs, stretched beseechingly towards him. The air was thick with their smell.

And nothing happened.

Nothing happened. They could not reach him. They did not try. They spoke, and waited, and spoke again.

And the Heron Man did not come.

Slowly, even as Ambrose glared at them across the little space, the beating of his heart began to ease. He was very tired.

He rested his head back against the stone fountain, and tried to watch them under lowered eyelids. It was cool, but still warmer in these flat lands than in the mountains.

Perhaps an hour later, he jerked up, realizing that he must have dozed. They were still there, but silent, watching.

There was nothing they could do to reach him.

He waited, and dozed again; woke, and dozed once more. Unhuman voices spoke as he dreamed, but he did not answer.

Some time before moonrise they must have slipped, or been ordered, away, for when he woke in the high moonlight he could not see them any longer. Not even the breeze stirred the leaves of the garden around him.

Now he was utterly alone.

# XV

## Shadows in Develin

n the early spring, the soldiers of Velis surprised the garrison at Bay. They were within the walls before the alarm was raised. Bay tried first to fight, then to surrender, but the attackers ran through the buildings in frenzy, listening to no cries. They killed the family, the men-at-arms, the servants and the children of servants – even the animals – and heaped the bodies in the great hall, and fired it over them. Then they returned to Tuscolo, the capital, and crowned their king in a ceremony to which no one was invited.

No one knew why Bay had been attacked. The first account to reach Develin was that Bay had sided secretly with Septimus, before his defeat. A later story was that it had been a private quarrel between Bay and some of Velis's counsellors, who had then persuaded the King that Bay would oppose him. The Widow of Develin sent careful messages of duty and submission to Tuscolo, and waited for news.

'These are the words of Tuchred Martyr,' said Father Grismonde to the scholars of the middle studies.

'"Men adore the power of kings, which is manifest.

295

Yet the power that is hidden is greater still. If the miser gives gold to a poor man, we have seen Raphael move his heart. When the coward knight turns upon his pursuers, there Michael rides upon his helm. And if a lying man speaks prophesy, you may look for Umbriel behind his eyes."

'Now,' said Father Grismonde, wagging his finger at the scholars. 'Some who seek to be foolish may ask if all good done by men is therefore of the Angels' doing and not ours. This was not the meaning of Tuchred Martyr. For the Angel to take its place within us, the coward must first find a seed of courage, and the miser must think of the farthing in his purse – be it only for an instant – a scrap of time. Then comes the power of Heaven, blessing, increasing— Yes, what is it?'

The scholar Cullen had stood to ask a question. You could do that, with Father Grismonde.

'Master – haven't the Angels all fled?'

'What? Fled?' Grismonde drew breath. 'No, of course not! Why should they?'

Cullen frowned. Perhaps he was surprised at himself. Everyone was thinking it, of course. But what had made him say it aloud? To the priest?

'People say they have,' he said.

Father Grismonde shook his head wearily. Even rank blasphemy no longer seemed to surprise him. With an obvious effort, he found the right degree of indignation.

'What – what is this? Idiocy! *Idiocy!* You are here to think! To learn – not to repeat nonsenses! If there is more such fool-talk I shall meet it with the cane. No, no, no . . .'

Ambrose did not know if the Angels had fled. But fled

or not, he did not trust them any more. They had sent him to the garden of Ferroux.

And Lex was gone, too. The last time Ambrose had seen him, he had been walking by himself on the winter tour, wearing a puzzled expression on his face. By the end of the journey he had disappeared. Four or five other scholars had also slipped away from the school since then. There were spaces on the benches that had once been crowded. And scholars were saying openly what they would never have dared to say the season before.

The 'power that was hidden' was the Heron Man. And there was nothing to be done but wait to see what he did next.

That night he was shaken awake in the darkness of his cell.

'Have you found it, yet?' said the Wolf.

'No.'

'You haven't looked, you runt! I know it's here. It's not in Tuscolo. It's not in Bay. I've been through both of them. It's got to be here!'

'I haven't seen it.'

'Listen.' His face was very near to Ambrose's own. His voice dropped to a whisper. 'I need the cup. It's nearly as important as my life – certainly more than yours.'

'I've not seen it.'

'Don't be stupid! I don't want to kill you. But I've got to stay ahead. I can't stay ahead without help. *He* knows that. He'll let me drink just twice more. Just twice! After all I did for him . . .'

'You took Velis's men into Bay.'

'Yes – I did. But it's *his* fault. If only he'd be plain with me, it wouldn't have been necessary. Anyway, the cup wasn't there. And now I need the cup more than ever. And that means *you* need me to have it. If I don't . . .'

His breath hissed.

'He knows I don't want to do it,' he said slowly. 'That's why he wants it to be me who does. And I will. If I have to, I will!'

The Wolf's head was so close that Ambrose could feel the warmth of his breath. His heart was beating thump-thump-thump as he lay eye-to-eye with the killer.

'That would give him everything he wanted,' he said slowly.

'If I have to . . .'

'I haven't seen it.'

'You know something. You know where it is.'

'I haven't seen it.'

The man sat back against the wall of Ambrose's cell with a gasp of frustration. 'You don't know what it's like! If I don't stay ahead, I'm finished. Velis – half the time he's like a wounded beast. If any of us goes wrong in his eyes, we're dead. And there's a lot of clever bastards around him who'd love to see my blood. That priest the Widow sent us – he's good, too. He nearly tripped me up over Bay. If I hadn't thought fast I'd have been marched out and had my head cut off. I can't relax. Not for a minute . . .' He ran his hands through his hair.

'All right, then,' he said. 'What is it you want?'

'What?'

'I need that thing. I've got to stay ahead. What do you want for it?'

Ambrose eyed his shape in the darkness. What could this man offer him? Could he possibly want anything that this man would offer?

'I could make you King,' the man said. 'I told you that once. I meant it.'

'No.'

'Don't be a fool. You'll only survive if you get strong. You've got the bloodline, from your father. You must be the very last male descendant of Wulfram there is. After a year of Velis, everyone will be sick of him . . .'

'No.'

'You can do it. I will help you.'

'I don't want to be King.'

'Don't be stupid! We're not playing girl-games here! The moment anyone knows whose son you are, they'll either try to make you King, or kill you to stop you trying it for yourself. Either you get the crown, or you get dead, one way or another.'

'I don't want to be King!'

Once more the man was on his feet, bending over Ambrose where he lay.

'Listen. I need that thing. I know it's here. If you don't get it for me, I've another way. And if I get it without you, then I don't care what happens to you – whether he gets you or not. You'll be finished! Better think about that. And hope I come back. Because right now, I don't think I will!'

He turned, and stepped towards the wall of Ambrose's cell.

'Wait!' said Ambrose, flinging off his blanket and climbing to his feet.

The wall was gone.

For a moment Ambrose saw before him a dimly lit landscape, jumbled with brown rocks and boulders, and the far sweep of what might be mountains. Low above the ridge at the edge of the world burned two lights, brighter than any star he had seen. Before him the Wolf was striding away, ignoring him.

Ambrose put one foot forward. It struck rock – not the dusty boards of the school, but a hard-edged rock. He looked around him. There was nothing here, nothing growing, nothing moving, except the figure of the Wolf, striding away from him, faster than Ambrose could follow.

This was where the Wolf came from, when he came. This was how he could appear inside castles like Develin; like Bay and Watermane. He came into them from this place.

The Wolf had learned his under-craft from the Heron Man. So the Heron Man must know this place, too. And so did his creatures.

This was where they all came from.

Ambrose looked at the nearest of the boulders that littered the landscape. It was large enough to hide any man – or thing – that crouched behind it. There were thousands like it, all around.

His nerve failed, and he drew back. The night of his cell flooded around him.

He stood in the close darkness, straining to see the Wolf. Perhaps he still could, for fleeting seconds longer, as he stood in one place and looked beyond it into the other. He thought he could see a man's head and shoulders, moving among distant rocks. Then the night was complete, and the Wolf was gone.

That was how they hid themselves – the Wolf, the Heron Man, the things he had seen at Ferroux. They walked among the brown rocks, and looked into the world. And unless you knew how to look, you would not see how close they stood.

Someone in another cell called a question, sleepily, in the darkness.

'It was just a dream,' Ambrose answered through the thin wooden wall around him. 'Sorry.'

He wondered how many of them he had woken. How many of the people around him were now sinking back into sleep, thinking that it had been Luke, just crazy Luke, having a dream.

It *had* been a dream; but not his. He had looked into the dream of the world. His mother had spoken of it, so long ago. He had had no idea that it would be so desolate.

And the Wolf was right. The cup he wanted was here, in Develin. That must be the 'stone thing' that Chawlin had spoken about at Ferroux.

And the Wolf had another way to get it.

Maybe he should not have sent the other scholars back to sleep. Maybe he should have spoken with them.

*The one thing they won't do is believe you.*

He was going to have to *make* someone believe him.

And it must be someone who would not only believe, but could do something, too.

Sophia woke in the dawn, from a dream about her father.

She had been walking with him in a moonlit garden where old, broken stones peeped from among herb-bushes and the paving was cracked under her feet. She had been telling him everything that had happened since he had gone away – everything – and he had been nodding as she spoke, because he understood. It was good to have him back. Everything depended on him. He was back in his place at last.

And then he said: *But why is it like this?*

She looked around at the stones of the garden, and the ruined buildings that lay in the moonlight. The roofs were gone. The doors hung upon broken hinges. She could not explain it.

*Why? Because of you, perhaps?*

She could not answer. Her father looked at her with eyes that measured all that she was. But when he spoke his voice was Chawlin's.

She woke.

Her heart was beating heavily. Her mind was a confusion of thoughts. She could hear cries at the gatehouse, the sounds of the door-leaves being opened, hooves in the courtyard as some early rider stirred about his business. The house was not ruined after all. It had been a dream.

Father had not come back – of course not. The wonderful lift that she had felt in her heart was sinking away. The dull dawn seeped in to fill the emptiness he had left behind him.

It had been Chawlin's voice. Father had spoken with Chawlin's voice. She remembered that Chawlin's smile had reminded her of her father. That was not right. She loved them both, but they were separate. How could she dream that they were not? The thought disturbed her. There should be places in her heart for both of them. One should not blot out the other.

She tried to recall her father, and to piece together what there had been about his looks or voice that had been different from Chawlin. He must have been older, by ten years perhaps. He would have been the same age when he left her that Chawlin was now. And he had thought a lot, like Chawlin . . . or had he?

Was she just assuming that he had been unlike her mother, who always decided things so firmly?

She could not remember.

After some time she woke Dapea, who was sleeping on her floor. Dapea was tired and cross. Plainly she did not think it was reasonable that her mistress should rouse her before dawn and demand to be dressed. They lit rushes at Sophia's table. While Dapea's hands were busy in her hair, Sophia sat at her glass trying to remember what Father's voice had sounded like, and wondering if she had ever known.

There was a scratch at the door. Dapea, still shivering in her shift, answered it.

'Lady Sophia,' said the voice of one of her mother's maids-in-waiting beyond the door. 'My lady wishes to speak with her – as soon as possible.'

Sophia jumped to her feet. She wasn't ready! Dapea was back with her, coaxing her to sit. Her fingers went back to work on Sophia's hair, while the Widow's daughter looked into her reflection in the rush-lit glass, and did not see.

Her mother had never sent for her like this – never this early. Something must have happened. What could it be? What that concerned her could the Widow think so urgent? Someone had told her about Chawlin. That must be it. That would be enough to make a mother summon her daughter at any hour of the day or night. She would be furious.

'There, my lady. You can go now. Angels go with you.'

Reluctantly, Sophia turned for the door.

It wasn't right, she thought, as she picked up her skirts and made her way through the dimly lit passages. Chawlin was *hers*. They had no *right* to make her give him up. She would defy them. She had done nothing wrong. She would refuse to stop loving him – they couldn't make her, whatever they did . . .

But it wasn't what they did to Sophia that would matter. It was what they would do to Chawlin. They would disgrace him, beat him, send him away and bar the doors. It was unfair! He hadn't asked her to fall in love with him! But they would make sure that she never saw him again. So she was going to have to deny it. She would deny everything. It was gossip, malicious, spread by some troublemaker in this house . . .

The council chamber was empty. She crossed it, to the door that led to her mother's private rooms. There was no sound within. She paused to steady herself. Her heart seemed to be fluttering wildly. She scratched softly on the woodwork.

'Enter.'

The Widow was half-dressed among her maids. Whatever it was that had troubled her had also got her out of her bed.

'Sophia.'

'My lady,' said Sophia, dropping a curtsey. That wasn't anger in her mother's voice. Not yet. It might just be worry.

'I have received a message, concerning you.'

'Yes, my lady?' So they *had* found out about Chawlin.

'It comes from the King.'

She meant it had come from Velis. The Widow was careful to call him 'King' now, even to her daughter. The pattern of the rug under her mother's feet ran with vines and fruit-trees at the rim. Sophia stared at it, trying to understand what she had been told.

'It came this morning. The riders who brought it had ridden all night. He himself will be here within three days.'

Velis would be here in *three days*!

'W-why, my lady?'

'The letter he has sent me . . .' The Widow glanced at a sheet of paper, curled like a new-born upon her writing desk. 'I have to take it as an offer for your hand in marriage.'

Sophia gasped.

'It is very – sudden,' the Widow went on, raising her arms to allow her heavy black gown to be dropped down over her head and body. 'I should have expected . . .' her head disappeared, and re-emerged with her long black hair all tousled by the passage of the cloth, '. . . a trusted ambassador, tasked to look us over, and to drop hints. I would then hint my replies in return. I would certainly have hoped for the courtesy of a month's warning before the entire royal pack of scroungers descended on my house. This King is not like that, it seems.' She scowled at the letter. 'He has even chosen to let me know what dowry he expects for you.'

'Why me?'

'It is logical. He has defeated his enemies – even some

who may not have thought they were his enemies. He still has to unite the Kingdom. By allying with us he gains the support of the last great house that has taken no side in these troubles. We are strong here in the south, where he is not. Still . . .'

'I – I won't do it.'

'Well, I did not suppose you would leap for joy. But you must understand that we have no choice, and very little time. That is why I called you at once. This will be all around the castle before noon . . .'

'*No!*' Sophia almost shrieked. 'He's a monster! You can't . . .'

Her mother approached her, deep in her black robes. For a moment Sophia thought she was going to embrace her, but she drew back. Her words, when she spoke, had sympathy in them. But they were firm.

'Sophia. We rule this house, but we also serve it. In this castle alone two hundred souls look to us for their bread, their warmth, their law – but above all to keep them safe. Beyond our walls there are thousands more. You know that. I cannot make an enemy of this King. Nor should I – we – surrender a chance to give all the Kingdom peace, by making an undisputed King strong. And . . .' She turned away. 'And, yes, he has let cruel things be done in his name. That does not mean that he is a monster in his own house. He is a young man – nearer your age than mine. His father and elder brother died in Tarceny's rising. His surviving brother was killed by Septimus, and I had some part in that. The house where he grew is a ruin. He has known nothing but enmity and war. He is swift, moody – I hear these things

306

from Brother Martin, whom I sent to him. But I do not think him a monster.'

There was a scratch at the door to the council chamber, and it opened.

'My lady, the counsellors . . .'

'Let them wait a moment yet!' snapped the Widow. She turned back to her daughter.

'Sophia. I have been pleased with you, these past months. You have worked. You have attended court and council. You have shown thought for others . . .'

'Yes – yes, but you don't know *why*!' cried Sophia, and stamped her foot. And before her mother could speak she ran from the room.

The council chamber was full of men, men in robes, men in gowns, men in armour, buzzing with the news that Velis would be in Develin in three days. The stores to be gathered, the ordering of accommodation, who was going to move out of their rooms . . . She pushed past them, their faces blurring in her tears. They saw she was weeping. She felt their embarrassment, and hated them for it. She was in the corridor now, running. She could hear the shock in their voices fading behind her.

To begin with, she did not know where she was going. Her feet carried her down stairs, through the great hall and out into the early morning. No one followed her. The rule about escorts had lapsed since the return from the winter tour. And no one remembered rules at a time like this. When she came to herself in the angle of the upper courtyard, she was alone.

She realized that she was looking for Chawlin. She would have to tell him. They would have to decide what to do together. Because the Widow was right. Sophia knew she was right. But she *could* not go to be Velis's bride. And she *could* not give up Chawlin. And she did not know what to do.

A door opened in the foot of the corner-tower, and out came a man. It was Denke, the disgraced Law Master, with scrolls under his arm. He saw her, and bowed his head as if to avoid her look. Of course, he no longer attended council or sat at high table. It would have been kinder to him and everyone if the Widow had dismissed him from the house altogether. Somehow she had never summoned the will. So he was still among them, barely speaking and barely spoken to, a living image of the listlessness that had fallen on the house. Heaven knew what meaninglessness he was finding to keep himself busy – teaching the scholars, perhaps.

Denke walked past her, saying nothing, with the same hollow look in his eyes that had been there ever since he had damned his own discipline at Ferroux. She watched his back as he passed under an arch and out of sight.

'I wanted to talk to you,' said a voice beside her.

It was Luke.

'Not now,' she said, crossly, turning away. She walked slowly, trying to think where Chawlin might be at this hour.

Luke was still at her side. 'It's important,' he insisted.

'Please leave me alone.'

'We're in danger.'

'I know that,' she said.

Did he know already? Would it be like this all day, with people running to her with their fears, wanting to know what she was going to do? Would Hestie talk at her about the Whore of Tarceny all over again?

'I want you to go to your mother. Tell her . . .'

'I've spoken with her already. Go away and leave me.'

'Not about this. They're after something that's in this house. That's what they want. You mustn't let them . . .'

'Who? What are you talking about?'

She kept walking as they spoke, hoping that he would see that she wanted him to go away; but he persisted.

'There's a man I see at night. He's one of Velis's counsellors. They want something from this house. You know what it is.'

Now she stopped.

'Velis – you're seeing one of Velis's men? How?'

Spies?

Then her mind absorbed the other things he had said. She remembered that he had heard what Chawlin had been saying by the fountain at Ferroux. He hadn't just been interrupting, then. He had been *eavesdropping*. She turned on him.

'If you tell anyone . . .'

'I haven't. I promise you. But he wanted me to tell him. He's threatening me. There are things – you don't see them, or if you do you think they are just normal. But they are not. They can come into the house. They want to kill me. Or he'll do it.'

The thought came to her, as clear as a voice in her head, that this was just a poor, demented boy who made fantasies and thought they were real.

She accepted it, because she had heard that voice before. There was no point being angry. But she must get away. She had important things to do.

'Luke . . .'

He had stepped back, and was watching her as though she had suddenly become unfriendly. His hand was on his pouch, which held those maddening stones.

'Luke. I'm upset, and I'm busy. Take your story to Padry and let him do what needs to be done.'

'He won't believe me.' He was still eyeing her carefully. He was calculating, she thought. 'But you've met him – the man I'm talking about. He was one of the riders that came here on the day you were out of the castle.'

She stared at him.

'How did you know about that?'

'I talk with demons.'

He is mad, said the voice in her mind. She might have said it aloud.

'Then who is that standing beside you?' the boy asked.

Sophia looked around. There was no one there.

'You *filth*!' she cried, furiously. 'Get away from me! Leave me alone!' And she ran from the courtyard and left him there.


Ambrose stood his ground in the angle of the upper courtyard, and looked where Sophia had been. Just out of the centre of his vision was a figure in a grey robe and hood. Somewhere in Ambrose's head a voice was screaming.

It was the Heron Man, standing there. Ambrose had an impression of a pinched nose, and deep lines on the face under the hood. That skin must be dry, like paper if he touched it. He could not see the eyes . . .

But he could feel them.

They were deep, like pits. They bore on him with the weight of years run dry of all weeping. They were tired,

310

dull, listless, as if all the malice of the Heron Man was only a crust upon the immense weariness within his brain. They looked at him, and they despised him. He felt like a tiny cockroach under pouring sand, drowning beneath vast sediments of time.

No! He could feel his hand on his pouch, clicking the stones again and again. The sound seemed light and very feeble.

No! Go away!

For long moments more the eyes watched him: slow, with that appalling heaviness. The mouth twitched – into a smile that mocked him.

The Heron Man turned away. In that instant Ambrose saw that his enemy was standing not in the courtyard, but in the landscape of brown stones where nothing grew. Then he vanished as he had come.

He was standing in the upper courtyard, and the monster was gone. He could feel how his heart beat and his breath staggered. He waited for his head to clear. The sky above him was still that of early morning. The sight of the Heron Man could have lasted only moments.

I saw him, he thought. I heard him and looked, and I saw him there.

They don't know him. They can't see him. I can.

What now?

He had to talk to someone. The Lynx was gone. She hadn't seen the Heron Man as he stood at her elbow. She was angry with him.

He could look for Chawlin. Chawlin still met him for practice bouts, as he had promised. But he was less friendly, after Ferroux. Ambrose knew that he had interrupted something important, then. But he did not think it was just that. Chawlin had not wanted to listen, in the garden. Why should he listen now?

And only the Lynx could speak to the Widow. She was still the best person.

He must simply try again.

It would not be easy to approach her now, with all the duties and business of the house around her. He would have to get a message to her. How could he do that? As a middle-study scholar, who was supposed to know his letters, he did not even have a writing slate.

His feet took him through the student kitchens to the School Stair, and up them to the library. The building was quiet. Everyone was out. Something must have happened to cancel lessons for the morning. He could not imagine what that might be. It had not happened before. But in this strange time it did not seem strange.

The presses of the library were full of scrolls and books and quires, each bearing the knowledge of years. And yet each was mere paper: paper on which his words might be written.

Tearing a work in the library would earn him the worst beating the masters could give him, if they found out. But even that seemed less important to Ambrose than his message. He was casting around the shelves for a suitable scroll when someone at the reading press on the other side of the passage sighed and sat up.

Ambrose jumped. He had thought the room was empty.

It was the master Padry, looking at him with bleary

eyes. There were scrolls open on the reading shelf in front of him. He must have been sitting quite still, with his head in his hands, for Ambrose to have missed him. There was a dead lantern at his elbow – here, in the room where no flame was allowed. From the crumpled look of his heavy green robe, he must have been sitting there all night.

'Boy.'

'Yes, master?'

'What is the second arc of the path of Croscan?'

Croscan?

He knew this. This had been in the lessons.

Touch the heart. Breathe.

'It is the path of the soul,' he answered. 'From defeat and ruin on earth to the ascent of the spirit through the spheres.'

'And what, on the second arc, is the import of the Moon?'

'It is the crisis of the soul, when Truth and Untruth meet. It is the Trial of Faithfulness.'

'Give me, then, three signs of Faithfulness – in any system. All are good, to me.'

Three signs of Faithfulness. Ambrose drew breath. Then he hesitated.

What was Faithfulness?

And he saw how his question was mirrored in the slightest widening of Padry's eyes. He saw the anguish within them.

Padry no longer knew the answer.

*What was Faithfulness?* If even a master had lost it . . .

But there was a sign – a very obvious one.

'The Lantern of Tuchred Martyr.'

313

Padry nodded. Ambrose could not tell if the master had forgotten even this, or if he had remembered it but thought it not enough.

'The oak leaf . . .'

'Oak leaf?' Padry frowned. 'Oak stands for strength, perhaps for Fortitude, but it has no purpose to cleave to.'

Ambrose wanted the oak leaf. It was his.

'The oak grows to the light, master . . .'

'And you have already given me a light. But – well . . . No, I will not quibble. A third, then. A good one.'

Ambrose wanted to say *a knight in the mist*. But that would mean nothing to Padry. And there was another, better one, as obvious to Ambrose as the Light of the Martyr.

'The hill people say it is the dragon Capuu, who binds the world together.'

'The dragon!' Padry blinked.

'So it is, so it is . . .'

Padry looked at the air in front of him, as if he was gathering his thoughts at last.

'Well,' he said.

'Well, if you know all that, then maybe what we do here is not in vain. If only One has learned, it may yet be enough . . . The Lantern, the Leaf and the Dragon. I will meditate upon those.'

He rose unsteadily from his place, and looked around him. 'What was it you wanted in the library?'

It had been from that very bench that Padry had dragged him to his beating. And yet it seemed to Ambrose that two humans on the edge of despair should trust one another.

314

'Paper,' he said.

'Paper?' Padry paused. 'Let me show you what I do when I am in need.'

He took the scroll in front of him and folded over the last finger's width of the bottom margin.

'Will that be enough?'

'Yes.'

Padry took from his pocket a sharp knife and, without hesitating for a second over the damage he did, carefully slit the scroll so that the folded paper came free. He handed it to Ambrose – a thin, straight scrap of blank sheet, with space for a dozen words.

'You will want pen and ink, I suppose. You may use mine. Take them to my cell when you have finished, and leave them there. I shall not need them this morning.'

He straightened, placed the scroll back into its rack, and walked slowly from the room. Ambrose sat in his place, and found the wood of the bench was still warm. Alone, and surrounded by the knowledge of centuries, he dipped the quill pen in the ink-bottle and began to scratch out his appeal.

He had only ever written on slate before – never on paper like this. It was harder than he had thought it could possibly be.

# XVI

## The Secrets of Develin

ophia was in the turret of the wall-tower, waiting for Chawlin. The sun was low under a mass of grey-purple clouds, bathing Develin in a gold light. It did nothing for her mood. This glory would slip from the stones in moments. Within, she was all anger and impatience.

Where was he?

She remembered his face when she had caught him that morning and told him about Velis. His smile had dropped, deadened all at once, as though the muscles in his cheeks had lost their power.

'We need to think,' he had said. 'We need to think.'

He had thought, and she had seen that his thoughts had led him nowhere. All he had said was: 'Meet me this evening in the wall-tower above the angle of the upper courtyard. It's a good place. We can talk there.'

It seemed to Sophia that there was not much to think about. Develin could not fight. Velis was too powerful, and the Widow would not do it. If she wed, they must be torn apart. She had thought wildly of poisoning Velis, somehow. But she did not know how. And she could not see herself doing such a thing. There was only one answer.

At her feet lay a coarse sack that she had brought across the courtyard and hauled up the steep stair. She touched it, as if to make sure that it was still there.

Where was he?

Footsteps sounded, coming up the tower. The trapdoor creaked open. Chawlin's head appeared through the gap.

'I'm sorry to be late,' he said, climbing onto the platform. 'Luke was following me, trying to find out where you were. He truly is crazy, I think, and now it is worse. I had to go and hide in the stables for a bit.'

She scowled.

'I don't want to talk to him.'

'I guessed not.' He cocked his head on one side to look at her, and the lines around his mouth were grim. 'So, then . . .'

She waited.

'So we now must face things as they are, and not as we would like them to be,' he said. 'There's no choice.'

'No.'

'I should have said this before,' he said. 'I am ashamed of myself. But it is useless that either of us should pretend about things that are not going to happen. You owe your mother duty, and I owe her a great debt. Even thinking that you may – step down to where I am . . . It's a betrayal. I've been stupid. I've liked your company too much. You would be right to hate me now. The only mercy is that we have done nothing but dream . . .'

He was saying they should give up, and part.

'. . . We both know it. You will have to – you will have to do as your mother asks.' He said the last words in a rush.

317

Sophia was silent for a moment. He was so obviously wrong that she could not feel more than mildly disappointed in him. *I've liked your company too much.* He was letting his head rule his heart, that was all. She only had to show him the truth.

'There is a choice,' she said. 'We can choose what we want. Or we can choose what we don't, because we're afraid. I know what I want. I need to know what it is you want.'

He sighed. 'It's no use thinking like that . . .'

'You have to tell me.'

'Sophia! You are – very dear to me. Indeed you are. But you are just at the beginning. For each two years that you have lived, I have three or four . . .'

'And I love you,' she said, for the first time in her life.

It stopped him. When he spoke again it was slowly, as though his words hurt him.

'Marriage is a big change – all the more so for someone who is young. There must be scores of girls every year who dream of escape when their betrothal is announced. Yet I only know of one who did . . .'

'So now it will be two!'

'Only *one* who did, Sophia. She ran to be the bride of Tarceny. And there was war.'

She stared at him. The Whore – the Whore of Tarceny. *He* was throwing that woman at her, now.

'Do not use that name to me! Do *not* use it!' she yelled in his face.

'I don't think you know yourself,' he said, as she gathered breath again. 'Running would change your life. It would change mine, too,' he went on. 'It's not been much. But it's not been bad either.'

'Do you like living near something, knowing you can't reach it?'

The sack lay at her feet, but she did not touch it yet.

'It's better that I do not . . .'

'Don't you want me, then?' (You do, she thought. You do. Why can't you say it?)

His forearms jerked in frustration.

'I don't think you know what you want!' he cried.

How silly. Of course she knew.

'I want you,' she said deliberately. 'I love you. I can prove it to you.'

'That's . . .'

'No, look.'

From the sack at her feet she lifted it. She heard him choke.

The large, roughly-cut stone cup lay in her hands. It was heavy and awkward, with its thick stem and a base like a two-handed goblet. Around the rim curled a vague form that might have been a serpent or snake.

'Michael's Wings! Why . . . ?'

'You wanted it.'

'Michael's Wings!' he said again. 'What if you had been caught?'

'I don't care.'

The council chamber had been empty. So had her mother's anteroom, with the writing desk and the secret drawer. The drawer had opened to the touch of her fingers. The key had been there. It had fitted the lock of the chest, as she had guessed it would. Within there had been boxes and heaps of letters, many of them in a hand that she knew had been her father's. At another time she would have seized on them and read them, to help her remember him. But she had not come for them. She had come looking for the cup, cut from plain stone, that Chawlin had brought to Develin. She had guessed it would be in the chest, and there it had been, nestling among the papers. She had taken it because she could.

She had taken it, secured the chest again, and was gone in less than a minute, with a sureness as if someone had been telling her that no one would ever know what she had done.

Chawlin turned it in his hands. All at once he let out his breath.

'I don't know . . . I don't know . . .'

'I thought you might know how it could help us.'

'I carried it. I never used it, or saw it used. Tarceny used it, and he was torn to pieces. It's dangerous. It must be.'

'I can take it back, if you don't want it.'

He shook his head. Of course he wanted it.

'No. No, let me think.'

He stood there, staring at the thing in his hands. Beyond him, the light was fading. The glow of the walls had slipped to a dull orange. It would soon be the hour for supper. The Widow would want to talk with her then, and afterwards, about her duty. This would be her last chance to speak with Chawlin today.

He must decide!

He wanted the cup. She knew that. If he wanted to keep it he would have to flee. If he fled, he might as well take her with him.

Still Chawlin knelt there, thinking, turning the thing at arm's length as if to find some hidden catch or crevice in it. The deepening shadows of the house settled on his face.

Awkwardly, as if he did not quite know what to do, but was being told by someone else, he put the thing down on the floor between them. Sophia crouched beside him. Chawlin rested one hand on the rim of the cup and then drew it away, palm still inwards towards the bowl. His lips were moving, soundlessly.

'What are you saying?'

'Just some words I— Look! Look!'

The bottom of the cup was filling, from nowhere, with water. It swirled brownly in the bowl. A scent of damp stone came to Sophia, recalling – what? She had smelled it before. At night somewhere. She could not remember.

'How did you do that?' she asked, shocked at the simplicity of the miracle.

'It – it came to me. I . . .'

'What do we do now?'

'Look,' he said at last.

'What for?'

'Ideas. Help, perhaps.'

'Let's look then,' she urged. 'We haven't much time.'

Still something about that plain stone bowl – maybe just a memory – made him hesitate. A hiss of impatience escaped her. He must have heard it.

He bent over the water in the dimming light. Sophia tried to peer in, too. She could see nothing. Perhaps it was just the angle at which she was looking at the water. But Chawlin began to murmur again, softly to himself. His eyes were fixed on the bowl. Something was happening, there. What was it? Why didn't he tell her?

'Rocks,' said Chawlin. 'Rocks. What place is that? No trees, grass or houses. It is not the mountains . . . Ho. Different now. Sunlight . . .'

Sophia looked at him, and at the water again. It was plain, a little brown and smelly, she thought. He seemed rapt in it. Perhaps the cup was speaking only to him, not her.

'There – found it! Did you see that?'

'No. What?'

'My home – the manor where I was raised at Greyfells. But there's no help to be had there,' he went on, half to himself. 'My uncle could not hide us, even if he wanted to. What about . . . ? Ah, that's how. There, can you see?'

It was just brown water.

'No,' she said.

'My keep, at Hayley in the March of Tarceny. It's all a ruin now. But it's not bad land, and there are few that live there.'

She knelt back, struggling with the suspicion that this was all a trick, and that he was just pretending, to humour her. But why would he be doing that? It was a risk for him even to be here.

Horrible thoughts came in a horrible time. She loved him. She must also trust him. She watched him, trying to guess whether he had made up his mind without saying so. He was intent on the bowl, and did not look at her. Perhaps he was using it as a way of putting off having to decide. Maybe she should not have shown it to him until he had done. But . . .

Something struck the side of the bowl with a sharp *rap!* and skittered away.

'What was that?'

'A twig. Someone threw it in from below!'

Who knew they were there? She jumped up to peer over the roofed parapet into the courtyard. A boy was down there, looking up at her.

'Luke!' she hissed, and stepped back out of sight.

They were both silent for a moment, listening for a step on the stair.

'So he managed to find us after all,' said Chawlin, still kneeling on the floor. 'He's clever, no doubt about it. I should have remembered that I brought him here. And he knows we are together. What does he want?'

'He wants to tell me his nightmares,' Sophia said bitterly. Why had she shown herself? At her foot was the twig that had landed on the platform. There was a small roll of paper around it. She picked it up, between a disdainful thumb and finger.

Chawlin was looking into the bowl again.

'It's changed,' he said. 'Why has it done that?'

'What can you see?'

'A man and a woman – in a mountain valley. He's a knight . . . It's not us . . . Why is it showing me this?'

Sophia's impatience was growing, and with it, the beginnings of fear. Already one person in the castle knew where they were. She did not like the way Chawlin kept poring over the cup. She did not like not being able to see what it showed him. She should have been more careful, she thought. She could have talked to him about it, before giving it to him. What they were doing was witchcraft – real witchcraft! Many people thought witchcraft was worse than murder.

There was so little time!

'Michael's Wings!' said Chawlin again. 'It is him –
Lackmere!'

'Who?'

'My old captain . . .'

'Can he help us?' (Chawlin! Remember what you are
doing here!)

'Maybe. He is no friend of Velis. He could be
anywhere on the edge of the Kingdom. Maybe he is in
exile after Septimus's fall. He looks fit enough, whatever.
Who is the woman, though? She is . . .'

Suddenly Chawlin exclaimed and bent forward, as if
to force a closer look from the narrow waters.

'What is it?'

'I know her – or knew her! Angels above . . . So *she's*
alive, too. Where has she been all this time?'

'Who?'

'That's the bride of . . . That's the mother of our
Luke . . .'

'He's orphaned.'

'Apparently not.'

'So you know his family then?'

Slowly, Chawlin withdrew his gaze from the cup. 'I
guessed . . .' He looked at her, then dropped his eyes as
though wondering how much to say. 'It changed – it
changed when his twig hit it. It knew him.'

Sophia peered out again into the courtyard. It was
empty. Luke was gone. Night was nearly on them. From
her vantage point she could see the upper walls of the
main courtyard, reflecting the glow of the braziers that
had been set by the doors of the great hall. Distantly,

the sound of the house gathering for supper came to her.

She should be down there.

'What does it mean?'

'I must think.'

Sophia nearly stamped her foot again.

'Why don't you *tell* me?'

He looked at her again. 'What do you want me to tell you?'

After a moment she said: 'Tell me what you are going to do.'

That was what mattered – not Luke; not the cup; not even that he loved her. What was he going to *do*?

'I will think . . .'

'You've been thinking all day!'

'Sophia. We're on the edge of a cliff. If we jump, maybe we can fly. But maybe we will kill ourselves. We need to be sure – both about what we want to do, and about whether we can do it.'

'There's no time! What if the King wants to take me away with him?'

'It's hardly likely, is it?'

'He's coming himself, the day after tomorrow. He thinks it's all settled!'

Chawlin pulled at his lip. The shadows of evening had grown about them. She could barely see his face.

'We could not just set out as we are in any case. It would take a day, maybe two, for me to gather the very least we would need. I may start storing it up by that fishing shelter you hid in the day we met. At the same time I want to think. And you must think, too. If, in two days, we are both sure – and I think we can – we will go.'

Sophia groaned. Two days!

'What was it Luke wanted?' Chawlin asked.

She looked at the twig. She did not care what Luke wanted. But she picked at the twine that held the scrap of paper, unrolled it, and lifted it in the last light of sunset. 'It says: *Please meet me at noon tomorrow on the chapel steps.* That's all.'

'Better to see him, if you can.'

'Why?'

'It will keep him quiet. I doubt he would carry stories of us to your mother. But if he were minded to – well, at least hearing him out will win us time.'

Sophia stared out over the parapet. Everything was suddenly difficult, and complex. The threat of marriage bore down upon her like a galloping knight. And now there was the threat of discovery, too. What would Luke do? She had no idea. The boy was gone. The stone angles of her home were empty. She had stolen the cup from her mother's chest. And she must stay here for at least two more days.

'What shall we do with that thing?' she asked, nodding towards it.

'Does your mother open the chest often?'

'I don't think so.'

'Then I'll hold it for now. It is safer than putting it back and getting it out again.'

He was going to keep it.

'I must go,' she said.

They embraced. She put her ear to his chest. She heard the warm heart thudding within it. Then she let him go. He pulled up the trapdoor for her. Even as he bade

326

her goodnight his eyes were going back to the cup, as if he wanted to peer into it again. But the water was vanished from it, without either of them seeing where it had gone. With a deep depression in her spirit, she began to pick her way down the stairs.

He had not even said that he loved her.

The hours that followed were long. She could do nothing except give promises that she knew she would betray if she possibly could. She stood in the Widow's chamber, answering her mother shortly and hanging her head, but swearing, when it came to it, that she did indeed understand her duty and would do as she was bid. The Widow did not seem to be reassured.

'Remember,' she said at least twice, 'you have not been out of Develin before, except to my other manors. There will be many things in Tuscolo and Velis for you that you have not seen. At your age you should rejoice at that.'

'Yes, my lady,' Sophia replied, thinking that the Widow did not sound very convinced herself. She was acutely conscious, as she stood there, of the secret drawer in the writing desk that she had rifled for the key, and of the emptiness in the bowels of the chest next door, where the cup had been. She did not think the chest had been opened in months. But what if someone did so now?

What if Chawlin was found with the cup?

Many times that evening she thought that she should not have taken the cup to him. She had known it was precious. She had known that it meant much to Chawlin. She had barely thought of the terrible reputation of Tarceny, and of what his thing might hold within it. It was dangerous, Chawlin had said. And yet he had taken it. She should have thought, harder and longer, instead of acting on the strange impulse that had crept into her head as she had passed down the living-quarter corridor and found the council chamber empty.

And yet the impulse had been right. Until he had seen the cup he had been ready to accept defeat and live apart. Somehow – she was not quite sure how – she had known that; and she had known, too, what might jolt him into seeing the world a different way.

At least he was thinking again. At least they had a chance.

She wanted to see him, and talk to him, and be sure that he would not try to persuade her to accept Velis. But that was impossible. For the next two days she must stay away from him altogether. So after her mother dismissed her, she wandered the house until it was time to lie down, and in the morning, after a sleepless night, she ignored her lessons and sought out unused rooms in the upper levels of the living quarters where she could be alone.

She tried to imagine what life would be like with Chawlin, if indeed they made their escape. He seemed to want to go back to his old keep near the mountains. That made sense – they should be as far away as possible from Velis (*she* could not call him 'the King') for as long as that man lived. In the shell of the keep they would build – she had no idea how – a cottage, perhaps, and live upon the milk of goats and bees' honey. And she would greet him when he came home from fishing the mountain streams and remind him of what he had been doing – and she had been doing – on the day they first met.

328

It was hard to believe in, but she tried, just as she tried firmly to believe that Velis was not so mad a lord as to take revenge on Develin when she disappeared. The Widow would be humiliated. She would be furious, too. Sophia could not help that. In a way, she thought, it was at least partly her mother's fault. She should have sent Velis's messenger away. She should not even be accepting Velis as King. She should have fought him from the beginning. Instead, she was just expecting that Sophia would do what was good for Develin.

At last she left her refuge and began to descend the stair to the main living-quarter corridor. She had, she thought, less than half an hour of liberty left. After that she must dress to meet the ambassador of Velis, who was expected shortly before noon.

And after *that*, if she could, she must slip away and let the boy Luke have his say at her. As if she didn't have enough to worry about already!

Bright sunshine slanted through the windows of the living-quarter corridor. The walls were barred with black shadow. A new thought came to her, almost naturally, just as the plan about the cup had come the day before.

The thought was of her father.

Father had always been a rule to live by when the world was stupid and unreasonable. Ever since her childhood she had been able to imagine him understanding, even encouraging her, when she ventured into things of which the Widow disapproved. Father wouldn't have allowed this dreadful offer of marriage. She tried to imagine him now, speaking calmly in the halls of Develin, while the messengers of Velis trembled at the softness in his voice.

It was difficult. The voice was wrong. And she could not stop herself from thinking that he might turn his eyes on her and ask: why is it like this?

*It's because you're leaving Develin*, the thought told her. *You're leaving him, too.*

She stood at the door of the council chamber, just as she had stood the day before. She was thinking: Father had lived here. All her thoughts and memories of him were set in Develin, their home. Now she was going to have to remember him from far away. She found that her image of him (peering from within the visor of his helmet, smiling, understanding) was already weaker than she had ever known it. She did not want to forget him.

*His letters are in the chest*, the thought said. *You saw them.*

The latch of the council chamber clacked in her hand.

The chamber was empty. The Widow was with the butler, hopelessly trying to decide how to take a week's supply of food and drink for a king's retinue (of unknown size) out of the cellars, and yet see the household through the spring without going to short commons. Sophia stood in the middle of the room, wrestling with the image of her father in her mind. Under the Widow's chair was the chest of secrets, apparently undisturbed. Letters from Father lay within it. She had seen them yesterday. She knew how easy it was to open the chest. The secret drawer was in the writing desk in the next room.

She knocked at the door, and there was no answer. She opened it. The Widow's antechamber, too, was as empty as it had been yesterday. She crossed to the writing desk, finding and pressing firmly upon the hidden catches – just as Father had shown her, smiling at the joke of the springing drawer when she had sat upon his knee all those years ago.

Did he smile now? Perhaps he did.

The key was a little-barrelled black thing. She took it, as she had taken it yesterday, and retraced her steps swiftly into the council chamber. She remembered Chawlin's warning about the risk of discovery and closed the outer door. Only the Widow would enter without knocking, and she was busy elsewhere.

She knelt before her mother's seat, and opened the chest.

The cup was gone from the middle of it. Around the space where it had lain yesterday was piled paper upon paper, small, folded, bound and addressed in her father's hand. She reached in for one.

Then, at last, she wondered at what she was doing. She had wanted something of Father's. Each one of the papers was written in her father's hand. But the names on the direction were not hers.

*To My Lady Develin, in Develin, to be borne by Special Messenger* . . .
*To My Lady Develin, in Armany, to be borne by Special Messenger* . . .
*To My True Love, The Lady Develin, in Develin* . . .
*To My Lady Develin* . . .
*To My Beloved Lady Develin* . . .

These words did not belong to her. They were for her mother – his wife, his love. Sophia could see that. She understood about love, now. Father was with the Angels, and

331

whatever was left of him on earth must rest here. All she could take with her would be wisps of memories. And for the first time she thought she understood the loss that the Widow had endured when he had vanished from the world.

Suddenly, somewhere, a trumpet sounded. She jumped.

The gate-horn! They would have seen the King's messenger from the gate-towers. She must go to her chambers to be dressed, quickly, and then down to greet the arrivals at her mother's side. She must go on playing the part she had set for herself.

She put her hand on the lid of the chest, thinking, Goodbye, Father. She was about to close it. Then another paper caught her eye. There was no direction. Instead, in writing Sophia knew as well as her own, her mother had scrawled: LUQUERCUNAS – LUKE.

Luke. She was due to meet with him soon. He knew she had met with Chawlin. What was it that the Widow kept in this chest about him?

Now the impulse that had lured her here, coaxing and wheedling, for the second time in two days, spoke. Clear as the voice of a man in her head, she felt the thought.

*Take it. Read it. If he wants to use what he knows against you, then you should know about him, too.*

And then, because she could, she picked the letter from among the others. It was crumpled. She straightened it. There was writing on it, in a hand she did not know. It read:

*To My Dear Beloved Friend Evalia diManey. One has come to loose Him. I beg you take care of my son Ambrose. Your friend Phaedra, of Trant and Tarceny.*

That was all.

Footsteps passed in the corridor, moving swiftly. Men murmured in hurried voices as they went by outside. There were calls from the courtyard. Ignoring the sounds, Sophia stared at the paper and read it again.

Luke – Ambrose.

*Tarceny!*

'Martin,' said the Widow, as the King's ambassador swung himself down from the saddle in the upper courtyard. ''Fore all the Angels, I had not dared hope it would be you.'

'I begged His Majesty that it might be, my lady,' said the priest. 'Since I knew his house and yours, and might serve both at once today. And I have been eager to see your courts again.'

He looked around him as he spoke, at the roof-lines, the towers, the faces that crowded into the courtyard for a sight of the royal messenger.

Eager? thought Sophia sourly. She sidled into her place beside her mother, trying to control her breathing after her run through the corridors. If Brother Martin had been eager to return, then he did not know this house as she did. It had become an evil place, all riddled with lies. She saw that clearly, now. It was almost surprising that Brother Martin did not. He was smiling broadly and nodding to the familiar faces he saw around him. Beyond him, his escort was dismounting – a valet, a bannerman and a dozen men-at-arms, all wearing on their chests the Eagle and Ship badge that Velis had adopted for his device.

333

Sophia looked at them suspiciously. They seemed ordinary enough.

'Come, let me embrace you,' said the Widow, and wrapped the monk in a brief and strong hug. 'We have much to speak of. I will not hide from you, Martin, that we are in some anxiety over this – proposal – of the King. And not least that it is so sudden. In faith,' she forced a laugh, 'I think my poor cellarmen will hang themselves in a row if they must feed his full retinue from tomorrow!'

'From tonight, my lady. This is the first thing that I have to tell you. For the King presses his pace. You must look for his banners before nightfall.'

'Tonight! How? Is he so eager to carry away my poor daughter?'

'He is such a man, my lady, that when he is set on a thing, it must be done at once,' said Martin as they began to mount the steps into the hall together. 'As for your poor daughter, I must confess to her and to you that I am responsible for this. For I have long been at pains to show him that he needs allies, not enemies, if he is to rule.'

'Do not mistake me. I would do much to spare my house the fate of Bay.'

'I swear to you, my lady, that what happened at Bay was an evil I could not prevent. But if the lives of Bay were precious, it seemed to me that the lives and learning in Develin were ten times more so, for their own sake and for all our wretched Kingdom. Therefore I have been the most eager of all Velis's people to persuade him to this course.'

'I do not fault you. But tonight! Angels have pity on us . . .'

The counsellors were crowding up the stair after them, eager to hear more. Sophia hung back to let them pass. She had no wish to be noticed.

The house was full of snakes, she thought bitterly. Brother Martin should have been a friend. Now she knew it was he who had hatched this plot to marry her to Velis. To save the school, of all things! And the Widow agreed with him!

And across the courtyard a figure was sitting on the chapel steps. It was noon, and the boy she had known as Luke was waiting for her there. He was sitting quietly, and all alone, looking her way. She could sense the appeal in his eyes even from where she stood.

*You* can wait, she thought, as she followed the others up into the hall. Ambrose of Tarceny? Child of the Whore! You can wait! I know who you are, now.

Your father killed my father, you viper. And you've lived in my house all these months, pretending to be a boy from nowhere. The Widow knew. Chawlin guessed. They did not tell me. They knew me too well. No one *dared* to tell me!

You can wait there for *ever*!


Ambrose sat on the chapel steps. He had watched the party of riders come up from the inner gatehouse, carrying strange banners, which he assumed were the King's. Was this the 'other way' that the Wolf had spoken of last night, already unfolding? Surely it was too soon. But if the King was coming here, then time must be running out. He needed to speak to the Widow's daughter – to the girl he still thought of as the Lynx.

He had seen her in the crowd. He had willed her to look across at him, to see that he was there. And she had. Then she had followed the rest of them into the hall.

He told himself that she would be making her way around inside the house, through the hall and the corridors to the back of the chapel, to emerge on the steps behind him. He began to rehearse, again, the phrases that he might use to convince her.

*There's something hidden in this house. I heard Chawlin talking to you about it at Ferroux. I don't know if he told you what it was. I'll tell you. It's a cup, and it's hidden because it is witchcraft. It doesn't matter how I know – just ask your mother if it is true.*

*That's what they want. One of the King's counsellors wants it. He wants it because . . .* No, better not try to explain all that. *That's what they want. They sacked Bay because they thought it was there. Don't trust them.*

The courtyard was quiet now. The horses of the King's troop were stabled. The crowd had gone in. One or two scholars sauntered around on the far side. Some castle folk were clearing out the lean-to next to the forge. No doubt they would need all the space they could make. They would need to put up tents around the walls too, just as the Widow's party had done when camping at the smaller manors on the winter tour. It was lucky the weather was warm and dry.

Was she coming?

What if she didn't come? She had not wanted to talk to him yesterday, but she had been in a hurry then. So he had given her time to think. If she still did not want to speak with him, he would have to find a place and time where he could make her listen. Or . . . no, he'd have to talk to Chawlin. He was supposed to meet Chawlin for a practice-bout that evening, by the river. If he could make Chawlin listen, then together they might persuade the Lynx. Then she could go to her mother.

It would take time. He did not know how much time they had.

Or he could go to the Widow himself. But how could he persuade her? How could he even approach her? He could not imagine himself explaining what he knew, and how he knew it, to the Widow.

He needed the Lynx to come, and come now.

The minutes seeped by. The sun was past noon. Shadows were beginning to creep outwards from the wall across the courtyard. The house was quiet. They must all be at the midday meal. Still he waited, because he could think of nothing else to do.

Someone was coming down the steps behind him.

He looked around. The Lynx was not there.

But there *was* someone on the stair.

'She will not come to you,' said a dry voice.

'She is mine, and she was the last. All this house is mine, now,' said the Heron Man.

## XVII

### The Rider in the Gate

mbrose scrambled to his feet.

'Call out,' the Heron Man said. 'No one will hear you.'

He can't touch me, thought Ambrose, clutching his pouch with the stones. I can run.

But he did not run. He felt running would be very difficult.

'And where would you run to?' said the Heron Man.

*Never listen to him, never speak with him,* she had said.

'You cannot hide from me,' said the Heron Man. 'I could have taken you the day you dropped your pouch on the stair. I could have taken you the day you placed them on the bench beside you as you ate. I did not, because I did not wish to. I have something to show you. Walk with me.'

Still thinking that he could run, run if he really had to, Ambrose turned. He walked down the steps and crossed the courtyard, and the monster went with him.

He did not look at the Heron Man. He looked fixedly ahead. Yet he could see him, from the corner of his eye, stalking beside him. Around the grey figure, and beyond him, Ambrose sensed another landscape – the place of brown rocks and boulders, stretching away far beyond the walls of Develin. The creature walked through it, within a pace of Ambrose's shoulder. Ambrose felt his feet trip and stub against things, as though the beaten upper court-yard were uneven and scattered with rough brown stones.

By the Wool Tower door stood two masters of the school, Pantethon and Father Grismonde, talking. They looked up as Ambrose approached, and looked away with an embarrassed air as if they knew they should be giving lessons, but would not do so that afternoon. They made no sign of seeing his companion.

'They despaired, one after another,' murmured the Heron Man in his ear. 'You saw it. What did you do?'

Pace, pace.

'The stronger they were, the more they suffered. And they have all come to the same in the end. What could you do?'

*Never speak with him.*

Ambrose clutched the stones in his pouch, but it made no difference. The step of the Heron Man forced him onwards. A scullion passed, panting, with a pail of scraps swept from the tables after the midday meal. He glanced at Ambrose and stumbled on.

'They see you, and you only.'

Ambrose walked – or was led – up the steps of the hall and through the pointed arch of the doorway. The long room was busy with people. The tables were being cleared after the midday meal and stacked against the wall. Scullions were sweeping the boards. Others were bringing fresh-cut branches to adorn the walls – for the coming of the King, Ambrose thought. It was strange that they could be doing such a thing when the horror walked among them.

In the middle of the crowds was the Widow, with her counsellors around her. They were talking earnestly, as if strolling in some palace garden with not a soul to hear.

'I cannot promise you a sure outcome,' one of them was saying. He was a bald priest in a brown robe whom Ambrose half-remembered. 'Nothing is sure with this King. But I believe that what you do is best for all in your charge, even for the Lady Sophia.'

'Hah. She does not think so. But if the King will have peace, then I must help him build it.'

'In all truth my lady, I have worn my soul thin through talking peace with this man.'

'It shall be worth your *soul*, so that you *heal* him at the same time,' said the Widow. Some of her counsellors chuckled, dutifully.

'The wheezing of courtiers,' murmured the Heron Man. 'Their laughter died long ago.'

Ambrose saw the bald priest look his way and frown, as if with recognition. His face was familiar. He did not see who stood at Ambrose's shoulder.

'Indeed, my lady,' said the bald priest. 'Would that I could. But I fear he endures me only because it makes others of his advisers less sure of themselves.'

'I would that you take care, Martin. I shall not forgive myself if your good words are repaid with his sword.'

'I take what care I may. He does not like to be asked to trust. And trust is what I must forever ask him, if he is to forge peace.'

'Faithfulness? Forgiveness?'

340

'Birdsong to him, my lady. He knows only Force.'

'Yet you do him a service, and greater than he can imagine.'

'And useless, of course. Useless,' whispered the Heron Man as they passed.

The bald monk was glancing back at Ambrose, again with a frown on his face.

'He is a fearful man, my lady. If he has cause, or even thinks he has cause, to believe someone plots against him . . .'

'The same thought had come to me,' said the Widow, firmly looking in another direction. 'We shall be careful.'

With a jerk of his chin, the Heron Man directed Ambrose away.

'They fear death,' he said. 'They fear you may be the cause of their death. And yet they have already died. Their bodies will only follow.'

They were all his. All the people of this thronging house belonged to the Heron Man. He moved among them, unseen, whispering thoughts, and they would never suspect that he had been there. They did not see him. They would never help the boy they had taken in. They would do as the Heron Man told them. One day, at the whim of the Heron Man, they would again move to take Ambrose's stones from him. One day they might simply kill him. And he knew now that he could not run. His mind could not make his own legs do it.

Ambrose's left hand gripped the white stones through the canvas of his pouch. He clutched them so hard that they ground into his palm. Don't speak with him, the pain said. Fight, but don't speak.

'The stronger you are, the more you will suffer,' murmured the dry voice in his ear. 'This is the truth. There is no one who knows it better than I.'

Still Ambrose gripped the stones, hard enough to hurt himself, so that he could be sure they were still there.

'How long do you wish to live like this?' said the Heron Man. 'It would be better to surrender them now.'

Pace, pace, pace through the hall, and he could barely feel the floor beneath his feet. Beside him the Heron Man walked in his country of dead stones.

'There she is,' said the voice, like a thought in his mind. 'Do you want to call her now?'

The Lynx stood in the minstrel's gallery, looking down at the long hall. She must have gone up there after lunch was over. If she had thought of the boy sitting on the chapel steps, she had ignored him. He was directly underneath her, now. She had seen him. She looked down into his eyes.

'Call her.'

Ambrose opened his mouth, knowing it was hopeless. Even as he drew breath, the Lynx turned and walked down the gallery to the dark little doorway that led out above the barracks. She walked slowly, to let him see that she had seen him, and that she did not care.

She was gone.

'You brought me here,' said the low, dry voice. 'You did this to them.'

Again the thought broke into Ambrose's clouding mind: *Never speak with him.* The enemy wanted him to speak. If he spoke, he could be tricked, trapped, persuaded . . .

'You looked for me, and so I came,' said the Heron Man.
*Never speak with him.*

A second thought came in answer to the first: *Never speak. Better, easier to despair.*

And whose thought was that?

He was dumb. He could not answer if he wanted to. He could not think if he wanted to. He could not tell which thoughts were his and which were not his. They were all his, as they warred in his mind, and he could not tell the right from wrong. When you do not speak you will despair.

Fight, he thought.

Fight, though it was hopeless, like a rabbit fighting the snare that tightens on its neck.

He stood there, and his mind was a fog. And he could no longer feel the stones beneath the canvas of the pouch. The strong ones suffered most.

His fingers held the long string of the pouch. The hand of the Heron Man was open, waiting for Ambrose to put the string into it. It was something he *could* do. His hand had already begun to move.

*'You!'*

The Heron Man jerked round. All at once a weight lifted in Ambrose's mind. He raised his head.

The hall was still. People had stopped in their tracks. They stood gaping, with their pails, rushes, trestles in their arms. They were looking at him.

Up the hall, the group around the Widow had turned and was staring at him. In their midst was the bald monk. It was he who had shouted. He stood with his arm raised, pointing: at Ambrose.

Not at Ambrose, but at the man beside him.

He had seen the Heron Man.

'Hold that man! Seize him – seize him!'

People nearby stirred. One or two took a step towards Ambrose, looking doubtfully up the hall as if they did not quite know who it was they were being ordered to seize and had no idea why.

'Hold him!' cried the bald monk, urgently.

Ambrose felt the Heron Man step back from his shoulder. He twisted and reached out – through into the other place. His fingers grabbed at his enemy's cloak, and he pulled. The Heron Man stumbled forward in his grasp, into the hall. He seemed to have very little strength. Ambrose backed as his enemy came, still holding the cloth.

'There!' cried a voice. Feet were running towards him.

Ambrose looked up into the face of his enemy. The eyes were bent on him in fury – bright as a snake's and deep as the rage of the pit. His knees sagged. He felt the robe slip from his grasp, and he fell forwards. Others were close.

Get him! he begged in his mind. Get him! But he knew that the enemy was gone, stepping away into the brown land where the fingers of Develin could not touch him. He grovelled on the floor, and there were people around him. Hands were on his shoulders: warm hands.

'Has he had a fit?' asked someone at the back of the crowd.

'Didn't you see . . . ?'

'Here, Luke boy. We'll get you some water . . .'

Pushing through the crowd came the bald monk. He knelt beside Ambrose.

'Did you see him?' Ambrose gasped. 'Did you see him?'

'I heard your mother's voice,' said the man softly. 'And then I saw him. Are you hurt?'

'. . . I don't think so.'

The crowd gave back around the Widow. She looked down at them both.

'Who was that with you, Luke? Where did he come from? Where is he, now?'

'He's been here all the time. I don't know where he went.'

'All the time?'

'Who was it?' asked someone. 'I didn't see . . .'

'Some priest, I thought . . .'

'Not a priest,' said the bald monk, rising to his feet. 'Not a priest . . . By the Angels, my lady,' Ambrose heard him whisper. 'What an evil you have borne in your house!'

'I know nothing of this. Who was he?'

'I barely know. But my eyes saw him last in Tarceny, on the day that Tarceny died.'

Someone in the crowd repeated the word *Tarceny!*

'It portends something,' said a counsellor. 'An omen.'

The Widow frowned. Then she said: 'I would know what you know of this, Martin, as soon as we may speak privately.'

'My lady, you shall. And it concerns – another in your house.'

Neither of them looked at Ambrose. The crowd was close around them.

'Does it? Well, you may bring them if you think it right. Once my royal guest is in his chambers and resting from his travels, you and I shall seize a moment then – around sunset, I guess. Come to the council chamber. And,' she said, looking around at the faces of her counsellors, 'I may wish to debate this in a fuller council when there is more time – when I myself have heard what lies behind this. Now, friends, we have enough to do to last us till Easter, yet it must be done before tonight. Let us be about it . . .'

'My lady!' said Ambrose. 'The King . . . May I speak with you?'

'Quiet, you boy,' said the Widow. 'Find your friends and stay with them, or go to the infirmary if you are unwell. Do not wander.'

Ambrose looked to the bald monk, who gave the slightest shake of his head. His mouth formed the word *Sunset*.

'To it, all,' said the Widow. 'The King lies here tonight. If his rest lacks comfort, I shall have hides . . . Yes, Merivane?'

A patient stableman at last caught the Widow's eye.

'My lady – is it yet known how many horses the King brings with him?'

'Oh, indeed. Martin?'

'My lady?'

'How many horses?'

'Some nine scores. And his wagon master will look to this house for more . . .'

'Nine scores!'

'Angels help us . . .'

Sunset, thought Ambrose as he watched the crowd follow the Widow slowly down towards the double doors. Sunset: the King would be here by then. But he could not

346

have blurted out the secrets of Develin in front of all those people. She'd have stopped him, even if he had tried. At sunset, alone, she might listen. She had seen the Heron Man in her hall. He could talk to her, now.

'What will the King think of this omen,' he heard a man say, 'that on the eve of his arrival a man is seen to appear and disappear in this hall, and cause a boy to have a fit?'

'Michael's Knees, Hervan,' cried the Widow. 'This is not so strange. With the King's appearance I swear we are all having fits.'

There was a burst of laughter from the men around her.

This time, thought Ambrose, the laughter was real.

Someone was singing in the open courtyard as the house assembled. It was one of the party attaching wreaths to the poles with which the king's men would be greeted. Whoever it was was trilling away with a careless purpose and joy, as if the king's men were not already riding up to the outer gates, and there were still all the time in the world to finish his task. And in her chamber Dapea had sung and done little dance-steps as she dressed Sophia's hair and dreamed of going to Tuscolo. It made Sophia realize how little song she had heard around the castle all that winter, in a place that was normally full of music. They had all gone plodding about in their grey worlds as if the sunshine would never again break through their clouds. She could not imagine why they should start singing now, as she stood waiting in her pale silks for the man that she dreaded. But they had.

And perhaps they deserved to sing, she thought. They had done what they had been told to do, and they had done it well. There were garlands on the gates and in the hands of girls. There were wreaths, going up around her on hand-poles, to be held out to the king's riders as they came. There were stirrup-cups, and posies for the harnesses of the leading horses. The midden heaps had been cleared, and the steps to the hall strewn with scented orange-petals – the very first of the year. The lowering sun flashed upon the polished helms and shoulder-pieces of the guard. Provisions had been coming in from the manors all day. Some were still stacked in carts, ranged along the courtyard walls because there had been no time to unload them. People around her were smiling. Develin stood like a bride, decked to meet her groom.

Sophia looked at her feet and fidgeted. It was all happening too soon. And the more that happened, the more preparations that were made, the more she felt that she was being steered like a sheep into her pen. Each garland, each stirrup-cup, was another push from a pair of hands she knew towards this marriage that she found impossible to imagine.

Where was Chawlin?

Beside her, the Widow waited in her black robes. Even for her King she would not change them. In the heart of that chattering crowd she stood like a rock, with her eyes on the inner gate. She had said no words to Sophia, but had looked at her long and carefully before they had gone down the steps together. Something was worrying her. Sophia guessed, from the absent way in which her mother had dealt with the final preparations, that it was not just the King's arrival. Maybe she had sensed that her daughter could not be trusted to play her part. If so, Sophia knew she would receive another talking-to before long.

Where, in the Angels' name, was Chawlin? She had not seen him since they had parted in the turret the day before. Surely he knew, now, that the King was arriving a day earlier than expected? Was he still going about his preparations?

Or had he given up?

Could he have done that to her?

The sun had touched the western wall. Beyond the gatehouse she could hear voices. The horn sounded from the unseen towers above the outer gate. She could hear the distant crack of the doors ceremonially opening before the King's party. The noise of many hooves rose from the outer courtyard.

'They're in,' said someone near her.

Hooves, hooves, hooves. So many of them, moving at a walk. The King had brought a great company with him. Sophia looked at her mother, but the Widow's eyes remained fixed on the inner gatehouse. The inner gate stood open. The gate-guards were looking out and down into the courtyard beyond. Then they straightened and held their long pole-arms upright. A single rider appeared there, framed against the light, wrapped in a cloak and with his head bare. Then there were a crowd of them, thronging in the gateway, filing inwards into the shadowed courtyard.

'Hoorah! Develin, hoorah for the King!' bellowed Hervan.

'Hoorah!' roared the house.

349

'Health to His Majesty!' cried Hervan, again.

'Hoorah!'

'Destruction to his enemies!'

'Hoorah!'

The riders advanced slowly up to the foot of the steps. Their leader gave no sign in answer to the crowd's cheers. He rode bare-headed, with a great mane of dark hair standing out from his head in all directions. A straggling beard fell to his chest. He wore mail, and seemed to be frowning.

Father Grismonde stepped forward. 'Now thanks be to Michael, Your Majesty, that he has guarded you, and to Raphael that he has guided your way, for you are safe come.'

'Develin does not greet me herself?' said the rider.

Beside Sophia, the Widow stirred.

'I hold it more pleasing in the eyes of the Angels that their prayers shall be said first, and by their priests, Your Majesty. As for greeting you, this I now do with joy, and I bid you welcome to my house.'

The eyes of the rider flicked around the crowd. Behind him, garlands were being handed up to his followers, who took them awkwardly. Sophia thought that the leaves and flowers had looked better on their poles than they did about the necks of armoured men.

'So. A swift answer,' the man said. Without any further word he swung himself down from his horse and stood before him. He was of middle height, little taller than the Widow. And beneath his hair and beard his skin was very smooth. Sophia realized suddenly how young he was. Surely he was not much older than she. His eyes were dark and his brows heavy. If his face had any expression at all it was the faintest puzzlement. Behind him others, who must be his aides and counsellors, dismounted too. At the back of his train mailed horsemen were still filing slowly into the courtyard.

So this was the man she still hoped to escape! She had known it would be dangerous. She now saw how very dangerous he might be. She swallowed. But she knew also that she was going to try – try really hard, even if it meant losing everything. She would need guile, and help. Where was Chawlin?

The Widow was sinking into a slow curtsey, the first that Sophia had ever seen her do. After a moment she remembered herself, and curtseyed too.

'My house is yours, Your Majesty,' said the Widow. 'And my homage also.'

'In truth, madam, I had rather have seen blood these past years than hear words of homage now. Blood spilled in my cause or, if it is my enemies', then spilled to their destruction.'

'Strength spent in battle may not last,' said the Widow, evenly. 'We in Develin have nursed ours in these sad times, and now we would lend it to you, to bring the peace.'

'Peace may mask traitors that battle will expose.'

'I have not heard that there are any here, Your Majesty.'

'I will not trouble you with what I have heard.'

The Widow rose at last from her curtsey, and looked her King in the face. If she was angry at what he had said, she showed no sign of it. Instead, she nodded to Sophia.

'My daughter, sir, the Lady Sophia Cataline diCoursi Develin.'

351

Sophia met the eyes of the man who would marry her. At first she wondered if he was at all interested. Then she felt she was being stared at, as if by a boy who wanted her to insult him, so that he could start a fight. She realized, too late, that she should have remained down when her mother rose. She curtseyed again. It was better to do so twice than stand in front of this man. She could tell already that he did not like being looked in the eye.

'Your only child?'

'My only child, and my heir, sir.'

'So. I have a gift . . .'

He looked around him, as if unsure which of his followers carried what he sought. Something was handed to him. There was a faint jingle in the air and his fingers touched her shoulders.

She had thought she would shudder when he touched her. She had braced herself to fight it, so that he would not guess how she felt. But his fingers clumped upon her skin with no more feeling than if she or they were made of wood. When they lifted, they left something heavy behind them. It was a necklace.

Gift-giving! Already! And of course she had nothing to give to him in return.

'My daughter is still choosing her gift for you, Your Majesty,' said the Widow. 'It will be the best that Develin can provide.'

'So,' said the King, carelessly. 'Madam, we have travelled fast and far. If my soldiers could be quartered according to their needs . . .'

'I have arranged it. And rooms are ready for you, Your Majesty. My chamberlain will accompany you . . .'

'In time, madam. I will speak with my counsellors first.'

He turned and left them.

Can I get up now? thought Sophia. No one had signed to her that she might. But it was stupid to stay in curtsey if there was no one to curtsey to. She rose. The King had marched off and was standing among his people, a few yards away. They were talking in low voices. Sophia could see the people at the back of the ring craning to hear what was being said. Hervan was murmuring to an officer on the edge of the group and pointing to the hall, where more refreshments waited. At last, still debating whatever it was, they followed him up the steps and within.

Beside her, the Widow let out a long breath.

'It seems we are dismissed,' she said.

'I feel like fruit left hanging on the tree,' said Sophia.

Normally she would never have said that – not to the Widow. But she was angry. She thought that a man that had come all this way for her, even if unwelcome, should have shown her more attention. He should have allowed her to speak, at least. And she was angry for her mother, too. No one had spoken like that to the Widow, ever. The Widow laughed with her people, but did not allow insolence. Now she had had to endure the crudest accusations in front of her house, and speak humbly in return. She must be seething.

'Stay with me, Sophia,' said the Widow. 'There will be more business yet.'

There was. The task of settling the royal following into the castle had been divided up among officers of the house. But of course there were problems. There was too much of this, too little of that. Men kept coming up to the Widow asking what to do. More wine was brought for the stirrup-cups, for the King's men were thirsty. The crowd diminished. Sophia wondered what it was that the Widow wanted to say to her. She found herself fingering the necklace that the King had put so casually about her, and looked down at it.

They were pearls – more and larger than she had ever seen. In the evening light they seemed almost blue. They were warm too, and no wonder. Whoever it was that had carried them for the King must have borne them next to his skin for days. What that man had so casually flung about her neck must be worth a half-dozen manors.

He had touched her! And yet there had been no feeling – no life at all between her and him when he had done it. His fingers on her skin, and such wealth passing from him to her! And no feeling. What kind of marriage could this possibly prove to be?

Now she shuddered at last.

The Widow was looking at her again. If she had seen the necklace, she did not comment on it.

'Come with me, Sophia.'

She led her daughter up the steps to the hall. Sophia realized that she must want to speak in private, and wondered what it was that she was going to say. Perhaps it would be a reproof for the way she had behaved on the steps – for failing to curtsey at the right time, or something like that. Perhaps it would be worse. The Widow was worried about something. It was beginning to look more and more as though that something was indeed Sophia. And the Widow must be angry after the way the King had treated her on the steps. Sophia realized that she might have to bear that as well.

They passed through the hall. The King and his counsellors stood clustered around the great hearth, where logs were blazing. A few of them looked up as the Widow went by. Martin was with them, and Hervan. The rest all seemed to be young men, armoured, violent, who watched each other and the world around them like wild beasts. One of them was leaning on the wall a few paces apart from the others, kicking idly at the brickwork as though he was tense, waiting for something. He looked familiar.

She stopped and stared. He did not look up. He was deliberately not looking up at her, avoiding her eye. But she had seen him before. He was a young man, with coarse, brown hair that straggled around his face. She remembered that face, looking down at her. He had winked at her.

'Sophia,' called the Widow from the door, in a low voice.

Sophia picked up her skirts and hurried after her.

She had seen him before, she thought, as they climbed the spiral stairs in silence to the living quarters. He had been one of the company of riders that had passed her on the road the day she had met Chawlin. Someone had said that one of those riders had been a counsellor to the King. Who? Just a day or two ago . . .

*He's one of Velis's counsellors. They want something from this house. You know what it is.*

Luke. Ambrose of Tarceny. He had said it.

He had said that he had met this man. How and where? What did it mean?

As to what it was they wanted . . .

355

She followed her mother into the council chamber. The Widow turned to face her.

'Something happened this morning in the hall, Sophia. It reminded me of the chest I keep here. I have not thought of it for months.'

The chest had been drawn out from under the Widow's seat. The little dark key from the secret drawer was already in the lock. The Widow lifted the lid for Sophia to see. The chest lay open, with only the bed of papers inside.

'Only three people living know of the drawer where I keep my key. Myself. Hervan, whom on this I trust more than myself. And you, for your father showed you the trick when he played with you on his knee.'

The Widow was advancing on her. Her face was pale as a wall. Her eyes were dark. She must have borne this inside her for hours, and all through the interview with the King.

'Where is it, Sophia?'

Sophia shook her head. She could not think. She knew it would be fatal to answer before she could think. And Chawlin would be in danger, too . . .

Could she deny it? She had no idea what her face had given away. Everything, perhaps . . .

'Dear Angels – what are you doing with it? What are you doing to us?'

'I – to keep it safe,' she managed.

'Safe? It is deadly! Safe? What do you mean?'

'They want it – the King.'

'The King? What talk is this?'

Feet were running in the corridor. Burne, one of the

house servants, appeared at the door, panting. A welcome distraction!

'My lady . . .'

'Outside, fool!'

'My lady – the king's men. They've arrested Hervan.'

'What!'

'And Brother Martin, too. They took them into the courtyard.'

'Arrested? What do you mean?'

'They said it was for Treason!'

More feet were coming up the stairs. Armoured feet – many of them. Mail jingled. The Widow listened for a moment, appalled.

'Out of sight, both of you,' she said. 'Quickly!'

Sophia hurried past her into the writing chamber. She looked back. Burne had not followed. He was gone somewhere – along the corridor, perhaps. The Widow was motioning her to close the door. She did so as softly as she could.

Feet scraped and clattered in the council chamber doorway. Armoured men were in the room. Sophia could not tell how many.

'Swords, you fellows?' said Mother. 'For one old widow?'

'You will come with us, my lady.'

It was the last time Sophia ever heard her voice.

## XVIII

### Sunset

mbrose stood by the river, watching the sun dip towards the crown of an oak tree on the farther bank. He was waiting for Chawlin, but Chawlin was late. He would wait another few minutes, then he would go.

The Widow had told him to stay with friends. Ambrose was not sure whether Chawlin was still a friend, but he was the nearest to a friend that he had. They still had practice bouts every week. Ambrose enjoyed them, because he knew his skill was improving and because they made him feel less helpless. So even after the terrible moments with the Heron Man in the hall, he had remembered that he was due to have a bout that afternoon, and had come to the riverbank as usual. But Chawlin was not there.

Time passed slowly. Ambrose began to fret. It would be a pity to miss the bout, but he could not stay much longer. He had to be in the Widow's chamber when she spoke with the bald monk about the Heron Man. He wanted to tell them about the fears that he had been carrying ever since he had fled the mountains, and of the new fears that had been piling within him since the Wolf had come to him two nights before. He wanted to speak with people who had seen the Heron Man; and he wanted to hear what the bald monk had to say. For the man had said that he had heard Mother's voice, there in the hall.

Ambrose remembered him now. He had been in the castle the day he arrived. He had said, then, that he had known her, and been her friend. So did the monk mean that he had looked at Ambrose in the hall and been reminded of her, so clearly that it might have been a voice speaking to him? Or had she really stepped up from under the Angels' Wings, by some miracle that only happened to priests, and spoken in his ear to point out the Heron Man where he stood by her son?

The monk knew the Heron Man, too. He had seen him before.

He was someone who knew! Someone who could help – at last.

The sun had touched the top-most branches of the oak. He could see the glare flickering through the highest leaves. Chawlin was now late by over half an hour. There was no telling when the Widow might begin her conference. Ambrose turned to go.

That was when Chawlin finally appeared. He was leading a donkey, laden with sacks, along the river path. Ambrose called to him. He looked up, surprised. Then he frowned.

'What are you doing here?'

'We had a bout,' Ambrose said.

It was obvious that Chawlin had forgotten. He did not seem pleased to be reminded.

'Angels! I'm busy enough already.'

'What are you doing?' Ambrose could not imagine what mission for the castle or the school would bring a scholar to the riverbank laden with sacks; but there were still many things about Develin that he did not understand.

'It's no business of yours,' said Chawlin, shortly. He began to unfasten the sacks from the donkey's back. Ambrose watched him. For a while Chawlin ignored him, but when he had all the sacks in a row on the ground, he seemed to think again.

'Ho, well. Since we are both here, and since we've promised it to one another, I suppose we should at least cross sticks once or twice before we go our ways. In fact' – he began to undo the tie around one of the sacks at his feet – 'I remember saying I would show you some iron. What do you think of this?'

From the sack he drew a short sword. The blade was dull, the hilt unadorned, but he swung it and swished it in quick, smooth strokes as though he knew exactly what he was doing. The donkey sidled a little away from him.

'Do you have one for me?' asked Ambrose.

'No. It took me enough begging and wheedling to get this one. We must take turns. One with the staff, the other with the sword. It's uneven, but then most fights are uneven. You try the staff first, since you know a bit about that now. I'll show you how I block with the sword . . .'

Ambrose picked his rough-cut staff out of the reeds where they left it after each bout. The sword was much shorter than a staff, but the way Chawlin held it made him look very dangerous. Ambrose did not like it. He understood the staff, and how it hurt if you were hit. This was different.

He swallowed. He did not like the look settling on Chawlin's face, either. It seemed like the face of an enemy.

'I can't be long,' Ambrose said. 'I have to be within the walls by sunset.'

'We've time for a few passes. Be careful, now. The sword is slower than the staff, but not much. And you may be surprised what I can reach.'

Ambrose advanced, holding his staff two-handed in the way he had been taught. Chawlin waited for him, balanced, with the sword held across his chest.

Ambrose stopped. Chawlin was quick – so quick Ambrose almost never touched him in practice. He did not think he had yet found out how quick Chawlin could be. He did not want to attack. He was – yes – he was afraid of Chawlin, and the sword.

He knew he was scaring himself. This was just a bout. That was all. Chawlin might have been angry with him at first, for asking for it. But he wouldn't *do* anything . . .

A rising sound from the roadway distracted him. Relieved, he stepped back a pace or two with his eyes on his opponent as Chawlin had taught him. Then he turned to look. Chawlin turned, too.

A small knot of horsemen were on the roadway, riding at full canter. A great banner danced over them. The long light of the evening showed the device clearly.

'It's the King,' exclaimed Chawlin.

The King himself? Not some messenger?

'What's he doing?'

'Riding from the castle. Why, I don't know. And he's left nine-tenths of his men behind him. Why this?'

*If you don't get it for me, I've another way.*

361

'He's going because he's already done what he came to do,' said Ambrose slowly.

'What is that?'

'He's got his men inside the walls.'

They stared at one another, and the shadow of the oak tree lay around them.

'They're going to do what they did at Bay,' Ambrose said.

That was what the Wolf had meant. That was the 'other way' he had spoken of in the night of Ambrose's cell!

Chawlin glanced at the road, and at the castle again. He hadn't accepted what Ambrose had said. He did not know what to do.

'I don't like this,' he said at last. 'We should go back, perhaps.'

'She'll be in the council chamber,' said Ambrose.

'Who?'

'The Widow. We can warn her.'

'Oh . . . yes.'

Chawlin hung where he was for a moment more. Then some thought, or conviction, came to him, and he swore. He started walking towards the castle, striding quickly. Ambrose had to jog to stay alongside him.

Then Chawlin began to run.

Ambrose hurried after him. He could not keep up. Chawlin was bigger, and far more powerful. He was getting further and further ahead. Ambrose's breath began to come in gasps, forcing itself out of his lungs as he tried to keep running. He had gone more than a hundred yards before he realized that he had dropped his staff.

He ran on, empty-handed, and the walls of Develin reddened with sunset.

Chawlin was not making for the gate. He was keeping to the river side of the castle, rounding the great corner tower and heading for the postern that stood concealed in its shadow. As they passed under the walls Ambrose could hear only his own feet, his breath, gasping with the run, and the endless ripple of the river. The towers and the wall-tops were silent. No sound came from within.

Chawlin had reached the postern, and was prising at it. He still had the sword.

'It will be locked,' panted Ambrose, as he came up.

'It looks it,' muttered Chawlin. 'But it's not. I've fixed the bolts from inside, so I can come and go without using the gate.'

'Why?'

'It's none of your business.'

The door cracked open. Inside, the passage was dark. They listened. Still there was no sound.

Chawlin led, sword in hand. They groped their way in. Ambrose did not know where he was in the castle. Chawlin did, it seemed. There were dark openings on either side of him, which might have been cellars. There was a light ahead – filtering in down a flight of steps. Chawlin hurried up them – one flight, two. They met no one. They heard nothing. They reached the level of the living quarters.

In the passage a woman was standing. It was one of the Widow's chamber-maids. She was doing nothing, going nowhere. She was holding her hand to her head, as if she was suffering a migraine.

'They've killed them,' she said. 'They've killed them.'
Somewhere, someone screamed.

Chawlin pushed past the woman and flung into the council chamber with an oath. It was empty. He passed on into the Widow's rooms beyond it. From the way he called and banged the doors Ambrose knew that there was no one there.

Ambrose stood in the council chamber, listening. He had not set foot here since the day he had come. The Widow's chair was empty. Someone had pulled a chest out from behind it and rifled it, leaving the lid open. The hearth by which he had crouched to warm himself was dead. The window that looked out over the hills was darkening with night.

A clamour of voices rose from somewhere – dreadful sounds, full of rage and terror. Feet were running, people sobbing, crying out. From the inner chambers he heard Chawlin exclaim.

'Michael's Knees! They're amok – the king's men!'

He must be looking out of a window into the courtyard. Ambrose stepped to the door, swallowing hard. He did not want to see what Chawlin could see. And yet seeing could not be worse than not seeing.

Another sound – the softest sigh of a robe – made him turn again. The Heron Man was sitting in the Widow's chair.

A voice was screaming for pity. It screamed, and stopped amid a series of dull thuds that must have been blows. There were more cries from beyond.

'It is because of you,' said the Heron Man.

He was plain to the eye. He was not hiding now.

Feet running, and screaming. A bellow that must have

ripped the throat that made it. Metal upon metal. Metal on flesh.

'It is your doing,' said the Heron Man.

'That's a *lie!*' yelled Ambrose.

'At their noon-tide halt the son of Lackmere went to his King. He said that the Widow kept the heir of Tarceny in her house in secret – the heir of Tarceny, and the blood-line of Wulfram. To this king it was very clear that the Widow was plotting against him. His plans were changed in less than an hour.'

'Chawlin!'

'He has done this because of you. His men hunt through every room and corridor for you. And they kill everyone in their path.'

Chawlin was at the inner door, swearing and breathing hard. He started at the sight of the Heron Man, and swore again. The Heron Man ignored him. His eyes were bent upon Ambrose.

'You could have warned the Widow, and you did not. Now they have cut the Widow's head from her body.

'You could have spoken with the monk. With the man who helped you. Now they have marched him into the courtyard, and made him kneel, and cut his bald head from his body, too. He lies beside the Widow, and their blood thickens on the cobbles. And the house-people will be heaped around them. Because of you.'

'You did it! You made him do it!' cried Ambrose.

'You could stop it,' said Chawlin, behind him.

The Heron Man seemed to shrug.

'I did not like to be chased from this hut of a farmer's daughter, as if I were a stray dog.'

Chawlin lifted his sword.

'Would you join the Widow then – a head shorter?'

'Do not wave your stick at me, oaf. Oh, I remember you. Did you think I did not? I remember everybody. You did not reach me in Tarceny. You cannot reach me now. Before you tried, I would be gone. And after that you would do well to walk with one eye over your shoulder. Do you remember what you saw, that day?'

Chawlin drew a long breath. The silence was torn with another scream.

Suddenly Ambrose could smell woodsmoke. There was a low, windy sound, that had not been there before.

'They've fired the house,' he said.

'Every man. Every woman. Every girl. Every pig or dog,' said the Heron Man.

'You must stop it,' said Chawlin.

'You have nothing to offer me.'

'For all the Angels – stop them!'

'You have nothing to offer me.'

There was another scream. It might have been a woman or a child.

'*There!*' cried Ambrose. He flung the pouch of white stones at the feet of the Heron Man. 'That's what you wanted, wasn't it? Now stop them! Stop them!'

The Heron Man did not even look at the pouch at his feet. He leaned forward.

'The Widow gave space for One in her house. One. So you may take One from it, alive. Choose whom it will be.'

Ambrose stared at him in horror. Names, faces, flooded into his mind: the sprawling, shouting, chaotic community of Develin; the Masters – Padry, Pantethon, Father Grismonde; the scholars – Rufin, Cullen; the scullions and serving girls whose hands had brought them food.

Who was already dead and who was still alive?

He was helpless.

'One.'

Suddenly, a name exploded from Chawlin.

'Sophia! The Widow's daughter!'

The Heron Man paused. His head turned slowly, as if he looked through the walls around him. For a moment Ambrose saw him, perched not on the Widow's chair but on a pinnacle of rock under a dull sky.

Then he said: 'Go to the hall. Be swift.'

He reached down for the pouch of stones. His finger and thumb closed on the very tip of the cord. When he rose, the pouch dangled from his hand like a dead rat that a man holds in disgust for a moment, before flinging it on a heap.

'There will be a price.'

He was gone, and the stones with him.

The room was misty with smoke. Ambrose coughed.

'Come on,' said Chawlin.

They hurried out of the chamber. There were men at the far end of the corridor, armoured, battering on a door. But the stair was free. They plunged downwards, Chawlin leading, sword held before him.

Ambrose followed. He had nothing else to do. He had lost the stones. He was as naked as a chick out of his shell. The air was full of smoke and the smoke was full of swords. He was going to be hunted. The only thought in his mind was to keep moving, keep moving. If he was moving they might not catch him. Perhaps he could go on running for ever.

Someone – a king's man in helmet and mail – had seen them, and cried out. Chawlin ignored him. In the hurry and confusion it was impossible to know if they were pursued. Everywhere men were running – chasing, fleeing, stumbling upon a new enemy and chasing or fleeing again to the kill. Chawlin kept ahead, down to the level of the hall and through the doors.

The smoke hung thinly in the great space. Ambrose's eyes were weeping, but he could see that the hall was empty. Chawlin groaned aloud.

'There!' cried Ambrose.

There she was. Perhaps she had been trying to reach the river-door. Now she came running blindly out of the kitchen doorway. A man was after her, lumbering in mail. He had a one-handed axe. She was quicker, but was running with her arm across her eyes. They could hear her sobbing – a high, broken sound, as she ran and did not see.

Chawlin lurched forward, bellowing. The pursuer turned on him, calling for help. The sword rang on the helm and the knee, and the man staggered. He did not go down.

'Sophia!' cried Chawlin. 'The river-door – quickly!'

The king's man was coming on again. Chawlin sprang back. He had no armour. Across the hall the Lynx had stopped and was looking at them.

'The river-door – both of you!'

The attacker roared, and swung clumsily with his axe. Chawlin dodged back again. Other men were crowding in

368

at the hall entrance. There were swords and pole-arms, dark against the smoky light beyond.

'Go! Michael's Knees – go!'

The Lynx was moving – back the way she had come towards the kitchens. Ambrose ducked around the fighters and followed her. Behind him there was a crash and a cry. He looked back. The soldier was down on one knee, clutching his axe-hand. The axe lay on the floor. Chawlin stood over him. The short sword swept in to the neck-joint. The man dropped like a puppet with its strings cut.

Beyond him men were swarming inwards, yelling. Chawlin turned and ran for the kitchen door. Ambrose bolted before him.

He did not know the way. The rooms were unlit, and full of smoke. His ears rang with cries. He could not see. He had lost sight of the Lynx – of Sophia. Where was she?

He turned right, and then left. The noises of pursuit were close. Maybe Chawlin was fighting again. Armourless, he had beaten that man with a speed and savagery he had never shown at practice. Ambrose felt feeble, useless. All he could do was run.

Surely he must be close to the river-door now. It hadn't taken this long when they were coming – or had it? He remembered that he had to go down a flight of steps to some cellars. He began to look for them. Maybe he had passed them already. He couldn't go back. If he went back he would run into the swords. He could only go on.

'Where are you?' he called. 'Where are you?'

He was moving in near darkness. If the shadow-creatures came, he had no protection. He must keep going. But he could not help slowing. Where was he?

'Chawlin! Sophia!'

Even now her name felt strange to him.

And there she was! A great burst of relief came on him. He saw her beckoning, and ran towards her. She seemed to be at the top of a flight of steps. He would be out in a moment. She turned, and he followed, downwards, stumbling. The way was rough. He could not tell where he was. He thought they had passed into the outdoors, but somehow they had done it without going through the postern. The light was dull. The air was dead. He could not see the river. Still he hurried after the woman before him.

His eyes were stinging with smoke. His feet told him that he was nowhere he knew. This was not the riverbank, mossy and slippery. They stubbed and stumbled among rocks. The way was level, when it should have sloped down to the water.

He stopped, and looked around him. The colours had changed. The castle was gone. The sounds of fighting and massacre were shut off, as swiftly as if he had woken from a dream. A deep humming ran through his mind, so low that he felt rather than heard it.

He was in the landscape of brown rocks, bare of trees and grass, under a dim sky. Far away, in all directions, he could see a wall of mountains, sweeping up towards the horizon. To his left two great lights like huge stars seemed to burn on the rim of the world. He looked back. The castle was nowhere to be seen. Nor was the river, or the banks of Develin. He was standing in the Heron Man's country.

The air was thick, as if it were almost water. There

was no smoke in it. Instead it was filled with the deep sound that he could barely hear. He could not see where it came from. It made him feel very heavy.

The woman he had followed was still there, a little way from him, beckoning urgently. She was not the Lynx. She was robed differently, and was slightly taller. She was the only other living thing in all that place.

He made his way towards her, dreading what he was going to see.

'Come, my darling,' she said. 'Quickly. They are already hunting you.'

He reached her, and looked into the eyes of his mother.

# PART III

## WAR

# XIX

## The Cup of the World

ophia moved in evil dreams.

She was waiting by the river-door again. The door was dark and smoking, and she wanted to run away. Chawlin was calling to her from the riverbank to come quickly. She knew that soon the man with the axe, all bloody, would come out of the postern and chase her again. But still she had to wait, while her mind screamed *Run! Run!* and the door fumed and coughed blood. Someone had not come out that should have come, and she must wait for them. Perhaps it would be Hestie; perhaps it would be her mother. Perhaps it would be the man with the axe. And she must wait.

A shape moved in the darkness of the postern arch. It was not Hestie, or her mother. It was Luke. He would have walked past her, but he stopped and looked at her.

*I'm sorry*, she said. *I did not know who you are.*

He looked at her a moment more, and then he left her.

She dreamed that she had gone to lie on the riverbank in the sun. Her mother came and stood over her, and told her crossly that it was time to get up and attend to her studies.

*Faith, madam,* she said pertly. *I study the art of sleeping.*

*Strange to study a high art in such a low place,* her mother answered. *As well to scoop the river-earth out of your hair and make your cup with that. I declare there is enough of it.*

'You're a dream,' Sophia mumbled. She knew her hair must indeed be dirty, because she was lying on the bank without even a pillow. Chawlin had offered to make her one from the bundles in the river-punt in which they had escaped; but she had been too tired to wait.

She could hear the river, rippling endlessly a few yards from her ear.

At last she opened her eyes.

Yes, she was on the riverbank, lying in full sun. There was a blanket about her feet. Chawlin must have laid it over her as she slept, but in the gathering heat of the morning she had already thrown it off. She was lying on the ground in the silks she had put on for the King. She saw that they were stained with mud and smoke. She thought there might be blood on them too, but could not see any. She remembered how her feet had slipped for a moment when she had run past someone lying in a passage. That had been horrible.

She lifted her head. Her body felt stiff from the hard ground.

Chawlin was sitting nearby, jabbing absently at the turf with the point of a short knife. The cup stood at his hip. He had not noticed that she was awake.

She sat up, and looked at the world.

The willow-leaves whispered and the river glittered in

the light. Empty green meadows, long with spring weeds, stretched on either bank. It was going to be a warm day. Weather like this should happen at another time.

'I dreamed about my mother,' she said.

Chawlin looked up. His eyes were tender. He must have been waiting for her to speak for some time. Yet he seemed to know how little words could do for her.

'Yes. I'm sorry.'

She would never see her mother again; or Hestie; or any of them. Beside her the river ran on and on, un-hurried. Already this much water had flowed under the walls that had been her home. How many tears would make a river as swift and deep as this?

She was still wearing the pearls of the King. They clicked softly against one another as she touched them. He had hung them so carelessly around her neck before destroying her house and life. Did wealth mean nothing to him? Or had he thought that he could easily take the pearls back again, soaked in her blood, when she lay dead with all the rest? He had barely looked at her. She thought of throwing them into the river; but she did not.

'Why did they do it?' she asked aloud.

Chawlin sighed. 'Sometimes I think we're driven to ruin everything we have.'

It had been something to do with the cup. Luke – she still thought of him as Luke – had tried to tell her that the king's men wanted it. He had said Develin must not trust them.

A pit opened in her heart. He had said that Develin must not trust them.

She had not listened to him!

She must have made a sound, then. Chawlin glanced at her anxiously.

'They are at rest, Sophia,' he said. 'They are under the Angels' Wings.'

'I . . . dreamed about Luke, too,' she said.

'He may have escaped.'

'How do you know?' She looked at the cup. 'Have you seen him?'

He shook his head. 'I've looked, but not found him yet. Do you know who he really was?'

'Yes.' But that did not matter either. Nothing like that mattered any more.

'Sophia,' Chawlin said. 'I need to tell you something.'

'What is it?'

'That I'm sorry for what I said in the tower. It feels very stupid now.'

In the tower? She could barely remember.

'It wasn't stupid,' she said.

'It was stupid because I said we have to face things as they are. Yesterday *I* was made to see things as they are. I was outside the castle when it started. The sensible thing to do would have been to lie low. I thought of it. But I knew you were inside. I knew I had to get you out. That's what I mean about being made to face things. Do you understand?'

He was saying that he loved her.

'Yes,' she said dully. 'Thank you.'

'Sophia,' he said earnestly. 'In all this dark, damned winter you were the one thing that was new and different for me. All the rest . . . In the end I could have left it. But I looked at the walls, and all I could see was you. That

378

was why I . . . That was why I had to get you out. I want *you* to understand that. Do you?'

He was looking at her as if he was begging her to forgive him. She did not see why he needed to. She looked at the river.

'I'm sorry,' he said gently. 'Perhaps this should wait for a better time.'

'No,' she said. 'No, I'm grateful.'

She did not feel grateful: not to be alive, not to be loved. She felt . . .

She rose and stumped off along the bank in search of privacy. Her limbs moved clumsily as they shook off her rough sleep. She remembered, too, how clumsily she had moved and thought the night before, and how she had sat in the stern of the punt all those dark hours, answering Chawlin shortly, or not at all. She had not been sleepy then. She had been dumb with what she had seen. She still was.

The pearls clumped untidily around her neck. Her dress was filthy. She had nothing else to wear. There was no one to help dress her. It was better not to think what had happened to Dapea.

Dapea, and Hestie, and her mother, and all of them – all of them! She was going to wake every morning and find that they were gone. She had even been fighting with them, betraying them, on the day they had died! And she might have prevented it. Luke – Ambrose – had been trying to warn her.

Why hadn't she *listened*?

What had made her hate a thirteen-year-old boy so much that she would not hear him?

379

Grief, when she could not cry, was like sickness when she could not be sick. There was no relief from the ugliness inside herself.

She sat alone for a long time as the river drifted slowly under the sun.

A little way along the bank was a small clump of snow-fishers, the brave plant that forces its way out through the wintry earth and drags the riverbanks into spring. She could see the white heads and silver-green leaves nodding in the light. For a while she watched them glowing while the river ran by.

At last, she picked one of them – just one. She was sorry to destroy anything; but she wanted to show Chawlin that the earth bore flowers, even now.

He was sitting where she had left him. He had the cup upon his knees. There was water in it, and he peered into the water as if to see something that moved there. He did not look up as she approached. So she dropped the flower into the bowl under his nose, and knelt beside him to kiss him on the ear. He was startled. Then he laughed.

His fingers picked the flower slowly out from the cup.

'I remember these. They grew in great masses along the streams by my keep at Hayley. I could spend a half-day among them, lying there with my fishing rod when the company of men grew dull . . .'

He looked up.

'How are you?' he asked, gently.

'Better,' she said. 'At least for a while. I want to tell you that you are wonderful. And wonderful things happen, as well as terrible things. And when we die, all that happens is that they stop happening.'

'I suppose you are right.'

'I'm very muddy,' she said determinedly. 'Have you anything I could change into?'

'Not a rag. But I have some coin. There may be a chance for me to buy something further downriver. When we have you dressed more plainly, it will be easier for us to go among other people without calling attention to ourselves.' His eye fell on her pearls. 'You should hide those at once. Next to your skin, if you can.'

The water had gone from the cup. Her flower lay curled and sodden in the bottom of it. She must have interrupted what he was doing, but he had not reproached her.

'Where are we going?' she asked.

'Downriver. Our punt will take us all the way to the lake. If you climb in now, I'll pass our things to you. We can breakfast later in the morning.'

The punt, now that she saw it in daylight, was a plain, narrow boat not much longer than the height of a man. Chawlin had moored it by pushing its nose into the reeds and jamming the punt-pole into the mud on its river-side. Most of the space in it was already full of bundles. She stepped unsteadily in and found a place to sit down. Chawlin passed her two rolled blankets and a water bottle. He carried the cup onto the punt himself, and set it at his feet. Then he drew the pole from the mud, placed the end against the bank and bent upon it. The boat moved slowly out into the stream.

'Now Michael guard us,' he said, in the ancient prayer of the traveller who sets out at the beginning of a new day.

'. . . and Raphael guide our way,' answered Sophia without thinking.

Chawlin swayed with his stroke, and found his balance again. As they moved into midstream the current picked them and drew them on. Sophia looked back up the river. There, beyond Chawlin's shoulder, the blue sky was smudged with a stain. It was too far to see where it came from, or to smell what it bore downwind; but she knew that it must be the smoke rising above the walls of Develin, where she had lived all her sixteen years.

Neither of them had spoken the last words of the prayer: *For we are far from home.*


Ambrose could climb no further. The slope of brown rock had grown steeper and steeper until he had been scrambling on his hands and knees. Now it ended in a wall that rose far above his head. On either hand it curled away until it was lost in dimness. Up, and to his right, the two great lights burned in what looked like a mountain-peak at the top of the wall. They did not seem to be far away. They wavered and grew with a noise like huge fires.

Beside him the woman stood.

'Put your hand on the wall,' she said.

It was his mother's voice, distorted in that strange air.

'Is it stone that you feel?'

He did as he was told. After so long among the brown rocks – he did not know how long it had been – he was moving as if in a heavy fever. Something about the air was fogging his mind. He could feel the wall beneath his hand. If it was not stone, he did not know what it might be. His eye, however, could pick out a pattern of lines and curves – huge curves – upon it. The pattern repeated itself. The lines were not smooth on the face of the rock, but marked with ridges, as though each was the rim of a lizard-scale the size of a castle-gate, overlapping another, and another, on and on upon an enormous, serpentine body that lay along the top of the slope.

'Now look up,' said the woman. 'Look at the light. Do you see?'

Ambrose looked at the fires on the mountain-peak.

The rocks were formed strangely there. The wall broke into massive curves and outcrops, the size of small hills. One great fire wavered and grew with a roaring like snows tumbling on mountainsides. Beyond it the second light was less glaring, but it trembled in time with the first, until he was sure that it had no light of its own but was simply a reflection.

What could reflect such a fire as that – standing upright on a mountainside like a huge eye?

An eye.

It was an eye in a head the size of a mountain, throwing back the light that burned for ever in its jaws. And under his hand was a body of scales, the height of a cliff, that seemed to curve all the way out of sight as if it would embrace the world.

'You have touched the hide of Capuu,' said the woman. 'No creature from the pit will approach him. This is why we have come as far as we have. You can rest now.'

His knees crumpled, and he lay on the ground at the foot of the wall.

Before him the slope dropped steeply. The huge space below him roiled with mists. The land at the bottom of the slope, across which he had marched and marched ever since Develin, was shrouded in it. But now he could see, across the face of the mist, across distances impossible to guess at, a line at the far horizon. It might have been a wall as high as the one against which his back was set. Slowly, as he looked, he saw that it must be the same wall. The curve of the vast beast behind him continued and continued to left and right, until at last it swept around to embrace the clouded lowland in one huge ring like the rim of a bowl.

'We are looking across the Cup of the World,' said the woman. 'It is clear to see, from up here. It is also clearer to the ear. Listen.'

The fire above the wall roared on and on. But she was not talking about that. She was looking down into the lowlands out of which they had climbed. He waited, but heard nothing – except the deep humming that was constant in this place. Down there, as he had stumbled across the floor of the bowl, it had been all around him, barely audible, pulsing upon his skin through all his long journey. Now he was above it, and out of it. And because he was out of it he heard it more fully. It was fathomless; but it had a shape that he knew.

'Someone is crying,' he said through a dry throat.

'Have you heard it before?'

'No.'

Except . . .

'It was there, every day we were in the mountains. We heard it in dreams, and also in the music that the hillmen have spun from the dreams that come to them. We lived in her shadow for twelve years, and within a half-hour's climb of the pool where her first tears fell. It is Beyah, the Mother of the World, weeping for the child that she lost.

She sits and dreams this place around us. Once it was her garden. Now these rocks are all she sees of the world.'

'Yes,' he said.

'The tears of one like that – what do you think they hold? Can you imagine the grief of a mother who has lost her child, swollen to the size of one that might be a god? Down there in the pit is her rage and her despair. Do you know what it is she cries as she weeps?'

'It's wordless.'

'It is not wordless. If you dived deep into the pool you would hear it. As you swam among her tears you would hear her cry, *"Let them eat their sons!"*

'And there was a man who embraced that cry as he sank to the deep. He has drunk from it for three hundred years, undying, and carries it into the world. Tell me his name.'

Ambrose shook his head.

'I don't know,' he said.

'I have told it to you myself. Tell me his name.'

'You mean the Heron Man.'

'That is not his name.'

'The Prince – the Prince Under the Sky.'

'His *name!*'

'I don't know! I don't know!'

She knelt before him, on the narrow lip of rock above the slope. She looked into his eyes with his mother's face. She took him by the shoulders with his mother's hands, and pulled gently, as though to bring him up to his knees.

Sunlight burst around him.

The great bowl, the mountain-head of the dragon, was gone. There was grass growing up between his fingers, as he held himself on hands and knees and hung his head to clear it. He was breathing in heavy, shaking gasps. He felt as if he had been under water for longer than he could remember.

Hands were lifting him. His legs staggered and banged into small branches. He sat heavily. There was an arm about his shoulders, steadying him.

'I know it is hard, that place,' she said. 'I have made you breathe too much of it. I'm sorry, my darling.'

Ambrose opened his eyes.

He was sitting on a fallen tree at the edge of a forest in a mountain valley. Before him was a steep, sunlit, grassy slope stretching down to more trees. There the bottom of the valley dropped out of sight, replaced by the wooded hillside opposite. He could hear a stream rushing somewhere below. Towards the lower end of the meadow a narrow track ran across the slope. A few insects were busy among the grass stems, although it was still early in the year.

'Oh, Amba,' she said, hugging him fiercely. 'I have been so frightened for you!'

He did not return her embrace. His head was still fogged. When she released him, he looked heavily around at the sunlit mountainsides. He saw the colours and the slopes, and the sky, and at the same time he felt that all he saw must be very thin, like a veil that might fall in an instant, leaving him under the eye of a huge creature ringing a wasteland of rocks, which was all that the Mother of the World saw of the thing she had made.

'His name is Paigan Wulframson,' she said, sitting beside him. 'Paigan, the son of Wulfram the Seafarer. I did tell you; but I suppose you weren't listening at the time.'

Her voice was no longer distorted, nor relentless, as it had been on the rim of the Cup. It had flesh, and breath. And it was scolding him – *I did tell you. I suppose you weren't listening* – as if nothing had happened to part them all winter.

Walking in that place, it was as if he had been dreaming of her. Even when she had offered him her hand as he stumbled, and he had taken it, he had also thought that this was not her, and that a time would come when he would wake and she would be gone. Now she was still here in the day, and his feelings were coming back to him. They were not comfortable.

He did not want her there. He did not want to weep, or embrace her. She might still be dead, even though she seemed not to be dead. Or if she was alive, she would be dead again soon, and he would have to lose her all over again. He would have to go through all that once more.

'You must remember his name,' she was saying. 'If you know his name you will remember that for all his tricks he is only a man.'

She had *left* him. She had left him to all the things that had happened to him!

'He acts like a demon,' he said sullenly.

'He is a man.'

'He wasted all the land by the lake.'

'That land was wasted by men, my darling. Partly because of lies he had told your father, and afterwards because of a badly made peace.'

'No one in Develin could see him. He made them all despair. Then he killed them.'

387

'The tears give powers over sight – among other things. You saw how he walks among the rocks of Beyah's dream, and yet speaks into the world. No one knows he is near, unless he chooses to be seen, or they know how to watch for him. And because they do not see him, they believe the thoughts that he slips into their head are their own. And so he mocks the Angels, who have charge of our souls. And he lies, he lies . . .'

Her voice trembled with a kind of hatred, and her fists shook in her lap as she spoke.

'I think he tells the truth mostly,' said Ambrose.

'Yes. Of course he does. And truth spoken with a false heart is the worst lie of all. But for all that he is a man, and the Angels have doomed him.'

Ambrose clutched his hands together.

'But don't the Angels lie too?' he said.

'No!' She shook her head. 'They do not lie.'

'Then maybe they've changed sides.'

'Amba! Why do you say that?'

'One of them spoke to me, at Ferroux.'

She looked hard at him. 'Are you sure?' she said slowly. 'Paigan Wulframson has many tricks.'

'It wasn't him. I'd have known his voice. And it showed him to me. It showed me how to see him, and see what he was doing. It said he was the father of the house. Then it told me to go into the garden and wait for him.'

She had told him to trust the Angels. And they never, never promised anything. They just watched. The thing within Lex at Ferroux had watched, passionless, while Grismonde fought his battle with the darkness and was overwhelmed.

What was the meaning of anything, he thought angrily, if the Angels behaved like that?

'Did he come?'

'No. But his creatures did.'

Her eyes widened. 'What happened?'

He shrugged. What could words tell her?

'They could not pass the stones. They reached for me, and spoke to me, but in the end they went away.'

'*They* spoke to you? What did they say?'

*Ando.*

'I think they were trying to say my name.'

'Your name! I see. I wonder . . . Ambrose, this may be important. The Angels do not "change sides". If it was an angel that spoke with you, it will have told the truth. They always tell the truth, even if we cannot see the truth as they do. And the father of the house of Ferroux was not Paigan Wulframson. Did his creatures say anything else?'

Questions, always questions; but she had no idea what it had been *like*!

'One of them said a word like "Anson",' he grumbled.

'"Anson"? It means nothing . . . Are you sure?'

'Yes, I'm sure!' he shouted. 'Of course I'm sure! And where *were* you?'

There! He had said it. He had said just a fragment of what he felt. There would be an argument now, but he had said it anyway. He hoped it had hurt.

She was looking at him with a dazed expression, as if she had finally understood what he was thinking, and yet was confused by it.

'Amba . . .' she said, using his child name again.

389

Ambrose drew his knees closer against himself. He was not going to answer.

'My darling,' she said. 'These past months have been bad for you. I am sorry. I am sorry I could not come before. But I have had to hide. When I came up out of the pool I could do very little. I have had to grow – back into someone that could help.'

'You did not come up. I waited for you.'

'I came up. I came up among the brown rocks of her garden, for the pool exists in that place, too. How do you suppose I know what Beyah cries? It was awful, Amba, awful. And yes, I did not go to a fraction of the depth that there is in that pool. I have barely tasted a drop of what Paigan must have done. Still, I was confused. When I spoke to Aun it was as if I was in a dream. It was a long time before I could see enough to understand what was happening in Develin. Thank the Angels that Martin was there to hear me! I could not have faced Paigan Wulframson on my own.'

'Why not?'

'He would have killed me.'

'They killed Martin, afterwards,' Ambrose said, accusingly.

'Amba!'

He glared at her. He saw her see his anger. Her mouth trembled for a moment, as if she was going to cry.

'Do you think that you are the only one who has suffered?' she exclaimed.

That was her. Ambrose had a sudden, painful memory of her standing with her stirring stick by the pot at home, driven beyond bearing as he whined for his supper. *Do you think you are the only one who is hungry?* And she had always served him first.

'Don't you see what has happened to me? I am like him! Like him! Don't you care?'

For a moment she was glaring at him. But she must have seen his expression change, for she softened her tone.

'No, Amba,' she said. 'I am not a monster. But the tears are in me now. In me. Can you imagine what that means? Nine-tenths of my living is among the rocks. I do not eat. I rarely sleep. I must drink, now and again, of the tears, but that is all. I fear his hunters, like you. I have skulked and hidden and prayed, in this hiding place and among the rocks, desperately afraid that they might catch me.

'But what I have also come to fear, as time has passed, is that he has chosen *not* to hunt me – at least, so long as I do not try to interfere with him or with the stones. I was at my weakest in the days after I left the pool. I had very little protection. I could barely move. The rocks around that place are alive with his creatures. And yet I lived until I could come away. Why?'

Her voice slowed, as if her words themselves were made of pain.

'I think he knows that if he lets me live, then I must go on living, like him; and that such a life as he lives in the end becomes worse than any death.

'Above all, he knows that if he lets me live, I must see my only child die. And I will, my darling. Whether we defeat him or not, one day I will.'

She stopped. Her face was drawn. Her arms were clutched tight around her knees. And he realized that she was listening, to some sound he could not hear. And he guessed that it was the Mother of the World.

'Capuu is a comfort to me now, and a shelter,' she said after a moment. 'But there may be a time when I cannot endure him any more. I tell you, it is very easy for me to see how Paigan Wulframson has become what he has become.'

Ambrose looked away across the mountainsides. His anger and his shock were both diminishing. He supposed, glumly, that it hadn't really been her fault. But there had been no one else for him to blame.

'I'm sorry,' he said at last.

Maybe she was waiting for more. But he did not know what else to say. Could he be sorry that she loved him? Sorry that he must one day die?

'Well,' she said. 'I am far back – far back – along the way that Paigan has gone. And I do not wish to follow him. I am not lost. But do not lay Martin's death at my door. Or any of them. It is already very hard to bear.'

'Yes,' he said, feeling guilty now. And, 'I'm sorry,' again.

And that was all. The sun was on the meadow, and the mountain breeze was cool. A butterfly landed on a high grass stem near his right hand.

After a little he asked: 'What are we doing here?'

'Resting where we are safe,' she said, as if no angry words had passed between them. 'Also I have asked a friend to meet us. I had hoped he would be here when we arrived. Perhaps he will come later today.'

'Did I dream what I saw – the dragon, and the Cup?'

'You may call it a dream. But your body has come a great distance from Develin. The nearest place in the

Kingdom is . . .' She looked puzzled. 'I used to know it. The city with the big shrines . . .'

'Jent,' said Ambrose.

Everyone knew about Jent. She had told him about it many times. She had been there. He hadn't. Why couldn't she name it now?

'I don't belong in this place any more, you see,' she said. 'Jent. Yes. We are some way from it, beyond the borders of the Kingdom. If you journey down the valley, which is . . .' she thought for a moment '. . . north, you would come to the southern reaches of the March of Tarceny. There. That is the answer to your question.'

So they were farther south than he had ever been. The full length of the Kingdom lay between himself and home. He ought to have realized, of course, because the woods on these mountainsides looked nothing like the scrubby thorn-covering on the hills he remembered.

Yet for her, the same brown rocks lay in each place, and everywhere. *Do you think you are the only one who has suffered?*

After a little she said: 'Are you going to tell me how you lost the stones?'

'I spoke with him,' he confessed.

She sighed.

'He was saying it was my fault, what happened in Develin.'

'And yet he must have hated Develin,' she said. 'Hated it. They were teaching people to hope. So he taught them to despair. They upheld Kingship; so he led them to abandon their king, and then he tortured them with their guilt at what he had swayed them to do. And when they escaped him, he turned his followers to kill them. I have seen him do this before.'

'We wanted him to stop the killing. That's why I gave him the stones. He let us have one life. He told us where we could find her, and we did.'

'My darling . . .' She shook her head. 'You see how he tricked you. Paigan Wulframson cannot order how each blow in battle falls. You gave him the stones. For that he sent you where you might save one life out of hundreds. With luck and skill you did, but you might have failed and been killed yourselves.'

'He said there would be a price.'

'Of course. Did he say what it would be?'

'No.'

'Who did he say it to?'

Ambrose frowned. 'To both of us. Well – to Chawlin mostly, since it was he . . .'

'Chawlin?'

'Yes.'

'There was a man I knew with that name . . .'

'I think he knew you, though he never said so.'

'I knew no wrong of him. But . . . Paigan Wulframson allowed Chawlin to see him, after going hidden in Develin all winter?'

'Yes. I didn't think . . .'

'Then we must guess that it was Chawlin he wanted to bargain with. And now Chawlin must pay a price, for a life . . .'

'I thought he was going to be killed at one moment, in the fighting.'

'I doubt that it would be so simple. Remember, Paigan

Wulframson has only to whisper to his creatures, any day from now on, and the life that Chawlin saved will be taken horribly.'

'Oh!'

Ambrose put his hand to his mouth.

The Lynx – Sophia. Hadn't they saved her after all?

'Remember where his power comes from,' she said grimly. '*Let them eat their sons.* Eat, corrupt, ruin, destroy. It serves him, but it also drives him. That is why he turns fathers against their sons, and friends against friends. That is why he prefers to turn a man to evil, rather than use a creature that is already his slave. That is why he will turn a good man, if he can find one, rather than use one he has already ruined. What price do you think Chawlin must pay, to keep his friend alive?'

After a while Ambrose said heavily: 'I suppose it must be me.'

He stared unseeing across the sunlit meadow, where the insects wove among the bright flecks of colour. He tried to think that Chawlin would not allow himself to be forced to choose. He had been a friend from the day they had met. Yet Chawlin had named her above all others in the house. The Heron Man could send his creatures to take her at any moment. What would Chawlin do? What would he, Ambrose, do in Chawlin's place?

He remembered the hours of practice he had had with Chawlin. He knew how fast Chawlin was. He had lost count of the times Chawlin's staff had found its way past his own. He knew he was a child still. What would it be like when Chawlin faced him with iron in his hand? He felt helpless.

'What are we going to do?' he asked.

'What do you want to do?'

. . . Helpless; and angry.

'I want to fight,' he said.

'So do I,' she murmured. 'So do I.'

She was looking down the slope, to where the path emerged from the trees. Ambrose realized she had seen something. And there was movement down there – something among the trees, plodding steadily towards them. He could not see it clearly until it stepped into the sunlight and became a pair of horses, and, at their head, an armoured man.

'At last,' she said.

Ambrose saw a short figure in a stained white-and-blue tunic, who looked familiar – and the horse, that big grey animal that followed him, he recognized at once.

The other beast was new . . .

'Mercy of Angels!' she exclaimed. 'What's that?'

It looked like a horse, although it was smaller than Stefan, and a muddy brown colour. But its head was the wrong shape, and so were its long ears. It was saddled for riding.

'It's a mule!' she said. 'The foal of an ass! I suppose – I suppose riding horses must be very few in the March, now. He has done his best. All the same . . .'

The man looked around him, and saw them above him. Then he looped the reins of his beasts around a small tree, and began to climb the slope towards them. Ambrose, trusting nothing, watched him carefully until he was sure.

'It *is* him,' he said. 'It's Wastelands.'

He was the same travelled, ragged figure that he had

been when they had parted at Develin, and his stained armour did not shine in the sun.

'What did you call him?'

'Wastelands. Should we go down to him?'

She shook her head.

'I am not Paigan Wulframson. I have not yet learned to walk in both worlds as he does. If I move, I must set my feet on the rocks of the Cup. Each place in the Cup matches a place in this world, but it is smaller. It is only a dream, after all. So a wrong step might bring me to the other side of this valley, or up to my waist in the stream. It is easier for me to be still. For now, let him come to us.'

'Does he know about our enemy, and his creatures?'

'He knows. He and I have spoken much since he fled from Septimus's defeat. And he too has had an evil winter since you rode with him. But you must not call him a wasteland. No man is all wasted inside himself, any more than our poor Kingdom, even now, is all destroyed. His name is Aun. He is, or was, the Baron of Lackmere. Of all the friends who helped me against your father – Martin, Evalia, Adam – he is the last. He will do his best for us.'

Ambrose frowned. After all they had lost, one fighting man did not seem very much. He remembered Aunt Evalia's voice, speaking by the fire at Chatterfall. Even then, she had known what must be done. The problem was that they had never had the strength to do it.

'Can't we get more help?'

'Not without risk,' she said.

'We should take risks then.'

She seemed to think about what he had said. 'Very

well . . . Although a man like Aun is not nothing,' she added.

'Are you going to wed him?' Ambrose asked.

She gave a surprised little laugh. 'My darling – what put that into your head?'

'I don't know.'

It had come to him, just then, as he had looked at her watching the man toil up the slope towards them. There had been something in her eyes that he hadn't seen before.

The knight climbed steadily towards them under the sun. Ambrose could hear the *clink, clink* of his mail as he moved.

'A wolf may watch the moon,' she said. 'But neither can wed the other. I am something else now. He knows that.'

Wolf? Why had she said that?

Oh, because of his badge. Of course. And that must have been why she called his son the 'young wolf' back home in the hills – because he came from the house with the wolf-badge. That was all. She hadn't been judging either of them.

'He wants to kill his son,' he said.

After a moment she answered: 'That must not happen.'

Butterflies fled wavering before Wastelands's armoured knees as he picked his way up the meadow towards them.

'It *must* not happen,' she murmured.

'You will find that he listens to you, as he did not before,' she went on. 'He knows that you know the enemy. You must decide how to fight, and he will help you.'

'Won't you be with us?'

398

'I will not be far away. But I told you that in some ways I am still a babe. I cannot go with you under the sun, and I must be wary how I travel within the Cup. No,' she said, seeing the expression on his face. 'The enemy moves in both worlds. Aun can see only this one. And I am forgetting this one, while still learning my way in the other. But you – you see both. I think you always have. Oh, I know. It's too soon for you. But there is no more time. And you have grown this winter, Amba. You have learned as well – perhaps more than you realize. You must find your own way now. And you must help the rest of us to find it, too.'

'Why do you think I can?'

'Because you already have done.'

She looked down at something she was turning in her fingers.

'In the darkest hours of my life, my darling, you sent this to me. You gave it to Martin to bring to me in Tarceny. "Give Mama," you told him. No, you do not remember. You were less than two years old. But I have treasured this, and when I escaped from the pool and returned to the house, I remembered where I had laid it. I have carried it since, and with it I have managed to hide and to protect myself from the hunters. And now I have it to give back to you.'

It was a white stone.

'It is, as they all were, a fragment of the bone of Capuu, cut from the broken teeth that stood around the pool. It will not make you a ring to hide in. It will not be enough, I think, to ward off all attack from the creatures of the pit. Nor will it keep you safe from any man who serves the Prince Paigan. But the enemy does not know where you are, yet, and it may help to hide you. Carry it, and keep watch, and be ready with a weapon. For your enemies are men or creatures. They are not ghosts. They may be wounded by a sure hand. Take care of it, my darling, for it is the very last.'

She looked up as the knight climbed the last few yards of slope to where they sat. He stood over them, breathing heavily.

'A sure hand,' he said. 'And I have a little iron, too. Also I have some hooves, to save our feet, and bread for our bellies. Where are we headed from here?'

Ambrose gripped the last white stone in his palm. He knew she had just given him everything she had to give.

'We'll go home,' he said. 'We'll go back to the pool.'

# XX

## The March of Tarceny

nce again he was travelling with Wastelands. He slept on lumpy earth and roots, and rose in grey dawns with his clothes all clammy from the dew. His days were straps and camp-meals and the hours of plod, plod, plod as the landscapes shifted slowly by. He remembered it all so well that Develin might never have happened.

Some things were different, and better. The wooded hillsides changed more quickly than the dull, flat lands on the other side of the lake. He had his own mount – the solid, rough-hided mule, with its air of peaceful indifference to all that came. He had not found a name for it and did not think he would. It looked as if a name would be just another indignity for it to endure. Nevertheless he was grateful to it, because riding its broad, swaying back was easier than he had thought it might be.

Better still, Wastelands had brought food for two, whereas before (Ambrose now realized) he must have been sharing what he had planned for only one. And they were both ready to talk, from time to time.

In a valley like any other, Wastelands pointed to a rock.

It had been roughly shaped into a short, square column, and stood where the stream they had been following tumbled over a cataract.

'The March-stone,' he said. 'In law we are now in the March of Tarceny, and therefore in the Kingdom. If we were ordinary travellers we would be under the protection of the King. As it is, I am an outlaw, and so I suspect are you. Therefore everyone we meet would now be our enemy, and the lords would be bound to pursue us, out of the duty they owe to the crown.'

Ambrose slid down from the back of his mule to look at the stone.

'However,' Wastelands went on, 'I do not think we shall meet many who have heard of this King, or will seek to apply his law. The March was ever a land of few people, and the wars and risings of the last years have made it more so.'

'And who is the lord here?'

'You, I suppose,' said Wastelands, as though it had only just occurred to him. He frowned. 'Tancrem of Baldwin was the last real strength in the March, although he only held the land in stewardship. When he was brought down, Septimus appointed others, but by then the March was war-riven and worth little. One of the stewards was killed by the Fifteen. I did not hear that the rest ever came to see what they had here. Now Septimus is gone. There is no lord. There are not even many manors or farmhouses.'

On the face of the stone was carved a disc, which might have been a moon, with a shape upon it.

'Who are the Fifteen?'

Wastelands grinned, bitterly.

'You have met them. It was they who hounded us to Develin – and pressed me close for three days after, until I won to Lackmere and could drop my own portcullis in front of their noses. They were knights of your father. They lost their lands here after your father's rising, but they have crept back to what was left and they wring from it what they can, riding like brigands out of the shell of Tarceny.'

'Will we meet them here?'

'I trust not. The March is a wide land. But if we stay in one place too long, then they may come looking for us.'

'Why did they chase us?'

'They do not love me. But they were on your trail before I found you. So I guess they thought you carried some treasure of Old Tarceny, or maybe news of where they might find your mother. Her, they would hunt to the death, for her part in Tarceny's fall. I do not know who told them where to look for us. It may have been this scarecrow-priest that is our enemy. It may even have been my devil of a son.'

The mule stood patiently in the narrow track while Ambrose clambered back into his saddle.

'Your son spared your life,' he said slowly.

The man shot him an angry glance. 'Eh? What's that?'

'He came to our camp last season, when we were sleeping in the old castle. He could have killed both of us, but he didn't.'

Wastelands had half-turned in his saddle, staring at Ambrose.

'How do you know this?'

'I spoke with him. He came by under-craft and woke me. He had a knife, but he didn't do anything.'

He realized that the man probably wouldn't believe

him. In a moment he would decide that Ambrose was either mad or a liar, and ride on. It would be difficult to talk to him about anything after that.

Wastelands sat stock-still in his saddle.

'You spoke with him? You talked prettily and let him go away?'

'Yes,' said Ambrose.

'Why didn't you *wake* me?'

'I was afraid,' said Ambrose truthfully.

'Afraid! Michael's teeth! I could have had my throat slit – would that have made you feel better?'

'No.'

'He killed his brother! For witchcraft – witchcraft, you hear? It's the same damned stuff that your father did. There's no other word for it. That's what you were dealing with!'

'It isn't right to kill your son.'

Now he had done it. Wastelands was staring at him, his eyes dark and his cheeks pale. What now? Was he going to start beating him again?

The fighter leaned in his saddle until his face was nearly level with Ambrose's.

'What business,' said Wastelands, 'is that of yours?'

'My mother thinks so,' said Ambrose defensively.

'*Does* she? And what's it to do with her, either? Listen. What's between him and me is my concern and mine alone. What he did in my house. And to my men and my friends and my King last winter, too. What *right* do you think you have to tell me otherwise?'

Ambrose looked into his eyes, and saw no speaking with them.

'Now ride on,' said Wastelands, in a voice that was not quite true.

Obediently Ambrose kicked at his mule, and kicked again until it ambled ahead along the path. Behind him, he heard Stefan follow. He did not look round. He thought the man behind him might be weeping.

After a while Wastelands spoke again.

'Could you sleep, thinking that I'd sit and chat with the scarecrow and his creatures if they came on us in the night?'

'No.'

'Your enemies are my enemies. Mine are yours. That's the way it works. That's why we can ride together, you understand?'

'Yes.'

'From now on, neither of us sleeps at the same time. You'll watch, then I'll watch, the night through. And if either of us see anything, we both rouse up.'

'Yes.'

'And I'll be sleeping more lightly in future.'

Ambrose heard the choke in the man's voice. And he felt like weeping, too.

*You have to find your way*, his mother had said.

He had tried. And what had happened?

It wasn't fair! He'd tried to do what he'd been told! And now he was left feeling ashamed – ashamed because he had tried to tell Wastelands not to kill his son.

He had not thought of Wastelands as a man who grieved. He had thought Wastelands looked at the world with a hard face and made his way through its misery as a fish swam in water – ruined farms, ruined houses; even, perhaps, the loss of Develin, and the Widow whom he had called a friend. Ambrose had wondered how he could be so callous. Now he knew that Wastelands carried within him a rage and grief that was deeper than anything the man saw. That was what lay in the pit.

*My mother thinks so.* What a thing to have said! He had said it because he had thought Wastelands would listen to her. But it had only made things worse.

*What right do you think you have?*

It was not right that a man should kill his son. That was true. And Wastelands knew it. He didn't want to do it – or why would he be weeping now? But he was still going to do it if he could.

It was not right. And yet what right did Ambrose have?

In Develin they had said that men followed their feuds only because they could find no other way. Wastelands could not find another way; and Ambrose had not found it for him. There was a part of the man's soul that was locked, beyond reach.

The enemy had him.

They jogged on along the path by the stream. The countryside had hardly changed with their arrival on the southern fringes of the Kingdom. The valleys were wooded and steep-sided, and outcrops of rock broke the tree-cover on the ridges. They passed no dwellings, ruined or otherwise. After some miles the path left the streamside and began to climb an easy slope. Ambrose followed it. His thoughts had abandoned Wastelands. Now, angrily, they pursued the Prince Under the Sky.

He had barely glimpsed his enemy, in Develin, until the enemy had chosen to show himself at Develin's fall.

That fleeting, despising figure: how could Ambrose find him now?

He had already been too long about finding him. He wished that he had not been so afraid, back in Develin. He wished that he had looked harder. He should have used his hours to go walking through the courts and rooms looking for the Heron Man. Somewhere, behind some door, his enemy had waited. They should have met, at a time of Ambrose's choosing. And when they had spoken, their words should have been like the quick quarterstaffs to each other; and Ambrose would have answered like an equal.

He still would – if he could find him.

Where are you, Paigan, my enemy?

And so his mind escaped into a daydream of the house at Develin. He saw himself passing through the house, perhaps with a weapon in hand, searching for the frail man in a grey robe. Door after door opened before him, and all the rooms were empty. The corridors echoed to his feet, and the silence closed in behind him. He searched and he searched. And here at last was the door to the scholars' hall. And when he put his hand upon the iron ring he knew that the Heron Man was waiting for him beyond it: waiting before rows of empty benches to begin his lesson.

Ambrose blinked.

The mule had stopped. It had stopped because his hands had been pulling at its reins. They were at the top of a ridge, looking north into another valley, with the same fleece of trees that darkened in the shadows of drifting clouds.

Wastelands passed, high on Stefan's back. He said nothing to Ambrose. He headed on along the path that would lead down into the valley.

'Wait,' said Ambrose.

His companion either did not hear him or chose to ignore him again.

Ambrose cleared his throat, and found the man's name.

'Aun,' he called loudly.

The knight checked, and looked back.

'Wait,' Ambrose said again.

'What's the matter?'

What was the matter? Ambrose was not sure. The feeling – the moment he had put his hand upon the door-ring in his dream – had been very strong.

'Have you seen something?' Aun asked him.

'No.'

It was nothing you could see. There was nothing moving in the valley ahead of him. He had not heard anything either. And yet he had felt it clearly for a moment; like a trick of memory: an ugly, familiar, sick feeling, as if he had been about to walk back into a room where something dreadful had happened before. There had been a scent in the air as if the trees had begun to drip water from their leaves, in droplets that smelled of the edge of pools. Perhaps he could still feel it; perhaps he was just imagining it. But his mind showed him shapes that might be moving in the woods ahead of him – or that might come there, and look there, or that were walking among the brown rocks in a place that was near to this valley.

The Heron Man was close; the Heron Man, or something that came from him.

'They're hunting us,' he said.

The man he had called Aun looked at him, and then at the trees again. Plainly he could see nothing.

'Have they found us?' he asked at length.

'No. Maybe they've gone, but . . .'

'But?'

Ambrose thought. Go on?

(Open the door? The door to the scholars' hall?)

Yes, he wanted to. He wanted to meet the Heron Man again. He wanted to hear him, speak with him, and *prove* to him that . . .

But not yet, surely. This was no daydream. Now that the moment was real, he felt the old fears slithering into his mind. He fought them. He knew he must not be so afraid. And yet at the same time he thought: Not yet. Not without more help.

His throat was sticky.

'Is there another way?' he asked.

'We could go back to the streamside and follow that. I think there was a footpath on the other bank. We could rejoin the road further on.'

Still Ambrose looked at the valley ahead of them. A minute ago Aun must still have been nursing their quarrel. Now he was ready to turn aside at Ambrose's word; because he was an ally in another man's war.

'Let's do that,' he said.

'Very well.'

They backed off the ridge and Ambrose felt better at once. He felt better still under the cover of trees.

The going along the stream was slow. The branches were low and they had to lead their mounts. They made only a few more miles that afternoon. Then, in a clearing by the bank, they came upon a hut. They saw the roof was whole, and that smoke rose from the chimney. Ambrose dismounted first, and Aun let him. The door was closed fast, and so were the shutters. But Ambrose guessed that there must be people inside, and called and banged hard upon the boards. At length a shutter opened.

'Lodging for the night?' he said brightly to the scared faces that peered out at him. It was a woman and her young daughter. They must have heard the riders coming and have been hoping that these two strangers would pass and leave them alone; but the woman unbolted the door and showed them where they might tether their mounts.

'Have you coin to pay them?' Ambrose muttered to Aun as they unharnessed the horses.

Aun's brow lifted in surprise.

'I have. Although they will give us food and bed for nothing.'

'Why should they?'

'It is the custom. Also they may fear that we would cut their throats.'

Ambrose felt his face harden.

'Better to pay them, while we can.'

Aun grunted, but said only: 'We should take watches through the night, still.'

Ambrose nodded. After feeling the enemy that afternoon he would certainly watch. If the Heron Man came to him, he did not want to be sleeping.

The hut was a single room with an earth floor strewn with belongings. The air within it was dark and smoky from the fire. The woman's husband arrived with fish that he had trapped in a pool. He was surly and suspicious, but

410

did not argue when his wife took his catch for their evening meal. While the pan began to sizzle on the hearth, Ambrose asked them questions about the March. They answered shortly. They had no lord or manor knight nearby. There was another family, half a day's walk further down the stream, but travellers were very few. They had heard of the Fifteen, and feared them, but had never seen them in their valley. They shrugged when Ambrose told them of the happenings in the wider Kingdom. Such things might have been taking place upon the moon.

The child, who could only have been six years old, watched them through the smoke and never said a word. Perhaps she had never seen armoured knights before.

Knight, he corrected himself. Aun was a knight. He wasn't. He did not know what he was.

'What was the old lord like?' Ambrose asked suddenly. 'The last lord of Tarceny, before the stewards?' He felt Aun glance sharply at him.

'Fair, as I heard,' said the man.

'More than fair, sir,' said his wife. 'There was good law then, and no brigands in the March either.'

'Better no law than a lord's law,' said the man.

'That's not so,' said his wife. 'When each time there's a horseman on our stream I think they'll put a rope round your neck – for me and the goat and a bucket of grain?'

'That's foolish,' said the man, and they both fell silent again in front of their knightly lodgers.

Ambrose asked no more questions. He watched the fish blacken over the tiny flames and let his thoughts turn as slowly inside his head.

After their meal he made a trade with the woman. He

411

gave her his scholar's shirt in exchange for a thin, black blanket and a rag of pale cloth. Then he begged from her the use of a needle and thread. He settled himself by the fire. Gradually the household went to bed around him, sleeping in huddles against the walls. He took his time over what he was doing. He did not want Aun to ask him about it until he was done. Let him suppose that it was an excuse to the household to be awake, and watching.

Aun went to sleep at once. The man and the woman lay still and made so little noise for so long that Ambrose was sure they were awake, distrustful of the strangers under their roof. He was sorry, because he did not want them to be afraid. But he knew that nothing he said would help them. His fingers worked slowly in the firelight, cutting the black cloth roughly into a broad rectangle with a knife that Aun had given him at the start of their journey. Then he took the pale rag and laboriously, cut by cut, ripped two rough circles from it, each as wide across as his spread hand. From each circle he cut a piece away, about the size of two of his thumbs together. At last he fumbled in the firelight for the needle and thread.

Stitching, especially for ornament or show, was not man's work. But Ambrose had learned enough to mend clothes and blankets in his mountain home, where even his child's hands were a help to his mother, busy with a hundred household tasks. And a scholar's life at Develin had been punctuated by the need to darn or mend his few things with whatever he could beg or borrow. It would have been better if he had had more light to see by. But these threads would not have to strain against muscle or stand the drag of skin, day in, day out. All they needed to do was to hold one piece of cloth to another, for show.

Gradually, carefully, he stitched one of his two circles into the centre of his black cloth, working obstinately on as the firelight dimmed and his eyes ached, and going over and over his stitches at the end to make sure that the line would hold. Then he found and placed two more logs on the fire, not for warmth but for light to finish his job.

Aun was asleep. The man and the woman were asleep. Across the room the girl had raised her head, and was looking at him with eyes that flung back the firelight. The last time he had seen eyes gleam like that had been when the monsters crowded upon him at Ferroux. Now it was a child's face, small and calm, watching the world as if it were a puzzle that she would one day understand.

He said nothing to her, but fumbled for his needle and thread again. It was not there. He had lost it in the dimness. He sighed, and began to feel around for it, spreading his hand flat on the earthy floor of the hut.

'It's by your foot.'

'What?'

'It's by your foot,' the child whispered again.

He found it and grunted his thanks.

She went on watching him as he slowly stitched the second disc onto the reverse side of the black cloth. He would look up now and again and she was still awake, lying propped on one arm among her blankets with her head raised to follow what he was doing.

It came to him that her home, although only one room and built of wood, was not so very different from the house in the mountains where he had lived with his mother, sharing all the chores as far as he was able to. It was far more

413

like it than the busy world of Develin where each task had its own man, and learning itself was considered a task. He wondered what this child saw as she watched him crouched by the fire, and remembered how only a few months ago he had sat in the court at home watching a strange knight, who had travelled in so many places and seen so many things. That man had become the Wolf – one of the enemy. Why should this child suppose Ambrose to be a friend?

He held up his cloth in both hands. It was now a small banneret, with the white disc stitched into the centre of either face. He would need to find a long pole or stick tomorrow to tie the corners to.

'There's a piece missing,' whispered the child with fire-light in her eyes.

He turned it in his hands and looked at the broken shapes of the discs on either side of his banner.

'Yes,' he said. 'There's supposed to be.'

'Why?'

'It's the moon. You are looking at the moon on a dark night. But there's something between you and it, so you can't see all of it. That's what that black bit means. I don't know what it is, yet, but I'll think about it. You should go to sleep now.'

She must have wanted to know more than that. But she laid her head down obediently. In the shadow of her blankets he could no longer see if her eyes were open. She did not speak again.

He wondered, for a moment, if this was another angel. Then he thought no, it was not. Or, she had as much of the Angels in her as there was in any human. He did not know her name – or the names of her parents either. He must remember about names. He could never speak with people properly if he did not use their names.

And when he spoke with the enemy? With Paigan Wulframson?

He sat, fingering the white stone his mother had given him. He did not think that the enemy had found him yet. He hoped it would not be here, hiding, with these people around him. When he met the enemy he wanted it to be because he had sought the Heron Man out face to face, as he had almost tried to do that afternoon.

Mother would say that even to want that much was dangerous. But he still wanted it.

He shivered. It was going to be colder, he realized, now that he had parted from his shirt. It would be some hours before he could wake Aun and take a rest himself. He picked up his new banner and drew it round his shoulders. Since he had sold his shirt for it, there was no reason why it could not be an extra blanket for him tonight. It was meant to bring him help, after all. It could start by helping him to keep warm.

The man and woman watched blank-eyed in the morning as he tied his banner to a long stick and slung it from his shoulder. They must have known what it meant. He wondered if they would tell their child, and if so, what they would say. He thought it more likely that they would argue among themselves again about whether it was better to have a lord than take their chances day by day with whoever might come to their door.

Aun looked darkly at the flag, but said nothing until

415

they had set off and left the hut behind them in its clearing. Then he reined his war-horse over to tower above
Ambrose.

'That is not my banner.'

Ambrose knew what he meant. If people saw a knight
riding with a ragged boy who carried a standard, they
would think that the standard was the knight's. And Aun
must have hated Ambrose's father, like everyone else.

But he was not going to be stared down this time.

'No. It's mine.'

He was expecting Aun to shout at him; instead, Aun
seemed to take him seriously.

'So. But in raising that standard you make two claims,
not one,' he said.

'I'm telling people who I am.'

'Who you are is the point; and more, who you could
be. Your father was not just lord of this March. Nor was
he the first of his house to be crowned King. People might
wonder if he will be the last.'

King? It was a king who had done what had been
done at Develin.

'I am not going to be King.'

'No? The land is still looking for one. No king who
rules like Velis can be secure. If you do not wish to be
King you will need to be sure that all men know it.'

'I am not going to be King. I'm just tired of hiding.
And if people are going to help me, they must know who
I am.'

Ambrose knew that Aun did not agree, and was
relieved when he did not answer. But at their midday halt
Aun astonished him by unbuckling his own short sword in

416

its scabbard and fastening it to Ambrose's saddle. Then he drew it, and handed it hilt-first to Ambrose, who stared at the faded oak leaf cut upon its pommel.

'I shall want this back in time,' he said. 'But it came from your mother's house, a long time ago. And of all my tools it is the most suited for you.'

There and then Aun made Ambrose stand before a mountain yew and cut at it with the sword, so that he could learn how to manage its weight and deliver the strokes that could break a mail-suit at the neck or cripple an armoured knee.

'Should we not fight with each other?' Ambrose asked as the iron swirled in his grip and dented the roots of the yew. It seemed much less heavy than it had last season, when he had lifted it with his half-starved arm from Aun's saddle.

'Better to wait until you have learned how to use that thing,' Aun answered.

'I want us to fight each other.'

'All right,' said Aun after a few moments.

Aun put on his helmet and shield and unlaced from his saddle a short, cruel-looking mace. And fight they did. It was slower than the quick flash of staves with Chawlin, because the sword was still clumsy in Ambrose's grip, and because they both knew that even a training-hurt might be serious on this wilderness journey. But Ambrose was happy as he panted and staggered and hacked at Aun, and tried the tricks that Chawlin had taught him. He felt he was becoming more dangerous. He wanted to be dangerous, after running for so long.

When they had finished, he cut a small strip of black

417

off his banner and folded the last white stone into it. Then he tied it tightly to the sword, where the hilt and blade met. That way he could use it to guard himself from the creatures of his enemy, and then strike at them in a single movement. Chawlin had told him often that the trick was to move from guard to strike in the blink of an eye.

And now he had the Oak, and the Moon, in one. Perhaps that was the piece that was missing, he thought. Perhaps the shadow on the disc should be the leaf of his mother's house. He could make it so, when he had time.

They mounted again. The path, a thread of stones and beaten earth, unravelled towards the heart of Tarceny. The stick of his makeshift banner bounced lightly at his shoulder as his mule moved forward. He could hear Aun's great horse, old Stefan, picking up the pace. The skies were clouded, but broken with blue and with gleams of sun.

He laughed, and rode north; and his ragged banner flew behind him.


Terrible things happened, and then wonderful things happened.

Not long ago Sophia would have called the dress that Chawlin bought for her terrible, because it was rough and stained and badly stitched. She had never worn anything like it before. But once it was on, she could look down at herself and imagine that she was some miller's daughter, living a completely different life. The truth of who she had been was hidden, like the pearls and the silk. It was locked away inside her secret self, until the time when she would choose to remember Develin, and how it had ended. Now she could be alive.

And never in her life had she felt so alive. Every day they travelled to a place she had not seen before. They drifted downriver in the punt, stopping at villages to join companies of pilgrims and pedlars for a meal or a night's rest. She liked the dirty lodging houses, and she liked them all the more for being crowded with fish-wives and journey men and clerks and tricksters and the hundred other sorts that still moved upon the river and roads. She woke with flea-bites, and scratched them, and laughed. Even when her hands got sore from her turns at the punt-pole she liked it, for Chawlin stroked her fingers and dressed the blisters, and she laughed again when he scolded her for not taking care. And one afternoon they rounded a bend in the river, and there before her was a broad estuary running out to the great lake of Derewater, that stretched the length of the western side of the Kingdom. She had never seen so much water all in one place before: a great, flat plain of wavelets, sparkling in the sun and so far across that the opposite shore was lost in haze.

'We should have a story to get us across the lake,' Chawlin said. 'I think we should be a brother and sister from Tuscolo, and our father can be a merchant who wants us to try to find some of his old trading partners in the March . . . What's the matter?'

Sophia had started to laugh again.

'Who do you think will believe us?' she said.

'About trading with the March? It used to be . . .'

'No. That we're brother and sister!'

They both laughed, then. And Sophia laughed so much that she got the hiccups, and Chawlin put his arm around her shoulders and kissed her, because he said it was a good cure for hiccups, and . . .

And *this* was love. When they lay together – under a bush or on a narrow pallet in a crowded boarding house, it didn't matter. All the meaning in the world found itself in the press of his body upon hers. And her head was pillowed upon his arm and his breath blew like a warm wind in her ear, and she knew that whatever else the world had done to her *he* was going to be there again and again and as much as she wanted, and she wanted him for ever.

'You save me,' she said, wrapping him in her arms.

'We were lucky, that's all.'

'No, I mean you save me now. Every day.'

He laughed softly at her. But it was true. Whatever she had done, he was the answer. For all her misery and failure and betrayals at Develin he was the answer, because he loved her.

So they played, for each other and for the world, that they were man and wife; although, as Chawlin said, few wives that he had seen went about finding their husbands little gifts of flowers, or brought him water that he had not asked for, unless they were still in the very first days of their marriage. And he had heard none – Sophia – that called their man 'husband', in the way that she so wished to do.

She loved him. She loved him so much. She had never had feelings like these before.

And he smiled, and teased her hair and let his breath linger on her skin. But he also spent much time thinking to himself, chin upon hand or with his fingers over his eyes, and he would not say what he was thinking.

On the estuary they came to a small town, which even in these days saw numbers of pilgrims making their way down to the holy city of Jent. There Chawlin went up and down the waterside looking for a boat. Sophia stayed with the punt, waiting and talking with travellers and fishermen, trying this gambit and then that, until at last someone she had given up on an hour before came back unexpectedly to say that he would buy the punt at the lowest price that Chawlin had said they should sell it for. Then she bought some food and a little wine (for which she guessed she was over-charged) and found Chawlin at the last jetty before the lake, stowing sacks in an open boat that he had acquired. It seemed very small, for a journey on such a huge water, but Chawlin said it would be good enough if the weather held. They paid the quay-guard to watch the boat and she persuaded Chawlin to come onto the hillside above the town, to sip the wine while they watched the sun set.

Chawlin sat in silence, looking at the gold light glaring upon the water and licking the under-bellies of the clouds with fire. She leaned against him, murmuring little thoughts now and again, but he answered only shortly and took mouthfuls from the flask. When he handed it to her she tasted it and decided that it was sourer than any wine she had known in Develin. But that was not the point. The point was that they had the freedom to drink it together, here, and not worry about who saw them or what might be thought of what they were doing.

And maybe – maybe they would stay out here together, if the night were warm enough, and love one another under the stars; and lie in each other's arms, and talk softly with the feel of skin against skin: the grass their pillow and all the world their bed.

'So we leave the Kingdom tomorrow,' she said.

'The March is still part of the Kingdom. But yes, it will be beyond Velis's reach.'

'How long before we can come to Hayley?'

'A week, yet.'

'Is it so far? I can see the mountains, I think.'

Beyond the lake the horizon was black, and a little higher than it should be, as if the sun were falling into a low bank of thick cloud.

'Yes. But Hayley is further north.' He gestured with the bottle, looked at it, and took another sip. 'The fastest way would be to sail straight up to the head of the lake before landing. But I'm no great sailor. So we'll take the shortest way across. I should be able to do that in a day. Then we'll follow the shore, at least as far as the harbour at Aclete. There are not many people there now, but it is the only place of any size over there.'

She put her arm around him and kept her head on his shoulder. He was speaking fairly, but under his words she sensed a mood that had not been there before.

'Is there something wrong?' she asked.

'It's – well, yes there is. I've had a shock, anyway. I met someone by the water. Or rather he – he came up to me.'

The way he said *came up* made it sound as though there had been something very unpleasant about the way this stranger had appeared.

'Who was it?'

'You don't know him. He's – he's no friend, anyway.

422

He wanted me to do something I'd no intention of doing. Then he threatened us. He knows who you are, you see.'

Sophia thought it must be someone who knew what had happened at Develin – who had seen them arrive and had recognized her. Plenty of travellers had passed through her home, when it had been her home. She supposed they were lucky to have gone unnoticed for as long as they had.

'What did he want you to do?'

He shook his head. 'I'd rather not talk about it.'

'We'll be safe over the water, though,' she said stoutly. And it would be another reason not to return to town tonight. They would have to hope that the bundles aboard the boat would be safe.

Chawlin grunted. He did not seem as confident as she thought he should be. He sat with his chin on his hand, like a man who had lost his way.

'Luke is over there,' he said suddenly.

Sophia sat up. 'He's alive?'

'Yes.'

Chawlin must have seen him in the cup, she thought.

'Are we going to meet him?'

'I'm thinking about it.'

Sophia thought about it, too. Something heavy stirred deep inside her, like a great beast shifting in its sleep. It was guilt.

'I want to talk to him, if we can.'

Chawlin shook his head. 'It's too far. It's out of our way.'

'Where is he then?'

'I don't know. I've tried the cup, but for some reason it is difficult to see him.'

Difficult?

At Develin, when people had told her something was difficult, what they had really meant was that they did not want to do it. She thought she could understand why Chawlin did not want to turn aside from their journey to go hunting through the wild lands. But he would if he knew it was important to her.

'Please, Chawlin.'

Chawlin sighed. He did not ask her what she wanted to say to the boy.

Sophia did not know what she wanted to say, either. But if Luke – no, Ambrose – was alive, then she had to speak with him. She could not speak to her mother, or Hestie, or any of the others whose lives she had helped to squander. She could tell Chawlin what she felt, but Chawlin did not stand for the dead. He was who he was, thoughtful, loving, capable – all those things. He was himself, and what he meant to her.

But Ambrose – a boy she had ignored and despised – he had been part of Develin, too. He had been one of those she had failed – and failed because she had not listened to him. And he was still living. If only he would hear her, she thought, it would be easier for her afterwards to bear what she had done.

*I didn't know you.* That would be part of it.

Not *I didn't know whose son you were*, but *I didn't know who you are*.

'We should try to find him, if we can,' she said.

Something like a hiss escaped from Chawlin.

'I wonder if we can get away with it.'

'What do you mean?'

'Not much. The light's going. Are you cold?'

She put her arm around him and snuggled into his shoulder again.

'No,' she said simply. 'Husband.'

'We can't stay up here all night, after all.'

'Yes we can. It's beautiful.'

The light, however, was dimming. The gold had gone from the lake. The last orange streaks were slipping from the clouds. The western sky was still bright in the afterglow of the sun, but the mountains were black and all the land was in shadow. The stars would be coming out, soon. She sat where she was, feeling her ribs and his lift against one another with their breathing.

Chawlin did not seem to be in the mood for embraces. He seemed to be looking about him at the hillside, as though he feared some interruption. And he was sipping quickly at the wine. After a while she heard him curse softly.

'Finished it?' she said; and then, teasing: 'I wanted some!'

He shook his head. 'No. There's some left. You have it. I'm drinking too much.'

'What's the matter?'

He did not answer.

'Sweetheart, what is the matter?'

'It's – it's difficult. And bad. Everything I do seems to be bad.'

'No! You're doing wonderfully, my darling! I wish I could be more help.'

'It's not that. It's two hundred people that I've . . . Two hundred and one, now. You said all that happens

425

when you die is that things stop happening. I wish I could believe that – and that if you're miserable, or mad, then it's even a relief when things stop . . .' He shook his head again, and ran his hand through his hair. 'I've drunk too much.'

'They weren't mad,' said Sophia. 'Some of the masters were strange. But none of them were mad.'

He gave a short, hopeless laugh, as if she had completely failed to understand.

What Sophia could understand was that the man she thought of as her husband was drunk, and she did not like it. She had seen drunkenness – rowdy drunkenness – at Develin. Someone or other would go bawling round the courtyards one evening, and next morning they would be sitting with their legs firmly clamped in the Widow's stocks. But Sophia had never seen sad drunkenness, like this, where the things that made the man what he was seemed to loosen and fall one by one to the ground. She did not like to think of Chawlin drunk. It was not his nature. It was as if he was being unmade.

'Tell me a story, then.'

'I've no stories at the moment.'

'Oh, sweetheart . . .'

She rocked gently against him with her arm around his shoulders. This night was not going to be beautiful after all, not with Chawlin like this. The shadows of the evening were growing, like groping memories come from the hiding places to which they had been banished during the day. They prowled at the edge of her mind, watching her. They wanted to tell her that whatever she did, she was theirs, even though she thought she had escaped them. She would

426

go back to them. Chawlin was already going back to them. They would drown together in tears that stank of dark water.

'My darling,' she murmured.

Something moved among the grasses on the hillside, and he started.

'What was that?' she said.

'Fox,' he muttered. 'Fox.'

Sophia got slowly to her feet, looking around her. Suddenly, a crowded lodging house seemed a better place to sleep after all. She no longer wanted to spend the night out here where strange things lurked and slipped among the grasses where she could not see them.

She had a feeling that the thing had not been a fox. But she had no idea what it might have been.

# XXI

## Blood and Black Water

t was bright mid-morning when Ambrose topped a rise and looked down onto the lake. He checked his mule and leaned in his saddle. Beside him, Aun halted also.

The water was immense, and blue today. From the ridgetop they could see far out over a broad bay to the flat plain of water beyond, running on and on to the east until it was lost in mists. Ambrose remembered the glimpses he had had of the lake on his last journey with Aun – on the farther shore, between the lights of Bay and the ruins of Trant. In his memory, everything had seemed brown or grey then. Now the sun had reduced the clouds to just a few large masses, with shadows that idled over hillsides and water like dull fish in a sea of light.

At their feet the ground dropped to a river valley that ran into the bay. Opposite them to the north was a great round-shouldered hill covered with grass, with woods clinging to its landward side. The top of the hill was broad and flat, and up there someone had built what looked like a beacon. The place must have a good view both of the lake and of the ways into the west and north of the March.

Aun pointed down the slope.

'Aclete,' he said.

Crouched between the bay and the foot of the great hill was a village or small town of about a hundred roofs, circled in a weathered palisade of old logs. It was a surprise to Ambrose. After days of travelling without seeing more than three huts together, he had begun to believe that the March was almost empty. He wondered how many people lived here. Some of the roofs had fallen or showed holes – not from burning, but from neglect. Of the two larger buildings that stood on either side of the bay itself, one at least was derelict. The nearer, however, was built of stone, and seemed to have banners outside it. Two or three small boats lay at anchor in the bay. Ambrose could see people moving among the huts. There also appeared to be a line of men standing along the road outside the palisade.

Had he seen this before?

He knew he had not seen this before. He had never stood here or looked down upon these huts in his life. The dream-like trick of memory he felt meant something else. He had felt it the day they had crossed into the March. Now he had it again – faintly, elusively, like a scent in a room that might be decay.

The enemy.

He wondered how close they were, on this bright day. He could not tell.

'They're not gallows, if that's what you are thinking,' said Aun.

'What?'

429

'Those men by the road.'

It hadn't been what he was thinking. But now that he looked more closely at the line of figures outside the gate, he realized that they were not moving in the way he would expect people to move. In fact, they were not moving at all.

He kicked his mule into a slow walk. Behind him, he heard Stefan begin to follow.

His feeling grew as they made their way down towards the town. He glanced left and right at patches of cover as he passed. He looked round to be sure that Aun was still there, and to check that there was no one else behind them on the road. Something of the enemy was here – or would come here, or had been here and was gone. But whether it was the Heron Man himself, he did not know.

He could see the line of men more clearly. They were standing at posts and bending forward. His mind made a jump. They were in stocks: not ankle stocks, like the ones in Develin, where the victim could at least sit during his long humiliation; but standing stocks that fitted around the necks and wrists of the man they held, at a height that made him bend forward. Looking at the posture of the nearest man, Ambrose saw that his back must be in agony. The pain was forcing his knees to give, in a desperate effort to straighten the spine, and his body was sagging, supported heavily on his neck and wrists, pinned in their close-cut boards. The victim was beginning to choke. He could not hold himself like that for more than a few seconds. He would have to will his legs and back into their tortured positions again – for as long as they could bear.

There! The man two along had almost fallen. A

430

woman was at his side, begging him to stand upright. The man's face was sunburned and twisted in its prison of boards. He was gasping. Ambrose could hear the urgent murmur of the woman's voice. There were nine men in the line, some with people standing by them, some fighting their battle with the cruel boards alone.

No one, Ambrose noticed, was jeering or throwing rotten vegetables at these people.

'What have they done?' he asked from his saddle. 'What have all these people done?'

A woman looked up, angry.

'And why should they have done anything?'

Ambrose flinched. He could not help feeling she was angry with him.

One prisoner was trying to look up at him from his bent position, but the board would not let him lift his head. By raising his eyes to the limit he must just be able to glimpse Ambrose's stirrups. The man in the next set of stocks had twisted round to get his head on one side, so that he could look down along his nose at Ambrose.

'How long must they stay like this?' Ambrose asked.

'To noon, perhaps,' said Aun beside him. 'To sundown, more likely. Come on. It's not our business.'

To sundown. They were fading already, with the heat of the day yet to come.

Always and everywhere, the enemy was before him, claiming the land for his own. And when Ambrose came he was gone, leaving his work behind him.

'Come on,' said Aun.

As Ambrose dithered, the knees of the man in the stocks nearest to him gave way again. He half-fell, and his

431

neck and head clumped against the boards that held him. He cried out. So did the woman, now struggling to hold him upright. Ambrose was down from the saddle with the oak-pommel sword in hand.

'What the devil are you doing?' said Aun sharply.

The boards were wedged into place with simple wooden pegs. By keeping a hand on the blade of the sword, a few inches down from the point, he was able to lever them out, one after the other. The upper stock-board lifted. The man tumbled free, groaning. The woman bent over him. Ambrose heard Aun curse, but he ignored it.

He stood over them, waiting to be thanked, but they were both too concerned with the man's hurts to think of him. After a moment he turned away, and saw the line of other stocked men still pinned. He made a further decision, and started to work his way down the row, freeing one man after another.

*You see?* he told the Heron Man in his mind. *I've come. It's not your land any more.*

Clunk, went another board.

*I'm here!*

It was so easy. Just a few moments of two-handed poking with his sword made the difference between torture and relief for these men. Any friend or wife could have done it, if they had had the will. It was not these wooden pegs that kept them off, but something else.

He looked about him. There was no sign of a guard over the stocks, although Ambrose realized that there must have been one. He turned to ask Aun if he had seen anybody, but to his surprise he saw that Aun was forty yards down the road, leading Stefan and the mule away from the huts. Ambrose supposed that he must be looking for some-where to tether them. The men he had released were sitting or lying where they had fallen. Those that had friends or family with them were being helped to their feet. To his left three still remained pinned in their stocks. His makeshift banner had fallen from his shoulder when he had tumbled out of the saddle, and was now flat in the dust.

And beside it was a folded blanket. And by the blan-ket was a flask of drink, and an apple. Someone had been sitting there. They had been sitting there only a few moments ago, because the blanket still bore the print of someone's seat. And whoever-it-was had gone in a hurry, because the apple was half-eaten. They must have gone as Ambrose rode up. He had not noticed them, and had not seen them go.

So there had been a guard, or a watchman. And where had he gone to?

He picked up his banner and brushed it off with his hand. Inside the stockade, a horse had begun to whinny.

*You can't frighten me*, he told the Heron Man in his mind.

He propped the banner against one of the empty stocks and went to release the next man. The pegs were pale in the weather-stained wood. They were newly made, he thought, to replace some other pegs that had held these boards before now. They had swollen, too, and wanted to stick in their places. But they shifted one by one under the point of the sword. There! The board lifted, and the man sank to the ground, groaning. Hoofbeats sounded behind him, moving at a heavy canter. He turned. Three horse-men had spurred out of the town gate. They were armoured and had helmets on their heads. Ambrose waited. He wondered if the Heron Man would glide softly out of the gates of the town after them. The horsemen thundered up to him and heaved their mounts to a halt in a cloud of yellow road dust.

'Right, Durbey!' cried a voice muffled in its iron helm. 'Grab that one and make sure he doesn't run.' They were flinging themselves down from their mounts in a clatter of iron. 'One poxy little squire in leather breeches and you think you can turn my town upside down. I'll have your ears for my doorpost!'

Ambrose realized that the man was talking to him. He could glimpse the eyes within the slit of the huge, closed helm that covered the man's head. He was wearing mail. They all were. But it had been thrown on in a rush. The helm was unlaced. They should have padded coats on under their armour, like Aun, to prevent the chain links bruising their flesh with each blow. They hadn't. They had come hurriedly, to stop what he was doing.

Ambrose looked hard, but could not see the Heron Man. That worried him.

To the Helm he said: 'They were hurting too much.'

'Hurting! What's that to you, you wart? Leo, grab him and cut his britches for me. First, I'm going to turn his buttocks black, and then . . .'

'Mar!' said one of the others, and pointed to the ragged banner.

The man in the helm looked at it.

'So you're with *them*, are you? That noser Orcrim sent you to have fun, did he? Well, he can buck out of my business. What he says doesn't go here. We'll have your ear off, to show him I don't hear him. And I'll cut it into fifteen

434

little bits for you to carry back to those bastards at Tarceny. Grab him, Leo.'

'I'm not with anyone!' said Ambrose. 'The banner's mine!'

'Grab him, Leo.'

The second man lunged for Ambrose's collar, but Ambrose twisted out of his grip and jumped back, raising his sword to guard as Chawlin had taught him.

'Put it down,' said the Helm in a different tone.

'Leave me alone!'

'I'm getting angry, boy. And when I get angry someone dies. Is that what you want? Put it down or I'll take it and spit you and leave you to wriggle on it.'

He could run down the road, calling Aun to help him. But even if they got away, these men would just put their victims back in the stocks again. And the Heron Man would have shown him that he was powerless. He had not got down from his mount to let that happen. The Helm must be made to see that he was wrong.

'I'm not with anyone. I'm with me,' he said, keeping his sword up. 'And . . .' He dug among his memories of the teaching at Develin. 'And I want to hear what you tried these men for, and when, and what witness was brought. That's the Law.'

'*Law?* Now he's telling me the Law! I'll give you law – the kind I run here. And I don't listen to anyone else . . .'

'A lord who is lawless loses his right to land,' said Ambrose remembering voices at Develin that had talked of land-right, and the Law, and the King.

He heard the breath hiss within the helm. The man was staring at him as if he had taken a body-blow.

435

It must be hard to hear, and see, inside a case of iron like that, Ambrose thought. Or to be heard, or seen, for who you are. It was a great, blind barrier between the man and the world: like never using anyone's name.

'So! It's like that is it? Right to the land, now, is it? If it's like that, then I know a good little game we can play with the law. Durbey, show me that fellow's neck, will you?'

One of his armed followers took the man that Ambrose had just released and forced him to kneel, pushing his head forward so that the back of the neck gleamed pale through the strands of dark hair. There was an angry red mark where it had been chafing against the upper board.

'Right. Now I put this one and his fellows in stock for a little for Disrespect. That's all. It was just something they needed reminding about. But *now* I say they were really plotting riot, and this one here's the ringleader. That means I can hang him, if I want to. But since I'm nice, and in a hurry, I'll do it with my sweet sharp sword here. Shouldn't take a moment.'

He flapped his hand. One of his fellows drew a great hand-and-a-half sword from the saddle of a horse and placed it in his leader's grip.

'Witnesses? Oh dear, there weren't any. All you've got is my word as a knight for it. But if you're *very* sure I'm wrong, you know what to do, don't you? Toot me a blast, Leo.'

One of the other armed men was fumbling at his saddle again.

'Toot me a blast, Leo!'

'Coming,' said the man. He held a short hunting horn

in his gauntleted hands, and blew a quick, harsh note on it.

'Right. Now by Heaven and by my hold on this land, I say this court is open. Let any who feel the right of this cause stand forth to prove it with his body before three blasts of the trumpet. Toot it, Leo.'

The horn sounded again.

'Right, I'm up. I say he did it. Leo? Durbey?' The other two nodded. One raised his hand, in the mockery of an oath. '*We* all say he did it. If no one says he didn't do it, I'll knock his head off at the third blast and make you a present of it. Going to help him out, are you?'

He meant a fight. He wanted Ambrose to choose between fighting the three of them, or watching them kill this man, who would have lived if he had not interfered.

He had fallen into a trap. When he had slid from his mule, he had thought he was undoing the work of the Heron Man. Now there was iron at a man's neck, and a sudden, appalling understanding of things he had not seen, and yet that he had seen before.

(*I will give you One*, said his memory. *There will be a price.*)

The Heron Man must be very close.

'This is an Ordeal, runt. If we say he did it and you say he didn't, we settle it in a fight. Don't worry. We're only allowed to come at you one at a time. That's the Law.'

(*Law bends before power*, said the ghost of Denke at his elbow.)

'Toot it, Leo.'

The horn sounded.

(*My darling . . . You see how he tricked you.*)

He had no idea if he could fight them. He supposed

437

not. They were stronger. They had mail, and big weapons. He was still learning.

The man he had rescued was whimpering now. He thought they meant it. Probably they did.

'Going to do it? No? Too bad, you could have helped him. Better still, you could have left him alone to get sore knees.'

'I'll do it,' said Ambrose.

It was his fault, so he would have to. And he was angry. He hated this lumbering, jeering voice that mocked everything he knew to be right. He stepped back and lifted his sword-point.

'I'm sorry you said that, boy,' said the Helm slowly. 'It's not my fault you did.'

Ambrose sidled onto smoother ground, wondering when the fight would begin. A voice called from behind him. The men straightened and looked up. Still he did not take his eyes off them, because Chawlin had taught him he must not.

Then a hand gripped him by the shoulder.

'Now that you've got this far,' said Aun dryly. 'You'd better let me do the rest.'

He was wearing his helmet. It was laced into his mail-shirt. He had dropped his cloak and was carrying his shield. His heavy, mailed gauntlets were on his hands. He must have been preparing for a fight all this time.

'So the pup's got a dog with him, has he?' said the Helm. 'Where did you spring from?'

'Not a dog,' said Aun, with a sour grin and a lift of his wolf-shield. 'Tourney, is it?'

'Ordeal,' said the Helm.

438

'Ordeal!' Aun glanced at the kneeling man. 'For the life of a townsman?'

'What's good enough for fine folk is good enough for mine. This is my ground. My law.'

'Better get into your saddles, then, the three of you,' said Aun.

'One at a time!' said Ambrose, finding his tongue again. 'He said.'

'One at a time,' agreed the Helm. He looked over Aun's shoulder at their horses. 'On foot.'

Aun shrugged. Ambrose realized how much of an advantage big, war-hardened Stefan would have given him over those three on their poor mounts.

'But . . .'

'It makes no difference,' Aun said to him, in a voice that was meant to carry.

'Damn right it won't,' said the Helm.

Then there was a bad time, which seemed to stretch for hours. Ambrose helped Aun to tighten the laces on his helmet. He knew he had nearly got the townsman killed, and then had nearly got himself killed, and now he was going to have to watch and see whether Aun would be killed instead. He wanted to explain what he had been doing, and why the Helm was so wrong. Aun did not look at him or speak to him. He had been arming while Ambrose was arguing. He must have known all along it would come to a fight. Ambrose felt stupid, and rebuked. On the other side of the road the three knights were getting themselves ready, making good the shortcomings in their gear with what they had between them, looking at Aun and trying to assess him. They were nervous, too.

'I'll have my sword back,' said Aun suddenly. 'I don't like that hand-and-a-half of his.'

The oak-pommel blade could not have half the reach of the big bastard sword the Helm carried; but it must be better than the mace would be. Ambrose put it into Aun's hand. There was no time to unfasten the pocket with the little stone in it. If Aun lost, he was going to lose everything.

When Aun at last stepped forward to take his place, Ambrose hurried to Stefan and took the mace for himself, in case he had to fight after Aun fell. Then he picked up his ragged banner. With a hollow, sick feeling inside himself he stood to wait upon the events that would never have happened if it hadn't been for him.

'Go to it, Leo,' said the Helm.

One of the men, armed with a sword and shield, stepped forward to face Aun. He was big, a head taller than Aun with shoulders to match. The two men crouched opposite each other, waiting. There was no signal.

'Go to it,' said the Helm again.

The other fighter took a step forward. Aun did not move. The fighter hesitated. He wore an open-face helmet, like Aun's but without a noseguard. Ambrose could see his eyes, fixed on Aun. When they come on at you, Chawlin had said, you go back to keep your distance. Or you attack. That was what the fighter had expected. Aun was doing neither.

The fighter moved forward again, just an inch this time. The point of his sword lifted. Even Ambrose could see the blow was coming.

It came, sweeping up and hard down. The wolf-shield lifted into it. There was a *crunch*, and Ambrose cried out

440

as he saw the blade split the wooden rim. The fighter was stumbling. Aun punched into the man's face with the pommel of his sword. The fighter dropped like a sack falling to the ground.

The point of Aun's blade hovered over him. The man did not see it. The sword lifted and Aun stepped back. The man lay there, moving one leg feebly.

The fighter's sword was still stuck in the rim of the wolf-shield. Ambrose ran forward to help Aun free it. At first it would not shift, for the wood gripped it fast. Aun must have used it to pull his enemy off balance and into his counter-blow. Ambrose had not known you could do that.

The sword wrenched loose and clattered onto the ground.

'Shall we get down to it now?' Aun said to the Helm. 'Or will you send me your other farmer first?'

The Helm grunted. He was not jeering any more. But he lifted his big sword two-handed and swung it *whoop-whoop!* in a figure-of-eight in front of him. Ambrose felt the air wince with it. He backed to the roadside, hurriedly. Aun circled, well beyond the reach of the sword. On the ground at their feet, the fallen fighter was trying to lift his head. The circling men ignored him.

*Whoop-whoop!* went the hand-and-a-half. *Whoop-whoop!*

He was quick. Ambrose was looking for the moment when Aun would try to duck inside the blow. Each time his mind thought *Go!* and his legs tensed, the sword was already whistling in on the back-stroke to cut off the head of a lunging enemy. Aun did not try it. He circled easily, at a long distance, sword dangling, shield half raised.

*Whoop-whoop!*

It was meant to keep Aun off. That was why he was swinging his sword like that – to keep Aun away. The Helm was afraid: afraid of the little man with the little sword, who circled him like a wolf. And Aun knew it. He knew who was going to win.

'Don't kill him, Aun,' said Ambrose suddenly.

The Helm grunted, furious. Aun did not answer.

Now Aun came, bounding like a wolf! The big sword swung to meet him. The shield was up – metal crashed and wood splintered. Ambrose saw Aun's counter-blow, delivered at the run, but it swished uselessly in the air. The Helm had jumped to his right – beyond Aun's reach – even as his own blow fell.

Aun spun to face him, panting. One corner of his shield was gone – clean gone with the blow from the big sword. Aun was moving his shoulder as if it hurt him. He began to circle again.

'I'll have your arm next time, old man,' the Helm shouted. 'Maybe your head, too.'

He was sounding more confident now. Aun did not answer. He went pace, pace pace, feinted a movement back and then pace, pace on in a quarter-circle around the man with the whooping sword.

Now he came again, shield to his head as before. The sword swung – low! Low for the knees; but Aun leaped it like a girl over a rope. The Helm was jumping away – already out of reach. And his foot caught in the feet of his fallen companion, and he stumbled, and crashed over backwards to the ground.

Aun was on him, dropping sideways onto his enemy's body with the short sword held high in his right hand. His shield clumped and dangled from one strap on his arm. His left hand caught the blade of his sword and brought the point down over his enemy's helmet. The Helm's hand flailed at Aun's upper arm but could not hold it. The point was poised.

'Don't kill him!' shouted Ambrose, running in. 'Don't kill him!'

Aun did not seem to hear. The Helm was swearing, struggling to knock the point aside. Aun was lying across him, half-pinning one arm with his body and hunching his shoulder against the blows of the other while he guided his blade down into the eyeslit. The man was bucking as he lay, straining to put off the stroke.

'Don't kill him!'

A horrible, ululating howl broke from inside the helmet as the point forced its way into the slit. Now Aun's left hand caught the blade higher up, and he lifted himself, putting all his weight behind the downward thrust. Blood spurted from inside the slit and ran over the metal cheek. The legs kicked. The free hand clutched at air. Then all the man's body was still.

Aun got up, slowly, and looked around. He stooped to pick up the hand-and-a-half sword.

'He could swing it well enough,' he said, panting. 'But he jumped the same way twice, and I knew he would. All I had to do was send him into his fellow's legs.'

The oak-pommel blade still dangled from his right hand, all bloody at the point. He lifted the hand-and-a-half sword in his left and looked at it.

'Pretty thing. Would have done for me if he had thought about his feet.'

*(Pretty shot, though. Smack, into the heart. I could do the same for you.)*

Ambrose looked around.

A ring of people surrounded them, townsfolk with women and children among them. They were all still, staring at the fallen man as if something terrible had happened. The fighter Aun had felled earlier was on his hands and knees, still with his head hanging as if he could not clear it from the blow. The other man was kneeling beside his fallen leader, uselessly unlacing the bloody helm. Ambrose looked away. He did not want to see the face of the dead knight.

At the roadside was the row of empty stocks, and in the last two the men that Ambrose had been trying to free when the Helm appeared. They stood with their backs bent and their heads and hands pinned by the boards as if nothing had happened on the road before them that morning.

He looked hard among the horrified faces of the crowd. He looked among the trees. He was looking for the Heron Man. He did not consider the small, triangle-sailed boat that was nosing into the bay.

'Stupid to end your life,' said Wastelands, 'on a mistake like that.'

Sophia thought she would have made a good spy. She did not ask questions as she strolled among the huts of Aclete looking for someone to sell her a few supplies. She took her time, and accepted water or ale at this door or that, teased the younger children who came to look at the strange woman from over the water, and let people talk to

444

her about what was on their minds. They wanted to talk – mostly about the fight that had taken place that morning outside the gate, when they had lost their lord. Now the town was leaderless. No one knew whether the armed men he had gathered about him would stay or go. No one knew if the men who had killed him would make themselves lords in his place. Someone said they were in league with a band of brigands who lived deeper in the March, who would surely come the moment they heard the news. Half the men in the town had gone off to a meeting with the new lords at the top of the big hill.

She made her way back to the bay, swinging her little sack of purchases as she went. There were not too many, for Chawlin's purse was getting slim. They needed more coin. She did not know how far it was to Hayley, and whether they would do better to sell the boat now, so that they could buy more provisions for their journey, or whether they should keep the boat so that they could travel faster up the lake. She plotted in her mind a conversation with some of the fishermen that could lead to her selling the boat for something approaching the price Chawlin had paid for it. The important thing, she knew as surely as if her mother had told her, was that she should not seem too interested in a sale. Someone else was going to have to ask about the boat first. Of course, no one who was interested in buying would make it so easy for her. So, said the ghost of her mother in her mind, she needed someone who was not buying themselves, but who knew someone who might, and would suggest it to both sides. The Widow had been good at these things – whether on the grand scale of politics or the smaller one of running the household. Sophia could see that now.

445

She was humming a tune as she walked. It was the slow, sad hill-song that Chawlin had taught her. She knew it was a lament, but she wanted to sing, and she wanted to sing this song because it was his.

It was good to be on land. She had not always felt safe in the small boat, caught in a big wind on the waters, and she had quickly grown tired of its cramped boards and the long, long waiting while it ploughed away at the waves. At least the two days spent sailing up past the changing hill-sides of the March had been better than the first, endless reach over empty waters. Even so, time had gone very slowly until at last one in the line of hills above the shore had swelled into the shape of the great flat-topped knoll above the town, to guide Chawlin to the harbour that he had remembered. And now they were landed and there were still hours left of the day.

She found Chawlin sitting with his back against the seaward wall of the big wooden house, screened from sight from the rest of the town. He had the cup on his knees and did not look up as she approached. She knew that he did not mean to let it seem that he had no time for her, but she wished that he would at least smile. And it wasn't doing him any good, that cup. His face was drawn.

'I've news,' she said.

'That's more than I have.'

'Is it safe to do that here?'

He looked around him. 'The building is empty,' he said. 'It used to be the chief house in this place. A woman lived in it. She was clever. She fooled me badly, once. But she's gone now: fled when the troubles came. Now they are using it as a storehouse. The guard is off somewhere today.'

'Up the hill,' she said. 'Most of the men have gone up the hill. There's a council going on there.'

'Ah. Is that what I've been seeing? It's been difficult. It's like trying to look at something that's always in the blind spot of your eye. And Luke must be in the middle of it.'

'Ambrose. They say he is.'

Chawlin drew breath.

'Close, then. Now I need to think,' he said.

'Why?'

*I need to think.* He said that a lot. Sophia did not see what there was to think about. They should climb the hill and wait for a chance to speak to Ambrose. It would not be easy, what she had to say. But that was her problem, and not his. And after that they could be on their way. Chawlin was talking as though this was something huge and impossible – or something that he really, really did not want to do. Why . . . ?

There! He was off again, looking into that damned cup.

'It's changed,' he said.

She wanted him to talk with her. She wanted to tell him how clever she had been among the huts (after all, she had found out things that the cup could not show him!). She wanted to talk about Ambrose. She wanted to talk about selling the boat. But she forced herself to be interested.

'What can you see?'

'It's a room. A big one. It's in a castle or a rich house. There are candles lit, so it must be night. There's a bed with a man in it. What . . . ?'

447

Sophia waited.

'Why's it showing me this? It's not done this before.'

'If it's at night, it can't be happening now,' said Sophia. And if it wasn't happening now, she did not see what help it could be.

'No . . . Maybe it was last night, or a few nights ago.' He watched the water for a while in silence. Then he said: 'I don't like this.'

'Why not?'

'He's got no one with him. He's . . . There's something coming. I can feel it. Why's it showing this?'

'What's coming?'

Chawlin was cursing, softly, to himself.

'*What's* coming, Chawlin?'

'I've seen this before . . . Is it this? In Tarceny. But I was there – I can't see me! What's this? Who is it?'

'Chawlin . . .'

'Wake up. Wake up, damn you!' He put his hands on the rim of the cup and shook it slightly, in his attempt to make whoever it was hear him. 'Come on!'

They must have come then. Whoever they were. He was dumb, pale-cheeked, staring into the opaque water. For a moment Sophia saw him try to look away, gasping. Then his eyes dragged him back to the bowl. His hand came up, cupped to shield his sight, but it stopped. The water had him.

'Chawlin, you're frightening me! What is it?'

His mouth moved, wordless. Then his eyes narrowed and his face hardened. He was watching something obscene – for long seconds.

'Chawlin!'

448

'That's – that's his arm. And that's a hand . . .'

She reached out and put her own hand over the bowl. He stared at it for a moment, as though it was something worse than anything he had seen in the cup. Then, painfully, he lifted his eyes.

'They tore him,' he said. 'Like Tarceny.'

'Who?'

'It was Velis. It was the King. And they tore him to pieces.'

## XXII

## Night on the Knoll

ow let the Lord of Tarceny speak,' said one of the townsmen.

For the third time that afternoon Ambrose rose to face the ring of men on the hilltop. As he did so, Aun caught him by the arm.

'This time remember, don't be clever,' he murmured. 'Just tell them what they've decided. Then it will stick when you've gone – or when I'm not here to back you up.'

Ambrose picked up his ragged banner and held it in his left hand, like a king's sceptre. The ghost of Denke reminded him to take a breath before he spoke, and to touch his heart with his right hand.

'Before the man Mar came to be ruler in Aclete,' he began, as though reciting a lesson, 'one of the boats in the bay belonged to Ham Graysson. Three boats belonged to Penn Cable.' He nodded to the tall, sparse-haired villager who stood among the crowd to his left. He had to get the details right. In the last case they had put to him, about the goat-flock, he had muddled them, and then he had made things worse by trying to invent a way out. The judgement had been argued over three times

450

until one of the older townsmen had managed to bring it to an agreement.

'Mar seized all the boats for himself, unjustly.' It helped if he described everything the Helm had done as wicked. Everyone else seemed ready to do so.

'Then he leased the boats back to their owners, demanding a share of one fifth of their catch and trade in return.

'When the boat of Ham Graysson was lost by mischance, Mar put him to work on one of the boats that had belonged to Penn Cable, increasing the share that he demanded to pay for the lost boat. Penn Cable received nothing from Mar for this. Yet Ham Graysson has now paid to Mar one third of the value of the boat that he had lost.' Ambrose paused. Some had said one half, some one third, some a quarter. No one argued with him.

'Ham Graysson must have a boat to win his living. Penn Cable must have some good for the injustice done to him. Therefore Ham Graysson shall keep the boat, and shall pay to Penn Cable one fifth of all his catch and trade for . . .' He hesitated.

'A year,' said a grey-bearded townsman.

'One year?' muttered Cable, incredulously. 'Ten, more like.'

'Two . . .'

'For two years,' said Ambrose firmly. 'After which no more shall be paid.'

'That is the judgement,' said Aun, because Ambrose had forgotten.

The murmur of voices rose around the ring. Penn Cable was shaking his head, as if he could not believe it;

451

but he was keeping silent and the crowd seemed to think the case was settled.

Ambrose looked around.

'Is there anything more?'

They had done the foodstores and hides, the herd (which had taken hours), and now the boats. An air of exhaustion hung over the gathering. Yet the Helm must have made hundreds of judgements in his years at Aclete. Any might be disputed now; and Ambrose knew that he would have to go on and on listening to people as long as they brought their quarrels to him.

'Enough for today, your lordship, I think,' said the grey-bearded townsman.

Ambrose sagged inwardly with relief. He hoped it did not show. He wondered what they all thought about how he had done.

Voices rose. The circle began to dissolve. Someone laughed. Someone else was calling out about some butts of wine down in the storehouse that could be opened (now, *they* hadn't been mentioned in all that wrangling over the grain and the hides). They seemed happy, for the most part: happy at the end of a day in which they had lost their lord.

'Will you be lodging with us in the town, sir?' said the greybeard.

Ambrose shook his head.

'No?' said Aun, surprised.

'We'd be pleased to offer you our best, sir – food and bed and wine.'

'No. We sleep here.' It was the one decision he had taken by himself all afternoon, and he felt quite firm about it.

Up here, on this big-shouldered hill, he stood in the light. It would last an hour more, maybe – a weak, liquid gold already welling with the cool of evening. Down below, and far out across the lake, the falling sun had left the land in shadow. And down there, by the huts, Mar had died, and the air had whispered of the enemy he could not reach. He did not want to go back down there. He wanted to remain on his island of light, as long as it lasted.

The greybeard looked nonplussed; but he shrugged. 'It's played its part for your family, this hill, sir. Your mother and father were married on it. And your first ancestor, sir. He waited for his bride here. That's why it's called Talifer's Knoll, after him.'

'Is it?' said Aun. 'Well don't let your young maids get ideas about their lord tonight. I'll be waiting with the flat of my sword for any that do.'

'No sir,' said the man, laughing wickedly as he turned away. 'We'll keep 'em under lock and key, right enough.'

'That's one mercy,' murmured Aun, as the crowd broke up. 'Useful man, that. Him and two or three others. With luck they'll be able to sort out the rest of it among themselves, now they know where their law is coming from.'

It was true. There had been three or four voices around the circle, all of them older men, that again and again had suggested things the rest had listened to. Disputes that had been close to fights at noon had been settled by evening. Ambrose had found that the less he said the better. His part had been to wait for them to decide, and tell them what they had decided, because when the words came from his mouth they would be the law. With the Helm dead he was the only one who could give it.

Whether he could protect them was another matter.

'Why did you kill him?' said Ambrose, watching the townspeople trail off the hilltop.

Aun shot him an angry glance.

'What do you think he'd have done if I hadn't? He'd have picked himself up, gone back into the town, shaken out his fighting strength – he must have some, to have kept the Fifteen off this place. That's what he'd have done right away, if he had realized you had a war-knight with you. And then he'd have been after us for our blood. It was us or him, the moment you set those men free. He was stupid enough to let us make it him.'

His name had been Mar. He had been a knight, or a soldier of fortune – no one quite knew which. But he had come out of the south some years ago with a small number of armed men and made himself the chief of Aclete. And he had settled the township's quarrels – not justly, they had kept saying to Ambrose: not justly at all, and they did not miss him. But not all his decisions had been bad ones – wouldn't Ham Graysson have starved if the Helm had not given him Cable's boat?

And how would Aclete deal with the Fifteen, now? That was for Ambrose to answer. He was Lord of the March, and the one who had brought Mar to his death. He hadn't wanted this. He didn't want any of it.

'Anyway,' said Aun, 'I don't like ordeals. I saw your mother face one just like that. They wanted to kill her. By good luck Septimus and I were there to put a stop to it.'

'What did you do to them?'

'Septimus forgave them,' said Aun flatly.

'It's important to forgive.'

'I don't think so. The leader's name was Baldwin.'

Ambrose said nothing.

'You're being damned prim about this!' said Aun. 'I could have got my head split this morning. If you'd been my – my squire I'd have had the hide off you for that. I promised your mother I'd let you do what you do and just make sure you stayed alive. And I will. And I'll lay my head on turf tonight if I have to. But *next* time I may do rather less letting and rather more making sure.'

He was angry again. Ambrose found it hard to look at him when he was angry.

'I was trying . . .'

'I know what you were trying to do. They taught you prettily at that school, I'll allow. But it wasn't going to work. You can speak about rule or law as much as you like, but out here it comes damned quickly down to the iron. That man had too much to lose to let him listen. Six months ago I'd have been the same. And as for forgiving – it's not free, not even for a king. It's like taking on debt. And a king who forgives too much pays with his life. Remember that.'

You think you're with me, thought Ambrose. And yet you kill without thinking.

Aun had turned away as if the talk were over, and was beginning to take wood from the beacon-pile to build up a small fire.

'How long until the Fifteen get here?' said Ambrose.

Aun looked up.

'Eh? You're counting on them arriving?'

'Yes.'

'You want to show them that banner and talk rule and law?'

'Yes.'

Aun swore. 'Are you mad or am I?'

'You think they won't come?'

'Oh, they'll come all right.' He frowned. 'Ordinarily I would say a day and a half to Tarceny – if they are at Tarceny – and the same back. But it can be done more quickly than that. And news travels like the wind. Aclete's strongman dead – that's news. You and your banner are news. We should be safe . . . until the evening of the day after tomorrow, I guess. If they don't night-march. If they do, it could be the noon or mid-morning. Now tell me why we should wait for them to come and cut our throats for us.'

'I don't think they will.'

'You think they chased us the length of the Kingdom last season just to ask the price of plum-fruit?'

'They were told lies about us. I know who did it. So do you.'

Aun gazed at him. In the long light half of his face was shadow. His cheek muscles were fixed.

You think you are with me, thought Ambrose. And yet you want to kill your son.

The man swore again, and stared into the pile of fire-wood he was constructing.

'What about diManey – your friend and your mother's friend?' he said at last. 'They killed him. Him and his wife. Do you remember?'

(The long room at Chatterfall. The people hurrying to get ready. Aunt Evalia with her hand on Uncle Adam's arm. And both of them dead within an hour.)

'Yes.'

'Do you care?'

456

Ambrose knew what he meant. How could he forget that? How could he hope for good from the men who had done it?

It was the Wolf who had killed Aunt Evalia. And yet the question was the same. And he had no answer to it.

'They'll attack Aclete, if we don't do something,' he said.

'The best we can do for Aclete is to get as far away from it as possible,' said Aun. 'The town must look after itself. We'll move at dawn. And you can have first watch.'

He bent to busy himself with the fire.

She had put a blanket around him, but he would not be still. Dazed, and with his mind turned inwards, Chawlin wandered through the huts of Aclete and out of the gate. She followed as if he were a sleepwalker whom she was afraid to wake. He climbed a little way up the knoll, still hugging his blanket around him. Then he sat down.

'It was a message. A warning,' he said.

'It wanted me to see them do it,' he said, a few minutes later. 'Those things – they're so *misshapen* . . .'

'You shouldn't look, if it's going to do this to you,' Sophia said.

She thought he had not heard her. But then, to her surprise, he said: 'I don't think I need to any more.'

'Good,' she said. And she thought: now that he's said that, I can hide the cup when he's not looking. Perhaps I could even throw it into the lake, so he can't change his mind. It would be better for him.

'So. Velis is dead,' she said. Anything to get him to talk.

'Yes. It makes no sense.'

'I can't think of anyone who deserved it more. What do you think will happen now?'

He shrugged, uncaring. 'I don't know. Some strongman among his followers will try to take the throne. It'll be more fighting, anyway. Perhaps a lot more.'

'Has any of them have a proper claim?'

'By blood? No more than he had.'

'I'll tell you one who has. Ambrose.'

She meant it as a joke. There was nothing kingly about Ambrose (although over the past few days as she had imagined meeting with him, she had begun to think that if the Kingdom could humble itself before this child it would be a better place indeed). But now she wanted to see Chawlin laugh again. She didn't want him to shut his eyes like that, as though even this were more bad news, more horror, more sorrow.

Chawlin! Do I have to shake you?

'He'd never have held it,' Chawlin said, looking into space.

'Well, he's already put down one lordling and held a court in the March. He's carrying the flag of Tarceny – did I tell you?'

'If he wants to reclaim . . . it's the right way. I wonder if he knows what he's doing.'

'I doubt if he's got the slightest idea.'

They sat in silence together. She put her hand on his. He did not move. Together they watched the lake greying in the dusk.

I'm not going to get him up the hill this evening, Sophia thought. He doesn't want to go. And he's had too much of a shock. He needs to rest. But if I wake before he does I'll take that damned cup and toss it into the water.

'Right,' he said suddenly, in a dead voice. 'Sophia, you should sleep in the town tonight.'

'What about you?'

'I'm going to stay here.'

'Why?'

'I've got to – I've got to think.'

'You can think in the town, with me. Two heads are better than one.'

He shook his head. 'They'll shut the gate.'

Sophia did not see what that had to do with it. She was sure he would be better off under a roof in the town, where someone could cook them a warm meal and maybe offer them wine. But if he wanted to sleep under the stars, very well. He just was not going to do it alone.

'I'll get our things from the boat,' she said.

'No. I want you inside the stockade. I want you to stay where there are people – in the light . . .'

'Chawlin!'

The sound of his name stopped him.

'Chawlin – what is it? What's frightening you?'

'You didn't see . . .'

'I don't see *anything* in that horrid cup. What is it?'

'It's those creatures. I – I saw the cockerel again.'

'But they're nothing to do with us!'

He wanted to say something to her. There was something he knew. What was it?

'Chawlin – what's the matter?'

'They are – to do with the cup,' he said slowly. 'They killed Tarceny. I saw it. Now they've killed Velis. And –

and they were in Develin. Yes, I think so. If I'd looked, I'd have seen them . . .'

Sophia stared at him. For a moment it seemed to her that all the world was haunted except herself. She was an island in a sea of madness. And Ambrose, and now Chawlin, were drowning in it . . .

Pictures rose in her mind.

An eye, red in the lamplight on a stair in Develin.

A voice, pleading by a stone fountain.

Something that was not a fox, slipping among the grasses on a hillside.

*The cockerel!*

Shadows moved in her head, hunched, hooded. Claws groped – blindly, but knowing she was there. She felt herself shudder. Where had she seen them? It must have been in a dream. She must be remembering a dream, that was all. She thrust the images from her head.

'We're scaring ourselves,' she said.

'They were in Develin,' said Chawlin. 'I'm sure of it now. If I don't do what . . . If we are not careful, they'll . . . We have to be careful. That's all.'

Sophia looked around her at the grey lake, and the grey slope of the knoll shadowed with the evening. Suddenly it seemed all too likely that she was being watched by things with unseen eyes. It was a feeling that was almost familiar, as if she had borne it for days without knowing. Nothing moved among the grasses or the low reeds. There was a shape on the shore that was probably a tree stump. But when you looked away, in this light, it *did* seem to be a figure of a hooded man, watching them.

460

'I'm staying with you,' she said.

He sobbed.

She put her arms round him, because she did not know what else she could do. His shoulders shook in her embrace.

'Soph . . . Soph . . .'

He was trying to say her name. He could not. She held him, but she could not reach below his skin.

I'm losing him, she thought.

Angels help me! I'm losing him.

Alone on his watch, Ambrose turned his sword in the fire-light. He hadn't wanted to take it back from Aun that morning, with the blood from the Helm's eyepiece on it. He had cleaned it, thoroughly. And yet he was convinced, each time he turned the blade, that he would see the stain there, dark in the light of the flames.

There was blood on the roots of the oak, he thought.

The night wind combed the fire and stirred his makeshift banner, propped nearby on its stick. The mule shifted where it stood by great Stefan. Aun turned in his sleep, muttering. Ambrose wondered what the Fifteen had made of the news, if they had heard about it by now. Had they laughed? Had they been angry, that he had tacked their own banner from mere rags? Most probably they had not known what to think. No one ever did.

No one did. That was why it was the Doubting Moon. There's a piece missing, the child with the fire in her eyes had said. A piece missing. What was it – a shadow, a bat-wing, a sign of doubt? Each of his ancestors had had his own answer. His father too must have had an answer, and

461

he had never learned it. Now they were gone, and they had left it to him.

His powers were the Oak, and the Moon: both stained; both corrupt. And so were the people who remembered them.

Uncle Adam – how could he forgive that?

How?

The ghosts of Develin whispered answers, but they were ghosts. Force had killed Faithfulness, and killed Forgiveness, and had left them bloody in the passages.

Because I need them!

And if they kill again? And again? Will you forgive them again? And what will your forgiveness matter – to anyone but yourself?

He had no answers. He felt only the need to hurry.

He needed to hurry. He was in his father's land, and his father was gone. He was in the enemy's country, and the enemy was always ahead of him. Where? Mocking, beckoning; that sick-memory, that scent of dark water – he knew it now. It showed him the mist in the bowl of the world, it brought him the cry that rose from the pit.

I need help!

But how can I forgive the help I need?

His hands played with the hilt of the sword. He teased the little pouch that he had tied there. He felt the shape of the last white stone within it: the pebble that had been cut from the bone of the dragon Capuu. He had seen Capuu. He should remember that. He had looked into the eye of the dragon that bound the world together.

He could remember that eye, looking at him. And he could remember the soft voice of a man, speaking in the wall-turret at Develin. The goddess stood for rage. But there was also the dragon Capuu. Capuu was a strength that endured.

And with strength, then yes, perhaps he *could* forgive.

Looking at it that way, how could he *not* forgive – since unforgiving was the pit itself?

'It is something close to that, perhaps,' he said aloud.

His legs were numb from sitting cross-legged. He rose to his feet and paced for a little. Then, quietly, so that he did not wake Aun, he began to build up the fire with logs from the beacon-pile. It was a warm night, but there was plenty of wood and he wanted more light. He wanted light to drive the shadows a little further off.

Light to beckon the armed men, hurrying through the night towards him.


Sophia dreamed of shadows moving.

They had been with her for so long, she could not tell when they had first come. In her dream-memory she had grown used to them. All they had done was watch her, and follow what she did. But now they were restless, shifting among themselves, sidling closer. They seemed to be expecting something. She did not like to think what it might be. She could see their shapes. She had begun to think that they had faces, although they were masked in all that shadow that hung like hoods or cloaks upon them. She thought that soon one of them would sidle close to her, and the shadows would part and she would see its face at last. She was horribly afraid of those faces.

One of them *was* coming closer. There were fingers, trembling as they were held out to her. A soft, cooing

463

sound came from it. She knew she was dreaming. And yet she knew she could hear it. She could hear the voice in her ear, saying urgently, *Wake up! They're coming. Wake up!*

She was waking. And she could still hear it.

It was a woman's voice, low and urgent.

'Wake up! You must wake up!'

Her arms pushed herself up from the ground on which she had been lying. Her head was dizzy with the plunge out of sleep. She was lying on a grassy hillside at night. Someone was crouching beside her, with a hand on her shoulder.

'You must not stay here,' said the woman. 'Go up the hill, quickly. Make for the fire and remain there. Are you listening?'

'Yes,' Sophia managed to say.

'Do not stop, whatever you hear or see. Whoever you meet. Ambrose is up there. If you can help him, he will help you. Do you understand?'

'Yes.'

'Quickly!'

Sophia put her hands to her head, trying to clear it of sleep. When she looked up she was alone.

There was almost no light – only the wide, pale-dark stretches above her and before her where the sky and the lake must be, and the deep-dark immediately around. Whoever it had been was gone into the night.

'Chawlin?' she said in a small voice, hoping that he was awake, too.

There was no answer.

She freed an arm from her blanket and felt around where she knew he had been lying beside her. She could not find him. She could not hear him breathing. The only sound now was the soft seething of the wind and the lake-water.

Her fingers touched blankets. They were empty.

'Chawlin!'

There was no answer. Chawlin had vanished. The night was full of shadows that watched her and did not move. And a faint smell, like water at the edge of pools, was stealing through the air.

'He killed the King!' exclaimed the Wolf, pacing in the light of the fire. 'He didn't warn me! He just did it!'

Ambrose stayed where he was, kneeling by Aun's sleeping form. He kept his hand on his sword-hilt and watched. He did not think the Wolf wanted to attack him, or to stab Aun as he slept. But he must have come for a reason. And he was more wayward than ever. He seemed unaware of how he stepped to and fro, or shook his fists before him as he talked. He might change his mind in a moment. Anything could happen now.

'He had no need to!' the man said. 'We were doing what he wanted. Why kill the King?'

'Did you find the cup?'

The Wolf scowled. 'No. I went through the place afterwards. They all thought I was searching for gold and laughed at me when I didn't find any. But he tricked me. It wasn't there.'

'It was all for nothing,' said Ambrose. 'The Widow, and all those people.'

'I know. I know. I wouldn't have done it if I'd known.'

'He tricked you.'

465

The man cursed. 'I've done everything he wanted! All the things he likes! And he'll only let me drink once more – once! This time it was just to get away from the king's men. They blame *me* for his death. I'm an outlaw – a sneaking, starving, grovelling outlaw! That's not fair! He was the one who did it. Why doesn't he treat me as he should? Why does he always want you? I don't want to give him you!'

He had stopped and was looking at Ambrose. Was he going to attack? Ambrose made ready to shake Aun by the shoulder.

'You've cost me a lot, you know,' said the Wolf. 'I could have cut your throat months ago. I could have given him everything he wanted.'

'Would he have given you anything you wanted?'

The man scowled again. 'Don't try to talk me round to your side, because you can't. I'm not a fool. I'm just not his worm, that's all. I play with him. He plays with me. We're equals, really.'

Ambrose waited. He did not think the Wolf was the Heron Man's equal. The Wolf had done nothing but complain: about the Heron Man, about the King's friends, about the way he had been treated. Maybe he had come here because Ambrose was the only person left in the world that he could complain to.

It was stupid. Aun might wake at any moment.

'It isn't *fair*!' exploded the Wolf, softly.

The wind flustered the low fire. It was full of night noises – leaves rushing, twigs dropping in the woods on the side of the hill. An animal – it might have been a marten – gave a high chittering cry. A bigger animal, perhaps a horse, blew noisily some distance away.

The Wolf lifted his head and listened, like a sentry hearing the chink-chink-chink of men riding in the dark.

'Don't think you can talk me round. I'm sorry about what's happened. But you can't give me what I want . . .'

I didn't try to talk you round, thought Ambrose.

There was the slightest movement under Aun's blanket. Ambrose looked down. Aun's face was at his knee, turned away from the firelight. The eyes were shut fast. His breathing did not seem to have changed.

'He can, if he decides to,' said the Wolf. 'And I'm going after him to make sure he does. But I've come out of my way to tell you one thing. Don't trust any friends you may meet, tonight or tomorrow. They're the ones he gave the cup to – just so I couldn't have it. They've led him to you. He knows where you are now. And one way or another . . .'

A branch cracked somewhere down the hill, as something heavy trod upon it.

'It may not come to that, of course.' He grinned.

Aun's blanket stirred again. Ambrose looked down. It was the same movement – a hand, creeping down under the cloth towards the belt.

Aun kept a knife at his belt!

Ambrose cried out. At the same moment the Wolf saw it, and cried out, too. Aun's blanket whirled from the ground and caught him at the ankle. He stumbled. Aun was up, springing at him, a knife in his hand. The Wolf yelled and jumped away. He staggered and nearly fell. Aun launched himself at his son again, snarling like an animal. The Wolf scrambled backward. As he did so Ambrose saw

467

the light change. In the dimness of the fire and a dull sky he glimpsed the brown rocks of another landscape. The Wolf was among them, cursing. Aun had missed his blow again. Now Aun stopped, on the rim of the other place, and the night closed again around them.

From somewhere unseen the Wolf's voice rose, cracking with rage and tears.

*'I didn't want to kill her! I didn't want to kill him!'*

The night wind breathed across the hilltop, and no other sound came.

Aun swore, and settled himself back down again. He was staring at the darkness where his son had disappeared.

'What was that place – where he went?'

'It's a magic that the enemy has given him. He can go from this world to that place and come back out again somewhere else.'

Aun grunted. 'It will be hard to catch the old scarecrow, if he knows the same trick.'

'He does it better,' said Ambrose.

Soft clinks told from somewhere on the hillside, borne to him on the wind. Aun had not heard them yet.

'So. Damned witchcraft. When I get hold of him . . .'

There were horses on the hilltop, moving in the darkness around them. Ambrose climbed to his feet.

'Yes,' he said.

Now Aun had heard them. He scrambled upright, swearing, and grabbed from the ground nearby the big sword that he had spoiled from the dead knight Mar.

'Back to back!' he hissed. 'Talk, if they let you. But if it's *them*, don't bother to talk of Law!'

Ambrose could hear the horses clearly, circling. He

tried to count them. They seemed to be all around. Here and there in the darkness metal gleamed and shifted with the faint glow of reflected embers. Twenty yards, he thought. I can't see them.

How did they get here so quickly?

But they were here.

He remembered, then, to stoop and pick up his own sword from where it lay among the blankets. Aun's hand touched his shoulder lightly, pushing him to his right, towards their mounts, which stood tethered at the edge of their camp. Obediently he stepped in that direction.

The horses in the darkness had stopped now. He could still hear them snorting and shifting where they stood. They seemed to be all around the fire in a ring. A dull clickety-winding sound broke into the night. Ambrose had heard it before, somewhere. Behind him, Aun stiffened and stopped his sideways movement.

Feet hit the turf, heavily, a few yards away. Someone had dismounted. Grasses swished in the night. One of the horsemen was approaching. Straining his eyes, Ambrose could see a pale shape floating towards them out of the darkness. For a moment he could tell neither its size nor its distance. Then it came closer.

It seemed to be the disembodied head of a man, with white skin and long white hair, that hung in the air about six feet above the ground.

# XXIII

## The Harvest of Pearls

ut up your swords,' said the head. 'We can shoot you where you stand.'

'You have a sweet shot among you then,' said Aun. 'For I have heard you wind just one crossbow, to pin two men and two mounts.'

The head grinned and shifted. Now Ambrose could see that it was indeed a man – a man in black armour, and his body barely showed in the light. He moved slowly and his face was old. On his shoulder, pinning a dark cloak, was the small, pale badge of the Doubting Moon.

'*Two* men?' He leered at Ambrose.

'My name is Ambrose Umbriel, of Tarceny.' His mouth was very dry.

'I had heard there was a pup who claimed that name. And do you know mine?'

'No.'

'You do not. Well, boy, my knees have become stiff these past years. I do not bend them for any name. And you *will* now put up your swords, or I will ask you less politely.'

Behind him Ambrose heard Aun ram his swordpoint

down into the earth. Ambrose did the same. It tilted, but did not fall. He could still grab the hilt quickly if he had to.

'Stay where you are,' said the white-haired man. He gestured into the night. Ambrose could hear more men dismounting from the ring.

He's a white lion, thought Ambrose. A White Lion. And then, with his pulse racing and his throat dry, he could not help thinking: Does he still have teeth?

Of course he does.

Mail clinked and leather squeaked. Figures appeared out of the gloom. One took Stefan and the mule and stood by their heads. Two or three more were going through their saddlebags. Others were moving around the fire. They were grouping their own horses, as well. More men came up to join their white-haired leader. Their faces were lined. Their eyes glittered in the firelight. A short, round fighter stepped forward, reaching for Ambrose's sword. Aun's arm shot out and caught the hilt of his own.

'Another step may cost you a head,' he said.

'Aun!' said Ambrose.

'Leave it, Hob,' said the White Lion. 'For the moment.' He lifted his voice. 'Anyone found anything?'

'Not here,' said a voice from the gloom by the saddle-bags. 'Some coin. Not much.'

The Lion and the man Hob exchanged glances.

'Didn't I say, last season?' said the man Hob.

'So you can skin that pup Raymonde for me when we catch him. If,' he added with a nasty grin at Aun, 'if his old man hasn't found him already.'

'Search them,' said one of the men by the fire. 'Or maybe they've buried it.'

471

'What are you looking for?' said Ambrose.

'The truth, first,' said the White Lion. 'Very important, the truth. It's like iron, or fire. Now,' he said, kicking at an ember, 'you have the remains of a good fire here. Not enough to turn iron red, no. But I don't need that. Just enough to get it hot. People tell the truth very quickly when they see hot iron, boy. What do you think?'

Behind him, Aun was breathing hard. Ambrose could sense how close he was to seizing his hilt again. And if he did that . . .

'You'll get the truth from me,' he said.

'So nice of you. So, you say you are the son of Tarceny. Believe me, there's not much to be proud of there now. I say this, and I live there. But it was a rich place, once. Many treasures. I remember that. Many treasures of different kinds. And I did hear, not long ago, that you carried some of them.'

'I can guess who told you . . .'

'The truth! Or by the Angels, I'll use hot iron!'

Ambrose swallowed. 'We didn't have any.'

'None? No gold, no jewels? Buried anything? Careful, boy, I'm watching you, and I'll know if you lie.'

'No.'

The men were grouping around him. He felt them willing him to tell of hidden gold. Wild stories gabbled through his head. He kept his eyes on the White Lion.

'There was a purse of copper I had once. I don't know if that came from Tarceny. I spent it getting across the lake.'

There was a long silence.

'We'd been fighting for two, three years after all,' said

the man called Hob to his leader. 'We were selling the furniture, by the end.'

'All right,' said the White Lion, suddenly. 'I never had much faith in that part of it. And yet I have a strong feeling – let's say I've heard from someone who should know – that the real son of Tarceny does carry a treasure. What might that be, do you think, if not gold or jewels?'

Ambrose hesitated. 'What do you mean?'

'*Guess* what I mean,' roared the White Lion.

Ambrose knew he had heard that voice before. It had bellowed out of the dark from the woods at Chatterfall, before Adam and Evalia had died.

He swallowed, and looked the Lion in the eye.

'You might mean a cup . . .'

'Good guess, but no. Try again.'

'A book then,' said Aun tightly, from behind him. 'A book that came from his father.'

'Not so good a guess. I heard that *you* had that, you moth-eaten old wolf. Try again.'

Ambrose was silent.

The White Lion stooped to look him eye to eye.

'Are you sure,' he said, 'that you have nothing from Old Tarceny? Not – one – single – thing?'

Slowly, reluctantly, Ambrose reached for the hilt of his sword and fumbled at the strings that held the little pouch there. The White Lion stepped back, out of reach of a sword-swipe.

Into Ambrose's palm fell the last white stone. He held it out to the man. Deftly a great black gauntlet picked it from his hand. The White Lion held it close to his eyes, peering at it in the weak firelight.

473

'That's one of them,' said the man Hob, at his shoulder.

'So that part's true,' said the White Lion. 'Is this all there is?'

'There were more, but I lost them,' said Ambrose.

'Careless. But I'll believe your name is Tarceny. So where is your mother now?'

'Dead,' said Aun, quickly.

'Somewhere else,' said Ambrose at the same moment.

The White Lion grinned and the stone was swallowed in the fist of his gauntlet.

'I do like the truth. But above all I like it to be simple.'

Ambrose watched him. If his men had believed in treasure, last season, he had not. It had been easy to convince him that none had existed. He had been hunting them for other reasons.

'Tell me, boy – what is it a mother loves most in all the world?'

There was nothing he could do but answer.

'Her child.'

'So, now. There's not a man among us but lost everything he had the day she let the good Baron here and his cut-throats over our wall. We lost friends, too. There's a lot to remember. Let us suppose that a mother has offended us. What is the worst revenge a man could take on her?'

They were all around him, standing over him like the rim of a great bowl.

'Come on. It's easy. I could do it now, and she would weep for the rest of her life. That's good revenge. Ask the Baron behind you. He knows.'

474

'I – don't think you want that,' said Ambrose, fighting to keep his voice steady.

'Don't I? Sometimes a man finds it hard to know what he wants. Last season, now . . . There were definitely some things I wanted last season. And in a moment I'm going to remember why.'

He did not want to kill. But he probably would. He did not want his quarrel with Mother, but it was still with him. And so he would do what he did not want to do. And he still had the white stone.

Ambrose had known he could not have help without risk. Well, he had taken the risk.

'I am going to the pool by the mountain of Beyah,' he said. 'I am going to fight the Prince Under the Sky. And I want your help.'

Did he mean 'fight'? *Find* might have been closer. And the White Lion was unimpressed.

'Help? A strange word. Not service, then? Surely you think you are entitled to our service? You've a banner there – at least I think it's a banner – with the Doubting Moon on it. It's nearly as ragged as some of ours. Boy, we have grown *very* ragged in Tarceny's service. Fifteen of us, now. Do you know how many knights your father had in the March? Seventy. Seventy manored knights. I ride these paths with their ghosts at my heel. And I can ride quickly. When I hear that some pup has put up the Doubting Moon on Talifer's Knoll, I can ride very quickly indeed. What happened to that fathead Mar, then? That was just an accident, I suppose?'

'He came,' said Aun, 'a little too close.'

The White Lion straightened. He was within reach of

Aun's sword, but this time he did not step back. Perhaps this stiff old man was as good in a fight as Aun was.

'I didn't do it to claim Aclete,' said Ambrose. 'And I want you to leave Aclete alone.'

The White Lion looked down at him again. With a careless gesture, he dropped the white stone into the grasses. At once Ambrose put his foot on it, to be sure of finding it again.

'I don't think you understand,' said the White Lion. 'You have come here with nothing. There's nothing for you to claim here, and nothing that you can give me. Anything that's worth having in the March, we can get for ourselves. There may be little. But there is Aclete, now. Mar's rabble can't keep us off without him. We can have that if we want. Or they can buy us off, if they want. But you can't. Not with a flag and a name.

'The Prince Under the Sky, you said. Does it surprise you that it does not surprise me? I know who you mean. That's not a small thing you want at all. And you want help. In this world, help has to be paid for.'

He waited. Ambrose was aware of an important moment passing, and yet there was nothing he could say. The man was groping, hopelessly, for something. But they both knew there was no treasure. There was nothing to offer him.

'Why should I do this?' said the outlaw heavily. 'No, don't wave your flag at me. Your house already owes us more than you can pay. I'm about to take the only thing you can give me. You've nothing else, have you?'

Revenge, said a voice wildly in Ambrose's head. Revenge on the Heron Man, for the death of their lord, your father!

476

'Well?'

Ambrose drew breath, thought about it, and then shook his head.

'No,' he said.

'No,' repeated the White Lion.

'But *I* have,' said someone from the back of the circle.

Ambrose looked up.

The Lynx of Develin was standing at the edge of the firelight, in a peasant dress all tattered from briars.

Of all Sophia had ever gone through, the moments after finding Chawlin had vanished were the worst. For long seconds she looked into the night, her limbs locked and her breath freezing in her throat. She knew – she *knew* – that in the darkness something was watching her. And she had a terrible feeling that she had seen it before. She could not remember it; but when she saw it, she would do. And then she must scream.

She could see nothing. She could hear nothing beyond the water and the wind. And still the shadows watched her and her heart sprang within her ribs like a trapped animal.

'Is . . . Who's there?'

There was no reply. Suddenly she felt sure that whatever it was would never reply. Perhaps it could not even speak. It watched her with a cold anguish. There was nothing she could do. So she stood up.

'Chawlin?'

Chawlin was gone. The voice that had woken her was gone. She was outside the stockade of Aclete. The towns-people were abed. She did not remember which way along the stockade would lead her to the gate. And would they open to someone screaming in the night? And what could they know about this?

Ambrose knew. He had always known. *There are things – you don't see them, or if you do . . . They can come into the house.* He had seen things she was blind to. She should have gone up the hill to him while it was light. But he was still there, and he could help her.

'I'm going, now,' she told the watching darkness.

Picking up her skirts, she began to make her way uphill.

She could not have said why she had spoken, or why she moved so slowly. She felt that it was very important that she should not show fear. Maybe, if she did, then whatever watched her would attack, like an animal. Panic was battering at her mind. If she cried out, or ran, then it would overwhelm her like a flood. She must not lose control. She must think. And she must listen.

Still there was no sound. If there was anything there, it had not moved when she had. (Maybe there had been nothing after all? But it did not feel like that.) She carried on upwards, trying to remember how long the slope was. A half hour's climb in the light, perhaps? How long would it take in the dark? It would take for ever, like this. Something – a briar – scored her ankle and caught her dress. She tore at the cloth, savagely, to free it.

Perhaps she would do better to try the gates of Aclete after all. She paused, hands on her skirts, looking upwards and trying to work out how far she had come.

And then something did move, on the hillside below her.

It was a long rustling sound of a great weight lifting

itself from where it had been resting among dry grasses, a few yards from where she had been camped.

Then nothing – no growling, no sound of anything worrying among her blankets.

What could make such a noise, and not move again?

With her heart galloping, she forced herself up the slope. Still her mind cried out, *Don't Run, Don't Run*. If she ran she would fall. If she ran she would never hear how close it was. And how could she run anyway, in the dark on a slope like this?

She was striding, and gasping with the effort. And now she heard it again, over the sounds of her breath and her feet among the grasses. Again it was slow – a swishing, creaking step that made her think of long limbs that could not be a man's. And it was closer. Or it was no further away than it had been. It was following her up the hill.

A horrible, horrible image came to her of the way a spider moves, slowly at first, and then with sudden speed upon its prey. Her mind hovered on the fringes of panic.

She swallowed. And she turned.

It must have paused within thirty yards of her. She could not see it. She could not imagine it. She could not think what might move so.

And what was its face?

*The cockerel! The cockerel!*

She scuffed uselessly around in the grasses for a stick, or a stone to use as a weapon. If only there was something to throw – even a pebble – she would have felt less vulnerable. Yet in this darkness there might be armour and weapons piled only feet away from her and she would never find them. Her questing foot struck into a patch of

479

brambles. She swore under her breath, and ripped the hem of her skirt free again.

The thing had not moved since she had turned. It knew exactly where she was. But it was not trying to catch her. Not yet.

'Go on then.' she muttered to herself. There was nothing else to do.

Go on. The most horrible dreams she had ever had were like this – darkness, trying to get away, pursued and yet not seeing what pursued her. And yet she could think. She could turn if she wanted to. She knew where she was going. She could hold horror away with her waking mind.

The thing stirred again, below her, and she whispered a curse.

But the slope was easing. And there was light – yes, light on the hilltop. There was a fire, there.

'Thank the Angels!'

Now she could hope. And now she had spoken of the Angels, she could pray as she went.

'Warrior of Heaven,' she whispered. 'Guard me, for my enemies . . .'

Oh Angels – what *was* it? She gulped.

'. . . For my enemies press close . . .'

The thing had paused again. Every step was taking her further away from it.

'Friend of the Hapless, guide me through the deadly places. Light of the peoples, Gabriel, attend me . . .'

She had always believed in the Angels that the Godhead had sent into the world. But outside the chapel of Develin, she had never given them much space in her thoughts. And she had never called on them like this, or felt the warmth of prayer in her struggling spirit. The fire was closer. She could see that there were people moving and standing by it. She could see horses. She could see the fringes of grass around her, lit by the faint glare.

She looked back. There was nothing. The sounds no longer followed her.

The ground was level at last, although still tussocky and difficult. She had reached the hilltop. She might run now, she thought, across the last fifty yards to the fire.

Then the night hissed at her elbow and she nearly shrieked.

'Get down,' said a man's voice. 'Get down!'

'Chawlin?'

She could just see the shape of him, sprawled full length on the ground.

'Get down. They'll see you!'

She crouched. 'Where have you *been*?' she hissed back at him.

'You've got to go back.'

She couldn't believe he had said that.

'I'm not going back!'

'You must!'

'I'm *not*. Do you understand?'

She could feel him staring at her, and she stared at him. Metal gleamed as he rolled his body slightly. He must have his sword in one hand. He was lying here, staring at the fire. He had no idea what the night held behind him.

'Those men would kill us,' he said. He was trying to keep his voice low, but she could hear the force in it. 'Or they'd kill me and kidnap you. And then you'd still be in danger. Go back!'

'I'm going over to them. That's what we came for, isn't it? To find Ambrose and his friends. What are you waiting for?'

'They're not friends! That's the Fifteen there. I saw them come . . .'

'I don't care. I'm not staying out here. And I'm not going down. Ever.'

'Sophia – trust me! You're not in danger down there. Not yet. Trust me. It will be all right. I've just got to do something, and it will be all right.'

'Then do it! For all the Angels . . .'

She saw his head turn towards the fire. The light glinted on his eyes, but she could not read his face.

'I can't. Not now. There's too many . . . I'd need a bow. There'll have to be another chance.'

*Do not stop,* the woman's voice had said.

'Then I'm going over.'

'Sophia!'

'No! I'm *not* waiting. I'm going. If Ambrose needs help, we can give it. They didn't kill us last time, these Fifteen, did they? Come on!'

'No!'

'I'm not staying out here! Come on!'

Without waiting for an answer, she got to her feet and strode across the top of the hill. She willed him to follow, but did not look back to see if he did. Her eyes were fixed upon the men and the fire. Brigands, cutthroats, swords – she marched towards them as firmly as if they were a pack of children playing in a courtyard at home. Horror of the darkness propelled her into the light.

She heard them talking as she approached. She could

see there was an argument going on – why, at this time of the night, she did not bother to think. She could see Ambrose in the middle of the crowd. He was looking and talking, she thought, like a man among men. The others were around them in a tight ring. She saw the weathered faces, tattered cloaks and pale badges. These were the same company that had ridden up to Develin the day she had gone to spy on the fishing. Their leader, a white-haired old warrior, was speaking to Ambrose. She heard his words. Some part of her mind, unclouded by horror, understood them.

They were brigands, but they were men. They had armour, cloaks against the cold, bellies that needed filling and purses that were empty. Now, in the light of the fire, she was back within her own world. And the words of the leader showed her at once what she could do. If Ambrose had not the means to buy them, she did. She stepped to the fireside and told them so.

Everyone was looking at her.

'What is your name, sir?' she asked the white-haired leader.

'Orcrim will do,' he said. 'What do you want here?'

'I am a friend of – of the Lord of Tarceny, there,' she said, nodding towards Ambrose. She almost said *the King*. Something in her wanted to say it. But she had learned enough politics to know that she must not make a claim like that until they were all sure of it.

Ambrose was watching her, too. There was something wary in his look, as if he was not sure he could trust her. No matter. Whatever he thought, he was going to have to wait.

'And, er – what was it you said a moment ago?' said the knight called Orcrim.

'That I can reward service, if service is given.'

'How?'

'That depends upon the service. But my family has never offered less than other houses. For a knight of long service, we would give . . .' She looked around her at the ring of faces. 'A manor. A manor for every knight here.'

'Manors!' said someone. 'Hah!'

'This is horse-droppings, Orcrim,' said another, angrily. 'What family dresses in rags and has manors to offer at a moment?'

The leader was watching her.

'It is a fair question, if ungently put,' he said. 'What family is this?'

'My name is Develin, sir,' she said levelly. 'Since my mother's death I have all the rights and dues of the lands of the house. At my last count, twenty-nine manors were held by the house direct, and many others are in our gift. Nine, altogether, are vacant, or in dispute . . .'

All those people and estates, leaderless after her mother's murder, looking to the reeking shell of her house! She had turned her back upon them. And yet they were still there, in the secret drawer of her memory. Once she had gone over these numbers imagining the day that she would see land given to Chawlin, to make him a man of standing. She had almost forgotten it. Now she felt them like a weight settling on her shoulders again.

'And if you doubt me, sir, I may tell you that I saw you and your fellows all on the road at Develin's gate, the day you came there not six months since. And there was a sixteenth man with you, who became counsellor to the Lord of Velis.'

'So. This is not proof, although I shall accept it for the moment. But it is in my mind that sad things have happened at Develin. So it does not surprise me much that you are here. But I doubt whether you are still in a position to dispose of these manors you speak of.'

He had jumped straight to the weakness in her offer. If she let him stay there, she would deserve his contempt. Keeping her voice level, she answered him, and put her argument together in her mind even as she spoke it.

'My mother is dead, and many of her people, by the treachery of Velis. No doubt that one thought to hand over our house to some lick-spittle, if he thought at all beyond the point of his sword. But Velis too is dead, now. And all the people in the manors and lands of my house know my right and my claim. If I approach boldly, and with a little strength . . .' Here she looked around the ring of men. '. . . I think I will swiftly be restored.'

'So that's it,' said one of the men in the ring. 'Fight first, paid later.'

'Velis is dead, is he?' said the leader.

'It's true,' said Ambrose. 'I have also heard it.'

The leader looked at him. Perhaps he was remembering that Ambrose's father had once taken the crown. If he was ready to think like that, then he would be ready to listen to her offer. But they must not be diverted into fantasies that were beyond reach. This man would need help with his men, in any case. It was time to lay some hard foundations.

'I was talking of a reward for life-service,' she said.

485

'For a lesser service – say a year, for it may be that long before I am home again – my house might offer the value of a year's harvest – the first harvest from your manors.' (*Your* manors. Now that they knew what she was offering, it was time to say it clearly.) 'I do not know the exact value of all of them. But my family has never counted pennies.' From her belt she drew a cloth, and unrolled it so that they could see. Men were crowding around her. She held up the pearls of Velis in the palm of her left hand. 'Here. Your first harvests.'

Someone drew a long breath.

'A knife?' She held out her right hand, carelessly. Someone fumbled at a belt, and gave her a knife. Carefully, so that nothing spilled into the darkness, she cut the chain. She held up the pearls, loose now.

'Here,' she said.

'Stand back a little,' the leader said to his followers. He drew his hand from his gauntlet and picked one pearl from Sophia's palm. He examined it, then turned away from the fire to hold it out at arm's length.

Far away to the west the clouds that had shrouded the sky were breaking. The moon, a three-quarter disc of light, hung low over the mountain-rim.

The man appeared to be trying to measure the size of the pearl against the disc of the distant moon.

'This,' he said, 'was what I was not expecting.'

For a moment more he weighed the pearl in his fingers. Then he dropped it back into Sophia's hand.

'You had better all sit,' he said. 'My friends and I will need to talk. Cradey, Endor – stay with them. They can keep their blades for the time being.'

486

Sophia sat, carefully gathering the pearls into her cloth again. Ambrose and the knight who was with him crouched by her, gathering their swords onto their knees. Two of the Fifteen stood nearby, wild-eyed men with weapons in their hands. The rest retired to the other side of the fire, where they sat in a circle and talked in low voices.

Sophia felt exhausted.

'Where is Chawlin?' Ambrose asked her softly.

Not *How did you get here?* Not *Why are you doing this?* But *Where is Chawlin?* The question turned a huge stone in her heart, and under it was emptiness.

He had not come out of the night with her. She had imagined, as she had walked to the fireside, that he would follow a pace or maybe ten paces behind her. She had believed, as she bargained with the old brigand chief, that he might be somewhere close, watching, and she had taken strength from the thought. But he had not come. He had been afraid to come.

She was safe, for the moment, from the horror that had followed her up the hill. At least, she was as safe as she knew how to make herself. And she had done what she could to help Ambrose when he needed it. But she was alone, and tired, and she had changed her course altogether. She and Chawlin had been travelling, she had thought, to a life of love and plain living in exile. Now, if she was to make good her promises to these men, she must return to Develin, where she would be the mistress. And what of Chawlin?

'Chawlin?' said Ambrose's companion. 'A man named Chawlin campaigned with me in this March, once. He became one of Baldwin's people.'

'And then one of ours,' said Sophia, dully. 'But I do not know where he is.'

Until she understood more clearly what Chawlin had been afraid of, she would not say anything that might give him away.

Ambrose had folded a white pebble into a cloth and was knotting it onto the hilt of his sword.

'They've found us, Aun,' he said quietly.

'Eh? Who?'

'The enemy – his creatures.'

'There was something on the hill,' Sophia said. 'It followed me.'

'Did you see it?'

'No.'

Ambrose looked at her, and she realized what he must be thinking.

'I'm sorry,' she said.

She was sorry for leading them to him. Sorry for never having believed him. Sorry that she had called it a cat in the shadows of Ferroux.

'I think they want me, too, now,' she said.

'Yes, they do,' said Ambrose.

'They were going to find us sooner or later,' growled the man whom Ambrose had called Aun. He was watching the gathering on the far side of the fire. 'At the moment I'd say we have bigger problems.'

Two men rose from the group and came over to change places with the guards.

'What are they going to do?' said Ambrose.

'Who knows? They want those pretty stones she's brought with her. One way or another, they'll have them.

They could try ransoming us, if they could find someone to ransom us all to. But they'll want the manors as well. So if they think they can trust your friend here, and if they think that there's a real chance they can get her back . . .' He was rubbing his chin with his knuckle, thinking aloud as he watched the Company of the Moon. 'Fifteen fighters, arriving suddenly at a lording that's in chaos . . . Friends everywhere – doors that will open. It's not impossible. And if life out here is as thin as he said it was . . . Hah, well, I for one would like to see the manor that could yield the value of one of those little stones in a harvest.'

'Faith,' murmured Sophia. 'What appeal was ever without poetry?'

The man stared at her. She raised her eyebrows at him.

'Angels blight me, if I didn't think you were your mother for an instant,' he said.

After that no one said anything for a while.

'All the same,' said Aun in a low voice, 'if they call me aside, or rise in a group, you run. Don't wait to find out what they want. Run for the night. And don't come back for anything.'

'I am staying here,' said Sophia firmly.

Almost as she spoke, the group on the far side of the fire broke up. Three men got to their feet and came towards them. The white-haired leader, Orcrim, was one of them. The second was a small, round-faced man. The last was another ageing knight with a circular cut of grey-white hair and a face like flint.

'We'll sit with you,' said Orcrim affably. 'If we may.'

The men settled themselves without waiting for an answer. There was a moment of silence.

'We have not made a good start tonight,' said Orcrim slowly, speaking to Ambrose. 'I suggest we begin again. And I'll begin roundabout, by doing something I've not done for a long time. I'm going to tell you a story.

'This story is about three knights who served their lord. They served him very well, and very closely, and were rewarded with high offices. One,' he nodded at the round-faced knight, 'even became the lord's chamberlain. One was his war-captain.' He tapped himself on the chest. 'And one was his seneschal.'

Sophia looked under lowered eyes at the third man, and wondered what kind of lord would gladly leave his home in the charge of that gaunt face.

'There is not much that even the most secret of men can hide from his closest servants. They knew that their lord obtained – powers – from one who seemed to be an old man in a priest's coat. Let us call that one the Prince. Since the powers given by the Prince brought success, there was little they thought wrong with that. Perhaps you would fault them. Others in the Kingdom might have slain them, lord and servants and all, or had them burned, if they could. But it did not happen, then at any rate.

'Yet it did not escape our knights that there was a price for power. One day the chamberlain understood that the lord would go to the Prince with his young son, then just a few weeks old. If he had gone, the son would not have returned. Yet our chamberlain warned his friends, the war-captain and the seneschal, that this thing might happen. And before a crowd of people, including the boy's own mother, they spoke such words to their lord that he did not ride, and the son lived – and no one knew what they had

490

done. Such was their loyalty to their lord – and to his line.

'Nevertheless my story has a sad ending, as you may guess. In less than two years the lord was dead, in a manner that you may know. And his servants were land-less, and remained so from that day to this.'

'So,' said Ambrose slowly. 'If you saved my life then – were you really hunting us for revenge last season? Is that what you are saying now?'

Sophia closed her eyes. Couldn't he see that this man was offering a truce? How like Ambrose to speak bluntly when others needed to talk in hints!

'Best we don't discuss that,' said Orcrim.

'Things get worse, things get better,' said Hob.

The third man said nothing.

'My point was that we understand something of your enemy,' said Orcrim. 'That, knowing him, we are maybe more proof against his tricks than any you could find who do not. Also that we *may* have grounds to make this our quarrel, too.'

'Is it this prince who is sending these – things?' asked Sophia.

'Yes,' said Ambrose. 'And he willed the attack on Develin. And I think he must have given Chawlin the cup . . .'

'No!' she said.

'No, I – did that,' she repeated, looking at the ground.

She was tired. Very, very tired. Chawlin had said the cup was dangerous. She had given it to him. And Ambrose was looking at her again.

'This is the proposal that my friends and I have discussed,' said Orcrim.

491

'You may travel in the March for a season, the three of you, with our good will, so long as you do us no harm. For the month ahead, twelve of us will ride with you and fight with you, if need be. We will do the same in the mountains, for the footsteps of Tarceny lead there and I think it is right that we should. Mind, I do not promise that we shall kill your enemy for you, or run great risk to do so, for I do not know his strength. But we will do what I think is in reason. For all this, I think it is fair that we take a toll, and the toll shall be the pearls you have shown us – however many there may be. I counted twenty, I think.

'At the same time I shall send three of my friends in secret to Develin's country. There, they will find out how things stand. They may even talk with men who owed service to the Widow, about how it would be if the Widow's daughter returned. I will meet with those three here a month from today. When I hear what they say I will decide if the venture you propose is feasible for us.' He looked narrowly at Sophia. 'You chose your words carefully a little while ago. You said a manor for each knight. Perhaps you did not know that there are only three knighted men among us. But I think every man who follows me is worth his spurs. So my price will be fifteen manors – if, as I say, your venture seems feasible at all.'

'I said nine were vacant,' said Sophia. 'I cannot do more in the first year.'

'I am sure my friends would be patient – within reason.'

'Very well.'

'Then I think we can sleep, and start fresh tomorrow,' said Orcrim.

'Three more things,' said Ambrose.

Orcrim had been in the act of rising. Now he settled again. There was the slightest sway in the way he held his head that told how tired he was. They must all be tired, Sophia realized – as tired as she. How did Ambrose dare beard him again?

'Yes?'

'Aclete shall not be taxed by you, or harried.'

'Nevertheless, you wish to take fifteen horses and riders for a week into the mountains, and we must eat. So I shall permit Aclete to make us a gift of supplies at least. They will count it generous if we do not ask them more before harvest. Next season, if we are still here, I may think again. Second?'

'There is a man nearby, I think. His name is Chawlin. He must be found and brought in. You may have to disarm him.'

'He's a friend. He mustn't be hurt,' said Sophia urgently.

'We will look. Third?'

Ambrose was looking at her. He had something he wanted to say to her. It must be about Chawlin. But he turned back to Orcrim.

'That you should give up your feud with my mother, and that she should also have your protection in the March.'

Orcrim's face hardened. But what he said was: 'In a way, I may already have done.'

'What! When?'

'How do you think we came so quickly? How do you think I knew you carried that pebble? Your mother reached us first, boy. I spoke with her at sundown yesterday. We were on the road to Aclete before Mar had even hit the ground.'

'Where is she?'

'Somewhere else, as you said. But she is not dead, despite what someone claimed earlier. She came to me on a pathside in sight of Tarceny walls. I could have lifted her head with my sword in an instant, but damn me, I didn't. I listened. Then I came here, thinking maybe I'd lift yours and be even with her anyway. But damn me, I haven't. And now I think we should all find some sleep, or I'll know I'm already dreaming.'

Sophia saw Ambrose draw breath to ask another question, and then think better of it. The men got to their feet. The fighter Aun rose with them.

'Chance has put us in different camps until now,' he said to the old brigand. 'But I know of no ill that you have done to me or to any friend of mine.'

'Now that is generous,' said Orcrim, as if to the men beside him. 'He remembers no ill of us, after all the things that have passed. What shall we say to that, Hob?'

The man Hob grunted and looked at his feet.

'Hob had a sore jaw to remember you by, from the ferry at Develin's river. But maybe it has mended by now. As for me . . .' His eyes narrowed as he looked at Aun. '. . . There *were* some things. One or two quite big ones. But I no longer seem to recall them clearly.'

Aun grunted. Whatever it was, thought Sophia, they both remembered it.

'So what leads you, then, to follow a child into such a fight as this?' asked Orcrim.

'An old friendship.'

'Oh, yes. And how will that help you when these things come close?'

'I did not hear that witchcraft was ever proof against iron.'

'Nor I. Sleep well, then. But not too long.'

The three men left them. The guards settled down by the remains of the fire, nursing their swords and talking to one another in low voices. Sophia threw herself full length on the grass, thinking that she could sleep for a week. Ambrose had lain down, too. But the fighter called Aun just sat, with his cloak around him, looking across the fire to where the Company of the Moon were arranging themselves for what remained of the night. Clearly he was going to watch, too, for whatever might come out of the darkness.

Sleep was drawing over her swiftly. The man's face hung in her sight, half-lit by the embers of the fire, staring after the enemy with whom he had spoken.

A child? she thought. That's what you think. But he's made peace between you two, and I helped him.

And you'd never have thought we could do it.

# XXIV

## Chawlin

hey did not find Chawlin when they combed the hillsides in the early dawn. The waving grasses bore no marks, the wind brought them no news. He had slipped away into the tossing wilderness of trees and scrub that covered the hills of Tarceny.

When the searchers regrouped at sunrise, Ambrose and Aun went down to Aclete with Orcrim and three others. They rode through the open gates and in among the huts. There they found some of the men who had been at the council the day before, and told them that the Fifteen had agreed to ride away and leave the village unharmed, in exchange for a fortnight's supplies for men and horses, and passage for three of their number in secret across the lake.

'It could have been worse, damn you,' said Aun, when one of the villagers started to mutter. 'Did you want to try fighting for it?'

Ambrose sat unhappily on his mule, waiting. He knew what it would have meant to his mother and himself if a troop of armed men had come to their home in the mountains and demanded a share of their stores. He could hear angry voices behind huts and down alleyways, complaining to the group of elders who were going around making the collection. And he hated the way that men were banging on their neighbours' door-posts and announcing a 'lord's tax' as they went from hut to hut gathering small quantities of meal and bread and dried fruit. He felt that he had betrayed them.

Orcrim looked at the growing pile of sacks and bundles.

'It's not enough,' he said to the nearest villagers. 'Tell them to double it.'

'You can't!' cried Ambrose.

'Can't I? I say I can.'

'You'll starve them!' He looked at Aun for support, but Aun glanced at Orcrim and kept silent.

'My lord,' said an elderly villager. 'Some houses, this is half what they have.'

'Then I'll have the other half,' said Orcrim.

'No!' cried Ambrose.

He didn't know what to do. He didn't want this man's help if they had to behave like this to get it. For a moment his hand touched the hilt of his sword. Then he realized that was stupid, and took it away again.

Orcrim must have seen the movement, but all he did was raise an eyebrow.

'Ask for something else,' said Aun. 'Something easier.'

Orcrim looked around. 'Very well. I want . . .' He paused. 'It had better be something useful. Oh, let's say half the horse-collars in the town. Horse-collars, you,' he said to the villager.

497

'My lord?'

'Horse-collars!' bellowed Orcrim. 'Time was, Aclete had fields all the way for a mile up the river. Don't tell me there are no horse-collars left in the town.'

'Yes, sir.'

'And pulleys. A couple of damned good, working, double pulleys. And hurry before I think of something more!'

'You can't . . .' Ambrose protested again. Aun leaned across and put a hand on his arm.

'Aclete can do it,' he murmured. 'They could have done the food, too. Don't argue.'

'But it's unfair!' Ambrose hissed. 'He can't keep demanding things like that!'

'Marketplace talk, that's all. I don't know what he needs them for, but if Orcrim comes away with pulleys and horse-collars, then it's pulleys and horse-collars he'll have wanted when we rode through the gate. You've helped. Don't get in the way now.'

The food was gathered and loaded onto donkeys for the short journey up the hill where it could be divided among the Company. Four shabby horse-collars were produced and added to the pile, with some short lengths of chain. Orcrim looked them over and complained, and then went with his three fellows down to the harbour, talking as though he was going to dismantle half the boats for the rigging and commandeer the rest to carry his men across the lake. Ambrose watched him go, helpless and angry.

'Your lordship.'

It was the grey-bearded townsman, standing at Ambrose's stirrup.

'I'm sorry about this,' Ambrose said glumly.

'We'll live, sir, I dare say. But if you please, this town has a gift for you.'

'A gift?'

'To welcome you home, sir, and to thank you for what you have done for us.'

They handed him a long pole, with a black cloth rolled and tied tightly at one end.

'It used to stand outside the old barracks, sir. And we've another we can put up when you're gone.'

Ambrose lifted it, puzzled. He was aware of all the people watching him, waiting for him to speak.

'Thank you,' he said. 'But you did everything, not me. And . . .' He looked at the pole and its roll of cloth. It was too long for a staff. It wasn't a lance. What was it?

Still they were watching him, waiting.

'You have to break the ties,' said Aun at his shoulder.

The ties were knotted around the cloth, with loops that came undone in a single pull.

The big, black banner of the Doubting Moon dropped from the pole to his stirrup.

Sophia watched the warm wind tease the folds of that flag, as it topped another rise at the head of the company. The air made it flap like a huge bird against the sky. They had given it to a man called Endor to carry, presumably because his horse would not shy under such a thing. Endor himself was a hairy, crazy-eyed man, and not one she would readily have thought could be trusted with a standard – let alone one of Develin's manors.

She wondered whether her father was smiling now, at

the grim joke that had cast her as an ally of the house of Tarceny.

She was tired and depressed. The going was bad. The old lake-road into the north of the March was narrow and stony, and the landscape was growing more rugged. The small grey mare she had chosen was a stranger, although clearly better than either of the other horses that Orcrim's spies had left behind when they had taken to their boat at Aclete. She was riding less well than she knew she could. She was more out of practice than she had realized. Also, she was not dressed for it.

The company crossed the ridge. From her saddle she looked back for a moment over wave after wave of hills cresting beside the bright lake-water, fading into blue in the distant south. Then the path dropped again, through pinewoods to another shallow stream. On the far bank there was a clearing. Ahead of her, up the line of horsemen, Sophia saw Orcrim splash through the water, overtaking the bannerman. On the other side of the stream he wheeled his big mount out into the clearing and began to wave the company past.

'Keep on,' he was calling. 'Keep on.'

They poured on under his urging, rider after rider through the ford and up the muddy path on the far side. Her horse checked at the edge of the stream and then found its way into the water after the others. Icy droplets kicked up and splashed on her bare legs. The mare waded steadily across in the wake of the bigger mounts ahead, then heaved itself up the bank. She saw there was a lonely hut under the eaves of the wood at the far side of the clearing.

'Keep on, my lady,' said Orcrim, waving her past as if she was just another rider. He had put himself between the path and the hut. Now that he had his supplies, he didn't want his men to stop there and waste time troubling the people in it. Perhaps there were some among them who might have done.

The mare was following the leading horses up towards more trees when a shout sounded from behind her. There was a man in the clearing, dressed in goat-hide, running after them. He was carrying something in his hands. He ran past Orcrim, past Sophia, and on up the path. Ahead of her, Sophia saw Ambrose check his mule, hauling it clumsily half-around. The man ran straight up to his stirrup.

'Well done, sir,' the man said. 'And good speed to you.'

He held up a hunk of bread, broken from a loaf that he was carrying in his hands. Ambrose took it.

'Thank you,' he said in surprise.

The man had turned and was coming back down the line of riders, sharing out his loaf as he came. He gave a piece to Sophia as he passed.

'Angels with you, sirs all. Good speed,' he was saying. Faces – a woman and children – showed in the doorway of the hut, watching.

'Keep on, there,' Orcrim called.

Ambrose was coaxing his mule around and trying to head it up the path again. Sophia had time to look back at the clearing and the hut and family within it.

'Why did he do that?' she wondered aloud.

The man Hob, his mouth half-full of fresh bread, was passing. 'There's a story running ahead of us, I guess,' he said. 'The young Lord of Tarceny has returned. He has thrown down the cruel master of Aclete. He has set its people free. He is going to take his throne, and restore justice and peace to all the land.'

'You did not say, "He has tamed the Fifteen,"' said Orcrim from behind. 'But that will be part of it. And it'll be on its way through the March, and maybe the Kingdom beyond.'

'Hah.'

Sophia looked at the bread that she was holding. A little warmth still lingered in it. Surely they had not baked it against Ambrose's coming. They had snatched their own meal from the oven as they had seen the Company pass. She sniffed it. It was moist and yeasty, and darker than the bread in Develin.

She tasted it. It was good.

'Why did you come to Develin, last season?' she asked Orcrim.

'Don't you know? I was chasing your young friend. Also that rascal from Lackmere, there.'

'What's that?' said Aun, looking round in his saddle.

Lackmere? Yes, Chawlin had called him that, too. She knew there was a small keep and holding with that name some way south and east of Gisbore, although she had never been there. So that was who this man Aun was – a fellow southerner, if not quite a neighbour.

'And your mother, of blessed memory, told me from her gate-tower – after much beating around the bush – that Lackmere had ridden by that morning. So off I went after him. I was most anxious to catch up with him then. So anxious, I forgot to ask the slippery-tongued woman whether he had ridden from her gates alone. Which, I guess, he had. Am I right?'

Orcrim's words were addressed to the knight ahead of them.

'You are,' said Aun. 'It seemed best, at the time. I was riding to join Septimus.'

'May he rest – though I have known better kings. So why are you in this now?'

'I told you.'

'A friendship, yes. Is that all?'

'That's all.'

'If you say so. But your girth's loosening, there. Stop a moment . . .'

Aun checked his horse. Sophia, guiding her mare past him, looked down. There was nothing wrong with his girth. Behind her, the two men muttered over each other's saddles. They let a space of several lengths open ahead of them before she heard them start again, talking in low voices all the while.

She could guess what Orcrim wanted to talk about.

The King is dead, the land in confusion. The boy has a claim to the throne. We have swords – not many, but how many are needed? And if Develin was restored, and friendly? And could Aun return to Lackmere, and from there provide spears?

You make peace between them, she thought. And they use it to plan more war.

She would have to watch this Orcrim. For all his affable talk he was subtle, and also ruthless, she guessed. She remembered some of the Widow's counsellors – more than servants, but always less than friends. If events really did

503

carry her back to Develin he could be very useful. (Why back to Develin? *Why* was this happening?) But she could see at once how hard it would be to stop him from controlling her, if he were the only man she relied upon. Now it was obvious why her mother had had so many counsellors, and why she had never favoured any of them above the others for too long – not even Hervan.

Her mother, her father, Chawlin – these thoughts were very strong this morning. A moment ago Orcrim had called the Widow 'slippery-tongued'. That had jolted. That wasn't her mother at all. What she remembered most clearly about that extraordinary, black-clad, heavy-voiced woman, was the open chest in the council room, piled with letters from the man she had lost. Her mother had carried that weight of dead love for twelve years. Where had she found the strength? Because she had indeed been strong. Sophia had never understood how much, or in what way. Perhaps she was beginning to – now that she knew what loss was. She could find so little strength in herself.

Chawlin! How am I going to get you back?

Oh, she was angry with him. And at the same time fearful for him. He had not followed her into the safety of the band of men. Didn't he see how he risked being attacked, by dreadful things out of the night? She had woken in the dawn with a horrible vision of a torn body, lying somewhere on the hilltop. Yet the Fifteen had found nothing. So Chawlin was still alive; but he did not want to be found.

At least he still had the cup. He should know where she was. When he saw that she was not a prisoner, but with friends, maybe he would come to them. That was the best hope. And then she would have to talk with him: about the cup; about the creatures; about returning to Develin.

Was she truly going to go back to Develin, after all? The plan had seemed obvious and clear on the knoll. Now she was wondering if it had been madness. Last night she had been woken by a voice. She had had no idea who or what had been speaking, but she had done what the voice had said. And within minutes she had left her man in the darkness and hatched a plan with the men he feared. Madness? But – but *something* had followed her in the night. She had not imagined that. She had heard it, and felt it watching her. And so she had gone to Ambrose at the top of the hill.

Her mount had slowed. She could hear Orcrim and Lackmere closing up behind her, their words becoming clearer. They had forgotten that they might be overheard.

'It's not as if he was the most convincing of candi-dates . . .' Orcrim was saying.

Lackmere grunted.

She urged her horse forward. She knew that she ought to try to hear what they were saying. But she did not want to listen to old men scheming this morning. She could see Ambrose ahead of her in the line. He had checked his mule and was looking back down the track towards her. Riders were passing him, one after another.

Orcrim was right, of course. It was hard to think of this child as a king in Tuscolo. He had grown a little, even in the time she had known him. He had lost, or somehow dealt with, the fearfulness she remembered from Develin.

But his body was still a boy's, and so were his voice and face. He could be taught, she supposed, to sit upright instead of slouching like that. He could be dressed in decent clothes. (He had not even a shirt to wear, and his bare arms showed under his leather jerkin.) He could be given a proper horse, and not that long-eared cross-breed. Yet none of that would make him truly a king. Sophia knew that if she were to step into her mother's place in Develin, she would find it hard to stay in control. Ambrose in Tuscolo would be a puppet.

His eyes followed her as she approached on the little mare. He was waiting for her.

'I want to talk to you,' he said.

'I want to talk to you, too.'

'Yes,' he said, and hesitated. She guessed the reason.

'You call me Sophia,' she said. 'I've spent years hating the name, but it's who I am.'

'Yes, Sophia.'

Whatever it was he wanted to talk about, he seemed in no hurry. They let their beasts amble side by side, while Sophia thought over the things she was going to say.

She had imagined herself pleading, perhaps even on her knees, before a pair of eyes that saw deep into her soul. Now, in the steep and sunlit March, with this boy on his ridiculous mount beside her, it was not going to come like that.

It made it more difficult, in fact.

'You tried to warn me what was going to happen in Develin,' she said. 'I didn't listen. I wanted to say I'm sorry.'

'It's all right,' said the boy.

That wasn't enough.

'I knew what you were talking about,' she said. 'You meant they were looking for the cup.'

'One of them was. The King thought your mother was a traitor, because of me.'

She thought about it. 'But it was the cup that mattered,' she said.

'Yes.'

'I could have listened. I could have come to you on the steps.'

'You weren't supposed to.'

Supposed to? Supposed by whom?

No matter. Whether she was supposed or not supposed, she knew what she had done.

'I didn't come,' she said, 'because I had chosen to hate you. That was wrong. I should have been hating your father, not you. Or . . .' She thought again. 'Or I shouldn't have been hating anyone.'

'I never knew my father. I don't know whether you should hate him or not.'

She shouldn't have mentioned his father. She, of all people, should have known better than that. Now she had complicated things, and they had been difficult enough already. *I did not know who you are.* How was she going to say that?

'Sometimes I think he might have been like Aun,' said Ambrose, dropping his voice and with a slight jerk of his head towards the riders behind them.

Sophia resigned herself to hearing the boy's ideas about his father. After all, it was hardly surprising that he should be looking for images. Hadn't she done the same

507

– with the childish memories of her father that she had clung to all her life?

'That might not have been so bad,' she said.

Ambrose looked at her as though he thought she hadn't understood him.

'Sometimes,' he said, 'I think he must have been more like Prince Paigan.'

Sophia frowned. She knew nothing but evil of the boy's father. And yet dead or alive, evil or not, fathers had a claim on you. Ambrose should not be putting his enemy in the place of his father. She had a feeling that could be dangerous, for all of them.

The path narrowed, forcing her to let him ride ahead. She followed him nose-to-tail.

'Tell me about this enemy,' she said. 'This – Prince.'

'The Prince Under the Sky. His name is Paigan.'

'I don't know him.'

'You've not seen him. But he's spoken with you. If you think, you may remember.'

'No.'

Ambrose turned in his saddle to explain. 'It's part of what I wanted to talk to you about.' He hesitated. 'Aun . . .'

'Yes?' She had no idea where he was leading her.

'He wants to kill his son.'

'No! Why?'

'His son – he is called Raymonde.' Ambrose said the name carefully, as if he were not quite sure of it. 'I told you about him. He's the counsellor who persuaded Velis to attack Develin. He's ahead of us somewhere now. I think he's going to meet Prince Paigan.

'Raymonde stole my father's book, which had been given to Aun to keep. To do that, he had to fight his own brother, and he killed him. At that time the Heron . . . I mean, Prince Paigan, was still a prisoner. He could not have said anything to Raymonde. But there was enough of him in the book to make Raymonde do it. That's what he is like.'

'Is he – this counsellor – a young man? He looks like . . .'

He looked like Aun. Of course he did.

The path was dark and muddy. The bright lake was lost from view.

'He's on Paigan's side. He thinks he isn't, really. But everything he's done is what Paigan wanted. He persuaded Velis to sack Bay, and then Develin, because he thought that the cup would give him power so that he would not have to depend upon Paigan. But that was another trick. It's Paigan's cup. It's all the same water from the pool. He'd have been as much a slave of Paigan as he is now, if he got the cup. The only thing he hasn't done is to kill me. Paigan tried to make him do it. And he could have done. But he hasn't.'

'Why not?'

'I think – it's his way of proving that he isn't Paigan's slave – not wholly. He's done everything else – he's sorry about it afterwards, but that has never stopped him doing it. This is the last thing he can refuse to do. And now he's lost everything he gained by helping Paigan, because Paigan has killed Velis, his king.'

So this Raymonde, this grinning monster of a man, was to blame for the deaths of Develin, more than anyone.

Some day Sophia hoped she would come up with him. It might not be right for a father to kill his son, but that did not mean that the son deserved to live, any more than the king he had served. She would remember it.

But the enemy . . .

'Killing Velis,' she said. 'It doesn't make sense. Why did the Prince do it?'

'Because his time is running out.'

'Really? He knows he will be beaten?'

'He's always known,' said Ambrose. 'He was told so.'

Sophia looked at him closely, searching for his meaning.

Oh yes, he was a boy all right. He looked like one and he spoke like one. He would let himself confuse his father and his enemy in his mind (and where might *that* lead, in a crisis?). And he was too embarrassed to hear her admit her faults properly. But for all that he saw things – things she did not. And when he spoke of them – of how she had not been 'supposed' to go to him on the steps, of the way the enemy worked, and of the enemy knowing he would be beaten – she felt something shift inside her; because she did not understand, and yet she knew it to be true.

He knew what they were fighting as no one else could. That was why they were all following him.

'Better a bad king than a good one,' Ambrose said. 'Better still, no king at all. Remember what Grismonde said – our blood would run and run. That's the way the enemy works. He wanted my father to kill me. Orcrim – he's not my father, but he was close to him. And yet Orcrim wanted to kill me, too. Raymonde told him lies to

510

get him to hunt us. Raymonde killed his brother; Aun wants to kill Raymonde. *Let them eat their sons.* That's what he must make us do. Sons, brothers, friends. He's been doing it for three hundred years.'

'I see,' she said.

Now the path was dipping downwards, twisting as it fell through the brown trunks all spiny with dead twigs and branches.

'That's why I have to talk to you about Chawlin.'

'What about him?' Sophia said, sharply.

'He's got to kill me.'

Down to her left Sophia could hear the sound of a stream. The sun would be sparkling on the water, there. But the beams could not pierce the thick shroud of pine-leaves above them. The forest slope lay in deep shadow, under the glare of midday. And for a moment she accepted what he had said. She knew why he had told her Raymonde's story.

Then she was furious.

'Don't be stupid!'

'He's spoken with Prince Paigan. I was there. It was in Develin, when the King attacked. Chawlin was told he could save one life. He chose you. Later he'll have been told the price was me. Now he's got to kill me, or the enemy will say his bargain is not fulfilled. That's why his creatures were following you. It was a threat, to make Chawlin kill me.'

Her hand, which had fallen slack upon her horse's neck as he spoke, slowly lifted the rein again.

'He's your friend,' she heard herself say. 'He was the one person who was sorry for you when you came to

511

Develin. When I thought you were dirt, he made me speak for you in council. He talked with you . . .'

Her voice failed. Memories crowded in her mind.

*Two hundred sentences of death. Two hundred and one now. I've got to do something, and it will be all right. I need a bow.*

Chawlin!

'Sorry,' said the boy, clumsily.

'I don't believe it.'

'Yes, you do.'

*Chawlin!*

'I gave him the cup,' she said. 'I did it.'

That dead look in his eyes, as he had drawn the blanket around himself on the slopes of the knoll yesterday evening: she had done that to him, to the man whom she called husband.

I gave him the cup. He had been safe, and sheltered. And then I gave him the cup. And now he's got to kill this boy, for me.

The path brought them down to the water, and to sun upon the broad mossy banks, and everything she had done was a ruin.

'I'm sorry,' said the boy again.

'I don't want you to be sorry! I want . . .'

There were no words for this – this smothering feeling in the sun of the March. No words could . . .

'I want you to forgive me!' she said.

'Of course.'

'Of course what?'

'Of course I forgive you.'

'Ho, Tarceny!' called Orcrim behind them.

Hot tears were lumping in her throat and clouding the

512

edge of her sight. She had stopped the mare. Ambrose was looking at her.

'Are you all right?' he asked.

'Tarceny!' roared Orcrim.

'He's speaking to you,' she managed to say.

Ambrose looked behind him. Up came Orcrim and Lackmere in a clatter of hooves. The rearguard followed.

'What are we all about?' cried Orcrim. 'Is this a picnic? Our enemy's things can jump on us in an instant, and you two are idling along on your own like a pair of babes. From now on we stay closed up. And I'll be telling men off to mind you. Don't get out of their reach, you hear me?'

'Yes,' she heard Ambrose say, humbly.

'Now let's catch up with the others.'

And now there was no escape. They were close before and behind her, even riding alongside her when they could. She was surrounded by men when she most wanted to be alone.

She fixed her eyes on her horse's neck and thought about Chawlin, and what she had done to him. She thought about Ambrose, the boy-seer who rode ahead of her: what she had done to him, too, and how he had forgiven what she had done.

It did make a difference, she thought again and again as the mare footed the paths towards nightfall. It made a very little difference.

She still had to forgive herself.

The sun was low and the air was beginning to cool. The riders filed out of the forest track into another valley. This one was broad and level, with a great open space of knee-high grass in its bed. The riders picked up into an easy trot to take advantage of the space.

Hoofbeats sounded from the back of the column, approaching quickly.

'Orcrim! Orcrim!'

It was the grey-haired knight with the hard face. He had been riding with the rear, and was now coming up at a canter to catch the leaders. Aun and Orcrim had halted their mounts and were waiting for him. Sophia saw Ambrose turn his mule back in a wide circle to hear what they had to say. Others of the Company were clustering around. She wheeled back to join them.

'Caw – what is it?'

'We are being followed,' she heard the grey knight say.

'Tell me what you saw.'

'We saw nothing. Barey heard someone in the trees a way back. He made me listen, but there was nothing more, then. But we stopped again, as we were coming out of the wood, and heard it. A man running, on the path behind us.'

'Are you sure it was a man?' asked Sophia.

'Why didn't you just snatch him?' grunted Orcrim.

'He was coming on carefully – fits and starts. He wasn't about to go falling into our laps.'

Orcrim looked about the broad glade. The sun had dipped below the western ridge. The grass and trees were all in shadow. The fringes of the woods watched them, unmoving.

'And now he'll have seen us close up and talk. If he's following us, he won't come running into the open, even if he sees us leave. He'll work round. But then he'll want to catch us up . . .

514

'So we'll move on as though we are not expecting anything. When we are a half-mile out of the glade, Caw, you and Barey can find cover, with' – he looked around – 'with Oram and Guildehard to back you up. Bring him in, unharmed if you can.'

'If he's sensible,' said Caw.

'If it's a man,' said someone else.

'Count on it being a man,' said Aun. 'And don't count on bringing him in.'

'What's that?' Orcrim glared at him.

'He's using Tarceny's witchcraft. You think you know what that means. But you've never tried to fight it. I have.'

'And?'

'Nothing goes right. You attack, they're waiting for you. You force-march, and they're ahead of you. You lie in ambush, and they do not come.'

Orcrim scowled. 'Did you find any answers?'

'The one that worked ten years ago,' said Aun, grinning, 'was a brave woman.'

Orcrim looked hard at Aun for a moment. Then, still scowling, he jerked his head at his men.

'Enough of this,' he said. 'Let's go.'

They moved off at a slow walk. Ambrose was alongside Sophia again.

'It's Chawlin,' he murmured to her.

'I know,' she said.

'If they bring him in, perhaps you should talk to him,' he said.

'That would be best,' she said, still looking ahead of her.

Of course she would talk to Chawlin. She just had no idea what either of them would say.

515

'Will they be able to disarm him?' she heard the boy ask Aun, as the trees closed around them again.

Aun shrugged. 'Depends.'

'What is he like, this man?' said Orcrim from behind them.

'Quick,' said Ambrose.

'Weak,' said Aun.

I don't know, thought Sophia. I don't know any more.

The path wound among the trees and darkened with the dusk. The riders were forced down to single file. Ambrose fell behind Sophia. She heard Aun bring his mount up as close as he could to speak quietly with the boy.

'Something you should know about that man Caw. You remember your grandsire's stone, in the chapel wall at Trant castle?'

'Yes,' said Ambrose.

'It was Caw who killed him.'

There was a short silence.

'Does Mother know?' she heard Ambrose ask.

'She does.'

A little while later someone further behind her said: 'They've gone.'

Sophia looked round. In the dimness the men were just a line of shapes, bobbing on their mounts among the trees. She could not count them. She had not heard anyone move off the path.

There was something awful about the silence that was falling on the forest.

They camped that evening in a dell under trees, a short way up a slope from the trackside. Orcrim would permit no fire. He stalked among the Company as they settled for the night, glaring at the shadows and cursing any man who made too much noise. Ambrose could feel his unease, and shared it. Sleep dragged heavily at him, after the nights of watching, but he did not want to close his eyes. He saw Aun roll himself in his blanket and settle at once. He saw Orcrim telling a tall man to come and be guard over himself and Sophia, and he saw the man make his way over and squat near them with a naked sword in his hands. He wondered what that sword had done at Chatterfall.

How could you forgive?

He rolled over, restless, and thought about something else. He thought about his rag-banner, which had become a blanket again, and about the device of Tarceny. He was still not sure what to do about the shape on the Moon. On the Aclete banner it was just the natural curve of the moon's shadow, at three-quarters full: neat, but not enough. He thought for a while about making it a hand holding a pearl. That had changed everything. He must remember to thank Sophia for what she had done. But there was still a piece missing.

He could not remember the name of the tall guard. He did remember that the first thing Sophia had done, when she had stepped into the firelight, had been to ask Orcrim his name. He must try harder about names. You call me Sophia, she had said. It's who I am.

He dozed, and in his dreams he walked into the library of Develin where she was reading from a scroll. He approached her confidently, because now he knew her name, and she would tell him where in the house he would find the Heron Man. But as he came up, it was no longer

517

Sophia. It was a man playing on a hill-pipe a tune that brimmed with tears. The piper looked up and the music died away. My name is Chawlin, he said.

Their swords wove between them. Chawlin was quick. He had always been too quick for Ambrose.

The Angels never promised that you would live, Chawlin told him.

His point was inside Ambrose's guard.

Ambrose jerked awake. He was lying in the dark of the dell, with a dozen sleeping men around him and the tall guard still sitting bolt upright a yard away. Beyond him there were horses standing against the night sky, and the shapes of more men with them. He heard low voices. Caw had returned.

'Did they catch him?' he called softly to the standing shadows.

'No,' said Orcrim's voice.

Shapes were moving in the darkness among the sleeping men – Caw's party trying to find places to lie down in the crowded camp. He could not see the sentries, although he knew they were there. The figure lying beside him was Sophia. He thought from the sound of her breathing that she was awake. She must have heard what Orcrim had said. He thought she was crying.

He lay back again, and looked up at the black weave of the branches against the dull night sky. The moon was high above thin clouds. It was nearing the full.

Nothing's going right, he thought. He's using Tarceny's under-craft.

*Under-craft prevails.*

## XXV

### The Voice of Heaven

hey travelled for three days, and the early spring went before them. Bright sunshine chased the heavy clouds, and insects thickened under the trees. The Company rode north along the lake-shore, and then turned west and north again into the March. They passed one farm where the family brought out gifts of food for the young lord and his people. They also came upon a ruined mill and some abandoned huts. Other than that they saw no sign of any man, and none of any creature except for birds and the occasional swift rustle in the forest that might have been game. Still the air among the Company grew more tense as the days wore on, especially towards evening. They talked little, and when they did they kept their voices low. They listened for sounds and watched the undergrowth for movement. Ambrose saw men muffling their harness with strips of rag so that they might move more quietly. Memories of shadows crept into Ambrose's mind, and his hand stole to the hilt of his sword to stroke the little pouch that held the last white stone.

In the far north of the March, where the rocky hills

reared up like small mountains, they came to a shallow stream running in a bed of boulders and grey shingle. Snow-fishers grew in white masses on its banks, and low trees, bare and grey, stretched their bony fingers over the water. Orcrim turned the Company right, upstream, onto a narrow ribbon of track that ran along by the river. Ahead, the mountains rose silently in line after line of disappearing blue: bare slopes and deep valleys, and crowns of cloud gathering above each peak.

Ambrose was looking around him as he rode.

'I've been here,' he called forward to Sophia. 'Sophia, I've been here. I came this way last season, before I crossed the lake.'

'Did you?' She looked round and smiled at him.

She did smile for him, now, although he knew she did not feel like smiling inside herself. And now that he could use her name, he liked doing so.

'There's a ruin along here, Sophia. A small castle . . .'

'That will be Hayley,' said Hob from behind him. 'We will see it from the next bend.'

'Hayley?' repeated Sophia.

'Will we stop there?' asked Ambrose, hopefully.

Orcrim's pattern was to start early, halt the company for the heat of the day, and then press on long into the evening. The sun was now rising high and Ambrose would have welcomed a rest. But Hob shook his head.

'Too soon. He's planning to pass the March-stone before nightfall. That's a long push from here. So he'll want to press on this morning and make the midday halt a short one.'

So by tonight they would have left the Kingdom again.

They would be in the real mountains, where he had lived his whole life. In a few days they would reach the pool, if nothing stopped them.

And then? Where was the Heron Man now?

The hillsides shifted as they passed. Among the grey outcrops a brown-stained rank of battlements shouldered into view. Hayley was a small, square keep, surrounded by a curtain wall, with no moat. Ambrose saw Sophia look up at it as they rode by. It must have seemed a poor place to her – no bigger than some of the lesser holds of Develin to which the Widow's court had travelled on its Midwinter passage. Still, he saw her watch the deserted shell closely as they sidled past it, and she looked back at it several times until the valley wound again and bore it out of view.

The path took them another league up the stream in bright sunshine, and then dipped across it at a ford among tumbled boulders and bare, grey willows. The leading horsemen rose into view as they followed the path up the steep slope opposite. One of them laughed and pointed at something he saw on a rock at the stream's edge. The riders passed. The same joke was repeated, but Ambrose could not catch it. He saw Sophia reach the far bank and check her horse, looking down at something on the rock.

'Sophia, what is it?' he called.

She looked back at him, but did not answer. Instead she set her mount at the slope in the wake of the others.

Feet dripping, Ambrose's mule climbed out of the stream. Now he could see that on the flat, bare top of the rock lay a bunch of picked snow-fishers. Their leaves were wet despite the sun, and the flowers were still fresh. Among the horse-clatter behind him, he heard Hob chuckle.

'What is it?' Ambrose asked.

'There are still some folk who live along the banks of this stream. Someone brought this posy down to their lover as the price of a cuddle, I guess. Then they hopped into the bushes when they heard us coming – or for some other reason.' He grinned, knowingly.

Ambrose looked about him. He had seen no sign of people, and there was nothing on the sunlit stream-banks to say that any were near now. The water rippled endlessly in its broad ribbon over the grey stones. The snow-fishers lay on their rock at his stirrup. If they bore any meaning at all, it was not for him.

'Come on,' said Hob. 'We must keep up with the others.'

The path wound upwards among tall bushes which quickly hid the stream from view. Then it broadened and climbed more easily up a cleft between two hillsides that were dark with thorns and low trees. Here, despite the high sun and stony ground, they kicked their horses into a trot to close the gap with the leaders. There was space to let the riders bunch up as they made their way between the hillsides. Ambrose could see Orcrim glancing to left and right. He hoped the old war-master was looking for a place with shade where they could halt, but he knew that it was unlikely. Orcrim was watching the thorns for another reason; and that could only be fear of ambush.

It would be a good place for it, Ambrose thought, if there was anyone who wanted to attack them. The high slopes were thickly covered and close to the path on both sides. The ground was difficult for horses.

'What's that?' said someone sharply.

Ahead of them, by a pile of boulders, a robed and hooded figure had risen to its feet. It seemed to be waiting for them.

'Careful,' called Orcrim to the Company as they approached. 'Look about you.'

Metal scraped in a scabbard. Ambrose glanced down at his own sword, but he needed both hands to manage his mule as it sidled on the stony ground, uncertain of what he wanted. Its movements carried him forward. The standing figure threw back its hood. He looked down into his mother's face.

'Well met, Count of Tarceny,' she said with mock gravity. 'Beneath your Doubting Moon.'

Ambrose was so startled that he could not say anything.

She stepped past the mule's head.

'A good morning to you, Orcrim,' she said. 'And thank you for bringing my son so far.'

'I am well paid for the present,' grunted Orcrim from his saddle. 'What is it you want?'

They were watching her, with their lined faces set like stone. Two or three had swords out. They had not lowered them. Ambrose could see Aun, at the back of the group, craning for a view. He was too far away.

She stood among the men she had betrayed and spoke with them.

'I want you to rest, and listen to me.'

'I had not thought to rest here. Why should I?'

'Because from here your road may take a different way.'

'Different?'

523

'You plan to cross the ridge at the head of this defile and follow the wooded valley that runs west and north into the mountains. If you go that way it may take you another four days to reach your destination, and your coming will be expected. I can bring you by another way, and within what would seem to you a single hard march – if you will listen.'

'What way is this?'

'I think you know it, Orcrim.'

When he did not answer, she added: 'Can you not tell me how my father's house fell so quickly to you, the year that I wed your lord?'

'Witch,' muttered someone.

'We can't stop here,' another voice said. 'We need shade and water.'

'We can water the horses later,' said Orcrim sharply. 'It won't kill them. Get out of my ear.' He frowned. 'All right, then. You can dismount. Let's hear what she has to say.'

'Why did you risk it?' Ambrose whispered to his mother, as they waited in the little shade thrown by a boulder for the Company to peg out their horses. 'They hate you.'

'And I do not love them, although I begged for their lives, once,' she said. 'But too many good causes have failed because their people could not hold together. And in truth, as we come closer to the enemy, it is no longer safe for me to make my way on my own. I, too, wish to come inside your ring of steel.'

'I thought you couldn't travel with us.'

'No. But you can travel with me. And that is what I intend.'

Something must have showed in his face, for she put her hand on his arm.

'My darling, it is a hard place, I know. But it will not be so long a journey as we made from Develin. And there is no other way that we can succeed.'

'Why not?' said Orcrim, who had come up to stand over them.

Around them, the Company was gathering, looking down at them. Aun was there. Ambrose looked about him, counting.

'Where is Sophia?'

Orcrim looked around and scowled. 'Gone for a bit of woman's privacy, I guess,' he said. 'I cannot do *every-thing* for her. Cradey – take a walk up the hill and make sure she reappears, would you? Now, mistress,' he went on, turning to Ambrose's mother. 'I know where you want to take us. Tell me why we must follow you.'

'I have told you about the stones, Orcrim.'

'And I have made some preparations – such tackle as Aclete could afford me; although I still lack baulks and levers.'

'That is good. But if you approach the ring as you plan to, climbing under the sun from the house on the mountain spur, you would need an army of craftsmen and horse-teams with you, for at least one stone has fallen to the very base of the pit beside the pool. And until you could raise those stones, you might wait for your enemy in vain, because he would have no need to come against you when you were strong and prepared for him.

'But within the Cup of the World, the ground is not the same. There, what is a mountain for you, may be a rise in the earth. A lake is a cleft, a castle may seem to be a pile of rocks. I have stood within the Cup and looked at the pool as it appears there. There the cliffs are shallow, tumbled slopes. Coming from within the Cup, we have a chance to raise these stones again, with the strength that we have.'

'How big are these stones?'

'Perhaps of a size with that one.' She indicated a boulder, larger than a man, that lay a little way from them. Someone swore under his breath.

'Can we bring horses through the Cup?' Ambrose asked.

'I have known it,' said Orcrim. 'But why should we do it now?'

'There is a man following you.'

'A friend who is an enemy, I gather. So?'

'As long as you are still days from the pool, I believe that the real enemy will be content to wait and play his game with our friend. Such devices give him the only delight he knows. But if he cannot stop you that way, he will sooner or later send his creatures against you, as he sent them to kill Tarceny, and Tarceny's father before him. Between here and the pool there are many places where the path can be attacked suddenly, and where horses will be disadvantaged. For these reasons it would be better to move quickly, now, and challenge the enemy on ground of our choosing – by the pool itself.'

'I have not said yes yet. What strength has he?'

'Do you not know?'

Orcrim scowled. 'Two men, we think. One behind, one ahead. But also things that are not men. I do not know how many.'

'I think – no more than seven.'

'Seven!' The riders looked at one another. Ambrose saw a face clear, a pair of shoulders straighten. These men had been marching towards an unknown enemy: shapeless, nameless and uncounted. Now someone had given them a number. Now the odds could be reckoned.

'Seven,' said Orcrim. 'Well, if that is true, it is not so bad.'

'How do you know?' Ambrose murmured to his mother.

'Because I have begun to guess who they must be,' she said, in a voice that everyone could hear.

'So that is seven, plus two, nine, and the old scarecrow too,' Hob was saying. 'Ten at most, against . . .' He looked around and hesitated.

'Fourteen?' said Ambrose, firmly counting himself. He looked around, too.

There was something wrong. The numbers were wrong.

'Who's that, there?' barked Orcrim.

They were one too many!

'Hold him!' cried Aun. 'Hold him!'

There was a scuffle on the far side of the group. Someone yelled and cursed. Swords leaped from their scabbards among the Company. A man broke free from another, stumbling among the thorns. He looked across at Ambrose. Their eyes met.

It was the Wolf.

'Back to the stream! The stream!' he snarled. 'He's killing one of you, now!'

Men were surging through the thorns to reach him.

He turned, and stepped away. For a moment Ambrose saw him, leaping among brown stones while the riders floundered in the bushes. Then he had disappeared.

Orcrim swore.

'When did he creep up on us? How much did he hear?'

'He was warning us,' said Caw, standing waist-deep among thorns.

Ambrose looked about him.

'Where's Sophia? Where is she?'

Sophia was on the path that led back downhill to the stream.

The air hummed with the warmth of late morning. All around her the bushes shrieked with the song of grasshoppers. She could see insects busy among the yellow thorn flowers. She could hear the distant rush of the stream water ahead of her. It was hard to believe in nightmares.

Nevertheless, she took care to walk in the very middle of the path, leaving as much space between her and the thorns on either side as she could. She went warily, looking to left and right for any sign of movement on the hillside. This was the first time in days that she had walked beyond call of the armed men she had drawn about her. And she had slipped away without attracting attention to herself, for she had not wanted them to know where she was going.

She was on her own. She knew that she might be in danger. But she had to get back to the waterside.

Down there, on the unseen riverbank, there had

been a bunch of white flowers placed so that anyone who crossed the stream might see them. They all had. They had ridden by the rock on which the flowers lay, one after another, and had sneered or chortled as they passed. The men had all read the message of the snow-fishers, and yet none of them had understood it. They had not understood it, because the message had been for her.

The flowers had said *I love you.*

They were freshly picked. There had been water-droplets upon the silver-grey leaves. Chawlin had laid them there that morning, knowing that she would pass and see them. He must be close. He would have laid them there, and watched the crossing from hiding, because if it had been important to him to send the message it would have been important also to know that she had seen it.

He must be somewhere near the stream. He would not know that she was coming. He could not know that the Company had halted, unless by chance he had looked into the cup. She would have to find him. And if she could not find him, she would at least take the snow-fishers, so that he would know, if he passed that way in the next few hours, that she had not only seen his message but had wanted to keep it, because it came from him.

*I love you.*

She had to speak with Chawlin. Ambrose had been right about that. She had to see the truth as Chawlin saw it. And, one way or another – with words, with looks, with all her heart – she had to draw him willingly out of hiding. The Company could not catch him. She could. She would bring him home.

If she could find him.

The sound of the stream grew louder. And . . . yes! Mingled in the flow of the water were the notes of a pipe, broken at first, but more and more clear as she made her way downwards. It was playing the lament-tune that Chawlin had taught and played for her on their journey from Develin to the March. He must be sitting by the streamside down there, alone and remembering, consoling himself with music in his desolation.

The path narrowed, snaking downwards. The trees and bushes pressed close on either side, and ahead of her where the path turned. She could not see more than ten feet in any direction. The pebbles rattled beneath her feet. She was nearly there, now. From around the next corner, she would see the stream.

The music had stopped. She stopped, too, listening. She heard Chawlin's voice.

'What are you doing here?'

He could not possibly have seen her. And he sounded tired. Ill and desperate. He had come all this way on foot, and alone.

'What do you want from me?' Chawlin said again.

'You know what I want,' a man's voice answered.

'I am trying, damn you!'

'You are not trying hard enough.'

There was something familiar about the second voice, too. It had a shape, a whisper or an echo in her mind that she remembered and did not know from where she remembered it.

'You want me to charge in, a dozen to one? This isn't a party of peasants or foot soldiers. They're always on the watch. You know that. I can't get to him. I'll just get my throat cut. How would that suit you?'

'Him, or her. I am becoming impatient.'

'You want me to get myself killed!'

'I do not want. I do not plan. Your debt to me is a life. I will have it by tonight.'

That voice . . . As in a dream, she knew she had heard it before, speaking to her, coaxing her to do this, to do that, and she had done them willingly. When had she dreamed that? She could not remember. But this was not a dream. A thorn-frond scraped lightly on the skin of the back of her hand. The pale brown pebbles of the path were hard beneath her feet. And a bee, a plain bee, could hum out of a yellow thorn-flower, even now.

Chawlin was silent. He needed help. Making as little sound as she could, Sophia crept down the path towards the last bend. As she reached it, she heard him speak again.

'Is it me you want? I tell you – I tell you that you can have me. Everything I have. Let them live – I'll bend my neck and give you my knife. Or I'll do it myself.'

No, Chawlin!

'Him, or her,' was the answer. 'That is the only choice there is. Choose now, and swiftly.'

'Damn you!'

Sophia crouched at the turn in the path, willing herself to go on. But her limbs were frozen. Something deep within her screamed that she must not, *must* not be seen by the one who spoke the Second Voice.

'I won't,' said Chawlin at last. 'He's a boy. I won't.'

'Him or her. You chose swiftly enough in Develin. One

531

name from two hundred. Your friends, your teachers, your fellow-scholars. You chose her. Do you choose that she should die, now?'

Horror crept into Sophia's heart. He knows I'm here, she thought. He knows I'm listening.

He wants me to hear what Chawlin says.

'He will die anyway,' said the Second Voice. 'You could still save her.'

'I choose . . .' said Chawlin, as if each word was labour. 'I choose to do nothing for you.'

'So now she will die.'

'Reach her if you can, then!'

'Do you think she is safe among her friends? She is not. You have called her out. You have chosen that she must die. Live long with your choice, and remember it.'

'Damn you!'

There was a ring of iron and a clatter among the stones of the streambed. She heard the voice make a sound of contempt. Then feet were floundering in the water. Chawlin must have leaped at his tormentor. He was crying: 'Come back, damn you! Come back!'

There was no answer.

She heard Chawlin groan. And she heard his feet splashing back out of the stream.

Now, Sophia!

She scrambled around the last corner of the path. Chawlin was leaning against the rock at the streamside, and he was alone. There was no one else in the valley. The sunlight rippled on the surface of the stream, and a breeze stirred the greening branches. The posy of flowers lay undisturbed on the rock at Chawlin's elbow.

532

'Chawlin!' she hissed, urgently.

His clothes were ragged and filthy. His sword, which he must have drawn to leap at his oppressor, hung limply in his hand. His hair was tangled. He looked weak. His eyes, when he looked up, had deep shadows under them, as if he had not slept. And there was horror in them as he looked at her.

'No!' he cried.

'Chawlin, come on. Come with me!'

He had pushed himself upright and was coming up the slope to her.

'What are you doing here?' he croaked. 'Where are the others?'

'Not far. I came back to speak with you.'

'Get back to them! Go, quickly!'

'Chawlin, you've got to . . .'

'Go!' He had reached her. His face was screwed up, weeping. He had his hand on her shoulder and was pushing at her, trying to force her up the hill. She fought him.

'Not without you!'

'They're coming for you!'

*They* were coming. Still she rallied, and clutched at his shirt.

'Not without you!'

'Sophia!'

'Come *on!*'

Something heavy moved in the bushes. Things were stirring in the streambed, like boulders that had grown limbs. The smell hit her – heavy, dank, like water that had never seen the sun.

They cried out, together, and lurched up the narrow path, twisting left and right among the heavy thorn cover.

She was panting already, but her legs leaped and pushed at the slope with the power of fear. Something blundered among the bushes to their right. The thorns parted. A grey thing the size of a stooping man scraped and shouldered through them. The path twisted again, carrying them away from it. Chawlin cried again, and there was terror in his voice.

'Help!' Sophia yelled. 'Help!'

It was too far to the camp. Her voice would not carry.

There was another of them in the bushes to her left! A ragged, threadbare hood hid a face too long and thin for any man. And it was gone. And it appeared again, yards further on, closer to the path, as if it had leaped unseen or gone around a rock in another world to re-enter into the day.

She could see them clearly. So horribly clearly.

'Help!' she gasped, uselessly.

Angels, help us, she pleaded in her head. And she ran.

Together they broke from the thorns. Chawlin was alongside her, still with his sword in his hand. She felt him stumble, and clutched at his arm to steady him. He was gasping – sobbing, she thought. He must be exhausted. Even so he was moving faster than she was. He was drawing ahead of her. She sensed his terror.

She stumbled.

The slopes of the cleft seemed to be full of moving shapes, some lumbering like moving rock, others flitting swiftly like rags upon the wind. There was a space ahead of them.

They don't understand about the path, she thought. They don't see it.

534

'Chawlin!' she cried.

'Keep going!' He was well ahead of her. He had not looked back.

'Chawlin!'

She was falling behind. For a moment she slackened her pace, looking around. And something leaped at her from the bare and sunlit hill.

She shrieked, and twisted. It was clutching her, and she was pulling at it. Fingers like filthy roots wound over her sleeve. Claws or thorns slit deeply into her arm. She shrieked again and backed from it. Up the hill, she heard Chawlin shout. She pulled and pulled again, knowing that the other things would be on her in seconds. The horrible, squat, hooded thing held her and dragged at her, and she felt her heels slip.

Something banged upon its head and bounced away – Chawlin's sword! A hood fell. She saw a face – a face like a huge and tortured bird, gulping, craning round at its attacker. It wore a circlet of gold.

Chawlin was weeping, yelling, striking at it again. It turned silently on him. Iron sang as though it had hit stone.

'Sophia,' he gasped. 'Go on.'

Sophia scrambled on her hands and knees. There was blood on her arm, where it had clutched her and let her go. She got to her feet. The thing had gone – it was crouching twenty yards off, looking at them. To left and right others were closing on them. Chawlin was beside her, sword up. He had come back for her.

He turned to look at her. For an instant he was still Chawlin – just Chawlin, fearful but rallying. Then he laughed. His face changed. A deep light came into his eyes.

'*Go!*'

She hung there, for the voice was not his.

'*Go!*' it bellowed.

She ran.

She ran, veering uphill to the left, where there was an open space among the things. Something flitted there, hunting for her as though it could not see her well. She dodged, stumbled, and ran on. Behind her she heard Chawlin shouting. She heard the sword strike, and she heard him shout again. The hills rang with his cry, and with the force of thunder. There were no words in it that she knew.

The slope was open ahead of her. She could see to the skyline. It was blue, with a wisp of white silver cloud. Her legs were trembling. She ran on.

There were people up there, shapes against the sky. They were looking down the hill towards her.

'Help!' she cried to them. They could not hear her.

A hundred yards down the slope behind her Chawlin roared and struck among his enemies. They had left her to get him. They would kill him!

'Help!' she called to the men above her.

They were moving, coming down the slope at a cautious jog on the bad footing. There were swords out among them.

They were so slow!

'Help him!' she called to them. 'Help him!'

Behind her the cry came again, rimmed with fire. He was still fighting.

Now the first of the Company had almost reached her. She saw the wild-eyed bannerman, Endor, waving a mace two-handed as he plunged on down the hill. She saw

Orcrim, calling *Close up! Close up!* as they scattered on the slope. Ambrose slithered past, sword in hand, a boy among men. Others were pausing in their career, calling to her – was she hurt?

'Help him!' she yelled at them.

Arms caught her.

'Are you hurt?' It was the woman who had been waiting at the rocks. The old chamberlain Hob stood on the slope a few yards away, looking at her.

'No,' she said.

'There's blood on your arm.'

The arm was nothing.

'I – I saw them.'

She had seen its face. The eyes, that had been like water. And yet deep within them there had been something tortured. Something human.

'It wore a crown,' she whispered.

The woman nodded. She was still peering at Sophia's arm. She had a pale, calm face. It was almost beautiful, in that place of all places.

'Have you a knife, Hob?' the woman asked.

The man drew one from his belt and held it out. Sophia looked at him. He had a sword, armour. What was he doing here?

'Please – go and help him.'

Hob looked down the slope.

'They've gone,' he said.

There was no sound down there, now.

The knife tore gently into Sophia's bloody sleeve. The cloth dragged at the torn surface of her arm. She winced with pain. She was feeling sick.

537

'Do you know who I am?' said the woman suddenly.

Sophia knew she was trying to distract her.

'No,' she said, and clenched her teeth.

'Four days ago, on Talifer's Knoll. Do you remember?'

She remembered darkness, and a voice that woke her. And then something had followed her. One of *them*.

'Why did you leave me?' she asked.

'I did not think that thing would attack you, then. But it might well have attacked me, as soon as the enemy knew I was with you. There. I'm sorry if it hurt.' The sleeve flopped bloodily onto the ground. The woman was lifting Sophia's arm by the elbow, peering at the mass of blood that bubbled thickly from it in three places.

'Is – is it poisoned?' Sophia asked.

'I do not know. But we should wash it. And we must stop the bleeding. Hob?'

Hob had picked up the torn sleeve and was knotting it.

'It's long enough. Wait a moment.'

They placed the knot in the pit of Sophia's elbow and made her bend her arm to keep it in place. Then they tied it, tightly, just above the elbow. She could feel the knot pressing into her arm, stifling the flow of blood to the wound.

'Keep it as high as you can,' Hob said. 'We'll get you down to the stream. Tell us if you need to rest.'

She was shaking as they led her, one on either side of her, down the slope again. Her knees were weak and her arm throbbed, and she felt sick. There was something strange about the way the woman moved beside her. She seemed to disappear, twice or three times, and for a few moments it would be only Hob beside her, holding her good arm to keep her steady. Then the woman would appear again, a few yards down the slope, reaching up to her. Sophia wondered if she was dreaming.

Below them, the men had gathered in a group. There was no sign of the creatures that had hunted her.

'Oh, Angels,' whispered the woman beside her.

There was something on the ground among the men. They were standing around it, looking down at it, talking. It looked like a bit of rotten blanket. As she came down the slope between her two supporters, Orcrim turned away from the group and took a step up towards them. He saw her, and opened his mouth. But he closed it again, as if he did not know what to say.

The men looked up at her. From their faces, she knew that there was something they had to tell her, but could not. She stepped among them.

The thing on the ground was Chawlin.

He was lying, huddled, by a low rock. His face and body were torn, many times, with long, bloody tracks, and a pool of dark blood was growing sticky on the ground under his body. She knelt beside him, and bent her head close to his, closing her eyes to the terrible marks upon it and begging, just begging, to hear the whisper of breath from his lips.

There was nothing.

'How close is your way to the enemy?' Orcrim's voice said from somewhere above her.

'We can go from here, or any place that you choose,' the woman said.

The voices seemed both distant and too loud. She

wanted to shut them out, so that she could hear him breathe.

'Then I would be moving as swiftly as we can.'

'Why now?' said Ambrose's voice.

'The enemy has struck. Now he must regather his strength, assess the success or failure of his blow, and plan his next attack. Now is the time to move against him.'

Please, Chawlin, thought Sophia. Please breathe. Please show me you are alive.

'We can't leave him lying like this,' said Ambrose. 'He was my friend, too.'

'A king should listen to his war-captain,' said Aun. 'You've had good advice. Take it.'

'We can't dig on this ground anyway,' said someone else.

Please, Chawlin! How can you be dead?

'I'm not a king,' grumbled Ambrose.

A hand had fallen upon her shoulder. They wanted her to leave him.

'A cairn, then,' said Orcrim. 'You've as much time as it takes us to water the horses, and to cut some poles and levers. Be quick. And no one is to wander off on their own. I want no party less than four strong. We've seen what can happen.'

They were pulling her away, murmuring in her ear. She let herself be pulled, because she had no strength to stay. She could not see. There was something wrong with her eyes. She put up her arm to wipe them, and found they were stinging with tears. When she had cleared them enough to look back to where he lay, they were already dragging his cloak over his face.

'That's his sword,' she heard Hob say beside her. 'Or part of it, broken. He must have backed up to those rocks in the end. Do you think he got any of them?'

'He was hurting them,' she whispered. 'I saw it.'

'If he didn't scare them to death,' Hob said with a forced chuckle. 'What a shout he raised.'

'It wasn't him,' she said.

'It was him, but not only him,' said the woman. 'I've heard that voice before, or one very like it. It said the last words my husband spoke, when he told Paigan Wulframson how he would end.'

Hob was silent for a moment, as if the woman had evoked memories that he did not want to recall. Then he said, 'What's that supposed to mean?'

'"When the – the fleeing man – turns upon his pursuers, there Michael rides upon his helm."'

Sophia knew the text. She knew the words of the Martyr. They read: *When the coward knight turns upon his pursuers* . . .

He isn't a coward, her mind protested.

Isn't, not wasn't.

Hob grunted with surprise 'Didn't do him . . .' he began. Then he stopped himself.

You were going to say, *Didn't do him much good*, Sophia thought savagely.

'Even Heaven has its price,' said the woman. 'Do you think we should go on? Orcrim said move in fours, and we barely count as three.'

They had come to the place where the path dipped into the close cover of the thorns. Less than a half hour ago she had been standing here, alone, and Chawlin had been alive at the streamside.

We've gone wrong, she thought. We made a mistake. Can't we go back to where we were? Can't we make just a little change, so that he could be alive again? On the hillside above her she could hear the distant clip, clip of stones going into place on the little mound under which they were burying him. Ambrose was up there, stooping now with a stone in his hands. Aun was there, too – the man that Chawlin had said was his old captain. They were sorry, but none of them had loved him.

And clip, and clip, and clip. She thought of the soul-less stones pressing against his face.

And now the world crumbled, silently. Its floor gave way in a pouring of dust and left her hanging in its void – empty colours, empty flowers, empty sky. Faces that came and went and spoke without meaning. Her eyes blinked, and opened again, and the colours were still there. A bee the colour of soot rattled lightly among the thorn flowers a yard away. And none of it was worth anything any more, because Chawlin would never be again.

'They'll be bringing the horses down in a minute,' said Hob. 'It would be safer if we could wait.'

'Can you wait?' the woman asked.

'Can you wait?' she said again, and the slightest shake of her hand on Sophia's shoulder told Sophia she was speaking to her.

'It's only dirt,' she mumbled.

And thirst. And pain. And the grey, empty ache inside her that would go on for ever.

542

Unseen in the streambed below, the waters poured by the rock where the white flowers withered meaninglessly in the sun.

## XXVI

### Torch and Tackle

hey were back at the outcrop of rocks where they had halted that morning. Ambrose was sitting on a boulder with his sword on his knees. Sophia was sitting on the rock beside him. Her arm lay in her lap, bound with the black, bloody cloth that was all that remained of the rag-banner.

'Group the pulling-horses and harness them up,' Orcrim was saying. 'Hob, you will take charge of them, with the women and you, boy, under his command. Those of you whose horses are not in the pulling-teams can stay with them for the march. Don't try to ride, because the going will be bad . . .'

'Will you need to ride?' Ambrose whispered to Sophia. She shook her head.

He did not know what to say to her. He could see that Orcrim was angry with her, for having slipped away unguarded. So were some of the others. And Sophia was not speaking either. Ambrose gave up searching for words of comfort. There were none. All that mattered was whether they would succeed or fail in what they were trying to do.

He felt that they were close to the end, but the end was not coming as he had thought it would. Chawlin was dead. It was not Chawlin's quick sword that would finish him. He had seen the things that afternoon, spread out on the slope below him. He had felt his heart crumble as he had run down towards them, waving his sword as though it were a child's stick. He could tell the men around him were nervous, too. Their eyes were down. Hands fidgeted with belts and sword-hilts. They had seen what the enemy could do. And yet they must fight them. The white pebbles were lost. The gaps in the ring must be blocked with iron, and with flesh and blood.

Ambrose was both glad and ashamed that he had been put back with the horses.

'These things,' said Orcrim. 'All right, so we've had a look at them now. What happened was that we came at them, and they made off. Remember that. *They* ran off. And they lost a man they thought was theirs. And if I understand it right, they'll be scared about the way they lost him. Damned scared, get it? They damned well should be, because when I think about it, it damned well scares me.

'So I want no mistakes. When we get there, every man but Hob is to be between the pulling-team and the pit. You can expect them to come at us. Don't give them an inch. Nothing is to get past us, or round us. We can hammer these things. But if the pulling-horses get the frights, and we lose them in that place, we'll never get them back. And if that means a stone stays flat when it should be up, we might as well not have come.'

His easy air had vanished. He walked among his sullen

men, punching one hand into the other as his voice punched their ears and told them what to think. He glared at Ambrose. He glared at anyone who met his eye. Perhaps he *was* scared, by something. Maybe it was the thought of angels watching him. Maybe he had been gripped now by what had to be done; and knew that he must make them do it.

'Let's have those horses lined up then,' said Orcrim.

The Company broke up, talking in low voices to their beasts and to each other. Ambrose made his way over to his mule and took it by the bridle. It did not want to come. Another hand caught it and drew it forward. It was his mother.

'I looked for the cup,' he murmured. 'If he had it, they took it before we reached them.'

She sighed. 'All the same, you did well to remember.'

'It was Aun that remembered,' Ambrose confessed. 'The old looter . . .'

Four horses had been picked out and were being fitted with the horse-collars that Orcrim had wrung from Aclete. They were grouped in pairs. Each pair was fastened with short chains to a stout baulk of wood that trailed crosswise behind them. Lengths of rope were being gathered around each pole. Hob was at the nearest, testing the fastenings.

'Seventeen mounts between us, and I've just two that know how to pull,' he was saying to another rider. 'And too much rope, not enough chain. *And* I've a crowd of frisky beasts to keep quiet when the fun starts . . .'

'Happy to change places,' said the other man.

That must have counted as impudence among the

Fifteen, for Hob cuffed him gently on the side of the helmet.

'You get yourself torn up a bit first. Do you good. Now, what have we got here?'

He was eyeing Ambrose and his mule.

'It might pull,' said Ambrose, hanging onto the bridle. He was glad to be under Hob, who seemed the friendliest of Orcrim's company, and the most ready to treat him as if he were really Lord of Tarceny. He would not have liked to be commanded by Caw. And of course Mother would have hated it.

'Done it before?' said Hob.

'I don't know; but it's quiet enough.'

'There's only four collars. I've two pullers and two that will do what they're told. And Orcrim will skin me if I hold him up longer. But it could carry some of the levers we've cut – or my rig. Come and give me a hand.'

Hob's 'rig' was a collection of fresh, stout poles, bound together with rope, that lay on the ground not far away.

'What is it?' said Ambrose, looking down at the pile. He knew the men had been busy cutting and binding it for more than an hour after he had returned, hands sore, from Chawlin's cairn.

'Hob's last stand,' said Hob. 'Or a bit of under-craft, if you like.'

'Under-craft?' said Ambrose sharply.

'Cunning. Using what you know. That's all "under-craft" means. I don't know how a master mason would shift a stone like we are going to, but I've seen enough of sieges and the like to know that we're going to have to pull *up*, not along. That's why this. Take that end . . .'

Ambrose lifted. Three poles came heavily up together in their hands. Ambrose realized that it was a great tripod, which would be the height of a man when erected. There was another one, and more loose pieces, left on the ground. They dragged it over to where Mother was holding the mule. The beast shifted unhappily, as though it guessed what was coming. Hob gave it a doubtful look.

'I don't think it'll be too much trouble,' said Ambrose. 'Provided it's with the others.'

Hob shrugged. 'It's the same with most of them,' he said. 'They'll be fine as long as all the others are behaving, and hell if they get the frights all together. But you give a real war-horse a job he doesn't like and he'll let you know about it.'

Ambrose glanced over at Stefan. The big horse seemed to be calm enough at the moment. Aun was standing by him, waiting. Ambrose saw the breeze stir stray hairs on the back of his head, and on the horse's mane.

'I'll take him when it starts,' he said. 'He knows me.'

He looked down at the tripod again. Suddenly he realized where he had seen such a thing before. He had been on Stefan's back, hiding under Aun's cloak. It had loomed at him out of the mist, a great, three-legged thing supporting the ferry-rope that stretched across the river to Develin's shore. It had been made exactly like this – three legs, tied together at the top and roped into a wide triangle at the feet. There had been a man kneeling at its base, working to throw it down so that he could not cross to the castle of lights. That had been Hob.

Hob was also looking across at Aun's back. His hand was rubbing his jaw.

'Come on,' he said abruptly. 'Let's get the rest of it over. Hurry, now.'

'Two more things,' Orcrim was saying, with his voice pitched to carry along the line. 'This place we are going into – I've been there. It's not meant for us. If you go wandering off you may or may not get out by yourself. But you'll never get back in. And you may come out more than a day's march from the rest of us. So stay together. I'll pass torches down the line, so we can see where we all are. It's not dark there, but it's not light either. Stay together.

'The last thing is – look out. We'll not be alone in there. I'm not counting on trouble before we reach the pool, but if they look they may see us coming. And Raymonde's ahead of us, too. Look out for him, and don't count him as a friend.'

Ambrose supported one end of a tripod while Hob lashed it roughly to the mule's saddle-bow. Mother had gone to the head of the line, so Ambrose had to hold the mule's bridle with one hand as well. He was thinking that Orcrim would give the order to move in a moment, and that they were not ready. The tripod was heavy. He could not stop it from wavering as he held it, and he could not stop the mule from shifting. Hob was whispering curses as he fought with straps at the saddle.

Orcrim came down the line and dropped some things onto the ground. 'Torches for you here, Hob. You mark the back of the line. No one's to get behind you, clear? And you keep my torch in view—' He broke off, watching. 'You all set, or not?'

'One more,' said Hob, turning from the mule. Ambrose

could tell that he wanted to shout at Orcrim for harassing him, and Orcrim wanted to shout back at him for being behind. They were on edge, even these two; and the others must know it.

'Hare,' said Orcrim to the next man up. 'Give a hand, here . . .'

It was the tall rider. His name was Hare. He must remember that. Hare. If he could remember their names, then they might be more to him than just the shadows that had hunted him from Chatterfall. He didn't want to think about that any more. He wanted to stop thinking now, if he could. Now they must just do what they had come to do.

Hare had dropped his reins and was helping Hob with the other tripod. Ambrose was free to steady the mule. It snorted and shifted, and he clung to the bridle and crooned at it, and all the while his mind yelped: Let's go! Let's go!

'Done,' said Hob at last.

'Good, then,' said Orcrim. 'Light torches, and let's be away.'

And that was the word to move. There was no more waiting; no more preparing. Caw came down the line with a torch already lit. Hob picked two more torches off the ground and lit one from Caw's. The head of the line was already in motion, shambling up to where Mother stood on the open hillside. Ambrose saw Endor walking at his horse's head, bridle in one hand, banner in the other. There was another horse and man on the far side of them. Ambrose saw the bright sun glint on the old metal of mail and spur. He sensed the loom of the brown rocks beyond them. Then horses and men faded into the air of the hillside. The next pair of men and horses was already reaching the same spot, and fading in their turn. He heard Hob swear softly beside him.

Two by two, the men and horses vanished into the air. Orcrim was gone. Ambrose thought for a moment that he could see the ghost of a torch-flare dancing among the stones where the head of the cavalcade had disappeared. There was Sophia, at the head of one pulling-team. And she too was gone.

'Come on, lad,' said Hob.

The horses ahead of them were moving. They were the last in the line – he, and the mule, and Hob with his torch held high. The tripods trailed and clattered over the rocks, and the mule jerked unhappily at the bridle he was holding. Hob had roped the back ends of the poles together to prevent them from splaying all over the place, but they snagged almost at once and Hob had to lift them over a low rock to free them. A gap had opened ahead of them. The last pair of horses was already disappearing. Mother was standing alone on the slope, beckoning urgently.

'Come on,' said Ambrose between his teeth, and urged the mule upwards towards her. It came in a clatter of hooves and timber. She was already turning, beginning to run, disappearing. For a moment they were alone on the hillside. He looked at Hob, with his torch flaming weakly in his hand under the bright sun. Then the world changed.

The light faded. The bright thorn slopes were gone. The colours had dulled to the twilight that lurks at dawn. The torch flared out, tinged with green.

He was standing among the brown rocks that he remembered from his journey out of Develin. Far away, in all directions, he could see the bowl of the Cup like a wall of mountains, sweeping up towards the sky. To his left two great lights like huge stars marked where the head of Capuu lay on the rim of the world. The deep humming that he remembered told upon his ear.

'Go on, go on,' Hob was saying, in the strange, flat voice of that place.

Ahead of Ambrose the company of men and horses toiled up an easy slope. They were shadow-figures, seen in twilight, and the sounds they made were dim. He could see his mother hurrying towards the head of the line, pointing to her right as if that was the way to go. Up there a figure waved a torch, repeating her signal. Men and horses began to turn; but Ambrose could hear no words. The mule snorted and jerked against the bridle. The tripods had snagged again.

'Talk to it,' came Hob's voice as the man lifted the trailing ends. 'Talk to it.'

Ambrose crooned, and the mule came. The tripods snagged again. Again they halted for Hob to free them. The gap between them and the rest of the column had widened.

Hob thumped him on the shoulder as they began to move again.

'I've brought siege engines over marsh, before now, for your father. This is nothing. Just keep moving.'

Why had he needed to say that?

Ahead of him the Company went in shadows and torch-flare. He was the last except for Hob. He looked behind him again, and Hob was still there. And Hob had turned, too, to stare at the empty landscape over his shoulder.

Then he turned back and saw Ambrose watching him.

'Keep going!' he hissed.

'What did you see?'

'Nothing.'

The air was heavy. It teased at his senses.

The tripods snagged, and snagged again. Each time Hob cleared them. Each time they dropped behind the Company, and had to hurry to keep up. The men ahead of them did not look back. How long had they been going? It already seemed like hours. She had said it would not be as long as the last time, but he could not remember how long the last time had been. It had been a dream then, or he was remembering it as if it had been a dream: a few images and the belief that they had lasted a life-time.

Still the Company trailed ahead of him. Still Hob trudged behind him, looking back over his shoulder. Did he sense that something was following them? Or was this just what the last man did? There was so much he did not know.

Ahead of them the bright sparks of the torches swayed slowly as the men marched, beckoning, reminding him that there was a world of light beyond this place, from which they had come and to which they would return. Just like that the Flame of Heaven fluttered on every altar in the waking world, to remind men that another world waited for them beyond the lips of death. Below the torch-sparks the men and horses walked, wrapped in thick shadows like cloaks that hid their forms. No one looked back at him. He could see no faces.

Were they truly men, these shapes he walked among? He remembered them drifting in through the gates of

Chatterfall like creatures from the pit. The memory seemed much nearer to him than the days of riding with them in bright sun, and camping under the sky. He wondered if those sunlit days had really happened. But surely, if he turned around, he would see Hob walking behind him as he had been only moments before. It would be Hob.

It would not be some stooping, crouching, Thing that loped along in his wake; closing and reaching for him . . .

He would not look round. Of course it would be Hob. It always had been. This awful, creeping feeling that it might not be . . . He would *know* if the enemy were close, just as he had known it in the March. It had felt like – what had it felt like? He could not remember. And he could not remember what Hob's face looked like. And he wondered whether the one walking behind him had a face at all.

He looked round then. And he did not see a face, because the man was also looking behind them. But when he turned back it was still Hob.

'Who's there?' Ambrose asked.

'Nothing,' the man said to him.

His eyes flicked away then, as if he did not want to meet Ambrose's look. Horrible worming thoughts still crawled in Ambrose's mind. A man on the outside could be a monster within. They had said they were proof against the Heron Man – but how could he be sure? They had hunted him before now. And beside him, Hob still walked in silence and would not meet his eye.

What was he thinking?

Speak to him, for the Angels' sake!

'Hob . . .'

'What?' said the man.

'Was it Orcrim who killed Adam diManey?'

(Why that? Why had he blurted out *that*, of all things?)

Hob scowled.

'No.'

'Caw, then?'

'Why do you want to know?'

'He was a friend.'

'Was he? I'm sorry, then.'

Ambrose decided that he was not going to answer further.

Hob said, 'I did.'

Ambrose stared at him.

'Don't you believe me?' asked Hob grimly.

'Why?'

'He fought us. He wanted to kill. I was among the first into the courtyard, so it was me he went for. If it had been any of the others I'd not have said who did it.'

Ambrose tripped and caught himself. The Company was fading into the brown rocks ahead of them, marked only by the lights they carried. The mule had halted. There was no one else. They were alone. Above him Hob's torch flared with a sickness of green, and the man who held it had killed Adam.

The killer was facing him, waiting for him to decide what to do.

'I'm sorry if he was your friend,' Hob said at length.

What *could* he do? Adam was dead. That was wrong and horrible. Aun had asked him how he could forgive it. Hob was not even asking to be forgiven. He remembered only that he had killed a man who would have killed him.

They must go on, side by side, as if this did not lie between them. It was that or walk alone. It was that or leave undone what they were trying to do. And Hob had not wanted to look at Ambrose. What thoughts had come to him as they walked side by side together?

They must go on.

They must.

Oh, Uncle Adam, staring at his death like a puzzle that was too clever for him!

Ambrose drew breath. 'Come on,' he said. 'Or we'll be lost.'

Hob nodded. Together they lifted the wooden tripods around a low, knife-backed rock and urged the mule on after the distant torches.

Uncle Adam. He *must* put it aside.

'Tell me about my father, Hob.'

'What do you want to know?'

'I want to know something good about him.'

Talk could be torchlight, too.

Hob paced in silence for a moment. Then he cleared his throat. 'Well, I'm here, aren't I?'

'For my father?'

'Pearls seem like good things when you haven't got them. But if it was just for a pearl I'd throw mine away and walk out of this place as fast as I could. Manors – well, that's going to be a different job. But your father . . . If he were alive and could look back, he would have wanted us to do this, for his sake as well as yours. Orcrim knows that. So do I. He was . . . Well, he was fair – and clever. He never did anything for just one reason. Oh, he was bad as well as good. I knew that . . .'

The ground was growing steeper and more broken. Beyond the dull rises, Ambrose could sense other scenes – peaks and valleys of the mountains among which he had grown. Once it was almost as if he was looking out of a window from a dark house and could glimpse a brilliant, blue sky and a ridge that still glittered in its coat of snow. For a moment he felt the cold air on his face and could see the little streams of water that poured down the bare rocks below the snowline, for the snow was melting with the coming of the mountain spring. But the line of horses had gone ahead of them and was plodding on through the barren land. He must follow.

He must follow, with the man who had killed Uncle Adam.

Hob stopped to light his second torch from the remains of his first, and to discard the old one. He had fallen silent again, turning over his memories. Ambrose paced beside him at the head of the mule, thinking of Adam diManey, who had been the nearest that he had had to a father in all his childhood. He wondered what he might say to the dead man, if he could.

Ahead of them – it seemed just a couple of hundred paces – the leading horses and men had paused upon a low rise. They were waiting. In twos and threes the Company came up to them, slowly. Still they waited, looking down to the tail of the group, with Hob, Ambrose and the mule lagging behind it. Ambrose could feel his feet moving heavily, his breath gasping as they climbed the slope to join the others. He was far more weary than a few hours' journey should have made him. Looking around, he saw drawn faces among the men, horses with their heads low. They were like a company that had force-marched through a long night, each imprisoned with their own thoughts. He saw Sophia, nursing her arm, her foot stumbling lightly as she made her way to sit down. He saw the man Hare, looking dazed. He saw Orcrim come walking among them, speaking as though he was drunk.

'Last stretch,' Orcrim was saying over and over to the men that he passed. 'She says it's the last stretch. Keep your hands near your iron and your eyes open. And as we go, there'll be something away to the right of us – something big and alive, she says. Don't mind it. Don't look at it, if you can help. Just keep going. Last stretch . . .'

He made his way back to the head of the Company. He seemed to be limping a little.

'Last stretch,' muttered Hob to himself. 'If we can trust her.'

*I'm here, aren't I?* Ambrose thought.

They were moving again, all together. After the hours of toiling in the lonely rear, Ambrose had almost forgotten what it was like to hear the clatter of hooves and feet all around him. The sounds had urgency in them – or perhaps it was in his own veins, that were beginning to beat with the thought of action. His sword trailed at his belt. Soon it would be in his hand. And what then?

The Company poured down a long slope which steepened sharply into a cleft-valley. Images danced in Ambrose's mind of mountains in the living world, beyond these low rocks and rises. He felt that he almost knew them, as if the peaks would be familiar when he saw them, but he was approaching them from a direction that he had never trod before. They were close, close.

And what was that, away to his right where the cleft opened into a broader valley?

At first he thought it must be a boulder, strangely shaped, but otherwise the same as any in that land. Then he wondered if it was an old man, sitting in a cloak and hood with his back to them. But it did not have a hood.

He could see what he thought was long, dark hair falling to the figure's waist as it sat. He supposed it must be a woman. It seemed to be weeping.

'Don't look,' came the word down the column of armed men. 'Orcrim says, don't look.'

Ambrose looked, and kept looking as they straggled past.

It was impossible to guess how large she was, or how far away. At one moment he thought she must be no taller than his own mother, sitting at a distance of a hundred paces from them. The next he imagined himself walking and walking towards her, mile after mile and watching her grow as he approached until she was the size of a mountain. And whichever way he walked around her, she would always have her back to him.

And she would never see him. And she would never listen. And she would never, ever, cease from weeping.

'Don't look,' said Hob.

Weeping, weeping. A lost child, and all the loss of all the world. Mar and Develin and Bay. Aunt Evalia, dead with her arms around him. And Adam diManey. And he must make peace with the killer.

'Don't stop,' said Hob urgently, beside him.

He *had* made peace. Why?

Because he must. Because if he did not, he must make

a corner in his heart that would be like that, like that. That endless rage and weeping.

'Damn you, come on!' said Hob. He dragged at the mule and it lumbered forward, leaving Ambrose last of all the Company.

Like a child in someone's arms over a vast gulf, Ambrose felt completely safe. He looked at the creature that was Beyah. He could hear her: that unending cry that shook the world. But it did not shake his heart. He had made his peace. He would hold to his purpose. All he could do now was beg the dead to forgive *him*.

Suddenly, he laughed.

He was still laughing when he caught up with Hob and the mule. Hob looked at him, frowning, but Ambrose could not explain. As he struggled up out of the cleft, following the line of march, he began to feel elated. And ahead of him were his men, whom he had brought to his place. His banner was black against the sky. Light-headed, he remembered that the moon would be full tonight. And if he lived to see it (and why should he not live?), he could make the moon on his banner full, too. He would remove the stain from it. There would be no more doubting. He could do it if he chose. He could do anything!

The slope eased. The Mother of the World was hidden behind them in the cleft. The eye of Capuu appeared as they climbed, away on the rim of the world. Before them, the ground continued rising gently for perhaps fifty paces. Then it dropped again among great boulders into what seemed to be a pit. Around the edge of the pit stood a number of upright stones, like sentries, like teeth. Ambrose knew them, for he had seen them in the living world. It

560

seemed a very small place, now that he saw it in all that wide land.

There was a gap in the ring, directly before them. A number of the standing stones lay headlong on the brown rocks, their bases protruding over small depressions in the ground from which they had been uprooted. One seemed to have disappeared. There was a hole, like the others, very near the edge; but the stone had gone.

'Horses go no further,' said Orcrim. 'Get them lined up.'

Warily, the Company made their way up to the rim of the pit.

It was not deep. The bouldered slopes dropped little more than the height of a man, to a ragged shore of stone around a pool of dark water. The surface was still. There was no sign that any creature, living or undead, had ever stirred in this place. Peering over, Ambrose felt the weight of an impossible depth beneath the water, sucking him downwards to the heart of the pit. The droning of the Mother of the World poured in his ears like a waterfall.

Below his feet, on the narrow shore, lay the last stone. In the living world, Ambrose remembered, it had fallen some fifty feet from the thorny cliff-top to the poolside. He had seen it from his shelter among the thorns. It had fallen close to the point where Mother had disappeared into the water.

She stood on the edge of the pit, looking down.

'He is aware of us, Orcrim,' she said in a low voice. 'Don't falter.'

Orcrim glowered at the black water. Then leaning out, he spat. Ambrose watched the flecks of white drift downwards to settle like snow upon the surface, and disappear. There was a rasp of iron as Orcrim's sword came free.

'The Moon is High,' he said in a loud voice to the Company.

'Hah, Tarceny!' called several voices.

'Under-craft Prevails!' roared Orcrim.

*'Hah, Tarceny!'* cried the riders.

'Iron of Tarceny!'

*'Ho!'*

Swords drew in a clatter of steel. The long blades wavered in the hands of the fighters like thorn-fronds in a thicket. No one spoke. They waited.

Nothing moved in the pool, or among the rocks around it.

# XXVII

## Stone and Steel

ll right,' said Orcrim at length. 'If he's going to give us space, we'll use it. Get the rig and the levers – Hob has them – and we'll hitch the pulling-teams to . . . to this one here.' His boot struck one of the stones. 'That looks the kindest . . .'

Sophia had stayed with the horses. She saw the group on the lip of the pool break up. Men came and unfastened freshly cut lengths of stout wood from their saddles. Endor and another man dragged Hob's rig forward to the lip of the pool. Ambrose appeared at her elbow.

'And *Watch for Who Comes*,' he said.

'Watch for Who Comes, indeed,' said the woman on the far side of him. 'Where did you learn that?'

'Sophia and I looked at a scroll in Develin. It had Trant on it. Sophia,' he said, 'this is my mother.'

'Yes,' she said.

His mother, whom Sophia had thought of all her life as the Whore of Tarceny. But there was no space to think about that now. There was no space to think of anything until the enemy who had destroyed Chawlin had himself been destroyed. That was what mattered. The pulling-horses

563

would have something to do with it. She would not let go of their bridles until it was done.

Her arm still ached and throbbed within its dark bandage, as it had done through all the long march. It looked and felt as if blood was still seeping into the cloth. But if she called attention to it they would only make her sit down. She pushed the pain and the sickness to one side again, and let the fingers of her good arm open and close on the bridle to remind herself that this was all real. This was not a dream, despite the world of stones in which she stood – despite the awful, awful figure of the weeping woman she had seen, and the horror that had curled around her heart as she had looked away.

Or if it was a dream, it was a dream that would be endless; and there was still something that must be done.

'Develin was a good place,' she heard the woman murmur. 'I'm glad you went there.'

'They suffered for it.' That was Ambrose again.

'That is another reason why we have come.'

Sophia opened her hand upon the bridle, and closed it again. The horse blew warmly on her knuckles, like the breath of a lover who lived and lay close.

Hob came up the line of horses. 'We've hobbled most of them,' he said. 'Those that will take it. But I'm not going near *him*.' He jerked his head at Aun's war-horse, which towered near them at one end of the line. 'Unless Lackmere comes back to do it. And I don't think he's going to. You'll have to keep him quiet. If he goes, they'll all want to.'

'I'll do my best,' said Ambrose.

Hob turned to the pulling-teams.

'You sit down,' he said to Sophia. 'Never handle horses with an arm like that.'

'You can't take both teams,' Sophia snapped.

'My lady can do it. Sit down.'

'No.'

'Michael's Knees . . . !'

'She can help me, Hob,' said the woman. 'I've barely touched a horse in ten years.'

Hob gave up. He took the head of the team on her right.

Strange how quickly they obeyed, even though they had hated her! And no doubt she could have managed the horses by herself with ease. But she would let Sophia help her.

'Thank you,' Sophia whispered.

They watched the men at the rim of the pool.

Around the fallen stone the two tripods stood, and a cross-bar had been lashed between them. Two small things dangled from it – the pulleys from Aclete. Half a dozen men clustered around the rig, stooping to work the ends of their levers beneath the stone. The rest – no more than another half-dozen – were spaced around them in a wide half-circle, at the edge of the pit and on either side, facing out with weapons in their hands. They had put on their helmets. Their frail shapes were clear against the sky, flanked by the stones that had stood for centuries.

'Steady, friend,' she heard Ambrose say to Stefan.

The endless, dreary moaning of the place throbbed in the back of her mind. She wondered if the horses could hear it too.

As she watched, one of the armoured figures picked up the big banner. He stood there for a moment, speaking with the men on the levers in words she could not hear. Then he lifted the banner, and swung it in a big figure-of-eight so that folds opened and the maimed Moon of Tarceny flew clear on the black cloth.

'Slowly now,' grunted Hob, and he began to walk backwards, leading both his horses.

Sophia had never led a pulling-team in her life, or controlled horses from the ground at all. But she spoke to her horse and tugged at its bridle. It hesitated. So did the horse of the woman beside her. Sophia's horse was the leader.

She pulled again, more firmly. *Come on, you.*

It came. They both came.

'Slowly!' said Hob.

For a few paces they were moving freely. Then she heard the flat jingle of the chains clinking taut, and the creak of rope. The horses halted, straining in their harness.

'Hah-sa,' grunted Hob to his team. '*Hah*-sa!'

Sophia saw her leader put one more foot down, and then lift it again. They were not moving.

'Right, back!' said Hob, who must have seen a signal from the rig. He put his hand on the chest of his leader. His team backed. Sophia's team copied them. The ropes and harness were slack again.

'Is that all they are going to do?' she heard Ambrose say.

'Little by little is the way,' the woman said. 'When I did this before, I had my hillmen camp by the stone we were raising – it was much bigger than this, but there was

566

only one of it. They dug and they lifted for four days, until it was done . . .'

Four days!

Four days for one stone. There were eight to lift, and one of them was down by the edge of the pool.

Ambrose must have been thinking the same thing.

'We can't last,' he said. 'Not for days in this place. And he may not even be inside the ring.'

'No. Most probably he is not. It would be too much to expect to catch him the same way twice. But his powers come from the pool, and must return there, and so must he. And no, I do not expect Orcrim to lift and haul for days without rest. We are showing the enemy that we have the means. If he does nothing, in the end his powers will be trapped again.'

'What will he do?'

'He will not do nothing.'

They waited. The men at the pit loitered around the stone, easing in small boulders to wedge it or to lever against. Sophia's team stood with their heads down. The ceaseless deep humming of the place ached in her head.

The banner waved once more.

'Hah-sa!' said Hob to his horses.

'Hah-sa!' she said, and brought hers into a shambling walk. The pulling-teams leaned into their harness. The tackle creaked. Looking up, Sophia saw the slight shift of the rig as it took the strain. The men around the stone had thrown their weight on their levers. One man was moving among them, rolling small boulders into the space beneath the stone. The banner swung again.

'Back!' said Hob. They backed teams and the ropes dropped. The lever-men rose, and rested.

567

'Under-craft prevails,' said Hob. 'Inch by inch.'

They did it again.

And again.

Sophia could see the stone had risen, now, and was propped at a low angle from the ground. The further it came up, she thought, the less easy it must be to find purchase for the levers. The pull of the team would matter more.

'If it goes as well as this for another hour, I will take us into the day again,' the woman said. 'We can camp, keep watch, and go back to it when you are all rested . . .'

There was a cry from the poolside.

One of the sentries was standing on the skyline, pointing with his blade at something down in the pit. There was horror and loathing in his voice. Other shouts sounded among the men. Orcrim was bellowing, gesticulating. Men left the levers and hurried to the cliff edge. Swords wavered against the colourless sky.

'Now Michael guard us!' said the woman.

'Michael guard us!' Ambrose repeated, staring at the skyline.

Behind Sophia one of the hobbled horses was beginning to whinny and struggle at the sounds of alarm. Hob cursed and left the head of his team. Stefan was snorting and shaking his head.

'Steady, friend,' she heard Ambrose say. 'Stay by me.'

A flurry of shouts broke from the hillside above them. The men had grouped in three places at the edge of the pit. As she watched, a man in the middle group stooped and swung his sword at something below them that was hidden from her. Others joined him. Metal rang and rang as if on stone. For a moment something like an arm – an arm of appalling length – reached up from the ground to claw at them. The men yelled and struck again and again.

'They don't feel it!' a man cried. 'Damn you, Orcrim, they don't feel it!'

'Turn them!' Orcrim's voice was shouting. 'Find the eyes if you can!'

The other groups were striking now – striking at things she could guess at but could not see.

'Turn them! Turn them!'

Whatever had attacked the first group must have dropped back out of reach a little way. The men were still looking down, weapons at the ready, as if it were about to come on again. Was it hurt? Was it wounded or just discouraged? She could not hope to know.

More yells, rising to a scream. The left-hand group was in trouble. One of them was half down. He was flailing at something that dragged at him from below, pulling him over the cliff. Two men had him by the shoulders and were trying to haul him back from the edge. Others were kneeling and hacking at the enemy – whether the same one or more than one Sophia could not see. More men were hurrying up to help.

Beyond them, at the extreme left-hand edge of the gap in the stones, something moved against the skyline.

For an instant she saw it – a hooded, crouching thing. It seemed to look towards the struggle at the cliff edge. Then it ducked down from the skyline and her eyes lost it for a moment. She saw it again as it leaped among the rocks. It covered yards in a single jump.

Her heart lurched. It was so quick!

'There's one over!' she shouted. 'To the left! To the left!'

It jumped again, and this time she could hear the *thump* as it landed. It was coming for the pulling-teams. And another was moving on the skyline beyond it.

A fighter was running back down the slope. He must have seen the thing and was racing to intercept it. But as she watched, he tripped on the rough ground and fell. The thing paused for an instant, and then leaped on him.

'Help him!' she screamed, turning to the nearest armed man. 'Help him.'

It was Ambrose. He dropped Stefan's rein, and ran.

'No!' cried Sophia. 'Hob! Hob!'

Hob had disappeared. She looked wildly around and could not see him.

Ambrose ran, struggling to free his sword. He heard Sophia shouting. He saw the fallen man beating with his hands at the thing attacking him. He heard the man cry out again as the talons tore into his mail. His own sword came free. Then he was on it.

*Clang!*

His blade rebounded, ringing as if he had hit a boulder or a tree stump. The thing raised its head and reached for him. He jumped back, and stumbled.

It was about to spring again. He had seen it move like a boulder off a catapult. He lifted his blade between them to show it the hilt, where the pouch with the last white stone still hung. It crouched.

Now he attacked, striking for head and limb as Chawlin had shown him. Its hood fell as it flailed at the blade. He saw a toad-like face – a thin circlet of gold: eyes

570

that looked horribly as if they had once been a man's. It bellowed with pain and the sound shook his very guts. Something answered it from his left.

There were two of them!

He glanced away, then back at the crouching thing. If he let his sword drop it would spring and finish him. He could not fight two. He could not keep his one stone between himself and two attackers.

The thing leaped, away to his right, landing in a cloud of dust and pebbles. Now it was between him and the horse-lines, between him and help. And the other one was approaching from behind him.

He whirled and scrambled away, passing the fallen man who still writhed slowly on the ground. His second attacker rose from the stones, groping at him. He saw a long face, horned like a cow, eyes the size of goose-eggs, claws like hooks. He beat at it and it wavered. He tried to dodge around it, to put it between him and the leaping thing. It moved to block him. He scrambled the other way.

Keep moving! Keep moving!

The poolside swung into view. They were between him and his friends. For the moment he could face them both, and guard himself with the stone at his hilt. But he was getting further and further away from help. The wounded man was trying to rise, but could not. He could see Mother and Sophia, pointing his way and calling. The horses were milling. He saw Stefan shy, and recover . . .

The leaping thing crashed among the rocks to his right and he turned to face it. The horned thing loomed slowly on his left, moving on long limbs like a spider's legs. He saw that it, too, wore a circlet of gold.

*Ando*, it said, shrilly, in a voice he remembered.

*Ando*, the other said, as deep as a cavern.

They were crooning to him – maddening burbles, with ill-formed words that he could not understand. He swung the sword to his left to check the horned thing, and back at once to the leaper. It was the leaper he feared most.

*Ando*, croaked the creatures, one deep, one shrill. *Andooh*.

He must attack.

He couldn't do it!

The horned thing had sidled further to his left. Now he could no longer check them both.

A man came leaping over the boulders, sword in hand. It was Hob, and he had no helmet. His sword rang on the back of the horned thing, and beat at its face as it turned.

'Ho, there!' yelled Hob. 'Tarceny! Help, Help!'

Again he swung into the attack, and the horned thing backed, groping at him. Talons slithered upon mail. Ambrose jumped to put his back to Hob, facing the other creature with the stone at his hilt. Somewhere men were shouting. They were coming.

'Here, Tarceny! Help!' cried Hob.

Ambrose heard a sharp ring of metal, and Hob's desperate curse. His sword must have broken. Ambrose could not turn round. He could not take his eyes off the crouching thing. But the crouching thing had lifted its head. It rolled its eyes at the coming wave of men. For a moment it hung like that. Then it seemed to shake itself, and leaped away along the slope. Ambrose whirled to face the horned thing but it, too, was slithering backwards.

'Round them, get round them,' came Orcrim's voice. 'Herd them back over.' The air was full of mail jingling

572

and the gasps of sweating men. Someone – it must be Endor – came up past Ambrose with his big mace raised. The horned thing was still retreating. Beyond it the crouching thing appeared on the lip of the pool, and dropped downwards, and was gone. The horned thing looked about it at the half-circle of armoured men, and swung its great eyes back to face Ambrose one last time.

*Andooh*, it said. *Anson*.

On its long limbs it crawled up the slope.

'At it!' came Orcrim's voice. 'Herd it over.'

Ambrose watched it go. Painfully, it seemed, the ancient thing crawled over the lip of the pool like a vast insect creeping into a crevice. Then there was nothing but the band of men leaning over the edge, staring after it as it disappeared from their sight. The creatures had retreated.

A sharp, heavy blow landed on his ear. Hob had cuffed him.

'Next time you are in a fight, stay among your fellows! And if you can't do that, remember to call for help.'

'Sorry,' Ambrose mumbled.

'Just remember it. Help – it's a good word. Now give a hand here.'

He strode toward the wounded man. Others were already standing over him. Aun was there. They were unlacing the helm. It came free. The face under it was pale and heavy with pain. It took Ambrose a moment to recognize him.

'Caw,' one of the men was saying. 'Caw, can you hear us?'

'Yes, damn you,' Caw said, thickly.

'Can you stand?'

'Don't – want to try . . .'

The mail had been torn like cloth from one shoulder. It was dark and wet. Blood had no colour in this place.

'Let's get our former mistress up,' said Orcrim's voice among the men. 'We need to bring him into the light. Better have the horses, too, and we'll all rest together.'

'Do you think they'll come back?'

'How do I know? If they were called off, then yes, they'll be back. If they just lost their stomach to fight, that may be another matter.'

Ambrose looked across the barren rocks. The horses in the line seemed to be quieter now. Mother was there, looking his way. Had she seen him in his fight? Of course she had. She and Sophia had called Hob to help him. There was Sophia, still standing at the head of her pulling-team, as if expecting to start work again as soon as the men got back. On the lip of the crest, Hob's rig stood like a low scaffold against the sky. There were men patrolling up there, watching the pool below them. From the way they stood and moved, Ambrose knew that the enemy had disappeared below the surface.

*Ando, Anson.*

He was shaking.

'There's a man down there,' someone said.

'Where?'

'There – he was watching. Then he ducked out of sight.'

He was pointing at an outcrop of boulders, a little way across and down the slope. Two or three of the Company started to walk over to it.

'Don't go too far . . .' Orcrim said.

There was a movement among the rocks. A man appeared from where he had been crouching and took to his heels across the slope. The leading fighter – it was Aun – shouted, and ran after him. Behind him, Endor hesitated. Then he was running, too.

'Aun!' Ambrose cried. 'Aun, stop!'

'Ho, there!' bellowed Orcrim. 'Stop. It'll be a trap! Stop!'

The men did not look back. Already they could not hear.

'It's Raymonde!' said Ambrose. 'Aun will kill him. He mustn't do it!'

'They'll have to look out for themselves,' said Orcrim. 'You stay here . . . Hey!'

But Ambrose was already moving. He heard Orcrim call again, and curse, but the sound died quickly in the air that hummed with the pain of the world.

His feet skittered on loose rock. He could see the runner ahead of him – Endor, that must be. He could not see Aun. He must hope that Endor still could. If they became lost in this place . . .

Next time, stay among your fellows! And already he was on his own again. But he could see the men ahead of him, jinking among the rocks. And he thought someone had followed him. He could hear the shadow of an armoured foot on the stones behind him. He did not look around.

The ground dropped at his feet. He plunged downwards, into the cleft-valley out of which they had climbed to reach the pool. He could not see where the men had gone, but as the slope grew steeper he angled to his left, along the hill. Ahead of him – he could not tell how far – the shape of a woman sat, weeping with her back to the world. And Ambrose leaped the rocks of her dreams, pursuing the unseen man who hunted his own child.

*Let them eat their sons!*

'Damn you!' he shouted at her. 'This should be a garden!'

But that vast grief would not stir for his voice. And another son was about to die.

# XXVIII

## Judgement

e had lost sight of the men. Where had they gone? Behind a rock – into a dip? He must find them quickly, or be lost himself.

He was not lost. He knew this place, even though his feet had never run or slid or skidded on these brown stones before. The low ridge he was following was like the echo of a voice he had known all his life. He remembered it.

He reached the end of the rise. The ground sloped away before him. There was nowhere for a man to hide. But there was a thinness to the air – movement, a memory of colour. He plunged forward, ducking his head as though jumping through a waterfall, and stumbled into the light.

He was out of the Cup. He had escaped from the brown stones. He was on a ridgetop path he knew, in the living world. The air was cool. The mountain-shapes were wreathed with mists. Far to his right the massif of Beyah rose, and her high snowfields gilded with the falling sun. He stood before the low gate-towers of the house that had been his home.

There were voices and movement beyond the

gate-mouth. The men, hunters and hunted, must have gone in. He hesitated.

The Heron Man was close. He could feel it. Where? An image swam in his mind of the door of the scholars' hall at Develin. Beyond it, the rows of benches, and the hooded enemy waiting to begin his last lesson.

Open the door?

The door hung ajar. Somewhere beyond it a man's voice cried out.

Hob appeared, with a curse and a clatter on the path beside him. He stared about at the mountain evening, understanding that for the first time in hours he was in the living world again.

'There you are,' he said. 'Thought I'd lost you. What is this place?'

'It's a lot of things. Come on. They've gone in.'

With Hob at his shoulder Ambrose plunged into the gate-tunnel. It was empty. So was the courtyard beyond, scattered with the droppings of goats that must have wandered wild on the hillsides all winter. The doors to the storerooms were open. Darkness lurked in them, but nothing moved there.

Sounds broke from the inner courtyard. An oath. Armoured feet on stone.

'Come on!' cried Ambrose.

'Careful,' said Hob.

They strode through the archway and into the last court of the world.

The air rasped with steel.

Two men were fighting between the fountain and the throne. One was Aun, in mail and helm, swinging the bastard-sword of Aclete two-handed against his enemy's guard. The other was the Wolf: Raymonde, Aun's own son.

He was bare-headed and had no shield. His sword was out-matched by Aun's weapon. His face was drawn in a desperate mask. As Ambrose watched, Aun attacked again, cutting for the head. Raymonde jumped back and stumbled.

'Aun, stop!' Ambrose cried.

Endor was there, leaning his elbows on the fountain rim. He was watching, but taking no part. He was waiting for Aun to finish it by himself.

'Stop him!' Ambrose cried.

Endor looked round at him, but did not move.

Ambrose turned to Hob. 'We have to stop this!' he shouted.

'Easily said . . .' muttered Hob, eyeing the fighters.

Raymonde lunged at his father, but Aun stepped beyond his reach and struck. The big bastard-sword slammed into the young man's left shoulder. Raymonde howled and dropped a bundle he had been carrying, but his mail must have held.

Aun attacked again, beating his son's guard away and charging into him. The two men staggered and fell together against the low wall that fringed the courtyard. Ambrose leaped across the paving after them. Twenty feet away the men struggled. Raymonde was pinned beneath his father. He had dropped his sword. Ambrose had seen this before.

'Aun, no!' cried Ambrose as he reached them. 'Don't kill him!'

Aun had his knife out, hovering for its mark. Raymonde's half-pinned hand groped for it. The knife lifted an inch beyond his reach. Ambrose caught it.

Aun's face was a mask, a beast, snarling. Ambrose couldn't hold the wrist. Where was Hob?

The knife-hand broke free. Again Ambrose caught it.

'Aun,' he yelled. *'Aun, I'm your King! Stop!'*

The man heard it.

Endor landed heavily on the fighters' backs, grabbing for the knife himself. Aun let it drop, his eyes on Ambrose's face. The four of them were in a tangle. Hob stepped round them. His splintered sword-point hovered above Raymonde's eye as he lay pinned at the bottom of the heap.

'You lie still,' he said. 'Up, the rest of you.'

They rose, Aun last.

'Now . . .' said Hob, uncertain.

'Prince Paigan,' said Ambrose to the fallen man. 'Your master. Where is he?'

'I am here,' said the enemy. 'I have been waiting for you.'

He was standing by the foot of the throne, where no one had been a moment before.


'So you have begun at last,' said the Heron Man. 'Now you will hear me.'

If we rush him, Ambrose thought feverishly, he'll just disappear again. We need to get close. How?

Behind him he could hear the men beginning to fan out.

'Stay where you are,' the enemy said.

580

The sounds of movement stopped.

'You have named yourself King,' said the Heron Man. 'Do you know what that means?'

He stood in his grey robe, with his hood thrown back. His head was small and hairless, his skin was like the bark on a wizened tree. On his brow was a circlet of gold, and in his hands he held a rough-cut cup of stone.

Ambrose took a step forward.

'One more step and I shall leave you. You will not find me. You will find only those I speak with, until you yourself are ready to listen.'

Ambrose stopped.

'Answer, as you have been taught. What must a king have, to rule in his kingdom?'

I must let him think he's got me, thought Ambrose.

'Answer.'

Touch the heart. Breathe.

'Power,' said his voice, clearly across the courtyard.

'What must a king do, to gain power?'

*Evil*, said the ghost of Denke at Ferroux.

Ambrose opened his mouth, and shut it again. He's playing with me, he thought. *I play with him, he plays with me. We're equals, really.*

At his feet Raymonde of Lackmere crawled across the paving, dragging his sword in one hand, like a dog to his master's heel. No one hauled him back. No one behind Ambrose moved at all. What had happened to them?

'You have seen what a king is,' said the Heron Man. 'You have seen what a king does. This is what you have chosen. To save one life, you chose it.'

One of us has got to get round behind him, Ambrose

thought. Aun, or Hob, or Endor. They've got to do it. I've got to keep him talking until then.

Still none of the men at his back had moved.

'Refuse it, and your friend will hunt his cub again.'

That was true. Ambrose knew it. He forced his mouth to move.

'What must I do?'

It had seemed the easiest thing to say.

'Go to Tuscolo, and you will die. The stronger you are, the more you will suffer. And sooner or later, you will die. You know this.'

Ambrose knew it. He could not be a king like Velis. He could only be a king like Septimus, and die as he had died.

He's playing with me, he thought. He knows I'm trying to play with him. And he's letting me try because it suits him!

'You trapped me!' he yelled. 'You sent him to bring me down here and trap me!'

'Why should I play games? Sooner or later every son of Wulfram traps himself. You have done the same.'

Ambrose remembered that he was the closest. Why wait for the others? His hand moved to his sword-hilt. But even as he groped for it, he knew he could not get it out and swing it before the enemy disappeared.

'You are showing weakness,' the Heron Man said. 'I only explain the choice you have already made.'

'What must I do?' Ambrose repeated.

Raymonde had levered himself up to stand behind his master. Ambrose could see, clearly across the space, how thin with hunger his face was. His beard was weeks old.

This man who had talked so lightly of the Heron Man; who had made a king and talked of making Ambrose king, hovered like a whipped servant at his master's elbow. And his eyes were on Ambrose.

But he was alert. He would make it much harder to catch the Heron Man from behind. *Why* didn't the others move?

'Men adore the power that is manifest,' said the Heron Man. 'Yet the power that is hidden is greater still. The throne in Tuscolo is high and canopied with gold. Great men cut the heads from each other in turn to sit upon it. But it is only a copy. There is only one throne in all the Kingdom that is real.'

Ambrose looked at the empty throne that stood under the open sky. He had sat in it so many times, imagining himself to be a king of armies . . .

'From here the fate of the Kingdom has been ruled, for nine generations. You know this now.

'It was mine. It is yours – if you would save a life.'

Was he offering to step aside? To give up being Prince? Could it be true?

Ambrose struggled. 'What about—?' he said, and stopped.

'Ask your question.'

'What about the power?'

'It is already yours.'

Ambrose did not understand.

'It was your father's. So now it is yours – by right. Come closer, and I will give. I do not fear your sword.'

Ambrose hesitated. He remembered that he had been trying to get closer. He couldn't remember what his sword had had to do with it. The men around him had faded. They had fallen back in his mind. Their faces were as distant as the mountains that had watched him, unspeaking, all the days of his childhood. Whatever he did, they would do nothing.

He took a step.

He looked into the eyes of the Heron Man.

He looked into those heavy, weary eyes, of the man who had played out his game over and over for three hundred years. Three hundred years of watching hopes shrivel like leaves in winter. He saw the truth in them. He saw the lie that embraced the truth, that coiled its smoky tentacles around it until the truth itself was changed. He knew it was there. But it did not matter, because underneath both he saw something else.

He saw a recognition of likeness.

*He's my uncle across nine generations.*

He took another step. Prince Paigan lifted the cup, and held it out to him.

Somewhere far off there was a cry, as if a beast had shrieked in pain. A hand and blade appeared for an instant over the Heron Man's shoulder. They fell. Ambrose saw the eyes jerk whitely in their sockets. The bald head lolled for a moment in its shoulders. Then the Prince was gone, crumpled at Ambrose's feet, and Raymonde stood over him, yelling and sobbing and hacking at the frail body with his sword.

Cries of outrage exploded from the men behind Ambrose. The cup rolled on the paving. Its rim was chipped from the impact of its fall. Ambrose scrambled for it, and looked up to see Raymonde standing over him, brandishing his sword and still screaming. An armoured figure – Endor – slammed into him, and bore him to the ground. The sword clattered away across the stones.

'You killed him! You killed him!' shouted Ambrose, cradling the cup in his arms.

'You! Why was it always *you*?' Raymonde screamed back.

He wrestled, but he was weak and Endor had his arms locked.

'Damn you!' he screamed, and spat.

'That's enough!' said Hob. 'Here,' he said to Ambrose. 'Put that on.'

He was holding out the circlet of gold that had fallen from the Heron Man's head. Ambrose looked at it, stupidly.

'Put it on, and get up there,' said Hob, pointing at the throne. 'We'll do this properly.'

Slowly Ambrose climbed the steps. The weathered stone writhed with carvings, beasts and powers, all dark and familiar to his eye. At the top he settled the gold circlet on his head, shuddering a little at the light press of the metal on his hair. It was awkward to sit with his sword hanging from his hip, so he worked his belt around until he could rest a hand on the hilt and keep the point from between his legs with his shin. Then he sat down.

The air was cool. The sun had gone. Masses of cloud were gathering along the crests and beginning to drape themselves down the ridges like huge, pale forests. To his right the peak of Beyah punched higher than all the others, and its face was half in shadow. The sky was pale gold, deepening to blue overhead. He had seen a thousand evenings like this in his life. He had forgotten how beautiful they were.

He was home.

In the crook of one arm he held the great cup. It seemed to be a plain, strange thing, to be the cause of so much evil. He could see the new roughness where a flake of stone had broken from it when it fell from the hands of his enemy. It seemed very heavy.

'An empty purse, a bit of stale bread, a book and a water bottle, also empty,' Hob said as he sorted through Raymonde's sack. 'That's all.'

'The book belongs to Aun,' said Ambrose. 'Give it to him.' He closed his eyes for a moment and felt very tired. He knew what the men wanted him to do.

'Now by Heaven and by the right of the King I declare this court is open,' said Hob. He was standing by the steps, just as Ambrose had seen the Widow's officers stand before her chair in the manor-hearings. No doubt Hob had done this many times for his father, the Lord of Tarceny. Endor had forced Raymonde to his knees before the throne and was holding him there.

So it was Aun who was standing behind his son with the drawn sword.

*Don't be clever. Just tell them what they've decided.*

'Who accuses this man?' said Hob.

'I'll do it,' said Ambrose, before Aun could speak.

He leaned forward, and used the man's name.

'Raymonde.'

The Wolf glared at him, tense. 'Don't forget I saved you, in Develin,' he said.

Ambrose ignored it.

'You killed your brother for that book,' he began.

'You know I didn't mean to!'

'You killed a woman at Chatterfall.'

'Damn you! What are you going to do? What are—?'

'You killed a woman at Chatterfall,' Ambrose repeated more loudly.

'Answer him, rot you!' roared Endor, and twisted an arm so that the man fell forward. 'Yes or no?'

'Yes – I'm sorry! I'm sorry . . .'

Still Raymonde craned to look up at Ambrose, and the cup.

The Cup.

'You led your King to sack Bay.'

'I know!'

'You led your King to sack Develin.'

'I know! I know!'

'You did this for the cup. And when you saw Paigan offer the cup to me instead, you killed him, too.'

'I helped you! I helped—' He broke off with a grunt. Endor had kicked him.

'You wanted him to be your father, and you killed him.'

No one spoke. Raymonde was staring at him in a kind of horror.

He's wondering how I knew, Ambrose thought. And I knew because I almost wanted that, too. While the Prince was turning everything I was taught on its head, I wanted it, too.

He drew a breath. They were all waiting for him. Any one of the things that the Wolf had admitted would be enough.

And the light was going from the sky. The air was full with the moist gloom of evening that would turn swiftly to night. The men before him were becoming outlines, and the clearest thing of all was the tip of Aun's sword.

Still they were waiting. Four faces, turned up to him.

Five faces. Away to his right the peak of Beyah loomed, silent. In this light it could have been a bowed head, too. Maybe even the head of a woman. Ambrose drew breath again, and held it. He could not hear, or feel, the sound of weeping.

*Let them eat their sons!*

Did she pause at moments like this, to hear what was done? Maybe she did. And when it was done, she wept again.

Five faces. One life. And all the lives the liver of this life had wasted. Aunt Evalia, the Widow, Bay with its lights and banners, all the scholars and masters of Develin whose wisdom lived on only in what he could remember.

One life.

'I will forgive these things,' he said.

Fiercely his hand gripped the hilt of his sword. Through cloth, his fingers clamped upon the last white stone. I needed you just now, he thought to it.

Capuu, enduring, I needed you. And I forgot you. And now I need you again, for I must beg all the hundreds who have died because of this man to forgive me for what I am doing.

The men were still looking at him, unbelieving. He spoke once more.

'Go away from here. Don't come back to this place. Don't look for the book, or the cup, or the pool again.'

588

'What?' barked Aun. 'You're going to save him? Let him go?'

'Save *him*?' cried Ambrose. And he jabbed his finger at Aun as if to pin him against the courtyard wall. 'I'm saving *you*!'

There was a moment's silence.

'You know,' said Hob. 'I think he has a point.'

'Which is more than you have!' Aun lifted his sword.

Hob looked down at his shattered blade, and shrugged.

'Straight back to the iron, is it, Lackmere? After the King has spoken?'

Aun glared at him, and Hob met his look. It was Aun who dropped his eyes at last. He turned away to stare across the valley at the mountains under their shroud. His head and shoulders were set, like rocks; but he said nothing.

'Let him go, Endor,' Ambrose said.

Endor stepped back. Slowly Raymonde got to his feet. He drew breath to say something. What could he say? I'm sorry? I didn't mean it? Nothing passed his lips.

Abruptly he turned and strode from the courtyard with his mail clinking and his left arm cradled across his chest. The sound of his feet receded.

Ambrose let out his breath. It seemed to be over. It really was over. Aun might never forgive him for what he had done, but he was going to be bound by it. And at his feet . . .

His legs carried him down the steps once more to stand over the body of his enemy.

'Is he really dead?'

Hob looked down.

'Oh, yes. Very.'

589

In death, Prince Paigan, son of Wulfram, looked much older. His hairless head was mottled like the skin of a frog. The eyes were sunk in deep pits in his face, and in the dusk the whites gleamed below lowered lids. The back of the head and one shoulder had been deeply gashed from Raymonde's sword. There had been very little blood.

Hob rubbed his jaw. 'Damned if the old fox didn't have us all spellbound at the end. Maybe it's as well things happened as they did.'

'We should bury him,' said Ambrose.

'Bury him? Dig up rocks? Not likely. And I'm not piling stones half the night for him either. We could burn him, if we had the wood.'

'There's wood in the storerooms in the outer courtyard. I could . . .'

'No. You go back and find the others, if you can. Tell them it's over, and they can come down. They'll be glad to hear it, I guess.'

Ambrose had almost forgotten the rest of the Company, arrayed by the stones above the pool. He wondered if Mother had brought them out by now. It was strange to think of them so near, and yet in another place where blood had no colour and from which no cry would carry.

'And take Endor with you, just in case. Lackmere and I will do what's necessary here.'

Aun was standing by the low wall of the courtyard, looking over at the unseen hillside below as if some vision or memory of a vision confronted him from the rubbled slope. He did not seem to have heard. But Ambrose understood that Hob was arranging things so that he could talk

590

to Aun alone. He must want to be sure that Aun would indeed be bound by the word of the new King. Perhaps that, too, was the kind of thing he would have done for Ambrose's father.

Ambrose did not think it was necessary; but he was grateful all the same.

He looked down once more at the crumpled figure at his feet. It was such a mean end, he thought, after all that he had been.

'You could put him on the throne and burn him like that, maybe,' he said. 'It would be right.'

'We'd never get enough wood under him. And it's more than he deserves. No, we'll find a flat spot outside the gates, I guess.' Hob rubbed his jaw again. 'No point in dirtying a throne, after all. That *is* yours, now – Prince Under the Sky.'

## XXIX

### Prince Under the Sky

mbrose dreamed that he was in Develin again. He was passing through the empty house, opening door after door, and finding no one. He was walking through the courts of his mountain home, which had somehow come to be in Develin, and no one was there. The fountain was still. The throne was empty.

He was late, and he could not find the man he was looking for.

Only in the last building, in a wall where it should not have been, did he find the door to the scholars' hall. It was shut. The iron ring, pitted and weathered, hung before his hand.

He opened it, and walked in.

The benches were empty. He went to the last one and sat down.

The master stood at the far end of the hall, facing him. He wore a grey robe, with his hood thrown forward around his face. Ambrose did not want to see that face. He knew what it would look like: very old, with eyes deep-sunk and the whites showing below lowered lids, and the mouth half-open in his last and sudden pain. He waited.

*The Angels lie*, said the ghost of Prince Paigan.

In the mountain sunrise he stood with his mother and with Aun, on the cliff above the pool.

'He was tricked,' he said. 'The Angels tricked him. And they tricked us, too.'

She laughed. 'Umbriel and all his brothers, tricksters? Do you wish to set the Church by the ears? What makes you think he was tricked?'

'They told him that the last of his father's sons would bring him down. We all thought that meant me. But I'm not the last of his father's sons – not of Wulfram's own sons. *He* was. He was the youngest of them. They meant him. He did it to himself!'

'But he was killed because you came to overthrow him. You did it.'

'I had nothing to do with it! He'd caught me! He was getting me to take his place. He was trying to make the prophecy come true in a way which would mean that he was still the real King. But he had already shamed Raymonde, tricked him, led him to kill all those people. He would not let Raymonde have the cup, and he killed the man Raymonde had made King. Then he stood with his back to Raymonde, and offered me the cup, his throne – everything he had let Raymonde think should be his. He was so sure that I was the one who was supposed to bring him down. In the end it was his own servant who did it. So really, he did it to himself.'

At the end of the ridge a faint column of smoke

stained the morning air. Paigan's pyre must have burned all night. They had built it from wood that his own hands had gathered, day in, day out through the summer. He had never dreamed what it would be used for. He hoped that it had burned hot enough to do its work.

She laughed again.

Around them the Company of the Moon were beginning to gather their belongings. Orcrim had judged that it would be better not to try to bring the horses or the wounded Caw down to the house in the half-darkness. He had also insisted on keeping watch by the ring, just in case the masterless creatures within it still wanted to attack. So they had made a precarious camp above the cliffs and sat out the night among horses which could smell water but had had nothing to drink since noon. Orcrim had forbidden any attempt to raid the pool.

It was bad ground for horses, up here. The barren undulations over which they had fought the creatures had become the steep, thorny slopes that Ambrose had lived among as long as he could remember. Even leading the beasts down to the track would be tricky work. He supposed that his mother could take the Company down to easier ground by passing through the world of the Cup once more, but no one would want to do that unless they had to.

Only the pool itself was the same – the pool, and the broken ring of stones around it. The same dark water sat still in the bottom of the cup the mountains had made for it. The same stones, like fists or teeth stood or leaned in their places. The stone they had been trying to raise remained propped with one end lifted perhaps a foot from the ground. The little boulders on which it rested seemed to be no more than rocks from the hillside, which had somehow crept in there.

Aun kicked at the stone and scowled. Ambrose thought he must hate to hear his son spoken of. But Mother laughed – she was laughing a lot, this morning – and put her hand on the baron's shoulder.

'You have made Aun angry with me,' she said. 'And Orcrim will be angry, too. For I had told them both that the Angels meant you should be victorious. Neither would have followed us so willingly if they had realized we were just the cat's paw.'

'Do this, camp here, fight him – I was the monkey man led by his own monkey!' growled Aun.

'A monkey you have made King – or Prince at least.' She seemed happy to tease all the world, today. 'What have you done with your crown, my darling? Not lost already, I hope?'

'It's in my pack,' Ambrose said.

He had taken it out and turned it in his hands in the mountain dawn, but had not wanted to put it on. The memory of the head that had worn it for three hundred years still lingered within its simple ring. It lay in the bottom of the sack that he was carrying.

'And what kind of king will you be, my darling?'

'I don't know.'

Paigan had told him the truth, he felt. As a king he must do evil, or die. Most likely he would do both.

'I should like to see the crown, and the cup, please.'

Ambrose dropped his sack upon the ground and picked them out of it.

'Aun,' she said. 'I think you have the book.'

'I was charged with it again, yesterday,' he said. 'For the second time. And I was not asked whether I wanted it.'

'Could you bring it, please, and let us discuss what should be done.'

Aun brought his hands out from within his cloak. They held a small, heavy book, bound in leather and iron.

'I have trusted it to lock and bar before, and both failed me,' he said. 'If I must watch over this damned thing again, it will not leave me until I go to the Angels.'

'And we shall raise a window to you in every chapel in the land – to the Knight who carries a Book that he can let no one read, and that he himself cannot. But I think this charge may be a short one. Give me the book first, then . . . Now, Ambrose, my darling. This is your father's record of all the things that he thought and did with the power that Paigan Wulframson gave to him. If you have wondered what kind of a man he was, you will find a great part of the answer on these pages. I have looked in it once, and found much there I wanted to read, of myself and of him. Perhaps there are things written in it about you, too, for he knew you as a small child. But the only man living who has read in full what lies on these pages is Raymonde of Lackmere, and what he found there set him on the path to the things he did. What shall we do with this book?'

'Destroy it,' said Aun.

Ambrose hesitated. His father's book! He did not want to destroy it – not before he had read it. He guessed that Mother did not wish to either. But the meaning of what she had said was clear; and he owed Aun much.

'We should destroy it,' he said.

At once she held it out at arm's length over the cliff. She seemed to weigh it in her hand, perhaps to sigh. Then she tossed it out into the air. It turned as it fell, and did not open, but hit the water in the very centre of the pool with a splash and disappeared.

'Gone,' she said.

Gone – the last trace of his father, on a few words he had uttered in doubt. There would always be a piece missing.

'The crown next,' she said.

'I want to destroy that, too,' said Ambrose.

'Why?' said Aun.

'Why?' said Mother.

'Kings cause evil.'

He saw Aun frown.

'Ambrose,' said Mother. 'We know you do not wish to be a king, such as Velis was, or even Septimus. Nor do you wish to be like Raymonde, who played games with crowns. But this is not the crown of Tuscolo. It is the crown of a power that is hidden.'

'*He* wore it. And those creatures from the pool – they wore crowns like it. I do not want to become him, or them.'

'Gold is gold,' said Aun. 'It's a sign, like any other. You were happy to ride here under the Doubting Moon, though men have been cursing it as a sign for a hundred years.'

'It means I have to have power – even if it's hidden, somehow. I don't want that.'

'Power is not evil,' she said. 'Power is choice, although often the choice must be between evil and greater evil.'

'Not to choose power can also bring evil,' said Aun. 'Or to let it happen when it should not.'

*Aun, I'm your King. Stop!*

Ambrose looked at his mother, but she said nothing. They were both waiting for him.

'He's right,' he said wearily. 'I've already chosen it.'

If he renounced it, Aun might start hunting Raymonde again. Paigan had spoken the truth about that, too.

'Very well,' said Mother. 'But now – or soon – you will need to choose what that means. What kind of a king would you be, if you could?'

'I don't know! Help me!'

'You're scared,' said Aun. 'Rightly. Most men who go hunting crowns end up losing their heads. But as things stand in the Kingdom, Orcrim and I judge that we could offer you the keys of Tuscolo in twelve months. And if we wait too long, somebody else will get them.'

Castles? Thrones?

Ambrose shook his head.

'I'm the Prince Under the Sky.'

'What does that mean?' said Aun.

'I don't know. I need to think about it.'

'Who will you rule?'

'I don't know!'

'Who does the Prince Under the Sky rule?' asked Mother.

'I . . .' He thought.

It's a lesson. Like in Develin. They are teaching me again.

'Anyone who listens to him,' he said.

Aun grunted. He was sceptical. But the more Ambrose thought about it, the more he liked the answer.

'When they want to come to me,' he said. 'We can do

as we did at Aclete. We can help them to find the law.'

'If you do this, others will make themselves kings,' said Aun. 'If they then hear witless peasants crying that you are the true King who gives justice in the face of cruel lords, they will come to hunt you.'

'He will sleep in hedges,' said Mother softly, looking at her friend. 'And he will hold his courts under trees in the rain. And he will beg for his food, and those who follow him will do also . . .'

'It's not that,' Aun said. 'Though I cannot keep a war-horse and a coat of mail by scrounging for bowls of broth.'

'You have done everything that could be asked of you,' she said. 'You could go home, to Lackmere, now. If Orcrim and the Widow's child take Develin . . .'

'No.'

Ambrose looked up, realizing that it was no longer he who was having to make a choice. He had fumbled his way to his answer. Now they were waiting for Aun.

The silence lengthened, as the man who owned him King frowned at the ring of stones.

'All right,' he said. 'Under the Sky it is, for now. Whatever that means. And I guess that means the March, where we are known. I hope we can find at least one black-smith who knows his craft well enough.'

'The cup, then,' she said.

Ambrose passed it to her. His arms felt very light when it was taken from them. He watched her turn it in her hands.

'So, my darling. You have talked of a hidden power. Here it is. Through the cup you can reach to the power that lies deep in this pool. You may see far, and speak far, and pass where no man should be able to pass. With it your father defeated armies that outnumbered his, took fortresses that were held against him, and even made himself King in Tuscolo, for a while. Prince Paigan gave some of the same powers to Raymonde, and with it he, too, made a king. Is this what you want?'

Ambrose frowned. He had almost taken it the evening before, from the hand of his enemy. He hated to think of that.

'No,' he said flatly. 'Why do you want me to?'

Her mouth twitched. 'I don't. But I did want to be sure. And if you had said you wanted it, I should have told you that for such power there is always a price. The Tears themselves demand it. You spoke with Paigan Wulframson. You saw what lay behind his eyes. I think you can guess what price he must have paid. You would do the same.'

'Can we destroy it then?'

Her fingers traced the chipped rim. 'Of course,' she murmured. 'It is just stone. It was cut from the rocks by the pool. I can show you the place from which it was taken. But – I am within this bowl, and so are seven others. Within this bowl, too, is the dream of Beyah, and in her grief she dreams of all the world. When it fell yesterday, I felt it. I do not know what will happen if we break it. I do not know what to do.'

'Who are the others?'

'Don't you know? They hunted you. They would have torn you to pieces if their master willed it. But they also knew you. They spoke to you. Do you remember what they said?'

*Ando, Anson.* Those lipless words.

Ambrose . . .

Grandson! It had been saying, 'Grandson'!

'One of them is my ancestor?' he said, appalled.

'One of them is all that remains of Talifer, son of Wulfram. Another was once Rolfe, son of Wulfram, the father of the house of Ferroux. He came to you in the garden, as your Angel said he would. He came to you as he was, leading his brothers. Why, I do not know. But he and his brothers were there when the Angel spoke through your father. No doubt they believed, as we all did, that the prophecy concerned you. So I guess they came to you to beg for help – or perhaps for pardon.'

To beg him for help. If there had been an appeal from those lipless throats, he had not heard it; any more than Chawlin had heard him when he had called for rescue. He had been as deaf as the man who had died.

'Can you think what evil had been done, to have such a price as lies in the bottom of this pool? At the founding of our Kingdom countless thousands were slaughtered, driven from the land, forgotten, so that Wulfram's sons, and his people, might divide it between them. Then Paigan trapped each one of his brothers, and brought them here, and confined them to a living death at the bottom of the pit. Here they have remained for three centuries, while their bodies deformed slowly under the grief of the tears the goddess has shed over what they had done. And only the gold remains as a sign of what they were.'

'Can they be cured?'

'Is that what you want?'

He remembered the wretched voices, pleading in the darkness by the fountain; the hand that had stretched towards

601

him; the voice of the Angel who had sent him to them.

'We must.'

'I thought this would be your answer, although at this moment I do not know how it may be done. But for this reason I have told Orcrim that we should not resume the stone-raising. No cure can come to them if they remain down there. And first we must decide what we are to do with this cup . . .'

She paused, looking into the empty dry bowl.

'I think – if I could be sure that in breaking this thing we would remove the Tears from the world altogether, I would say it should be done, even if I and seven others must be removed also. And if I could be sure that neither I nor they would be changed by destroying it, I should again say that it should be done, simply to remove a thing that has been used to work evil. But I do not know. And so I do not dare speak.'

'I can imagine no world without grief,' said Aun.

'We will keep it, and guard it,' said Ambrose.

'Septimus gave the same order,' she said. 'And it could not be obeyed.'

'We will be more careful,' said Ambrose. He could not permit them to destroy it if there was a risk to her. And perhaps there was some point in being King, after all, if it meant they had to agree.

'Who will take it then?' she asked.

'You should,' said Ambrose.

Still she turned the bowl in her hands, as if poring over memories. She was not laughing now. 'Well,' she said. 'Until we think of something . . .'

She was interrupted by a cry from behind them.

'Orcrim! Orcrim!'

'Oh, he's awake,' sighed Mother.

Caw had passed a poor night, shifting restlessly in pain from his wound. Hob and some of the others had watched over him by turns, talking with him when he was able to talk, trying to ease his fears as the darkest hours passed. Hob had said that he had seemed to relax a little at first light. By the time Ambrose was up, Caw had dropped into a shallow sleep.

'We'd better see,' said Ambrose.

He turned and made his way through the camp. Aun followed him. Around him members of the Company were loading their horses and tightening straps for the first stage of their journey back to the March.

'Orcrim!'

'I'm here,' said Orcrim, coming up to stand over the wounded man, who lay wrapped in cloaks on the ground. He was carrying the banner of the Doubting Moon. Like Mother, he seemed to be in a good mood this morning. 'How are those scratches?'

'You're going, aren't you?' gasped Caw.

'The job's done here. We're off to Aclete with my lady Develin, to see if we can nip over the water and sort her out at home. With luck we'll sort out a nice place for you at the same time.'

'Help me up,' said Caw.

'Oh, no. You're staying, my man. We'll lift you down to the house, but that's as far as you are going. I was planning to ask your former mistress to make sure you don't starve.' He bowed slightly to the woman who had appeared at Ambrose's side.

603

'How – thoughtful of you, sir,' she said coldly.

'No, damn you!' said Caw.

'. . . And you can come down to Aclete nice and easy in a month or so,' said Orcrim.

'Orcrim! She'll poison me!'

Orcrim gave a look of mock surprise.

'I don't think so. You won't, will you?' he said to her.

'She'll look after him,' said Ambrose. 'So will I.' He turned to her. 'It must be us,' he said. 'They'll need everyone they've got, when they reach Develin. And you told me you begged for his life, once.'

'Yes,' she said. 'Although I have never begged to bear his company.'

'I beg that you should,' said Ambrose. 'For a month, at least,' he added.

'You have already asked much of me today,' she said. 'And I rose so joyfully this morning.' She sighed. 'Well, Caw,' she said after a moment. 'It seems our Prince has passed judgement on both of us, and sentenced us each to a month under the same roof. May Umbriel count it as atonement for what we have done.'

Caw stared helplessly at the sky, and did not answer.

'What about you, Old Iron?' said Orcrim to Aun. 'Are you coming with us?'

'No, I will stay here.'

'What will you do?'

'As before. I will keep *him* alive, as long as I can.'

He jerked his head towards Ambrose.

'And – the things we spoke of?'

Aun grinned. 'We'll not march on Tuscolo this season, I think.'

'So?' Orcrim waited for a moment, as if expecting Aun to say more. Then he shrugged. 'One thing at a time, maybe. Well, my lord,' he said to Ambrose, handing him the banner. 'After forty years I am leaving the service of the Doubting Moon. I am sorry for that. But before summer I look to have a hearth of my own in Develin, and some good southern vines. If anyone here comes to my door while I live, there will be warmth for you of one sort or another that you will find good, I swear. And maybe we can talk of other things again. My lady?'

Sophia had come up, leading her horse.

'Are we ready?' she asked him.

'We need the litter for my friend here. Hob!'

'A moment,' called Hob, from where he and a few others were bending over something on the ground.

'A moment, he says,' said Orcrim cheerfully.

Sophia gave Ambrose a quick, tight smile. Ambrose did not know what to think, or say. She had lost so much, and suddenly she was leaving. There were all those dangers ahead of her, as she tried to go home. *Goodbye, good luck. I'm sorry about Chawlin.* Words could say so little. And there was no time now. The Company was on the point of going. A smile was all the farewell that would pass between them.

He watched her lead her horse a little way down the difficult slope to where the horsemen were forming. He had liked her a lot – more than he had realized. She was a good person. She was also very strong. Even looking at her now, dusty and grieving, he could see the way she carried herself. He could imagine a kind of glow coming from within her that would lift her and at the same time touch those around her. He thought that if ever she

605

managed to take her mother's seat at Develin, people would quickly look up to her. Perhaps one day he would be able to go and see. He hoped so.

The litter appeared – a frame of wood made from the heavy tripods and the levers, with a bed of rope wound to and fro to support a man's body. They lifted Caw onto it. Four men took their places around it. Orcrim was calling from the head of the line, waving with his gauntlet. The Company began to move, slowly, scraping and clattering as they coaxed their mounts down the steep rocks. Caw cursed as the litter-men began to lift him down the slope, a pace at a time, feeling their way. Ambrose stayed where he was, watching them go.

'That's the way he was thinking of,' said Aun suddenly, pointing to where Sophia was bringing her horse down to the faint track that ran around the end of the ridge. 'If you wanted it. Wed Develin now, and you would have a better chance at the throne than any man alive.'

'No,' said Ambrose.

'If you don't take it, someone else will.'

Ambrose thought that Orcrim and Aun knew a lot about how the Kingdom worked. But they did not know Sophia.

'I think there's going to be a Widow in Develin again.'

One by one the Company passed. A man took a moment to raise his hand in salute. Others copied him. Ambrose shook out the folds of his banner to let them see the Moon that they were leaving. He remembered that there must have been a full moon last night. But he had not seen it rise because of the high horizon of the mountains, and he had not seen it set either. He had slept, and he had dreamed. And now it would be waning again, clouded by new doubts, as it made its way upon its endless journey through the sky.

There's a piece missing. There always would be. That was what the Doubting Moon meant.

There would be fear. There would be grief that could only be endured. He could not part the Cup from the World.

He could only hope that people would listen to him.

By late afternoon the Company were picking their way along a scrubby slope that fell to the valley floor a thousand feet to their left. Near the head of the line, Sophia allowed her horse to follow the leaders, while the flies of the hillside wove around her ears. Her eyes alternated over the path immediately before her and the big view out across the valley to her right. She could see the blue of the sky and the detail of the distant ridges. She could look back and still pick out the knuckle of rock where they had left Caw with Ambrose, his mother, and Aun in that strange house. She could see the huge peak of Beyah that rose far beyond, white-capped and purple-sided with the shadows of the clouds.

She saw the beauty in the mountains; but it did not speak to her.

An hour before, the little track they were following had passed by some huts of a curious, circular build that she had not seen before. The men had said that they were the dwellings of hillmen, but that they must have been abandoned in the last season. The low stone walls and little dark doorways were shells that had once held life, but were now empty. Perhaps life would come back to them after the defeat of the enemy by the pool. But no life would come back to her heart.

It was already more than a day since Chawlin had died. Sophia could not believe that it had been so long. She felt that she had been distracted by other things. The war to avenge him had passed, and she felt that she had done little in it – mostly to have marched with the others in dark places, while her arm throbbed and the horses misbehaved. The horses were behaving now, but her arm still hurt and hurt: another distraction.

And Orcrim had been trying to talk to her for much of the day. He wanted to hear about Develin – about who on the manors might support her, about the attitudes of the towns, their status, and their relations with her mother – all the things he needed to know for his campaign. And of course she should tell him. All that would matter, soon, to all of them. Her hours and days would be full of it. She would no longer be able to remember Chawlin as he should be remembered.

She had woken knowing that he was dead.

Somewhere ahead of her lay his grave, under a pile of stones in the foothills. She did not know when they would pass it. She had an idea that it might be days before they reached it, and yet already she was looking at each new view that the mountains showed her, trying to pick out where it might be. Flowers would not grow on it, on that bare hillside. The best that she and he could hope for would be sunlight, and perhaps a gentle covering of moss on the shaded side of the cairn, as the fist of the world closed over him for ever. Such a poor grave, for the man who had lit her life. And already the tides of politics would bear her beyond it, hurrying her on to errands in the south. She would pass, unable to improve what he had been given, or even to stay and weep.

The days ahead of her would be meaningless – busy, and smiling for the sake of the people around her, but meaningless. She would go back to Develin, if she could. She would gather and protect the people she had left behind. She would have men repair the fire-damage, find what remained of the dead and bury them. She would see that her mother and the others who had been lost were remembered. She would re-found the school, for their sake. And perhaps there were still men in the Kingdom who, as masters and counsellors, could speak the things that would help her bear the disorder of living. But still Chawlin would lie out here, beyond the lake, beyond the March, in a little lost valley where few came and none understood whose story had ended under the cairn of stones.

Ahead of her, the leading rider called and pointed upwards. Immediately behind him Orcrim rose in his stirrups and, shading his eyes, studied the skyline. She looked up. The path they were on was rising slowly to the crest ahead. They must have seen something up there, against the sky. She glanced upwards, but there seemed to be only rocks. Nothing moving. No life.

Orcrim was looking back at her.

'What is it?' she asked.

'Someone on the path ahead of us. He's gone over, now.'

Someone on the path ahead. Well, one person was not

going to be a threat. And very likely whoever it was would run off and hide when they realized that a troop of armed men was following them. She saw Orcrim and the leading rider watching the rocks by the path as they approached the skyline. They had a habit of expecting ambushes, these men. She supposed that was good. As usual, it was needless. The rocks were empty. The path was safe. They crossed the ridge and looked down into a new valley, shallower and narrower than the last, with a stream running in the bed of it. The shadow of the hillside filled it almost to the brim. Only the rocks on the far ridge burst once more into the gold sun. Evening was coming. Sophia guessed that Orcrim would want to camp somewhere along the stream below them.

The ridge lifted like a curtain behind them as they began to pick their way down. It cut out the view of Beyah at last.

Almost at once the men were pointing again. Looking forward, she could see what they had seen – a man walking along the track ahead of them, some way down the hill. They would overtake him before long. Orcrim was looking back at her. He was expecting her to say something. He was waiting to hear what she wanted to do about the man on the path. She thought, and realized why.

It would be Raymonde of Lackmere.

Had he seen them? He was not acting as if he had. He would have quickened his pace at least, or taken to the hillsides where the horses could not follow him. But he must hear them soon. The clipping and scraping of sixty hooves on stone, the repetitive clatter of pebble after pebble rolling away beneath them – he would have to be deaf not to know that they were coming.

She knew what judgement Ambrose had given on him, when they had caught him the evening before. But surely he was not counting on that to protect him.

He had brought Velis's men to do murder in her home.

He had done other things, too. He had killed his own brother. Did Ambrose have the right to forgive that?

He had done no good that Sophia could think of. Worse, he had lived, where Chawlin had not. It should have been the other way around.

They were getting nearer. He would reach the valley floor before them, but not by much. Surely he had heard them by now. He had not looked back.

Orcrim was looking over his shoulder at her again. His question was clear on his face. A word, even a nod of her head, and this man would pay with his life for all he had done. She needn't even watch while they did it. She could just ride on, and let them catch her up. It seemed a very little thing, his death – too little, to pay for the grief of Develin, for Chawlin, and all the rest. But it was all that there was to be had.

Chawlin. Could she bury his memory beneath the bodies of enemies?

She could do it. She could do it, because she could.

She did not even have to do it. She could simply have her troop ride past him as though he were not there. They would leave him his life, but treat his life as if it was nothing. Because it was nothing. He did not seem to be carrying anything – food, blanket or even a weapon. She had no idea how he planned to live on his way through these mountains. And probably, after they had passed, Orcrim would nod secretly to one or two of the men; and they

611

would drop back and finish him anyway. And she would never know or need to know that it had been done.

Her mind was shut like a box, and she did not know herself what answer lay within it.

The man limped on before them. He did not look strong. He was cradling one arm as if it had been hurt. He knew they were coming up behind him. He knew who they were, and that they might kill him if they chose. He was trying not to look around at them, but in a moment he would. There! He had done it. He was too weak to rule himself. And yet he did not care enough to try to save his skin.

They were on level ground now, by the banks of the stream that ran with the opaque grey-blue of glacier water. The bright faces of snow-fishers showed in clumps along the banks as the colours around them dimmed in the mountain-shadow. For a moment the horses could ride alongside one another on this ground. Orcrim and his leading rider pulled back, and let her come up to them. They were still waiting for her command. It would be her first order for them in her service. Her first order would tell them much about the woman they now followed. Was she ruthless? Was she weak? They would watch what she did, and draw their conclusions.

But her mother had never let that sort of opinion sway her. Why should she?

She steered her horse around the limping man, wide enough to be well out of reach, and looked down at him. He was making what pace he could on the level ground. He kept his eyes ahead of him. He was ignoring her.

'Look up,' she said to him, irritated.

He looked up. His eyes and cheeks were hollow, his long hair all tangled. He was glaring at her. He would not ask for mercy.

But there were snow-fishers on the banks beyond him, bright as the tears that the world wept at evening. Her answer came like a drawer at the touch of a hidden spring.

'Bring him one of the spare horses,' she said to Orcrim, without looking around. 'He can ride and eat with us, as far as the March. After that, he may go where he wills.'

She kicked her mare on, riding ahead while her orders were passed down the line. She did not want to look at the man she had saved. This evening, when they camped, she would have to speak with him. Heaven alone knew what she would say.

She did not think she could forgive him. But she supposed she did not have to.

That had been done for her.